THE RED DRAGON

And there was the dragon, winging away over the rooftops. The body of the beast was russet-colored above and golden beneath, the sunlight glancing off its scales as though off burnished metal. The four great limbs were drawn up against its underside with the claw-tips dangling, and she saw the horned head turning this way and that, as an eagle's does when it scans the ground for prey. Then the dragon dipped one wing and banked, and she saw the sharp dorsal scales, like a row of spearheads all along its spine; and the flat scales flanking them were not russet but red as blood, or roses, or rubies. She could see the webwork of veins in the giant crimson wings as the sun shone through them, standing out against the pellucid membranes like the veins of a leaf.

There were other dragons too, higher up—a dozen or so sinuous red-golden shapes dropped out of the clouds above the mountains. For all their great bulk, they glided as effortlessly as swallows . . .

PRAISE FOR BOOK 1 OF THE DRAGON THRONE *THE STONE OF THE STARS*

"Baird blends an accessible style . . . with a rich mythology in this delightful fantasy . . . sure to please fans."
—*Publishers Weekly* (starred review)

"A cast of appealing heroes . . . This series opener provides a strong contribution to the epic fantasy genre and belongs in most fantasy collections."

—*Library Journal*

"Remarkably effective."

—*Challenging Destiny*

"Sparkles with original touches and characters . . . I anxiously await the next volume."

—TheRomanceReadersConnection.com

THE STONE OF THE STARS

Also by Alison Baird

The Dragon Throne
Book 1: The Stone of the Stars
Book 2: The Empire of the Stars
Book 3: The Archons of the Stars

THE STONE OF THE STARS

THE DRAGON THRONE • BOOK I

ALISON BAIRD

NEW YORK BOSTON

Cover design by Don Puckey
Cover Illustration by Steve Youll

Aspect
Warner Books

Time Warner Book Group
1271 Avenue of the Americas, New York, NY 10020
Visit our Web site at www.twbookmark.com

Printed in the United States of America

Originally published in Trade Paperback by Aspect
First Mass Market Paperback Printing: July 2005

10 9 8 7 6 5 4 3 2 1

to Clan Baird

of Duck Cove, Pocologan, and St. Andrew's-by-the-Sea:
remembering magical summers,
and stories told on the beach

Acknowledgments

This book has been many, many years in the making, and my debts are numerous. My thanks to Jaime Levine at Warner Aspect, for giving me a chance; my editor Devi Pillai; and my amazing agent Jack Byrne, for finding a home for this tale. Many thanks also to Andre Norton, both for her own inspiring work and for graciously helping a newcomer to find a foothold in a vast and intimidating industry.

Thank you to my English teachers, Susan Smyth and Dr. Margaret Swayze, for encouraging a schoolgirl with a budding urge to write. Thank you Judy Diehl and David Plumb, for being among the first to read the book and for offering your many helpful suggestions. Thank you to all of my writer friends who over the years have lent your support and encouragement to my quest for publication: to Avril and Frances Tyrrell, to Terri Neal and Marian Hughes and Louise Spilsbury and Jan Stirling, to Josepha Sherman and Julie Czerneda. And thank you to my wonderful and supportive family, especially my parents, Violet and Donal Baird. I could not have done this without you.

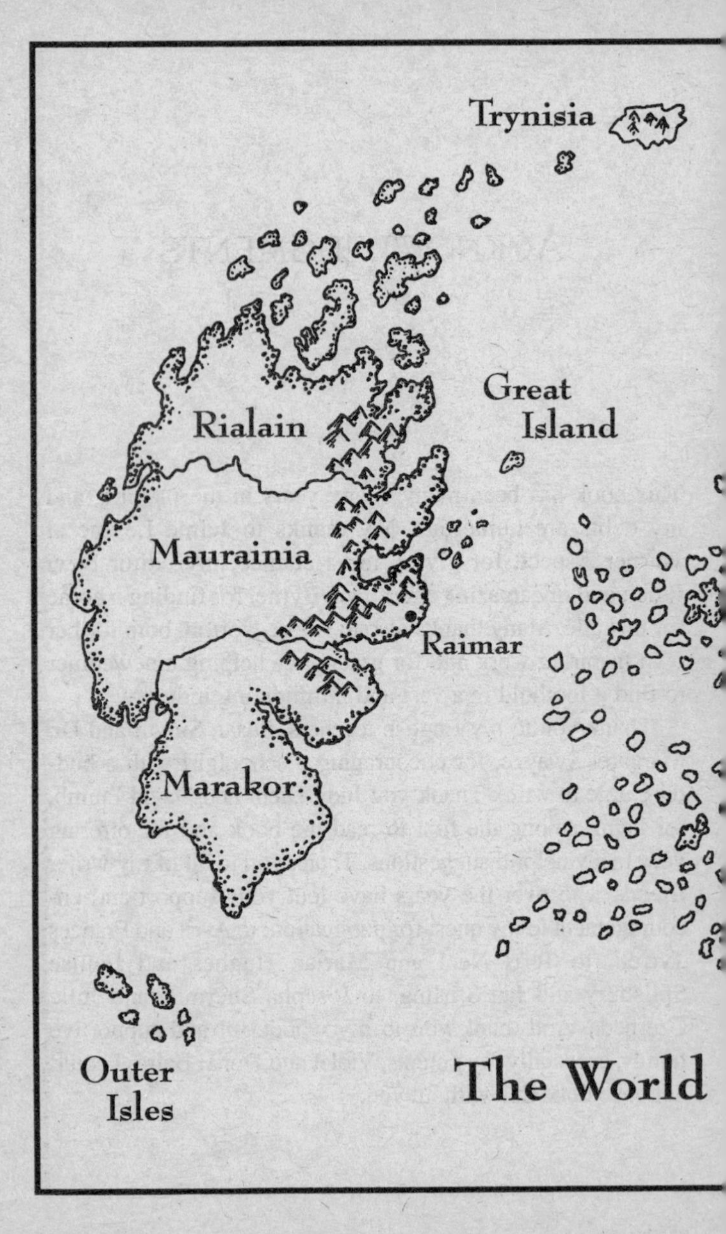
Trynisia
Great
Island
Rialain
Maurainia
Raimar
Marakor
Outer
Isles
The World

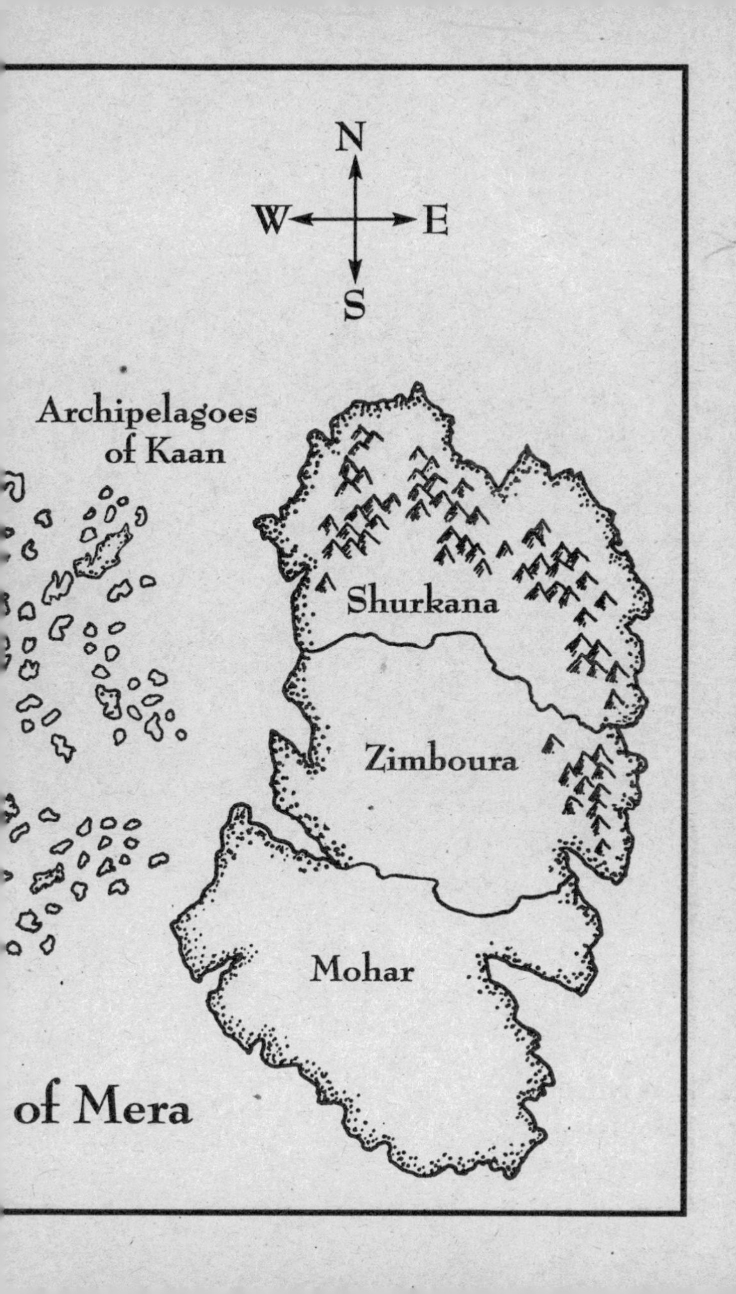
N
W
E
S
Archipelagoes of Kaan
Shurkana
Zimboura
Mohar
of Mera

Prologue

In the beginning were the El, whom the ancients call the gods: the first children of the Maker. They woke in the deep before Earth and Heaven were made, and they beheld the Creation. And when it was completed some of the El chose to dwell amid the stars of Heaven; and they became the Elyra, the high gods. Others of the El chose to dwell upon the Earth, and they became the Elaia, who have many other names: the genii, the faeries, the gods of land and sea. The Elaia delighted in the making of things, in shaping wood and stone and gems and ores: it was they who crafted the enchanted talismans that guided the heroes of old. But before that time, in the very dawning of the world, they fashioned a treasure for the Elyra. It had the likeness of a gemstone, clear as water and cut with many facets, small enough to hold in the hand. Though formed of the stuff of Earth, it shone as though all the stars of Heaven were contained within it, and so it was called the Meraalia, the Star Stone. The Elaia made it to show the high gods that things of the lowly Earth could be as beautiful as those of the sky. And

Modrian, who was then chief of the Elyra, accepted the gem and set it in his crown.

But still Modrian cared nothing for the mortal world or for its creatures, and he used the latter as he pleased, for servants and for playthings. At this the gods became divided, some siding with and others against Modrian. But the greater number opposed him, and led by the bright god Athariel they waged war on him and his minions until the stars shook in the firmament. In the last great battle Athariel struck the crown of Modrian with his sword, and the sacred Stone broke loose from its setting. Down to Earth it fell, shining like a shooting star; and it came to rest in the north of the world, on the summit of a mountain that ever since that time has been called Elendor, the Holymount. There the gem remained, long after Modrian was defeated and confined to the Pit of Perdition, which he himself had made for the imprisonment of others.

Now, the name of that land into which the Star Stone fell was Trynisia: it was a place of ice and bitter cold until the Elaia went to dwell there and by their arts made it green and fruitful. In those days many of the Elaia took mortal mates, and out of these unions came the Elei, the Fairfolk. Being a divine race, they could work many kinds of magic, and their time upon Earth was many times greater than that allotted to other mortals. The Elaia brought the Fairfolk to dwell with them in Trynisia, and instructed them in their arts, and made them wise.

Elarainia, goddess of the Morning Star, looked on the Fairfolk with special favor. Often she descended to the Earth and walked among them in the likeness of a woman, sharing her knowledge with them. And the children of the gods loved her, and called her Queen of Heaven and Queen of Night, for her star shone more brightly than any other. Many of them she took to dwell with her, in her own land that lay beyond the world's end. And she bade those of the Fairfolk who remained in Trynisia to leave the Star Stone on the mountaintop and watch it well, lest those who still served Modrian should come and take it for their own dark purposes. For the powers of Earth and Heaven were bound together in the Stone, and it was said that it would one day defeat its former master when he returned in might to conquer the world.

So the Fairfolk built a fane upon the mountaintop, called the Temple of Heaven, over the place where the Star Stone lay. The years passed, and a great city was founded upon the summit, a holy city where priests and sibyls and astrologers dwelt: Liamar, City of the Star. Dragons guarded its gates, and gryphons guarded the temple, and in the city were many wonders made by the Elaia and their children: enchanted gems that commanded the weather and the waters, shining stones that gave light in place of lamps, and a magical crystal that revealed to Eliana, queen of the Fairfolk, all the doings of the world. But of all wonders the greatest was the Star Stone. Heavenly spirits attended it, and the temple was a place of awe. At times a bird of fire was seen to rise from the Stone and fly about the temple: the holy Elmir, the Bird of Heaven itself.

Many were the pilgrims who sought the holy city, for in time the Elei sent out sailing-vessels to all the ends of the Earth, befriending the peoples there: and so the Commonwealth was formed, to be the earthly counterpart of the Celestial Empire above, harmonizing Earth and Heaven. But even as the Star Stone was a source of awe and reverence, so did it become a source of strife among men. As the heart of the Elei realm it was hateful to the Elei's foes, the cruel and warlike rulers who yet worshipped Modrian.

A day came when the sorceress-queen of the Fairfolk, Eliana the Wise, gathered her people together and spoke to them thus: "Although he cannot ever leave his prison in the Pit, the dark god has many servants still. Some of these are mortal, and some are mighty spirits, and both shall strike many blows against us. Wars shall rage on the land, and stars fall from their places on high; and darkness shall cover all the Earth for a time. And in the end this land of Trynisia will be but a memory, a tale told to children by the hearth. Then Modrian shall send forth a great warrior to ravage the world in his name. The dark god's power shall be in this man and shall rule him, limb and mind, so that it will be as if Modrian himself has come again in a new form. All shall flee the prince of the Dark and the dread hosts that follow after him."

The Elei were filled with fear and sorrow, and begged their queen for words of comfort. Then she spoke to them this prophecy: "Do not despair, for the forces of the light shall also have a champion. The Queen of Night shall bear and bring forth a maid-child, and she shall be called the Tryna Lia, Princess of the Stars. With her mother's authority she shall reign, throned upon the moon; and she shall summon out of the heavens a mighty host to challenge the enemy. And she shall seek for the sacred Stone of lost Trynisia: for it will give to her the power of Earth and Heaven that alone can defeat the power of Modrian.

Whenever you behold the Star of Morning in the sky, remember this and know that there is hope."

In this way the Elei first learned of the Tryna Lia, the one who will descend to the Earth and make war against their foes. But the hour of her coming was not then revealed, nor does any mortal know when it shall be.

—apocryphal text, circa 1080 N.E.
The Royal Academy archives, Maurainia

THE STONE OF THE STARS

Part One

THE PROPHECY

1

Ailia

". . . AND THE EVIL DAYS CAME that Queen Eliana had foreseen," Ailia recited, spreading her arms in a wide sweeping gesture. "Modrian, still prisoned in the Pit, commanded his servants to assail the world on his behalf. The evil spirit Azarah obeyed, snatching stars from out of their places in the heavens, and casting them down upon the Earth below. Some lands were burned, and others drowned in the sea, and the moon's face was marred and darkness fell over all the world. Even the blessed isle of Trynisia did not escape the day of destruction. Then those Elei who still lived fled the ruin of their realm: some went to dwell in Eldimia, the land of the goddess of the Morning Star, that lies beyond the world's end; and others went to live in the mortal lands, where in time their race dwindled and died. And so the Elei have all vanished from the world. But their sorceress-queen promised them long ago that the triumph of their enemy would not last forever. The Fairfolk who fled to Eldimia shall return again, and their ancient Commonwealth be restored, when the Tryna Lia comes to rule the Earth."

She and the village children were—or rather, should have been—gathering kindling in the thin belt of woodland that Ailia had named the Enchanted Forest. Most of Great Island's timber had been felled in bygone ages for firewood and lumber, leaving behind only forlorn and isolated copses like this one. Its wind-worn trees bowed inland, and huddled together as if for shelter. Yet as Ailia told the story, the little wood was altered in the eyes of her listeners: its stunted trees seemed to grow taller, the green shade beneath them deeper. And Ailia too was transformed as she spoke, becoming in turn each character she described. Standing straight and regal before them, she seemed, in the dim otherworldly light that was half of her making, to become the Faerie Queen Eliana; and when she spoke of Modrian the Fiend her voice became a hissing whisper, and her audience grew pale and still.

It had been Ailia's intention to ease the tedium of their task by telling stories. But as soon as she began the tale both she and the children completely forgot the kindling. They saw only the Fairfolk and their sacred gem, and the holy city on its mountaintop, and the fiery rain of falling stars. When at last she finished they all sat in silence for a while. The spell was lifted, and the children saw before them only a girl who looked slightly younger than her seventeen years, slender and of medium height. Her clothing was as plain as theirs, a white linen blouse under a tight-laced brown bodice and skirt, with a frayed old apron tied at her waist. Yet still there was something different about Ailia, something that was not quite like other people. Perhaps it was her eyes: they were so very large, with irises that in the shade seemed dark gray but in the sunlight showed a purplish cast, the color of the small pieces of amethyst the children sometimes found lying among the rocks. The hair that fell loose about her back and shoulders was oddly changeful too. Under the trees it was fawn-colored, and seemed dark in contrast with the pallor of her face; but when she stepped out of the shadows, the sun, streaming through the nebulous outer layer of flyaway hairs, made it look almost like spun gold.

The youngest child in the group was the first to find her voice again. "Tell us another story, Ailia! Tell us about the time the Stone was stolen," she begged, fastening doe-brown eyes on the storyteller.

Ailia raised her left arm and pointed to the southeast, where the slate-blue sea showed in narrow panels between the tree trunks. "Once upon a time, in the days when Trynisia still prospered, there was a king in far-off Zimboura whose name was Gurusha, and it was said that his father was an evil demon in mortal guise. He commanded the Zimbouran people to worship a god called Valdur, who demanded terrible sacrifices, and all the while he plotted the end of the Commonwealth. Every new-knighted Paladin in Maurainia had to make a sea voyage to Trynisia, to pray in the Temple of Heaven before the Star Stone; and so Gurusha dispatched a group of warriors to steal the holy gem away. They entered the temple by stealth, disguised as pilgrims, and seized the Stone and slew the knights who guarded it. Fleeing back to Zimboura, they presented the Star Stone to King Gurusha, who placed it on the forehead of the idol of Valdur."

The children had heard this tale many times before. They knew of the holy war waged by the old Commonwealth against Zimboura, with its terrible battles fought far away beyond the sea. They knew the combined forces of Maurainia and Trynisia had won the final victory. Yet still they hung on Ailia's every word.

"King Brannar Andarion of Maurainia went himself to the palace of Gurusha, and called the Demon King forth to do battle. And Gurusha answered his challenge. He was dreadful to look upon, and his immortal sire's dark power was in him. But Andarion too was no common man, for his own father was of the faeries. The two kings met in single combat, and Gurusha mocked Andarion as they fought. Then the Maurainian king waxed wroth—"

"He waxed *what?*" interjected one of the older girls.

"He got very angry," explained Ailia, "and pierced Gurusha to the heart with his sword." She snatched up a stick from the ground and made a thrust with it. "Then the minions of Valdur were filled with dismay—"

"What's a minion?" the girl asked again.

"Elen Seaman, would you *please* stop interrupting! It makes me lose my place in the story."

The other children glared, and Elen subsided. "They laid down their arms," Ailia went on, "and sued for peace. The Paladins went to the chief temple of Valdur, and destroyed it; and King Andarion declared that the god of the Zimbourans was in truth an evil fiend, none other than Modrian himself in another guise, and his worship was banned." Ailia let fall her stick-sword. "And so the war was ended, and the Stone returned to its rightful place in Trynisia."

"What a tale!" breathed Lynna, the youngest girl. "It makes you wonder, doesn't it—where the Fairfolk came from, and whether there really was a Star Stone."

"I'll wager there wasn't," Elen Seaman scoffed. "Papa says"—her face took on a lofty and learned expression—"Papa says the Elei just made up those stories to impress our ancestors."

"Where was Trynisia supposed to be?" asked Kevan, the carpenter's son.

"It lay far away, to the north," answered Ailia. As she spoke those words, she felt a little thrill and her heart yearned northward, for a far-off land of jeweled palaces and bright cities surrounded by ice and snow. "Far, far away," she repeated. "No one is sure how far. And Eldimia, the land of the Morning Star, was farther still—beyond the world's end."

"The world hasn't *got* an end," Elen interrupted again. "It's round like a ball, my papa says. There's no edge you can go beyond, or fall off of. And my papa is a sailor, and he's sailed all around the world, so he should know! And all that rot about gods and goddesses, when you know there's really only one God, and One Faith. None of this is *true*."

Ailia sighed. "It's only a story, Elen." She would never have confessed it to these children, but deep within she longed to believe in it all: not just the Elei and their ancient wars but the magic, and the flying dragons, and the precious Stone that fell out of Heaven.

"I wish there were knights nowadays," remarked Kevan. "*They'd* stop King Khalazar and his armies! Ailia, are the Zimbourans going to go to war with us again? Some of the foreigners down by the harbor say so."

Ailia looked again to the far-off horizon behind which Zimboura lay, unseen yet threatening, like the approach of night. She shivered: and for an instant the old stories no longer seemed so remote. "Of course not," she said with an effort. "There hasn't been a war in hundreds of years. Now, you had better get your kindling, you lot, and so had I."

She went back to picking up fallen branches. What, she wondered, would she do without these children to tell stories to? Beyond the little copse the landscape was bleak: fields that grew nothing but hip-high grasses, great whalebacks of granite that thrust up through the thin soil. The little houses of Bayport village clustered together at the sea's edge: with so little arable land available, most of the Islanders had to support themselves by fishing.

This is a terrible place, she thought with a shudder. *Why have I never noticed it before now?* But in her childhood everything had been different. In those days Great Island was not Great Island at all, but the magic isle of Trynisia, or the faerie-land of Eldimia, or Maurainia in the golden age of Brannar Andarion's reign: whatever she had imagined it to be. And Ailia, together with her cousins Jemma and Jaimon and the other barefoot village children, had lived a long idyll of make-believe: had been kings and queens, knights and wizards, had fought dragons and won wars. There were no myths or legends on the Island. The hardened and bitter exiles who first arrived on these windswept shores were preoccupied with survival, and in its sparse and stony soil romance never took root. At least, it did not until that day when, inspired by a collection of wondertales from the Old Country that she had found on her father's bookshelf, Ailia took it upon herself to address the lack. She made up a local mythology in which every tree, knoll, and boulder had its origin in some fabulous feat of yore, and told the tales to her delighted play-mates. The great submerged rock outside the harbor that daily endangered the fishing boats was a petrified sea monster, transformed by a hero with a magic talisman; a gnarled old crabapple tree with pure white blossoms had sprung from a magic apple brought from faerie-land; and so on. In her thoughts many features of the surrounding landscape still went by the names she had invented for them—the Mermaid's Rock, the Ogre's Cave, the Enchanted Forest.

At the memory Ailia both smiled and sighed. Those childhood friends had grown up, grown away from her. Jemma was a wife and mother now, Jaimon a sailor on a merchant ship traveling distant seas. Loneliness over-whelmed her suddenly, and with it a feeling akin to des-peration. *I almost wish that there* could *be a war. At least it would be a change*—

Kevan Carpenter gave a sudden shout. "Sail—sail! The packet's coming!" He jumped up on a tree stump and pointed.

Ailia swung around, the kindling spilling from her apron. Far away on the western sea a mass of white can-vas scudded like a cloud. One of the sailing ships that brought Great Island its mail and goods and news of the world was approaching the bay.

With a little cry she darted forward, outrunning even the fleet-footed children in her haste to reach the wharf. Would there be any mail for her? A letter from Cousin Jaimon perhaps, telling of his voyages on the high seas? Or perhaps even *the* letter—the one from the Royal Academy in Maurainia, stamped with its official seal?

Her heart pounded in time with her footsteps as she swept through the little village and on toward the harbor.

THE CROWD AT THE WHARF was a motley one, and as shrilly excited as the gulls that wheeled above it. With refugees pouring in from the Antipodes to seek haven here, Great Island at times was like the world made small. First had come the westerners, Maurainian and Marakite and Rialainish merchants and missionaries, returning in haste to the Continent. Then as summer ripened, native Antipodeans began to flow out of the southeast to Great Island's shores: Zimbourans with their sallow faces and coal-black hair, robed and turbaned Shurkas, even a few dark-skinned Mohara people out of the desert lands; they had all fled to this, the most far-flung of the Commonwealth's colonies, a stepping-stone to freedom. Many of the refugees could not afford to go on to the Continent, however, and had to stop here. They already filled the only inn to capacity.

To this inn Ailia came whenever she was able. Her parents would never permit her to enter its common-room full of rowdy sailors, but she liked to linger outside it on mild summer evenings. Perching on an empty keg or packing-crate, she listened eagerly to scraps of conversation that wafted out of the windows along with the reek of tobacco and the sour yeasty smell of stale beer. There were songs and tales of the sea and alien lands: stories of whales and pirate ships; of the strange pale lights—said to be ghosts of drowned men—that glimmered upon the rigging of ships in southern seas; of wrecks and buried treasure. With the arrival of the refugees, the tales had become more dramatic than ever before. There were harrowing accounts of the civil war in Zimboura, of the legions of the God-king storming cities and of the blasts of cannon fire that sent people screaming and running like panicked beasts. There were tales of perilous flights across the ocean in cramped and wallowing vessels, of tragic partings and families divided. She felt a pang of sympathy for these unlucky people, driven so far from their homes; but she could not help feeling a certain fascination too. What must it be like to live through such times? And the fugitives brought with them an aura of foreignness: tantalizing hints of their exotic homelands were revealed in their faces, their clothing, their accented speech.

Ailia ran up to join the crowd on the wharf, squeezing between the tightly packed bodies as she gazed with hungry eyes at the packet. The ship was a fine new one, square-rigged, with a sea-green hull. The figurehead was a mermaid, wide-tailed and golden-haired, and the ship's name was proudly proclaimed in gilt letters at the bows: *Sea Maid*. Ailia gave a long sigh of blended envy and rapture. To think that this very vessel had sailed distant reaches of the ocean, visited far-off ports of call! How glorious to be a sailor and roam the world!

And then the sight of a sandy-haired young man striding along the ship's deck made her spring forward with a cry of incredulous delight.

"Jaim! *Jaim!*"

The young sailor turned at her call and waved to her. "Hello there, coz!"

She struggled past the people in front of her and bounded up the gangplank. "Jaim! We've not had a letter from you for so long! When did you sign on with this ship? Are you on shore leave now? Did you get to Maurainia, and the Academy? They hadn't any message for me there, had they?"

"One question at a time." He smiled, swinging his haversack onto his shoulder.

So that was that; had there been any news he would have given it to her right away. Swallowing her disappointment, Ailia continued with her interrogation. "But the books, Jaim? Did you bring me some books? You promised, in your last letter—"

Jaimon grinned. "And here I thought it was myself you were so happy to see." He lowered the sack again and rummaged in it. "Here you are—I couldn't find the complete works of the Bard of Blyssion, but here are his ballads anyway—and the *Annals of the Kings*—"

With a little squeal Ailia seized the two shabby old volumes, hugging them to her chest. "Oh, thank you, Jaim! You don't know what this means to me. I'd give *anything* to be a scholar. I'd hoped to hear from the Academy by now, whether I was to be accepted or not."

Jaimon looked troubled at that, and did not meet her eager eyes. "Well, Ailia—you know it's hard to get accepted there, even for men," he said. "And it's fashionable right now among wealthy folk to have an educated daughter. Only the ones with money get in, as a rule."

"But I applied for a scholarship," Ailia replied. "Though lots of people apply for those too, I suppose. It isn't fair, Jaim. I want so much to know all about history, and the poets, and philosophy. I've read all of Papa's books ten times over, and no one else here has any that are worth reading. And reading is as close as I can come to seeing the world." She was silent for a moment, feeling the ship's deck rolling and swaying beneath her feet, moving with the sea's own rhythm. "If only I were a boy, I'd stow away on the *Sea Maid*, and sail off with you." She spoke in a light tone, but at her own words a fierce longing filled her.

"You wouldn't want to be a boy," said Jaimon, tweaking one of her straggling locks. "There'd be no hair-ribands for you then, no sighing over romantic ballads—"

"Yes—well," Ailia amended as they descended the gangway together, "I just wish that girls could do all the things that boys do. Look at you, going off to be a cabin boy when you were only fifteen—sailing all over the world, when all I can do is stop here at home!" She glanced over her shoulder at the ship. "I've half a mind to do it. Stow away, I mean."

Jaimon chuckled. "You wouldn't like it. When they caught you they'd put you to work in the galley."

She laughed with him. "Well then, I'll disguise myself in male attire, and become a sailor."

"Even worse! They'd have you swabbing the decks. Believe me, a life at sea is no life at all."

"*You* don't seem to be suffering, Jaimon Seaman!" She thumped him on the shoulder with one of the books. "Oh well: I must go home now, I suppose. I'd invite you to supper, Jaim, only it's my turn to make it and you know my cooking is awful. Mamma has tried her best to domesticate me but it's been an uphill battle for her. Anyway, Aunt Bett will want you to sup with her, of course. But you and she might drop by afterwards—and Uncle, too, if he's back from fishing. Will you, Jaim? It would be such fun—like old times. And I do so want to hear all your news."

"Of course. Tell Aunt Nella to expect us. There's something I must talk to you all about."

"Really? What is it, Jaim?"

"I'll tell you later." He smiled again, but it seemed to her now that there was something not quite right about the smile—it seemed stiff and forced. He turned away, and reluctantly she left him. After a few paces she halted and turned back to ask him yet another question. But it never left her lips. Her cousin was standing motionless, staring out to sea: he was facing, she saw, south and east to where Zimboura lay.

AILIA'S HOME WAS A peculiar structure, assembled by her father out of the odds and ends of his shipbuilding trade. Some of its windows were small round portholes, and its roof was made of an old ship's hull, the inverted keel serving for a ridgepole while the gunwales formed the eaves. Perched atop a gray granite outcropping not far from the shore, the house looked for all the world like a piece of sea wrack deposited by a high tide.

Ailia sat in her little bedroom, her mind filled with gloom as she gazed about her. The wooden bedstead, one chair, night table, and washstand all stood in the exact same places they had occupied since her earliest childhood. Her books were neatly lined up on the bookshelf that her father had made from planks propped up on stones: even with the two new additions they were so few in number that she was forced to fill up the empty space with other things. There were treasures gleaned from the tidepools: seashells, pebbles, crabs' carapaces, some hollow glass globes of the kind fishermen used to float their nets. Above the shelf was a round porthole-window, framing a view of meadow and sea. The latter's gentle heave-and-sigh had lulled her to sleep at night and filled her days until the sound seemed a very part of herself, like the pulse of blood in her ears. Any changes in the order of life on the Island were cyclical, not permanent: the turning of the tides and of the seasons, the transits of sun and moon.

She sighed and took up her comb. Her hair was inconstant in more than its hue: it changed its moods like the sea, on some days lying straight and smooth, on others rolling in waves. At the moment, however, its color was unmistakably mousy, and it had arranged itself in a mass of involved and intricate tangles that caught in the teeth of the comb. As she struggled to plait it she was aware of a growing frustration. *I always wanted hair like the princesses' in faerie tales, golden hair that was long enough to sit upon.* It was one more item in the long list of things life had denied her. Adventure was another. Why did she crave it so? Adventures, when they happened at all, happened to men and boys. For a girl there were but two possible destinies, housewifery and spinsterhood: and both meant a life confined to the home.

Sighing at the injustice, she left the bedroom and went down the small narrow passage to the main room of the house. Its rustic simplicity was strangely adorned by her father's collection of exotic objects, gathered by him in foreign lands back when he was a sailor on a merchant ship. There was a sextant and a brass ship's clock; the polished shell of a sea turtle; the huge white egg of a moa on a carved wooden stand. From the west wall stared an ebony ceremonial mask from Mohara-land, curiously elongated and with narrow slits for the eyes, which Ailia had found rather frightening when she was small. There was a magnificent conch from the Archipelagoes of Kaan that made the mussel and scallop shells in her own collection seem shabby little things, and a great spire of ivory that looked exactly like the horn of the unicorn in *Bendulus's Bestiary*, though her father said it was really a whale's tusk. There were several framed sea charts and maps of exotic lands hanging on the walls, some that her father had been to, some that even he had never seen.

Her mother stood by the fieldstone hearth, stirring the pot that hung bubbling over the fire. She dipped out a mouthful and tasted it, grimacing slightly. "Is something wrong with the chowder, Mamma?" Ailia asked. "Did I forget the onions again? Or is the cod not cooked through?"

"It tastes well enough, but it's watery. You'll never get yourself a man if your cooking doesn't improve." Nella glanced at Ailia's neat braids. "And you really should be wearing your hair up now—that's proper for a grown woman. It's high time you started acting your age, miss."

"I hate being my age," Ailia answered, not angrily but with a quiet sadness. She looked away from her mother and ran her hand up and down the smooth polished ivory of the whale's tusk.

Nella's earth-colored eyes dwelt thoughtfully on her daughter. "Ailia, you know it's time," she said. "Time to be seeking a man, and a home and family of your own."

Ailia made no response to this statement, too often heard of late. The only men she knew really well were Jaimon and her father and uncle. She thought of the village fishermen and shipwrights, of their bellowing voices, the brutish strength of their backs and arms as they hauled on nets, or hefted loads of imported lumber from the dockyards, or hammered away on whale-ribbed skeletons of ships. She had dreams, fostered by faerie tales, of romances with handsome princes: but they were dreams only, and she preferred it so.

Nella turned to her husband in appeal. But Dannor Shipwright was as always imperturbable, his sea-gray eyes watching without expression as Ailia ladled chowder into his bowl. "There's young Kurth Fisher," Nella continued, taking her own seat at the table. "He's got a boat of his own now, and no sweetheart yet. And then there's Armyn Cartwright, widowed only last year: a better, kinder man you'll never find—"

The ladle halted in midair. "But—he's so much older than I am!" Ailia exclaimed. "As old as Papa—and I couldn't look after all those children of his!"

"Why, you like little ones—telling them tales—"

"That's different!"

"You must learn to care for children, Ailia, or how will you manage when you've infants of your own? Your cousin Jemma's only a couple of years older than you, and she's got two babes already."

Ailia sat down and stared into space. The figure of a woman floated before her like a ghost: a grim-faced graying fishwife with crying children tugging at her skirts. Ailia saw many such women in the village, but this one was different: her eyes held a hunger keener than a knife's edge, a hunger that had nothing to do with food. It filled Ailia with fear, for the woman was herself.

"I don't want to get married," she said quietly, "ever."

"And what do you plan to do then, miss? Enter a nunnery? You can't live with your father and me forever. You came to us rather late in life, you know, and I want to see you settled. It's of your own good I'm thinking."

Again Ailia made no reply: there was a peculiar lump in her throat that made both speaking and eating difficult. Her mother said no more. Three different silences—placid, affronted, and dismayed—blended over the tabletop with the steam from the chowder-bowls. As soon as the meal was over Ailia leaped up in haste to gather and wash the dishes.

"Hello in there!" came a shout at the door, to Ailia's vast relief. Jaimon stood in the open doorway, the mead-mellow light of early evening spilling in around him, and behind him were Aunt Betta and cousin Jemma with her two little sons. As they entered in a babble of conversation Ailia felt her mood lighten. Her father and Jaimon now dominated the conversation, with their tales of ocean voyages. As she scrubbed the chowder-pot she listened to the men's talk, journeying with them to faraway places: to bath-warm seas where the fish were bright as butterflies and the Archipelagoes lay in long necklaces of emerald; to the coast of Mohara-land, where crocodiles sunned themselves on the mud flats of the deltas and dark women stooped to fill clay pots with river-water. Even the stars were different here, and the moon hung upside down. The men's talk moved northward along the Antipodean coast, and she followed them to Zimboura. Ships of the Commonwealth had once put into the ports of that heathen land to load the wares of the desert caravans, silk and incense and ivory; but even the sea-weary sailors never cared to linger in its teeming, violent cities. Farther to the north lay rocky and rugged Shurkana, where the elephants and rhinoceri grew woolly pelts, and the fierce proud Shurka people dwelt in their mountain fortresses.

The conversation crossed the ocean then, traveling to the great western Continent: moving along the sunny southern coasts of Marakor with its vineyards and fragrant orange groves, then north again to the storied forests and mountains of Maurainia. There crumbling ruins—towers, temples, aqueducts—bore mute testimony to the ancient reign of the Elei.

"The Elei claimed to be descended from their own gods," Jaimon explained to her mother. "The gods came down to Earth from the skies, they said, and took human wives and husbands, and taught them how to read and write and build and farm."

"Imagine!" said Nella. "They were as heathen as the Zimbourans, then."

"They had a great civilization, though, Aunt Nell," her nephew told her. "Its art, its buildings—*we've* nothing to match it, nowadays. And they had it when our forefathers were dressing in skins and hunting with spears."

"The stories say the Elei came from the island of Trynisia," put in Ailia, all pretense at dishwashing abandoned, "way up north. It was full of beautiful palaces and gardens." Again she felt a little thrill of delight at her own words.

"Trynisia's only a story, Ailia," said Jaimon. "No one has ever found it. It was just an imaginary country."

"Do you really think so?"

"Of course. Remember, the stories say that Trynisia lay in the far north, but they describe it as a *warm* country! And all that rot about dragons, and faeries, and buildings covered in gold and jewels! The king's sent expeditions into the north sea, and they've found nothing up there but ice."

Nella waved her hand impatiently, as though at a bothersome fly. "Never mind all that nonsense. What is the news these days? Has the king's daughter wed yet? And what of this new tyrant in Zimboura?"

"Khalazar." All the animation dropped from Jaimon's face. "He's overthrown King Jandar of Shurkana, so he rules all the Antipodes now. The sailors from the merchant service say he'll make his way westward next, to the Southern Archipelago."

"He's got his own people believing he's some sort of god, hasn't he?" Dannor commented.

"So I hear. Power-mad, that's what he is. He wants to rule the whole world." Jaimon shook his head.

"The world!" Jemma tightened her arms around baby Dani and looked with anxious eyes at her little boy Lem, who was sailing a toy boat across the worn planks of the floor.

"Now, don't you fret, my dear," Aunt Betta soothed. "You know those heathens have been fighting each other since time began. It's nothing to do with us."

There was a short silence broken only by the chimes of the old ship's clock, ringing out the watches of a vanished vessel. Then Jaimon spoke again.

"Things have changed, mam. The Shurkanese capital fell to the Zimbouran army in only *three days*. It's these new cannons, they say: they're a hundred times stronger than catapults or battering rams. Walls just crumple before them. You're wrong if you think it doesn't really affect us. Now that he's got all of Shurkana's lumber and pastureland, King Khalazar can afford to build a bigger fleet and feed his armies. Next he'll take the Archipelagoes of Kaan, to harbor his Armada. And then he will be within sailing distance of our island."

He paused at this point to let his words sink in, but the faces turned toward him were blank. None of them could imagine anyone wanting Great Island. After a moment Dannor said as much.

Jaimon raised his eyebrows. "No? It would make another fine base for his ships—one not so very far from the Continent."

"Oh, do you really think it will come to that?" cried Jemma in alarm. "Attacking the Continent?" The baby woke and began to mewl.

Jaimon gave a slight shrug of his shoulders. "We'll see. If he takes the Archipelagoes it will be a sign that he's preparing for war against the Commonwealth. We can only hope our king will send warships to defend us."

"He will, if it comes to that," opined Dannor in his slow, considered manner. "The Commonwealth protects its own. And I say this tyrant won't dare touch a Commonwealth colony."

"Anyway, the fishing boats are coming in now, by the sound of it," said Aunt Betta, turning toward the door. "I'm off to help with the catch, tyrant or no tyrant. Jemma, you just stay here and mind your little ones."

Nella looked over at Ailia. "Why don't *you* help your aunt, Ailia? I'm sure she could use a hand. Leave the dishes to me." She and Betta exchanged an odd, conspiratorial glance. It made Ailia feel uneasy.

She followed her aunt down the well-worn dirt track that led to the harbor. The sun had gone in behind the hills, taking the golden light with it; in the west the sky was rimmed with rose, and to the east the line between sky and sea was already lost in shadow. Halfway to the wharves Ailia stopped short and gave an exclamation. "It's much cooler down here by the water, isn't it, Aunt Bett? I had better go back and get my shawl."

Before her aunt could say anything Ailia sprinted back along the path. Betta called after her, but she pretended not to hear.

When she arrived at the house she slowed to a walk. Stealing up to the front door, she stood listening to the conversation within. The baby was now crying lustily and she had to strain to hear the adults' voices. She felt guilty to be eavesdropping like this, and struggled to justify it to herself. She had to know what they were talking about in there. She was quite certain, from the looks she had seen her mother and aunt exchange, that it was not about wars or tyrant kings. It was about her.

Finally she heard her name spoken. "Ah, this is foolishness, Nell," said her father. "Tell Ailia. She's got a right to know."

"Tell her what, Dann? That she won't be going after all? Let her apply for the scholarship, you said. Give her something to hope for. I told you at the time I didn't approve of giving her false hopes."

"I thought," answered her husband after a pause, "that if she were to apply to the Royal Academy and be rejected, she'd resign herself to life here, instead of always thinking she'd have had a chance if only we'd let her try."

The letter! Ailia thought in dismay. *Jaim brought it—why didn't he tell me? Perhaps he couldn't bear to break the bad news—*

"Well, this is a pretty kettle of fish!" Nella continued.

"Just listen to this: 'The essay was exceptionally well-written . . . a scholarship available as of this autumn . . .' And 'payment for your sea-passage and for the return trip of your chaperon.' "

"The payment for the berths is here in this purse," said Jaimon's voice. "In money, of course—they don't barter over there."

There was a rustle, a clinking sound, then silence. At last her mother spoke in a hushed voice. "I've never seen real coin. Is that silver? It's so bright, so beautiful—and there's so much of it!"

Jaimon laughed. "Too much. Those Academy folks must think our island's on the other side of the world. We could send the whole village to the Continent with that!"

"Well, it must be sent back to them," Nella said. "What a fix! Bless us all if the girl didn't go and get herself *accepted* at the Academy, and what's to be done when she finds she can't go is beyond me. She'll be even more miserable than she was before. Jaimon, this is all your doing. *You're* the one who egged her on."

"Why can't she go?" said Jaimon's voice.

There was a moment's stunned silence. The heart of the eavesdropper leaped.

"What'll she do here?" continued Jaimon. "Marry some fisherman? Spend her life mending nets and gutting fish? She couldn't bear to live like that, and you know it!"

"Only because her head's been filled up with foolishness out of books," said Nella. "We should never have let her have them: they've given her wild ideas. As for marriage, you and Ailia used to get along so well, I'd thought you and she might make a match of it one day. Cousins do marry sometimes. But you up and went off to sea, and left her here all alone."

"Look here," Jaimon said, "Ailia and I are good friends, always have been. But she doesn't want to marry me, and why should she? Why marry at all, if she doesn't want to? With what she learned over there she could be a teacher, or something."

"It's out of the question," Nella replied. "No Island woman's ever gone away to be educated."

"You make it sound like something shocking, Aunt."

"She is our only child, Jaimon. And—if she goes she might never come back."

Her mother's voice had changed—there was a hint of a quaver in it, and Ailia stood aghast, her heart wrung now as well as her conscience. As she began to back quietly away she heard Jaimon say, "I couldn't wait to go to sea, but since I left there hasn't been a day when I haven't thought of this place and the folks at home. Ailia might love the Island more if she went away from it for a while."

But Nella had recovered herself. "I'll not have her making an ocean voyage with the world in such a state. I'm amazed your parents will let you go to sea again—and you're a man, not a slip of a girl. Ailia is not going anywhere alone, and that's final."

There was no comment from Dannor, which could only mean that he agreed with his wife. Ailia turned away and headed down the path, feeling dazed. She had never really believed she would be accepted at the Royal Academy, she realized now: it had just been a daydream, a faint hope that had nonetheless raised her spirits and made life endurable for a time. She had not allowed herself to think of what she would do when the rejection finally came. And, incredibly, it had not come after all: she had been *accepted* at the Academy—and she had not really thought what that would mean, either.

My head was in the clouds, as usual. Me, travel across the sea—go live in another country all by myself! No, I wasn't thinking. Of course they would never have let me.

"Where's your shawl then?" Aunt Bett demanded when Ailia joined her at the wharf.

"Oh," Ailia murmured. "I—I don't really need it after all."

Some of the fishermen's boats were docked, others were just coming in to shore. She had once loved to see them glide in out of the deepening dusk, the lamps at their bows and mastheads glowing, returning to the safety of the harbor and leaving the dark and dangerous sea behind. Now she yearned to take a boat herself and sail away—far across the sea, to the distant horizon, to the End of the World. She watched dull-eyed as her Uncle Nedman brought his boat in and secured it to the wharf, and he and his son-in-law Arran Fisher hefted the nets to spill out their catch of herring in a large glistening pile. Ailia joined the fishermen and their families as they gathered by the boats in little knots, pulling fish from the piles, slitting them open with the long gutting knives and tossing the offal into the harbor, where a few lingering gulls fought over it in a flurry of wings and jabbing bills. The birds' indignant screams drowned out the few murmured scraps of conversation; most of the men and women worked in a wordless day's-end silence, seldom raising their eyes from their beslimed and bloodied hands. Beyond the docks the sea lipped the shingled shore and then fell back with deep sighs, as though it too were weary.

In the absence of talk, Ailia was once more left to her troubling thoughts, and she looked about her for some distraction as she worked. The sky above the tossing forest of masts was now candled with stars, flickering as if a breath might blow them out: but though they wavered they shone undimmed, for the moon had not yet risen. In the north was a dance of light, shifting and shimmering like sun-ripples on a boat's hull: the aurora borealis. Ailia remembered what an old fishwife had told her about it long ago: " 'Tis the lights of the Fairfolk's cities reflecting in the sky. They hold high revels in their kingdom tonight." Perhaps Jaimon was wrong and Trynisia was real after all, and some Elei were still living there, and she would go look for them one day . . . Or perhaps she would sail west, follow the wheeling motion of sun and moon and stars to the Continent, and Maurainia . . . But these were only idle fancies and at last she knew it. She looked at the *Sea Maid*, swaying at anchor with sails furled, and she felt a stab of longing sharp as any physical pain. If only she had been born a man, like Jaim! Or *anything* but a woman! Birds could migrate each year to the southern isles, and perch in the carved eaves of heathen temples, seeing with their little ink-drop eyes wonders that she would never know. *This island is the only place I will ever see. Only this, until I die.*

Averting her eyes from the scene before her, Ailia fixed her eyes on the stars instead and let her mind wander among them, far from the stench and slimy feel of the dead fish in her hands. Dannor had long ago taught her the names of the major stars and constellations—as a sailor, of course, he knew the night sky by heart. Her own name meant "Lodestar" in the old Elei tongue—an appropriate name for the daughter of a sailor, though she thought it quite romantic too. "Faranda—Berilion—Anatarva," she murmured the star-names below her breath while she worked, as though incanting a spell. Two planets were visible tonight: yellow Iantha, high in the zenith like a spark flown out of a fire; and low in the west a great welling droplet of water-blue brilliance, brighter than anything else in the sky. That was Arainia, which old poems called the Morning Star, though sometimes it shone in the evening as now. Down on the point, in the squat stone tower where the sea-beacon burned, a statue of the goddess Elarainia still stood in a tall niche. She was carved of gray stone, one hand raised in a protective gesture as she gazed out to sea. Her face was worn away by storm and flying spray, but one could still make out the shape of a starry diadem above it. To sailors in olden times Elarainia was a guardian spirit: Almailia, Star of the Sea. The Patriarchs of the True Faith, however, disapproved of polytheism in general and female divinities in particular: her name had not been invoked on the Island for hundreds of years.

Overhead the Merendalia, the Starry Way, laid its luminous track across the night, and to either side of it were arrayed the constellations of late summer: the Sphinx, the Centaur, the Dragon with his starry coils. As Ailia looked up at them her heart filled, as always, with a poignant yearning. To the ancients the constellations were not mere guides for navigators, but the dwelling places of their gods, stellar states within a Celestial Empire. And long ago the Elei (so the old tales said) had journeyed to this sky-country, the homeland of their divine ancestors, riding upon winged dragons or in magical flying ships.

"What in the world?" exclaimed Aunt Betta, setting down her knife.

Ailia, in the act of passing a fish to her aunt, turned to look at her in puzzlement. Aunt Bett was staring and pointing seaward, as were all of the other villagers. And now Ailia saw the lights shining out there on the darkened sea, dozens and dozens of them. More fishing boats approaching shore? But all the boats were in: and anyway Bayport's entire fishing fleet wasn't half so large. These lights might have belonged to a lamp lit town adrift upon the waves. And they were drawing closer as she watched.

The herring slipped through her fingers to the ground. *Could it be King Khalazar?* she wondered, and felt her heart lurch beneath her ribs as she sprang up. *Was Jaim right—is the Armada coming here?*

As the fisher folk stood gesturing and exclaiming to one another she turned and fled back up the path toward her home.

THE VILLAGE WAS IN AN UPROAR. People streamed down to the harbor, lanterns in hand, and somewhere a man's voice was shouting—the town crier, probably. Staring out through one of the kitchen windows, Ailia could see the lights swarming around the wharf, and imposed upon them the transparent reflection of her mother's figure as Nella rushed to and fro, flinging clothes and pots and loaves of bread into an old sea chest of Dannor's.

"What are you doing, Aunt?" Jaimon demanded, coming in the front door with Betta and Dannor.

"We must go," Nella babbled, "away from the sea. We'll go inland, to the barrens—"

"Be easy, Nell," her husband interrupted. "The ships are not Zimbouran after all. They're Kaanish."

"Kaans!" Ailia cried. "But why have they come *here*, Papa? Does this mean the Archipelagoes are—"

"The southern islands are taken," Jaimon told her. "They say Khalazar has annexed them, and the Northern Archipelago will be next. It's just as I said: the Armada is on the move."

Ailia darted past him out the open door and stood at the top of the path, staring down at the harbor and the alien vessels there. There was one large ship, but most were not much larger than the fishing boats of the Islanders. All looked weather-beaten, some lying low in the water as though they had sprung leaks, with waves lapping at the staring eyes painted on their prows. Their ribbed sails were tattered, and their decks crowded with people.

She hastened back inside again. Jaimon was arguing with her mother. "Aunt Nell, if the Zimbourans come here they will take the whole island. Coast and barrens and all. It's no use hiding out in the wilds. They'll hunt you down and kill you."

Nella made no reply, only put her hand to her heart. Jaim swept a grim gaze about the room. "The Kaans are only stopping here to get a few supplies, and mend their ships if they can. But even if they can't, they're still sailing on—as soon as possible. They would rather risk drowning at sea in those rotting tubs than wait here for the Armada. Now do you understand?"

"But what can we do, Jaimon?" wailed Aunt Betta. "We can't leave the Island."

"No," Jaimon admitted. "Not right away, at any rate. You should go to the Continent, to Maurainia; but fishing boats will never cross the ocean, and the Kaans' boats are overcrowded as it is. That leaves only the *Sea Maid*, and my captain says he doesn't believe in the danger. He has a cargo to pick up in the Northern Archipelago, and he'll not change his course—not unless he's paid in money. The fool!"

"But we have money!" Ailia cried, leaping forward. "We've got all that silver coin from the Academy."

Her mother stared. "How did you know—"

"I overheard," Ailia interrupted, and turned to Jaimon. "There was enough to send the whole village, you said."

He looked a little taken aback. "I was only joking. The silver's meant to buy passage for two."

"But on a proper passenger ship, Jaim, with cabins and everything. Wouldn't a cargo ship cost less? Your captain might take more of us for the same amount." Ailia faced her father. "Please, Papa! I'm sure the Academy people won't mind us using it, in an emergency like this. We needn't stay in Maurainia forever: only until the danger is over, and we've earned enough money to come back again. And the Kaans must come with us too—they will never make the crossing in those leaky boats of theirs. If we haven't enough money for all of them couldn't we pay the captain the silver we've got, and promise him the rest on arrival? We can earn it when we get there. And anyway someone *must* get a message to the king. Once we're on the Continent we can tell him what's happening, and ask him to send some more ships to pick up the other Islanders. Or even some warships, to defend the Island. We must take the *Sea Maid* to Maurainia—" Ailia was obliged to stop at this point, as she had run out of breath, but her eyes remained fastened on her father's.

"I'm not leaving," said Dannor, his face set in obstinate lines. "The Island's my home. I told you, Khalazar won't dare touch it."

"You don't know that, Papa!" exclaimed Ailia. She felt a sharp, cramping sensation somewhere in the region of her stomach and suddenly thought, *This is what real fear feels like.* It was not in the least romantic. "You heard what Jaim said—King Khalazar wants a base for his ships, so they can attack the Continent!"

Jaimon stepped forward. "Uncle," he said, "Ailia is right. There may not be enough silver to buy passage for the whole village and the Kaans. But we could at least send away our women and children, and theirs too, until this threat has passed. You needn't go if you don't want to. I will be on board, and I can leave the ship when we get to Maurainia and look after Ailia and the others—until we're certain it's safe for them to return."

Ailia watched her father with a strange blend of fear and elation. *Please let him agree, please . . .* Dannor ruminated, stroking his bristly chin, and as always the many lines and furrows in his weathered face made his expression impossible to read.

Then he looked up at his nephew and gave a slight, almost imperceptible nod. "Very well, then," he said.

2

Damion

FATHER DAMION ATHARIEL STOOD ALONE before the gate of Heaven.

It reared up from the green hill's crest, gleaming in the tropical sun: two tall pillars of white stone, placed about ten paces apart so as to form the posts of an invisible gate. Each was adorned with a carved dragon, its stone coils wound around the pillar in a graceful spiral, its horned head resting on the capital. "Spirit-gates" like this one could be found throughout the Archipelagoes of Kaan: they were very old, dating to the days of the Elei Commonwealth, and their use and significance were now unknown. There was never more than one to an island, and they were never located on roads, or near the ruins of old cities where a gate might be expected: they stood always in isolated places, leading from nowhere to nowhere. The Kaanish people in the city below declared that this gate was wizards' work, and that it led to the spirit world. Though the Maurainian missionaries had walked between the pillars time and time again to disprove the superstition, nothing could induce the Kaans to follow them.

There were, Damion acknowledged, similar superstitions in his own country. A pair of old standing stones in northern Maurainia was believed, at least by the locals, to mark a magic portal to the faerie world. But those ancient menhirs were crude things compared to the spirit-gate. He walked closer to the right-hand pillar, examining the sculpted dragon. It was a beautiful creature, lithe and sinuous and scaled like a carp, with only a superficial resemblance to the fire-spouting beasts of his own western mythology. The "dragons" of old Elei and Kaanish lore were not monsters, but celestial beings like gods or angels. Their proper dwelling place was the spirit plane, but they manifested in the material world whenever they chose, and always used their magical powers for good. The heroes of Kaanish legend did not ride out to slay them, but rather to seek their help and guidance. Celestial dragons used this gateway, it was said, flying back and forth through it invisible to mortal eyes. It was still against the law to erect any building on the summit of this hill, for such a structure—so the Kaans explained—might obstruct the paths of the dragons' flight.

Damion sighed. It was to eliminate pagan notions like these that he and other missionaries of the True Faith had journeyed from Maurainia to the Archipelagoes. The Faithful were particularly suspicious of dragon-worship, for in western lands the dragon was a symbol for the Fiend, Modrian-Valdur. But now that he had lived here for a time, Damion's feelings were curiously mixed. He found much in the eastern traditions that was both beautiful and inspiring. He stepped back and gazed at the vista framed by the stone posts. No otherworldly realm lay there: merely a view of the hillside's feathery foliage, the tiled roofs of the city of Jardjana, and the jewel-blue expanse of its harbor and bay. In the distance loomed the green volcanic peaks of Medosha, the sacred island, where none but the highest Kaanish priests ever set foot. Many other islands reared out of the sea beyond, blue and dim with distance so that they might almost have been low-lying clouds. And on the far horizon sprawled real clouds with towering summits, like islands still larger and more fantastic in shape.

Damion stepped between the pillars and descended the grassy slope of the hill. This island of Jana, with its bustling port city, had been his dwelling place for the greater part of a year. Exotic and strange as it had seemed to him at first, it had now become like home to him. The steep-roofed buildings, with their ornate carved eaves and fierce-looking ceramic door-guardians; the houses of the poor, built on stilts over the water because of the scarcity of land, so that they resembled spindly-legged birds wading in the tide; the riot of smells—incense blown from shrines, fresh fish, spices, cow dung, the ripe refuse of the gutters; the short-horned water buffaloes, smaller cousins to those of the Antipodes, that carried peasants and huge straw panniers to market; the open-air stalls with barrels full of mangoes and coconuts and clambering crabs . . . all these things were familiar now, like a garment grown more comfortable with wear. But not until this moment had he realized that he loved the Archipelagoes. And now he must leave them. This last walk around the city was his final farewell.

In the early days Damion had walked the streets of Jardjana with his cowl drawn over his head, as much to ward off the Kaans' inquisitive stares as to counter the rays of the sun. His white ankle-length robe marked him as a priest of the True Faith, but the Kaans of this day and age were accustomed to seeing the garb of the western religion in their streets; it was the young man's coloring that had drawn their attention, the fairness of his skin and hair and his astonishing sky-blue eyes. But now passersby paid no heed to him. Panic-stricken citizens rushed past him along the hill path with all their belongings bundled on their backs, fleeing the city for the dubious safety of the hill country farther inland. Refugees from conquered islands thronged the streets and alleyways below, some trying to set up crude shelters in the gutters. In the midst of this confusion the beggars squatted among their hovering flies like heaps of discarded rags.

The Zimbouran king had ordered all citizens of the Commonwealth expelled from the island domains, which he declared annexed; Jana's governor, knowing that other islands had already fallen and that his own warships could never match the Zimbouran fleet, offered no resistance. People from the western Continent—merchants and missionaries, for the most part—crowded the harbor inns: they would be able to get any berth available, as they had money. Most of the natives could only stare hopelessly at the few ships remaining, and wait for the invading Armada. One small black-hulled Zimbouran galley, rowed by slaves, had already arrived in the harbor this morning.

Tales of Zimbouran savagery abounded in the city. When they conquered a country, they burned whole villages to the ground and put hundreds of people to the sword—"just to frighten the rest," one trembling Kaan told Damion. There was no reason to doubt the man's word. It was well-known that Zimbouran rulers meted out such treatment to their own people; they would surely not hesitate to do the same to foreigners. A few Kaans, driven to desperation, had set out in fishing boats and makeshift rafts in a dangerous attempt to cross the leagues of open ocean separating their island from the nearest Commonwealth colony.

And now we are leaving, abandoning them to their fate.

Damion's bleak thoughts were interrupted by a commotion in the street ahead of him. Craning his neck above the crowds, he glimpsed a number of black-clad priests standing on the steps of a building, an exquisite structure whose gilded spires reflected in the shallow moat surrounding it. It was a native shrine, its shape an imitation of the Sacred Island. But the clerics on its steps were not Kaans. They were Zimbourans, tall and almost deathly pale: they had likely come here from the slave-galley. As Damion watched, one Zimbouran priest descended the steps and walked right into the throng, which parted and eddied around him as though he carried some deadly contagion. Mere days ago, Damion reflected, this man would have been pursued and beaten by the crowds for daring to go near one of their holy sites.

Now no one dares touch him, and he knows it.

To avoid a confrontation with the priests, he turned quickly toward a side alley. Even as he did so there was a clatter of boots along the main street and a little procession of dark-clad men appeared around the corner. He recognized these as Zimbourans also, and withdrew into the alley to watch them stride past, imperious as a parade of conquerors despite their small numbers. They knew the island was theirs now. A stout, bearded captain walked at their head in black leather battle dress. In the heat his face had turned from the usual Zimbouran pallor to deep pomegranate. His dozen underlings followed, one man lagging somewhat behind. At the sight of this last figure Damion caught his breath in surprise.

This was no Zimbouran: the man's skin was dark as mahogany, his black hair curly rather than straight. He must be at least half-Mohara, though how such a union could have come about was baffling. The Zimbourans considered the Moharas a lower caste, and the two races were forbidden to intermarry. It was a wonder this improbable half-breed had been allowed to live, let alone been made a soldier. He wore a defiant air; his black leather tunic was open at the front, showing much of a well-muscled chest, and on his left ear gleamed a brass ring from which an animal's claw—a lion's, perhaps?—dangled. A fierce mustache shadowed his upper lip; beneath the heavy brows his dark eyes were like smoldering coals. For an instant those eyes met Damion's own, and suddenly the fire in them rekindled: they flashed briefly with anger—or was it disdain? Then the man deliberately looked away and walked on. Damion stared after him, wrung with pity and indignation, until he disappeared into the crowds along with the rest of the procession. He must be a slave of the Zimbourans—but why, then, had he shown such resentment to a western priest?

The guardsmen, Damion realized, were heading for the shrine. There was another flurry of activity there, followed by shouting, and then a sound Damion had never heard before tore the air.

It was a man's scream—harsh, despairing, filled with pain.

Damion could see the Zimbouran soldiers, standing tall above the slight island people: their leader seemed to be carrying something in his arms, a roll or bundle of dark brown cloth. Some sacred relic, no doubt, snatched from the shrine in an act of deliberate desecration. The crowd moaned. And then it gave a great roar: there was a flash of movement, and the heavy, sweating captain stumbled and fell ignominiously, vanishing along with the bundle into the press of bodies below. Had somebody actually dared to trip him up?

At the back of his mind Damion knew that things were growing dangerous and he should leave, but still he remained, riveted by the unfolding drama. Someone was fighting his way through the mob. The young priest saw no one, but there was a trail of jostled bodies and gesticulating arms, like a disturbance of undergrowth when an animal darts through. The Zimbouran leader's head and shoulders reappeared above the crowd: he had managed to get to his feet again, but he no longer held the bundle. His face was redder than ever, red with rage. He yelled at the crowd in Kaanish.

"Stop him!"

The commotion in the crowd was moving in Damion's direction, toward the side alley. Peering through the overlapping bodies, he glimpsed a thin, wiry figure weaving in and out through the tangle of limbs. A boy of about fourteen years, it looked like, clad in beggar's rags with a dirty cloth wound turban-style about his head. Damion saw to his astonishment that the boy's face was as fair-skinned as his own, with a freckled nose and wisps of blond hair straggling under the turban. This street waif was a westerner! Pale blue eyes flicked up at Damion, then away again, as the youth struggled through the milling bodies.

Under one arm he clutched the cloth bundle.

Shouting, the Zimbourans beat their way through the crowd with the flats of their swords, parting it by force. Two black-clad soldiers lunged simultaneously for the thief, who dodged neatly, making the men collide with one another. He rolled on his side to avoid another attacker, then was on his feet again, sprinting down the alley toward Damion.

"You, priest—come with me!" The waif grabbed Damion's hand and yanked him into the alleyway.

Damion found himself running along beside the youth. "What is it? What have you got there?"

"No *time*," came the breathless answer. The street waif gave a swift backward glance, followed by a foul and explicit Kaanish curse. "I can hear them coming! Take this to the monastery, Father, while I try to draw them off down that other alley."

Before Damion realized what was happening, something was thrust into his arms, and he found himself the possessor of the contested bundle. He gaped. "What! Wait a minute!"

But the youth only gave him an impatient shove. "Go *on!*" he yelled, then sped off down the other alley. There were shouts as the pursuers caught sight of their quarry, and a pounding of booted feet.

Damion stood rooted to the spot, stunned. *I mustn't panic,* he thought, still unable to believe that any of this was really happening. He watched, in a curious detached way, the Zimbourans approaching. They shouted, seeing Damion standing there: a priest of a rival faith, with their stolen prize in his hands.

Damion pondered no further. He whirled and sprinted wildly down the narrow lane and on through a maze of interconnecting alleys beyond. In his confusion it never occurred to him to throw the bundle away; if anything, he held it to him more tightly than before. All he could think of was the rage on the leader's face, and the hoarse scream he had heard coming from the shrine. Glancing down at the dirty brown cloth of the bundle, he saw with a queasy feeling that a smear of red on it had rubbed off onto his robe. Blood . . . ?

The back alley proved to be a veritable obstacle course, with supine beggars, meandering pariah dogs, rubbish heaps, and laundry lines strung inconveniently across it. He ducked and dodged as he ran, and was soon out of breath, but dared not stop: he could still hear booted feet clumping behind him, and gathered from the grunts and curses he heard that the pursuing soldiers were encountering the same obstacles. He risked a frantic glance over his shoulder: no sign of them. Kilting up his robes with one hand, he put on a desperate spurt of speed, despite the growing stitch in his side.

He did not even know to what deed he had become an unwitting accomplice: he only knew that it was too late now to turn back. Would his pursuers believe he had nothing to do with the seizure of this bundle? They might have done, had he surrendered it to them at once. But now they would be certain that he was part of some plan, that he'd conspired with the turbaned boy to snatch . . . *whatever* this thing was.

The heat was overpowering, but he could not pause even to mop the streams of sweat from his brow. He blinked as it ran into his eyes. Speeding around a sharp corner, he crashed into a broken handcart lying discarded in the middle of the alley, and fell his length on the pavement. For a moment he lay stunned, gasping for breath. Then with an effort he took up the fallen bundle and struggled to his feet again, leaning for support on the side of the overturned cart. There was a fiery jab of pain in his left ankle as he put weight on it, and his shin was barked and bleeding. Wincing, he forced himself to limp on for a few paces. The alley widened out into a small oblong space between buildings, their walls flaking and blotched with damp. The space was dominated by a huge rubbish heap composed of everything from filthy rags and torn clothing to rotting vegetables. Flies swarmed noisily above it. At the far end an archway led into another dingy alley. He must keep running—but his ankle was hurt . . .

The soldiers were drawing nearer. Suddenly Damion knew he would never outrun them, lamed as he was.

His eyes swept around the court, then settled on the rubbish heap.

"IT IS TRUE, BROTHER: the Zimbourans *are* coming. A slave-galley has arrived in port, and the royal Armada is less than a day away, according to reports that I have heard." Abbot Shan's face and voice were calm as he spoke these words, but Prior Vale blanched.

"Dear God in Heaven," he murmured.

Within the walls of the Monastery of Perpetual Peace, perched on the second highest of Jardjana's hills, the atmosphere was that of a fortress under siege: never had the building seemed so ill-named. Its monks had broken with tradition to offer the sacred inner spaces of their cloister as a safe haven, and its once-silent hallways rang with the clamor of the refugees.

"I think, my friend, that you and your Maurainian brethren had best leave while you can," continued the Kaanish abbot in his deep, tranquil voice. "Your mission here is ended. I am glad I could give you shelter this day, but before long even these walls will not be sufficient to protect you. The Zimbourans have no love for the peoples of the western Commonwealth, as you well know. There are ships in the harbor still, and the guardsmen from the Maurainian merchants' compound have agreed to escort all their people there. Gather up your monks, Brother, and join them. Tomorrow you will have no guards, and no more vessels to flee to."

Prior Vale gave a sober nod. "I'll go fetch the Brothers at once."

He heaved a great sigh as he hurried out of the cloister and into the central court. This monastery was a triumph of the Faith: a former pleasure-palace, donated to the Order by an island noble who converted some years ago. The monks had since labored to give the buildings a more austere atmosphere, painting over decorative murals and transforming the women's solar into a chapel. The building represented many decades of mission work—and soon it would all come to nothing. In the courtyard birds and cicadas twittered and thrummed complacently in the branches of stately cypress trees, while water plashed in the blue-tiled basin of a fountain. The sweltering heat pressed down upon the prior's head as he crossed the court toward the missionary monks gathered at the fountain's edge. "Still no sign of Father Damion?" he queried, wiping his brow.

They all shook their heads.

The prior groaned. Damion Athariel had been raised in the orphanage of his monastery back in Maurainia, and ordained to the priesthood a little over a year ago. Though he was a fine theologian for his age and strongly committed to mission work, the prior often worried about him. "If there's trouble of any kind, one thing's for certain," he fretted, his annoyance masking a rising anxiety. "Damion will manage to be right in the thick of it." How like him to go for one last walk about the city only moments before news broke of the Armada's approach!

The prior went back inside and stood in the main hall, blinking as his sun-dazzled eyes readjusted. People milled about him in the dim light.

"A Zimbouran galley is here, with priests and soldiers—and there are more ships on the way!" someone shouted. The crowd in the hall buzzed at the news, like a hive struck by a stone. Prior Vale, forcing down the panic that rose in his own mind, fought his way to the Kaanish monks stationed by the main doors. Yes, they said, Father Damion had gone out; but no one had seen him return.

"I am sorry," one monk told him, speaking with the same quiet fatalism the abbot had shown. "But there is nothing to be done. I understand you were close to this young man, and I promise that if we find him we will take him in. But you must get your own people down to the harbor before very long, or none of you will be able to leave."

Prior Vale knew it was useless to argue. As he turned away there was a fresh outburst of cries and exclamations from the other end of the hall. The refugees were scattering in apparent panic. *Not the Zimbourans already?* he wondered, staring in alarm at the scene. Then he saw a lone figure, swathed entirely in rags, limping in at the door. The man's face and hands were completely covered, and even from here the prior could smell the foul odor of decay that emanated from him.

Dear God—a leper! The man's fear of the Zimbourans must have driven him to seek sanctuary here, despite his terrible illness. One of the monks hastened toward the ragged figure and, standing at a safe distance, remonstrated with him. In response, the man unwound his headcloths to expose, surprisingly, a healthy, youthful face surmounted by fair hair. He called out something to the monk, who came forward looking bemused, and handed him what appeared to be a bundle of dirty rags.

Prior Vale started. "Damion Athariel!" he shouted, rushing forward. "For the love of Heaven, what do you think you're doing? And where have you been?" He felt weak at the knees with relief.

"Down in the city, Father," Damion replied. He began to struggle out of his foul-smelling rags, like an insect fighting its way out of a chrysalis.

"What games have you been up to?" Now that Damion was safe, Prior Vale was free to be angry. "A priest of the True Faith dressing up as a leper! What do you mean by this behavior? What were you doing?"

Damion bent to massage his shin, wincing: apparently the lameness at least was unfeigned. "I . . . well, the truth is, I've been having a bit of an adventure, Father. I've been hiding at the bottom of a rubbish heap—sorry about the smell—and to get back here safely I had to disguise myself with these rags. No one interferes with a leper, so—"

"What did you give to the Brother just now?"

"I don't know."

"Don't know?"

"I haven't had a chance to look at it yet. I just wish I could have helped the lad who gave it to me, even if he did land me in a mess. I hope he got away from the Zimbourans . . ."

Zimbourans! "Has the Armada come, then?"

Damion stared. "Armada? No, it was just some soldiers off a galley in the harbor. Is the Armada on its way, then? That would explain why they were so bold."

"I should have known this was another one of your escapades," complained the bewildered prior. "Yes, the fleet's on its way and we're leaving, thanks be, so you'll have no more chances to get yourself into *adventures*."

"Brother Damion?" The monk who had spoken with Damion at the front door had reappeared. "The abbot would like to speak with you in the chapel, as soon as possible."

"I'll be with him directly," Damion answered, wondering, *Why in the chapel?* He turned to Prior Vale. "And the Kaanish monks, Father? Are they leaving with us?"

"No, they're staying here, of course! It's their country, after all."

Damion looked troubled. "I hate to leave these people, Father. I was beginning to like this place—to feel I belonged. I wish there was something we could *do*, instead of just turning tail and fleeing back to Maurainia. It makes me feel like the proverbial rat abandoning ship."

"I always did think," the prior muttered when Damion had moved out of earshot, "that that rat showed a certain amount of sense."

* * *

ABBOT SHAN MET HIM at the chapel door.

"You sent for me, Father?" Damion asked.

The abbot nodded. "Come in."

Inside lay a cool stone interior, the tropical sun pouring through tinted windows to pool in molten hues along the floor. Damion entered, then stopped short. There was another person in the chapel, seated in an ornate gilded chair to one side of the marble altar—a figure clad not in the white western-style robe worn by the monks, but in garb more like that of a Kaanish holy man: a robe richly patterned with red, gold, and saffron, and a tall golden headdress fringed with scarlet tassels. From behind the tassels light blue eyes gazed at him out of a fair-skinned face.

The face was that of the street waif.

But now that the grimy rag-turban was gone, a braid of long blonde hair was revealed hanging down the figure's back, and the slender silk-clad body showed curves that the ragged shirt and baggy trousers had concealed.

"You . . ." Damion lost his tongue; sputtered; found it again. "You're a *girl!*"

She grinned at him from underneath the fantastic headdress. Now that her face was clean, he noticed its features more: they were strong and regular, not pretty in the classic sense, but with a bone-firm beauty of their own. "You didn't guess?" she said in her clear contralto voice. "I only wear boy's clothes when I'm down in the city. It's safer that way. Here at home, though—"

He stared. "Home? Are you saying that you *live* here?"

"Yes. I've lived here all my life." The girl turned from him to the abbot, tassels swaying around her face. "May I go now, Father?"

"Yes, Lorelyn. Return to your room and pack your things: I will summon you soon."

Lorelyn. In the old Elei tongue the name meant "Daughter of Heaven." As the girl rose he noticed how tall she was, her head on a level with his. She swept out of the room with a rustle of her silken robe, and the abbot gazed after her with pensive eyes. "The ways of God are mysterious to men," he observed when she had gone. "We have tried for years to forbid Lorelyn from leaving the safe confines of the cloister, but always she would climb the walls and steal out to walk the streets on her own. The girl has no real understanding of danger, having led such a sheltered life here. When we warned her of the risks facing one of her sex in the city's alleys, she merely assumed male attire, taking discarded clothing from trash heaps. We thought her willful and difficult, and all along it was a plan of the Almighty to thwart our enemies. He intended that she should be down in the city today, and do what no one else dared."

Damion stared at the abbot in perplexity. "Father—why is a *woman* living in your monastery? Where did she come from?"

"We do not know," the abbot replied. "She appeared quite mysteriously, sixteen years ago: we arose for our dawn prayers one morning and found her sitting on the grass in the central court. It was as though she had dropped down out of the sky; indeed, some of the Brothers called it a miracle. She was very small then, scarcely old enough to walk and speak, so we could not question her. We do not usually take in orphans—ours is a contemplative order, and we never leave the walls of the monastery once our vows are taken. But she was a special case."

Damion was puzzled. The child of a Kaanish beggar might be smuggled into a monastery as an act of desperation, but there was no such thing as a poor westerner in the Archipelagoes. Only merchants came here as a rule, apart from the celibate missionaries. Was she illegitimate? She did not look like a child of mixed race—and if she were unwanted wouldn't she have been abandoned at birth? Why would her mother wait until she was old enough to walk?

"Her unexplained arrival is not the only curious thing about her," Abbot Shan continued. He gestured to Damion to sit in a pew and the priest was glad to obey: he was beginning to feel slightly giddy, and his twisted ankle was throbbing. The abbot sat down beside him. "She hears voices in her head—the voices of saints and angels, or so we believe. As a small child she would often laugh at nothing, or babble away at empty space, or follow with her eyes things no one else could see. Sometimes we could not reach her at all: it was as though she dwelt in a world of her own, some realm apart from this earthly one."

"What do these, er, voices say to her?" Damion asked.

"She cannot say: she does not hear them clearly enough."

"I beg your pardon?"

"The heavenly voices are indistinct—she says that it is like hearing people talking in a closed room some distance away. The sound of the voices comes through, but not the words. In time, though, I am sure they will become clearer. We believe that she is a holy being, and will one day be a prophetess—perhaps even a saint."

Remembering her rough and reckless behavior in the alley, Damion felt the girl was an unlikely candidate for sainthood. But he restrained himself from saying so.

"When she has reached an even higher state of grace, no doubt all will be made plain to her," the abbot continued. "She will converse with saints and angels, and convey their revelations to other mortals. We have been instructing her in the holy scriptures and the lives of the saints, to prepare her for the role she must play."

The poor girl's mad, Abbot—mad! That's why her parents abandoned her: they must have seen the signs. None of what Damion thought showed in his face, however: it was a mask of attentive concern. He had no wish to offend a good and kindly man, who was sheltering Damion and the western monks at his own risk: a man who might well be dead in a few days' time.

"We would be grateful if you would take Lorelyn away with you, to Maurainia," said the abbot. "Her fair coloring stands out here, and the Zimbourans will kill her if they find her."

"I will take her to the Continent," promised Damion, thinking: *I can leave her with the nuns at the Royal Academy. They'll care for her, give her shelter and schooling. Perhaps she can even be cured.*

"If, as we believe, she truly is a saint, then she has some great destiny to fulfill. Perhaps she has already done it, by taking the relic from the Zimbourans."

Damion now noticed the cloth bundle lying atop the altar. "What *is* this relic, Father?" he asked.

The abbot stared into space for several moments before replying. "Five hundred years ago, before the last Zimbouran invasion, brave monks of your country brought the True Faith to the Archipelagoes. In those days there was a monastery in Jardjana that guarded a great secret." He looked at Damion. "You know of the Meraalia—the Star Stone of Trynisia?"

"The Star Stone . . ." The words came to Damion along with a memory: the musty smell breathing from the pages of ancient books, long happy hours spent with the other orphanage boys in the Royal Academy's library. "Yes, of course: it's mentioned in the scriptures, and in some of the apocryphal writings too."

A soft gleam lit the depths of the old man's eyes. "Then you know the Stone was a holy gem, made by the angels—whom the ancients called the gods. And the angel Modrian, whom we call the Fiend, wore it in his crown before he was cast out of Heaven. The Fiend plots to seize it again, with the aid of his earthly servants, to keep its power out of his enemies' hands."

"So," Damion ventured, translating the abbot's words, "the Zimbourans want to find the Stone."

"Of course. For to them, also, the Star Stone has great significance: it belonged to Modrian whom they call Valdur, their god. They wish to return it to him—or rather to his new avatar, that great warlord whom the Fiend will send to challenge us, a man in whose mind and body Modrian-Valdur will dwell."

"King Khalazar." Damion nodded. "I believe I understand now. If Khalazar were to display the Stone before his people, it would prove that he is their god returned in human form? And he would have the priesthood under his thumb as well. But why doesn't he simply pretend that he has it? Any large gemstone would do—"

"You do not understand," Shan said. "Khalazar *be-*

lieves in the Stone, as devoutly as we—as firmly as he believes in his own destiny. A false Stone would not give him the powers he needs to defeat his prophesied adversary." Shan rose and went to the altar, and Damion followed him. Carefully the abbot peeled away the stained layers of cloth, revealing a wooden box about twice as long as his hand. The sides were intricately carved, with six-pointed stars and crescent moons in a repeating pattern, and on the lid was a relief of two gryphonlike creatures facing each other, with another star between them. The stars had tiny blue gems at their centers, and the eyes of the gryphons were chips of some yellow stone—topaz, perhaps, or yellow diamond.

Damion stared from the box to the abbot and back again. "You're not saying the Star Stone is in there?"

"Not the Stone itself, no." Shan lifted the lid—it was not hinged, but came straight off like a pot-lid—and took from the box's interior a small parchment scroll. It was obviously very old, brown with age and webbed with fine cracks.

"What is it?" asked Damion.

Shan opened the scroll slowly and with infinite care. "The relic of which I spoke was the lost scroll of Bereborn. It is told among us that a knight of that name came here long ago after the fall of Trynisia, bringing with him a scroll from the holy city of Liamar—a scroll that the monks of Saint Athariel here on Jana guarded throughout the early days of the Dark Age."

"Oh, yes, I remember that story now," Damion said. "But wasn't the scroll destroyed?"

"It was. At the start of the Dark Age the Zimbourans returned to the worship of Valdur, and they raided the

Archipelagoes, sacking the temples of all other faiths and burning their holy relics, including those of the western monks on Jana. But though the sacred scroll was destroyed in that raid, it was said that one day its prophecies would reappear in written form. We thought that meant a miracle would occur, but as you see, the explanation is much simpler."

Damion cast a dubious eye at the aged parchment. "Are you trying to tell me that's . . . a *copy* of the scroll?"

"It was found only recently," said Shan. "The Zimbouran attack of five centuries ago was a sudden one: it seems the monks only had enough time to conceal their extra copy of Bereborn's scroll before the marauders came with sword and torch. The good brothers were slain, and the secret of the second scroll was lost—until recently. The priests of the Kaanish shrine, wishing to conceal their own sacred treasures from King Khalazar, searched yesterday beneath their floors for hiding places and came across—this. Their shrine, you see, was built upon the original foundations of the old western monastery. Their high priest sent word to me this morning of his find, and asked if I wished to have it. He was going to dispatch one of his brethren to deliver it to me. But the Zimbouran priests invaded the shrine, as you saw, and had Lorelyn not been there to take the scroll from them in turn, it would now be on its way to Khalazar."

"What does it say, Father?" Damion asked. From where he stood he could see that the first section was written in Kaanish characters.

Abbot Shan was silent for a moment. Then slowly he began to read aloud. " 'I, Brother Haran, servant of the One True Faith in this house of God, am honored with the great task of copying the holy words of our most sacred testament, the scroll of Bereborn, in this year of 2530 of the New Era. The scroll, old when first it came to us, now suffers greatly from age, and the abbot fearing it will soon fade beyond legibility bids me prepare a copy so that when the original shall perish, its holy truths shall not.

" 'These words were written by the enlightened people of the north, whose land is now lost. The scroll of Bereborn from which I copy them was itself but a copy of an older document: and so no man can say how ancient are these words I must now write.' " The abbot paused, then pushed the scroll over to Damion's side of the altar. "The rest is in Elensi," he said.

Damion, like all western clerics, was schooled in the old Elei tongue. He looked down at the lines of crabbed writing and read aloud: " 'Hear now the words of Eliana, highest among sibyls: Behold, the Queen of Heaven shall bring forth a maid-child, the Princess of the Stars, in whom shall lie the hope of the world. For a warrior prince shall rise up in Modrian's name, and ravage the Earth like a dragon spreading war and ruin.' " This much was familiar to Damion: there were similar prophecies of the Tryna Lia and her adversary in one of the old apocryphal writings. But now it continued: " 'By these signs shall ye know her time is come: the sun in the land of the west shall hide its face at noon; and a great star shall shine by day; and many of the sons and daughters of men shall arise and prophesy. In those days the Princess shall walk the Earth, and shall seek for the Stone of Heaven where it lies upon the holy mount. For with it alone can she conquer the warrior prince, the vassal of the Dark One; and he will pursue her across land and sea, to wrest the Stone from her.' "

The passage ended there. Beneath this last section of text was a crudely drawn map of some unfamiliar landmass surrounded by the sea. And that was all.

Shan placed a trembling hand upon the parchment. "The prophecy's reappearance cannot be an accident: it must mean that the time of the Tryna Lia's coming is very near."

Damion's eyes drifted up to the fresco painted on the wall above the altar: a flight of angels, armored as for war, battling a horde of hideous bat-winged demons. In the foreground of the scene a black-scaled dragon with a jeweled crown between its horns was attacking a white-robed female figure. She also wore a crown, and set in it was a starlike object surrounded by rays of light. "To defeat him she needs the Stone of Heaven and the power it confers," Shan continued, also looking at the mural. "And now King Khalazar has learned of this scroll, and is seeking it. He must *not* find it! He may well be that evil prince of whom the scriptures speak, the rampaging monster sent to destroy us. And in this, the oldest version of the prophecy, the Tryna Lia's victory is not assured. Her enemy can wrest the Stone from her, and leave her weaponless!"

"But how can he do that, if the gem has the power to defeat him?" Damion felt obliged to point out this contradiction.

"I do not know. Is the Tryna Lia vulnerable in some way, divine though she may be? Could he use surprise or trickery? I have studied the prophecies and the writings concerning them for many years, but I never imagined such a thing. I always believed her victory was certain. I have not told my brethren of this, not with the Zimbourans coming to take our island: they might face martyrdom, but not the death of all hope." His hands clenched and unclenched, in a visible effort at self-mastery. "You see the importance of this parchment—with the sea chart showing where Trynisia lies. What if Khalazar had seized it, and arrived on the Holymount *before* the Tryna Lia? Only you and Lorelyn prevented this from happening."

Damion was staring at the mural again. He tore his eyes away from it and answered in a neutral tone, "That was a piece of luck."

"Some might call it that," Shan answered. "I prefer to call it providence—or as we say here in the east, destiny."

Damion said nothing. With the almost childlike enthusiasm of all converts, these Kaanish monks took a literal approach to scripture, embracing not only its teachings but many of its obviously mythical passages as well. And the Tryna Lia did not appear in the Kantikant, the Holy Book of the Faith, but only in apocryphal writings. Wishing to be tactful, he did not say that works like this parchment were abundant, and of dubious origin. Nor did he say that in his own country the celestial Princess and the land of Trynisia were interpreted as allegories, with the former representing the Faith triumphant and the latter the state of holy enlightenment. The present crisis must be fought with acts of organized resistance, not with the aid of supernatural relics. But he could not bring himself to say these things to Shan. They would not reassure him, but only add to his doubt and fear.

The abbot, however, seemed to guess his thoughts. His dark eyes looked deep into Damion's. "It was no accident that put you and Lorelyn in the right place at the right time, to save the scroll." He put the parchment back inside the box and replaced the lid. "It is clear that you were both chosen for that task. Now you must take this ark with you to Maurainia."

"Damion!" Prior Vale's voice cried outside the door. "Are you in there? We've got to go *now!* Some hired guards are going to escort us through the city to the harbor. But they say they won't wait a minute longer!"

"I'm coming, Father," Damion called back.

The abbot thrust the carved box into the young man's hands. "God go with you, Brother," he said quietly, "and guide you back to your own land. More than your own safety is at stake now."

THE WALK THROUGH THE crowded streets of the port was a blur of confusion and fear. Wild-eyed faces surrounded them, a din of panic-shrill voices besieged their ears. The guardsmen were forced to beat back not only the Zimbouran soldiers but also hordes of terrified Kaans who begged to be taken aboard their ship. Damion could not meet their eyes: he felt as guilty as though he had betrayed them personally. Through the chaos he heard the captain of the guard shouting at them to keep moving. The girl Lorelyn, walking at his side in a concealing monk's habit, its white hood drawn up over her head, kept stopping to look about her: at last he had to seize her wrist and pull her along with him. But with his hurt ankle he could not move very fast himself, and the two of them fell to the very back of the line. Their group was last to reach the docks, and Damion and Lorelyn were the last two people to hasten up the gangway of the Maurainian ship. As they set foot on deck it cast off its moorings.

As for Lorelyn, she showed no fear because she felt none. Of the Zimbourans she knew little, save that they were the enemy. But the monks had reassured her that the enemies of the Faith could not triumph, and she held firm to the hope that the Kaans would escape harm. The ocean voyage that lay ahead held no terrors, for her destination was not an unknown but an answer. Even had the monks not told her so, even had she not been fair where the Kaans were all dark of hair and eye, still she would have known in every bone and sinew that she did not belong to these islands. Out there, beyond the farthest isle of the Archipelagoes, lay her real country: perhaps it was this land of Maurainia to which Father Damion was taking her. But it was not the thought of finding her true home that made Lorelyn stride forward to the ship's bow and gaze with eagerness at the cloud-piled horizon before her. A sense of purpose drew her, as undefined as sunlight muted by mist, but stronger now than she had ever felt it. This, even more than the half-heard susurration of voices at the margins of her mind, made her believe what the monks said of her: that she had been born to fulfill some appointed destiny. And with every yard the ship advanced she sensed that she drew closer to it.

A sailor perched on the rigging above her gave a yell and she turned, distracted, to see everyone on deck staring astern. Jana had already grown hazy with distance, blending back into the blue island chain. There was a little tug at her heart, as if an unseen cord binding her to the island had at last stretched far enough to be felt. Then she saw against Jana's fading outline the black shape of the vessel pursuing them. Though it was still some distance away, she could clearly see its oars rising and falling in rapid rhythm, and the black star emblazoned on each of its three-cornered sails.

Cries of alarm went up from the crowd on deck, but the captain laughed in scorn. "Zimbouran fools! That poky old galley will never catch up with the *Dolphin*, and they know it. They're just trying to give us a scare. They could hardly care that much about a lot of monks and merchants, and what else would send them after us like that?"

"What indeed," Father Damion remarked. But he spoke the words under his breath, and only Lorelyn heard them.

3

The Angel and the Scroll

"WELL?" JAIMON PROMPTED. "What do you think?"

Ailia was silent. She had seen many drawings of the famed Royal Academy in books, but this was the reality, rearing up before her in the dying light of evening. Gargoyles ramped about its roofs like strange wild beasts on the slopes of fantastic mountains: gryphons, dragons, horned imps at motionless play in the gloom beneath the shadowing towers.

"It's magnificent," she replied at last, half whispering.

They had been in Maurainia for several weeks now, in the capital city of Raimar, and the Island girl still woke some mornings afraid that she had dreamt it all. Travel, for Great Islanders, was an unheard-of thing. A "trip" to them was a wagon ride across the Island's interior or along its jagged coast, and many of them died without ever venturing far from their homes. Ailia's feelings were not so much those of a traveler as of an old-time explorer, arriving on the coast of an unknown continent. She was amazed by everything she saw: from the high-towered sea walls, raised in olden times to defend Raimar from Zimbouran naval assaults, to the streets of the city beyond, broad and bustling with carts and carriages, and paved instead of earthen. Beyond the rooftops swelled the dome of the High Temple of the Faith, burning gold amid the verdigrised domes of lesser temples: a sun surrounded by its vassal planets. Then there was King Stefon's marble-fronted palace, with the royal banners on the roof flaunting their device of sword and crown. Even the tall plane trees lining the main boulevards were wonderful to her, after the little spindly trees in her "forest" at home. And never in her life had she seen such crowds: every street held enough people to fill a village.

And over it all, looming high above the city on its steep, wedge-shaped escarpment, reared the gray broken curtain walls of Brannar Andarion's old fortress, with the towers of the reconstructed keep rising out of its ruin. The keep that now housed the Royal Academy. In the dusty, waning light of early evening walls and towers seemed painted on the sky.

But it was real, all of it; she had come to Maurainia at last.

She and her relatives spent the first night at an inn in the lower town, not far from the wharves. In the cramped room that she shared with her aunt, mother, Jemma, and the children, Ailia had lain awake until dawn staring at the strange steep-roofed buildings outside the window, and listening to the clop-and-rattle of carts passing through the stony streets. It was reassuring to see, high in the night sky above the rooftops, the very same constellations that shone down upon the Island: the Centaur, the Unicorn, the Dragon. The stars were shifting to autumn now. In the east rose the constellation of Modrian, a worm devouring its own tail: the worm's eye was the star Utara, and in these clearer skies it burned as red as fire. Lotara, the worm's tail, shone not far away. Legend claimed there was another star near it, where the worm's mouth was: Vartara, a black star invisible to human eyes, that engulfed light instead of giving it forth. And there to the north as always was the Lantern Bearer, who held in his hand the steadfast polestar, beacon of navigators. Ailia had seen it on the ocean voyage too, shining above the masts at night. It was comforting—as though a part of her home went with her.

In the daytime she and Jaimon went out into the city on foot. They entered the High Temple, passing between the tremendous pillars of its doorway into the vast, vaulted interior, where long sunbeams from the dome's central lantern slanted down through pungent clouds of incense, and huge stone statues of the saints stood watch over the Shrine of the Flame. She would never forget it to the end of her days; nor the thrilling moment when an open carriage guarded by liveried horsemen drove within ten paces of the sidewalk where she and Jaimon stood, and they saw riding in it a girl of Ailia's age. She was gowned in gold brocade and her fair hair, falling in ringlets about her shoulders, was crowned with a circlet of real diamonds—for this was Princess Paisia, Stefon's daughter and only heir, on her way to a royal engagement. "I thought your eyes were really going to fall out of your head that time," Jaimon teased Ailia.

But there was no money for a prolonged stay at the inn, and they were soon obliged to move into the hostel where the other Islanders and the Kaanish women were staying. Conditions there were poor, the food and bedding inadequate and the dormitories crowded. It was decided then that Ailia should go on to the Royal Academy, where she at least would be properly fed and housed, while Jaimon found work to earn their passage home. And so she had come at last to this place for which she had yearned so long, taking the steep climbing road that led to the faerie-tale towers. But her pleasure was shot through with guilt.

"What's the matter, coz?" Jaimon asked her, noticing her subdued look.

"Oh, Jaim, I feel like such a fool," she moaned. "It was my doing: I brought everyone all this way for nothing."

Ships had been dispatched to Great Island in response to their news, both warships and smaller vessels to evacuate the women and children; but it was reported that most of the Island women did not want to leave their homes and husbands, and the governor would not make them go. "They are so brave," Ailia said, "choosing to stay and face the danger with their men. I don't know how I can ever go back and look them in the eyes. And King Khalazar *didn't* attack the Island after all, and now there's even talk in the city of a peace treaty."

Jaimon took her firmly by the shoulders. "Talk! Rumors, you mean. These city folk don't know everything, and they believe what they want to believe. Khalazar is a dangerous man, and war may happen yet."

"You're only trying to make me feel better," she mumbled.

Manfully he resisted the urge to laugh, and kept his voice and face solemn. "As for those other Island women, well, it remains to be seen whether they were brave or foolish. If Khalazar does come, they may yet be sorry they stayed behind."

But Ailia's conscience pricked her, and her own expression remained tragic. "It *was* my doing, Jaim. I threw everyone into a panic about the Zimbourans, insisting on our taking ship and going to Maurainia." Her great gray-purple eyes turned up to meet his. "I think perhaps—deep down—what I really wanted was just an excuse to leave the Island, and come here."

"Ah, so that was your nefarious scheme!" He grinned. "Well, now you're *here*—at the Royal Academy, where you wanted to be. It's too late to go back. Why don't you just enjoy it?" Jaimon began to walk around the outer walls, pulling Ailia along with him. "Look! This is Haldarion, Ailia—the oldest fortress in all Maurainia. Just think of the history it's seen. The Elei were still ruling their Commonwealth when these outer walls were built!"

"And King Brannar Andarion lived here with his court and his knights," said Ailia, "five hundred years ago. And he wanted the Paladins to be well educated before they could serve their kingdom: that's how the first Academy began. He invited famous philosophers here from all over the Continent to teach the knights, great thinkers like Elonius the Wise." Here—it had all happened *here*. Her eyes seemed to strain from their sockets as she gazed.

"So you have been reading those books I brought you."

Ailia nodded. She knew the present Academy's history too. The main keep had been completely rebuilt during the reign of Harron III, great-grandfather of the present king. Harron's dream had been to restore the entire fortress to its former glory, but in the end he had run out of both funds and time, and the ruinous curtain walls and outer watchtowers continued their slow disintegration. Already some of the battlements, with their weathered stone and rambling greenery, looked more like natural rock formations than anything raised by human hands. Doorless entrances gaped from ivied walls like the mouths of caves, and in the empty towers crows and owls roosted. The moat was a wide grass-grown ditch, spanned now by wooden bridges.

Not all the damage had been done by the mere passage of time. Five centuries ago Haldarion had fallen to a siege and been stormed, and what remained of it after the battle was quarried during the Dark Age by peasants, who fenced their fields and built their cottages with the plundered stone. Their present descendants, the inhabitants of the nearby villages, were uneasy about the ruin: it had an evil name, and its past lingered like an unquiet spirit.

Beneath the brooding keep there lay a network of tunnels, it was rumored, spreading out through the countryside like dark and secret roots. No good could come of the place, the villagers insisted, and they clutched their holy mandalas whenever they spoke of it. Nothing could persuade any of them to pass near the crumbling walls once the sun had set.

"But what are they afraid of exactly?" Ailia asked.

"Well, there's that old story about Prince Morlyn—Andarion's son." Jaimon pointed to the top of one vine-matted wall. Looking up, Ailia saw a stone monster perching there. It had been carved to look as though it were snarling, but time had worn away its fangs and left it with a toothless, gaping grin. Batlike wings were furled at its sides, and its talons clutched a shield whose device had long since been weathered away. "That was his personal emblem, the dragon," Jaimon continued. "There's an old story that the prince's spirit walks the castle ruins in the dead of night. Do you believe in ghosts, Ailia?"

"Of course not," she replied, a little too loudly. The grim wall with its dragon guardian suddenly looked sinister in the failing light, and she gave a tiny shiver.

Jaimon laughed and led her back through a gap in the curtain wall. Within lay the outer bailey, now greened over with neatly clipped grass. "That's the old monastery, over there," he said, pointing to a large rectangular structure between the Academy and the chapel spire. "It was restored at about the same time as the keep was, and today it houses a hundred monks of the Order of Saint Athariel. The Paladin knights were once members of that order too, and took holy vows like monks, and lived in the monastery when they weren't away fighting Maurainia's enemies."

"I know," said Ailia. "And then in the Dark Age the Inquisitors called them heretics, and executed them for witchcraft and idolatry. Some Paladins escaped and lived on in secrecy, but in the end the order died out." To think that *she*, Ailia, was going to be a student where the Paladins themselves had once studied!

Jaimon grinned and led her toward the building. "Go on inside."

"Are women allowed in?" asked Ailia, hesitating. "I thought we had to stay in the convent." They had passed the white stone cloister earlier, on their way to the inner keep: she had left the small tin trunk containing all her possessions there. The girl students lived with the young novice nuns in the Postulants' Wing, which jutted out from the inner cloister: though she had glimpsed the white-shrouded forms of the Holy Sisters through the gates of the convent proper, she had not met or spoken with any of them yet.

"On Holyday you're allowed in—the girl scholars all worship in the main chapel, once a week, and dine in the men's refectory, so the poor novices can hold their fast with the senior nuns and have some peace and quiet! Come on in, I'll show you the way." He strode up the gray stone steps of the Academy and into its yawning doorway.

She followed him timidly, along wide corridors floored with slate. The windows were set high on the walls, admitting little light. From a large oil portrait, dark with age, the narrow-featured imperious face of an old-time noble gazed accusingly down at her. She wanted to apologize to him for her unseemly intrusion. "There's the chapel," her cousin said, pointing to a pair of massive oaken doors at the far end of the hallway. "They'll all be at worship in there now. Go on in."

"Aren't you coming in too?" she asked, shrinking back a little.

He shook his head. "I want to get back down to the city before nightfall. Go on," he urged her. "The Academy girls will all be inside. Their head prefect is a tall girl with chestnut-colored hair, Arianlyn's her name. She's a good sort, and will look after you. I met her the last time I was on shore leave, when I came to ask about your letter, and I got to know her quite well. As well as the nuns would let me, that is."

Ailia offered him a faint smile. "I wondered how you knew so much about this place."

He grinned. "Say hello to her for me." She looked small and vulnerable, he thought, with her big eyes wide and fearful and her hair pulled severely back from her pale face. He thought of what might lie ahead for her, and it made him pause. "Ailia—there's something I want you to remember."

"What is it?"

"It's about Great Island," he said. "People here say it changes everyone who lives on it: that a little of its granite gets into our souls, and that's why Islanders are so hard and grim and obstinate. So they think, anyway, but there's more truth to it than they know. The fact is the Island makes us strong, as strong as stone; and that's why we can weather things that other folk can't. Soft earth can be blown or washed away, but rock endures. Never forget that." It was with an effort that he made himself turn and walk away down the corridor. As he went he whistled a jaunty tune, as much for his own comfort as for hers.

Ailia gazed after him until he turned the corner and vanished from her sight. Feeling terribly alone, she went up to the great heavy doors, pushed one open, and entered the chapel. Rows of young men and women were seated inside, and a few raised their bowed heads to stare at her. But she scarcely saw them. The chapel itself held all her attention at once.

It was, of course, nowhere near as large and imposing as the High Temple in Raimar, but it had a beauty and majesty all its own. To Ailia it seemed as though she stood in a forest—if a forest could be made of stone. Great columns like the trunks of century-old trees reared up around her, branching at their tops into majestic vaults and a stone foliage of intricate traceries. Angels soared like birds among those branches, caught by the sculptor in the frozen instant of spread-winged flight. Directly ahead lay the sanctuary, where the Sacred Fire burned: the eternal flame of the Faith that was never allowed to die, but was kept perpetually alight by the priests. The brazier stood on an altar of marble; beyond reared the crenellated ramparts of a carved stone screen, and in this was set the sacred portal, through which only an ordained cleric could pass. For worshippers the curtained door represented the limits of human knowledge, and the forbidden sanctum beyond the mystery of the Divine. Upon the marble battlements stood bronze figures of angels in knightly armor. The largest angel, she knew, must be Saint Athariel, patron of the monastic order that had once included the Paladins. At his feet Modrian-Valdur—a coiling bat-winged shape, half man, half dragon—seemed to topple from the ramparts as his assault on Heaven was repulsed. As Ailia gazed up at the statues a bell rang out clear and pure from the chapel tower high above.

This was no reconstruction, but the original chapel of Haldarion, spared out of reverence by Brannar Andarion's men during the siege of the keep: here the knight-priests had come to worship alongside their brother monks, gazing on the figure of the warrior angel who was their divine model. Now the scholars of the modern Academy attended services in the chapel, together with the monks and the little boys from the monastery orphanage. The boys' choir sang the opening hymn of the service as she walked into the main aisle: she could not see them at first, in their minstrel's gallery immediately above and behind her. Their pure high voices seemed to come down to her from the vaulted ceiling, as if from the mouths of the stone host hovering there.

Overwhelmed, she seated herself in a pew to drink it all in. Presently the hymn ended, another bell chimed silverly behind the sacred portal; the crimson curtains parted, and a procession of clerics entered the sanctuary. To Ailia's awed eyes they seemed more like otherworldly creatures than living men. All but one were clad in the gray hooded habits of monks. The last man's robe was white, the alb of an ordained priest. He must be the chaplain, though he looked very young: in his early twenties, she guessed. When the monks had filed into their pews he went and stood by the altar, where the light from the Sacred Fire fell on him. Ailia gazed at him with wondering eyes. He was handsome—no, more, he was *beautiful*: a word that she had never before thought of applying to a man. His face was clean-shaven, his eyes a deep blue, and his hair blond—not flaxen but gold-blond, with the hard bright gleam of the metal it suggested. As he stood there the fire gave to his fair skin a warm alabaster glow, haloed his hair, and lent a lambency to his eyes so that they blazed like the blue core of a candle-flame. And the same artist who had cast the bronze archangel's idealized features might have shaped his face.

Ailia gazed at him, entranced. Then he moved away again, and the moment was past; but though it had scarcely encompassed two heartbeats, she knew that in her memory it would live forever. Long after the clerics had concluded their liturgy and retreated through the curtained door she sat there in a state of bliss. That was an angel she had seen, without a doubt: a mortal one, but an angel nonetheless. For angels were messengers, and this one had come to her as the emissary of a realm of beauty, a larger world than she had ever dreamed existed.

The other worshippers filed out of the chapel, and Ailia, coming back to herself, hastily rose and fell in behind the female students as they walked out into the hall. What a lot of them there were, all talking at once! And what fine clothing they had on! Ailia was wearing one of the postulant's gowns her mother had sewn for her. It conformed to the nuns' specifications, white in color with long tight sleeves, confining bodice, and voluminous, ankle-length skirt. But it had been hastily made of the cheapest cloth available: beside the other girls' more expensive gowns of white satin or brocade it looked shabby. And they all wore their hair down, in curls or braids tied with ribands. Did young Maurainian girls not wear their hair up, then? She felt gauche and provincial, and recalled suddenly what Jaimon had told her: as a rule, only daughters of wealthy families got into the Academy.

The other girls fell silent, seeing Ailia behind them. A chestnut-haired girl turned toward her. "Can I help you?"

"I'm looking for the head prefect," Ailia answered, overcome with shyness.

"I'm Arianlyn Rivers," the other replied. "What was it you wanted exactly?"

"I—I'm a new student," she stammered. "I'm Jaimon Seaman's cousin."

There was an incredulous outburst as the girls eyed her.

"Did she say she's a *student?*"

"*Whose* cousin?"

"What's your name?" demanded a thin, dark-haired girl.

"Ailia Shipwright," she answered.

"What an odd name," observed another girl, a pretty blonde whose hair fell in silken curls about her shoulders. "Where are you from?"

"Great Island."

The girl looked blank.

"One of the Colonies, Belina," the dark-haired girl told her. "They name themselves after their fathers' occupations in places like that."

"You don't say? How terribly quaint!"

"I've heard of Great Island. Is it still a penal colony, then?" another girl asked.

"What!" Ailia exclaimed, indignant. "Of *course* it isn't! It hasn't been for ages—" Then she saw from the girl's gleaming eyes that the question had merely been a taunt.

"Well, Lorelyn," said the dark-haired one, turning to a

tall girl with long flaxen braids, "here's another refugee to keep you company."

"I suppose you had to win a scholarship to come here?" suggested another girl.

"That's right," Ailia acknowledged.

"That explains it, then," said the other, with a knowing look at her companions. Ailia squirmed at her tone, feeling rustic and poor, and horribly out of place.

The girl named Lorelyn took a sudden stride forward, her long braids swinging. "All right, you lot, that's enough!" she ordered in a ringing voice, glaring at the other girls. "Leave her alone!"

There were some sniggers, but no more comments. "Well," said Arianlyn awkwardly, "back to the convent, everyone: it's nearly dinnertime. Look, there's Sister Faith waiting in the hall for us. Ailia, you come along with me, and tell me how your cousin is." She spoke in a kindly tone, such as one might use for a very small child; but there was no reply. Turning, she saw that Ailia was gone.

The Island girl had fled down the hall as soon as the other girls shifted their attention to the nun. Her brief happiness had completely evaporated, replaced by a miasma of doubt and anguish. *Why did I come here? I don't belong—I never shall! That's what Jaimon was trying to warn me about. If I stay here they will eat me alive.* Another voice inside her spoke of enduring rock and the Island's honor, but it was faint and quailing as she remembered the girls' knifing eyes. *I can't go back to that. I can't—I can't—* Ahead of her the corridor came to an abrupt end in another set of high oaken doors. Not caring where they led, wanting only to put some physical barrier between herself and the source of her misery, Ailia pushed one door open and ran inside, slamming it behind her. For a moment she leaned against it, breathing hard, her eyes half shut. Then they flew wide open. Staring at the scene before her, she gave a soft low cry of amazement.

This room was huge, at least as large as the chapel: and it was filled with books—*filled* with them. Books old and new, from small cloth-covered volumes to great tomes bound in calfskin, occupied wooden shelves that ran all the way around the walls. In the center of the room were more tall shelves arranged in rows, and long study tables scattered with volumes carelessly set aside by students hastening to dinner. The shaded lamps on the tables shed a muted golden glow over the whole chamber. It was the Academy library: she was standing in the very midst of all the knowledge in the world. No one else was in the room, as it was now the dinner hour. Even the librarian was absent, a curt notice on his desk announcing his return in half an hour. She had the place entirely to herself.

She darted forward, snatching up books from the tables. Why, here was Dainar's *War of Heaven*! She opened the heavy brass-bound cover, flipped through the yellowed pages with their dark old woodcuts: and there before her eyes the great-winged angels flew, and held court in paradise, and battled with evil demons among the clouds. She glanced at another book, then pounced on it in turn. The *complete* poems of the Bard of Blyssion—at last! And there beside it was *Bendulus's Bestiary*. Her father had a copy, but this was a rare early edition with hand-painted illustrations. Strange beasts pranced across its pages in full and glorious color: dragons, unicorns, lion-bodied sphinxes with the heads of women.

She ran to the shelves. There was a copy of Galdiman's *Theogony,* and *The Annotated Apocrypha,* and the *Chronicles of the Seven Kingdoms*. Books that she had never heard of, others she had encountered only as tantalizing titles referred to in other works: here, at her fingertips. She piled them up gluttonously in her arms. There was a *Grammatica Elensia,* for students of the old Elei tongue. And what was *this* small leather-bound book, here on the corner of a shelf? She pulled it out, releasing a puff of dust. Its cover was embossed with a gilded dragon rampant, but there was no title. Shifting the stack of books to her left arm, she opened the cover with her thumb to read the title page. But there was a picture opposite the page that momentarily distracted her: a woodcut of robed people dancing in a woodland grove beneath a great shining star.

She headed for a study table, poring over the picture as she walked. And so it was that she did not see the two men in front of her until she ran full-tilt into one of them. She recoiled, the books tumbling from her arms onto the floor.

"Oh—I'm sorry!" she apologized as she knelt to pick up the scattered volumes.

The man she had collided with looked annoyed. He was middle-aged and nondescript, black-haired and blunt-featured; she might have taken him for one of the Academy magisters, only he was not wearing the long black gown of a scholar. Behind him stood another man of far more remarkable appearance, young and tall with skin that gleamed in the lamplight like polished mahogany. Looking at him, she was reminded of her father's wooden Mohara mask gazing inscrutably from the kitchen wall.

"Where is the Jana scroll?" demanded the middle-aged man abruptly. "I cannot find it." He spoke with the faintest trace of an accent.

"I beg your pardon?" Ailia asked, still stacking books.

"Come, you must know where it is," the man said with undisguised irritation. "You reshelve the items, obviously, as well as dust them."

He thinks I'm a servant, thought Ailia, humiliated anew. "I'm a *student,*" she corrected, with as much pride as her groveling posture would allow.

The man raised a disbelieving eyebrow, but continued. "Even so, you must surely know of this famous scroll. It was brought to the Royal Academy barely a month ago from the Archipelagoes of Kaan."

Ailia rose, struggling to balance the tottering pile of books in her arms. "I'm new here. I don't know where anything is."

The man's eyes narrowed. His dark-skinned companion stood silent and still behind him, a tall, intimidating presence. All at once Ailia was aware of the stillness of the great half-lit chamber, of the maze of corridors that must separate her from the refectory where the Academy's inhabitants were now gathered.

"You've been instructed not to speak of it," said the man in a soft low voice, "haven't you?" He advanced upon her and she automatically stepped back, still clutching the books. "But of course, I understand: the document is very valuable, your magisters are right to be cautious. But it is all right." He gave a slight bow, his hand to his chest. "My name is Medalar Hyron. I too am a scholar."

"You are?" Ailia backed into one of the study tables. Unable to retreat any farther, she held the books before her like a shield and asked, "Then why don't you ask the magisters? I'm sure they'd be glad to help a scholar."

The man's heavy face darkened, and for a wild instant she thought he was going to hit her. He opened his mouth again, but before he could speak another voice cut in.

"May I be of assistance?" it asked.

He whirled around; his companion was already staring at the doorway. A blond young man in a priest's white robe stood there, looking in at them with a slight frown on his face. Ailia gaped at him. Wasn't this her "angel" from the chapel? It almost startled her to see that he was real—that he could enter ordinary rooms and move among ordinary mortals like any flesh-and-blood man. How long had he been standing there, watching them?

"I am Father Damion Athariel, chaplain to the Academy," the angel said, coming forward into the room. "I'm sorry, but I must tell you the library is closed after the dinner hour. If you wouldn't mind coming back tomorrow . . . ?"

For an instant the dark-haired man seemed about to argue; then he shrugged his shoulders. "But of course," he replied in a smooth voice, turning to the other man, who had stood like a statue all this time, not saying a word. "Come, Jomar. We will return another day." He strode out the door, followed by his silent companion.

"Were those men bothering you?" the angel asked Ailia.

She shook her head, speechless.

"Did they say why they were here?" he persisted.

Ailia found her tongue. "They were looking for something, the man said. The scroll of . . . of Jana."

The angel gave a little exclamation under his breath. He went to a little low door in the wall that she had not noticed before, marked "Archives." Taking a key from a bundle that hung from his cincture, he unlocked the door and stepped inside. When he came out again he was holding a box of carved wood in one hand. He set it down on a study-desk, removed the lid, and took from it a roll of parchment. For a long moment he gazed down at this, looking like the Angel of the Apocalypse with the scroll of revelation in his hand, and seeming deep in thought.

"I had better put this someplace safe," he muttered at last, as if to himself. He placed the scroll back in the box. Then he saw Ailia setting her books down and edging toward the doors. "*You* needn't go," he told her.

"But—you said the library's closed," she said.

"Only to people from outside the Academy," he explained, "not to the students. It is your library, after all."

With that, he headed out the door, the box tucked under his arm. The treasure trove of books was once more hers to explore in blissful solitude. But Ailia remained rooted to the spot, gazing after the young priest. Now she knew his name: and it was beautiful, she thought, as beautiful as he was. So great was her delight at this discovery that, without thinking, she spoke the name out loud.

"Damion Athariel!"

4

The Eve of the Dead

"WHAT IF THERE REALLY *is* a Star Stone?" Damion mused aloud.

He was standing at one of the windows of the receiving room, looking out at the High Temple. It dominated Raimar's central plaza with its grand pillared portico and triumphant dome, its snow-white marble and gold leaf brilliant even in the mellow autumn sunlight: the chief of the houses of Aan, One God of the One Faith. Beneath that golden dome, deep within the inner shrine it sheltered, burned the Sacred Flame: the original and eternal flame, from which the holy fires of all other temples of the Faith had been lit. The Maurainian prophet Orendyl (so the scriptures said) had seen a thunderbolt strike this spot, and on drawing near had heard a divine voice speak to him from out of the flames. Obeying its command, he had founded a new faith that spread along with the Heaven-lit fire that inspired it. For he never allowed that fire to die out, but constructed over it a little shrine to keep off rain and snow; after his death his followers had kept it burning, and so had their descendants in turn. For nearly three thousand years now it had burned unceasingly, while a continuous traffic of pilgrims came to light votive tapers from its flames. Five hundred years ago the High Temple was built over the shrine, to house and protect it in turn. In addition to its grand façade, the Supreme Patriarch's palace and other administrative buildings surrounded the plaza with their own imposing architecture. In the plaza's center a bronze colossus stood on a towering pedestal, one arm raised skyward: Orendyl, drawing the attention of mortal men to God. During storms thunderbolts sometimes struck this statue, linking the hand of the prophet to Heaven with a bond of fire. It was a place of power, this, the hub of the greatest religion in the world: the place from which holy edicts, pardons, and dispensations emanated like the rays of the sun.

"What if the Stone really does exist?" he said again.

"Oh, Damion!" reproved Father Kaithan, crossing the room to refill his friend's goblet. "Sheer rubbish."

"That's what I said to myself at the time—no, no more, thank you," Damion said. He glanced around the receiving room's elegant interior, then back at Kaithan's amiable, rounded face. He had gained considerable weight since Damion last saw him. "You're looking well, Kaith," he said, seating himself in a tapestried chair.

"We all live well here at the temple," replied the other, returning to his own seat. "Even minor clerics like me. What hypocrites we priests are! We like to put on noble airs about our great sacrifices, forswearing wealth and wives. But the truth is, most of us hadn't any chance at wealth, nor even of marrying well, and are much better off being men of the cloth. *You,* though, Damion—with your looks you could have had any girl you wanted, perhaps even a rich one. But not for you the happy hearth, and brats gamboling at your feet. Oh, no: you must be a missionary, and go sailing off to distant, barbarous lands—"

"Hardly barbarous—"

"You haven't changed a bit, Damion." Kaithan gave a plump chuckle, and took another sip of wine. "Back at the orphanage you were always ranting about knights and quests! You may talk to me of mission work, but you were really seeking adventure. Trust you to find one—the Stone of Trynisia, no less!" His second laugh was loud and hearty.

"I wasn't talking about a magic gem," said Damion, nettled. "I know that's just a faerie tale. But what if that whole tale were based upon a germ of truth? What if there *were* a stone—just an ordinary bit of rock, I mean, that the Elei once revered back in olden times? A shooting star, for instance. The ancients believed in a literal Heaven, and any object that fell out of the sky would be holy to them. And if their veneration for this bit of sky-iron went on long enough, the whole thing might grow into an organized religion. Look at what *we* have done, with one lightning strike." He waved a hand at the view outside the window. "Now suppose this sky-stone is still lying in a shrine somewhere, on some long-forgotten island up north. What if a Zimbouran expedition were to come across it one day, and bring it back home with them?"

Kaithan shifted in his chair. "No one would believe it was magical nowadays."

"*We* wouldn't," Damion corrected. "But the Zimbourans would. They have never been enlightened, as we have: they still believe in all their old superstitions. There are even people on our side of the sea, Kaith, who might believe in the thing. We have our share of fanatics, including some of the clergy. Look at that eclipse of the sun we had last month. Lots of people thought it was an omen of some kind. Imagine if they had read that sentence in the scroll about the sun hiding her face at noon. Do you see now why one little stone could shake the Faith to its foundations? Or even cause another holy war? If that scroll *is* the key—"

"My dear fellow, that's utter hogwash, and you know it," declared Kaithan. "I've talked to scholars here who had a look at that scroll of yours. It's nothing but a fraud. The parchment it's written on isn't more than a few centuries old, they say."

"It's supposed to be a copy of an older document."

"Which was very conveniently destroyed, making it unavailable for study. *Pah!*"

"Well, what of the sea chart?"

"More nonsense. No one will ever find Trynisia or the Star Stone, because *they don't exist.*" Kaithan thumped the arm of his chair for emphasis. "You spent too long in the exotic east, my friend. It's made you even more fanciful. Sacred jewels and lost scrolls—honestly, Damion!"

Damion gave an impatient wave of his hand. "I'm not saying it's really the scroll of the Apocalypse—we both know that's nonsense. But there are people who believe it *is,* and one of them is the king of Zimboura. If his servants had placed it in his hands, he might well have taken that as a sign for him to start a holy war."

"Ah, but fortunately Damion Athariel thwarted his evil scheme, and saved the world!" Kaithan laughed again as Damion set his goblet down and looked around for a cushion to hurl. "Oh, come: you must admit it sounds rather—"

"Silly, childish, incredible: I know! That is exactly what *I* thought at first. But now I'm not so certain. The Zimbouran king wants the Stone. He thinks it is the sign of his destiny and will help him to rule his people—not to mention all the rest of us. And now he knows where the scroll was taken."

"And I think your imagination's running away with you."

"Is it? Two Zimbouran intruders turned up in the Academy a few weeks ago. I was at dinner when a servant came to the high table and told us there were strangers looking for the library. They were half-breeds, chosen because they didn't look obviously Zimbouran, but I could tell. And I'm positive I recognized one of them, a Zimbouran-Mohara man. I saw him on Jana, walking with a column of the God-king's soldiers. Can you look me in the face and tell me there's no connection?"

"Oh, pish-posh: foreigners all look the same." Kaithan drained his glass. "Now, what about this girl of yours, this saint-in-the-making? *She's* what really intrigues me." He grinned.

Damion groaned. "She's not a saint, and she's not *my* girl: I wish people would stop calling her that! 'Father Damion, your girl was late for class again; Father Damion, your girl has knocked over a votive vase and broken it.' Lorelyn means well, but she's a great strapping lass and clumsy as a bullock in a glassblower's shop, poor thing."

"Does she still hear her 'voices'?"

"From time to time, but she's been told not to talk to anyone about them. The odd thing is that, voices apart, she seems perfectly sane."

"It needn't be insanity. Has she been seen by a physician?" Kaithan asked. "There could be something wrong with her hearing."

"I never thought of that," Damion admitted. "Thank you, Kaith: I will ask the sisters to look into it."

"As for King Khalazar, why not let him *have* the scroll? If he wants to go off to the north pole looking for a bit of stone that doesn't exist, then let him! He might oblige us all and get himself shipwrecked: there's many an arctic expedition that hasn't returned. But if you really are worried about that wretched piece of parchment, then take it and burn it, and that will be the end of the matter. I see nothing to be afraid of, myself. There is no real reason to believe the Stone is anything but a myth—like everything else the Elei told our poor benighted ancestors. The truth, my friend, is that you *want* to believe in those stories, deep down inside. And so you've convinced yourself there is some truth to them; and now you're frightened of your own imaginings!"

A little silence fell while Damion tried to think of an answer to this. "We're not little boys anymore, Damion," Kaithan added. "We have been taught to read everything—the Holy Book of Books included—through the eye of reason. And reason must surely tell you that I'm right."

"But we're priests, Kaith—it's our duty to take some things on faith," returned Damion. He was beginning to suspect that his friend might be right, after all, but he still could not resist arguing with him.

Kaithan shook his head. "The Age of Faith is over, Damion. We clergy must accept that, or we will be left behind. Look at us—wearing these archaic robes, pronouncing ritual phrases in a dead language. We're relics of a bygone age, that's what we are—and so are most of our beliefs. God, now, and heaven—you don't actually believe in a bearded old gentleman sitting up on a cloud somewhere?"

Damion stared. "Well, no, but—"

"Precisely. The Deity is—well, an idea. A splendid idea, that has served us very well for a few thousand years, but the world has changed since Orendyl's day."

"Kaithan!" Damion exclaimed. "You're saying you've lost your faith!"

"No, I'm not saying that." The other man smiled, but his eyes did not meet Damion's. He gazed into his empty wine goblet instead. "Not at all. But we must keep up with the times. We mustn't be so *literal.* You've said it yourself, my friend: if we don't learn to use our minds we will be forever panicking at eclipses, or waging wars over sacred pebbles, or believing that a girl with bunged-up ears is a saint. Who was it that made fun of Orendyl's lightning strike a moment ago?"

"I didn't mean—that is—well . . ." Damion floundered.

"You see?" Kaithan spread his plump hands.

Damion looked at the floor. "I suppose you're right," he conceded at last.

"You're not offended, old friend?"

"No, no. You've said nothing I haven't been thinking myself." But Damion's heart felt lead-heavy as he stood and took his leave.

AUTUMN WAS NOW IN ITS PRIME. For a month or so the weather along Maurainia's east coast had been almost summer-mild, the trees and meadows untouched by frost, the air heavy and still. Great ponderous cumuli drifted across the sky like slack-sailed ships in a windless sea, and the distant hills and mountains were blurred blue with haze. Then a front came in from Rialain to the north: it struck the slow-sailing clouds and swept them before it, and beneath their flying shadows the sere, harvested fields seemed to flow with a motion urgent as a tide. The sun grew paler, cast sharper shadows; the trees gave up their green, and in the harsh new light their scarlet and gold and vermilion foliage glittered like uncut gems with a thousand sun-bright points. Summer had left the land at last.

With its passing the last flowers withered, and the wind rattled through the stiffening stalks in farmers' fields. Migrating geese haunted the night with their high unearthly cries; bears and little burrowers sought the tomblike holts where they would sleep the winter away. In the countryside villagers who still followed the old traditions lit huge communal bonfires to light the night, beat upon pots and pans, and hung horn lanterns painted with goblin faces in their windows to frighten away wandering shades. For this time of year, when the land's life began to ebb and fade, was also the season of the dead. Even the Royal Academy, that bastion of reason, was not immune to the change. The turbulent air entered its stone buildings like an army of restless ghosts, twitching curtains from windows, slamming doors, leafing through the pages of books lying open on desks. And waking superstition.

"The prince is walking again," declared one of the girl students as they crossed the Academy's central courtyard together like a flock of trouping doves, their short white capes fluttering in the wind.

"Prince?" echoed Arianlyn, staring. "What prince, Wenda?"

"The ghost of Morlyn—King Andarion's son," the girl replied. She spoke with a kind of fearful relish. "You remember, the one who dabbled in black magic when he was alive."

"Black magic! Hogwash!" exclaimed Janeth Meadows. She was one of the more intelligent and sensible girls, the daughter of a magister.

"It's true," interjected Belina White. Her rather bulging, gooseberry-green eyes were filled with fear. "About the ghost, I mean. I've heard stories too. In the ruins he's always dressed in his Paladin armor. But in the chapel he wears his monk's robe with the hood up, and all you can see inside the hood is darkness, and two eyes like burning coals—"

Wenda Dell gave a little squeal, and Arianlyn, remembering her duties as prefect, looked as severe as she possibly could. "Don't be silly, Belina. You know there are no such things as ghosts. They're just a pagan superstition. Spirits of the dead don't hang about on the Earth, they go to Heaven."

"The good ones do. But what about the bad ones?" Belina persisted. "Some of the boys at the Academy have *seen* him. Ferrell Woods and Burk Armstrong both saw him one night, riding out of the ruins on his ghostly black horse. And Dail Moor once saw him too. Dail went downstairs to raid the buttery in the middle of the night, and when he got to the main hallway he saw two eyes in the darkness ahead of him—just *eyes,* glowing like candles. He turned and ran as fast as he could!"

"It was probably just the head magister's cat," Janeth said.

"Is his cat as big as a man?" retorted Belina. "It's all true, I tell you. The prince haunts the old original parts of the castle, the ruins and the chapel, and the library—it used to be the monks' old scriptorium, you know. When the librarians go into the library in the morning they find books and scrolls lying on the tables—even though they've tidied the place the night before, and locked it!"

"The village people have seen him too," Wenda added. "There's a shepherd up Kairness way who saw him one night on the old path that leads to the castle, with old Ana walking beside him."

"What nonsense you two are talking!" said Lusina Field in her sharp voice.

"Yes—utter rubbish," agreed Janeth. "Why would Ana be strolling along with a ghost?"

"Well, they do say she's a witch," Belina put in. "She lives all alone on the Mistmount, the villagers say, in the Faerie Cave. And she can—"

"Girls, girls," reproved Arianlyn, "how can you listen to such foolish tales?"

"Yes, only fools listen to tales. And only fools tell them," commented Lusina, with a sidelong glance at Ailia Shipwright.

The Island girl flushed at the sneer in the other's voice. Her reputation as a storyteller was by now known throughout the convent, much to her dismay. Since that first miserable day she had never been at ease with her classmates, and had turned instead to the little girls of the convent orphanage, helping the nuns with them and telling them the tales that had enchanted the Island children. She had told them the story of the Unknown Knight, who was so modest about his valorous deeds that he never raised his visor lest anyone should learn his identity; and of Lady Liria, who disguised herself as a page so that she might follow her beloved Paladin into battle; and of Ingard the Wild Man, who was raised by wolves in the Dark Forest and lived in its groves like an animal until King Andarion bested him in a fight and became his friend. The orphans loved all the tales, and now whenever they caught sight of Ailia they would follow her about in an eager, pleading train: "Could you tell us about Lady Liria again, Ailia? And the Brazen Horse, and the Magical Flying Ship . . . ?" Her classmates, seeing this, teased her without mercy.

"How is your cousin Jaimon, Ailia?" asked Arianlyn, trying gently to change the subject.

"He's well, thank you," replied Ailia, giving her a grateful look. "He's found work down at the docks, and has been providing for both our families."

Jaimon had paid her a couple of visits, and had told her that both her mother and aunt were growing homesick and wished to return to Great Island. "I told them it's too early yet," he said. "We still can't be sure King Khalazar won't attack. If anything, it seems more likely he will, now that King Stefon has called his warships back from the Island. What better time to launch a surprise assault? I can't understand what he is waiting for. His Armada is strong enough."

"Zimbourans are terribly superstitious, aren't they?" Ailia suggested. "Perhaps he is waiting for some sort of omen."

"That might be it. Though you'd think his augurors would be quick enough to provide him with one. There is something very odd about this whole business."

Ailia, recalling the conversation, felt anew the sensation of being wrenched apart. Of course she should hope that the Zimbouran king would not launch a war. But in that case her mother would certainly expect her to return home, leaving the Academy and its daily lectures and its wondrous library behind.

"Well, give your cousin my regards," Arianlyn said.

"Poor Ari! You'd better give up on handsome Jaimon," Lusina mocked as they entered the library. "He's already been promised to his cousin—isn't that right, Worm?" She turned to Ailia. "On Great Island first cousins marry, don't they?"

"Heavens! Do they really?" exclaimed Belina, opening her gooseberry eyes very wide.

"Not often," Ailia said. The air in the great chamber was cool, but she felt suddenly as though she were stifling.

"But it's really quite reasonable," continued Lusina, looking down her high-bridged nose at Ailia. "Living on that rock out in the middle of the sea, you'd be bound to get a little inbred. Why, that would make a good story for you to tell, Worm! A tale of a fair Island maiden and her undying love for her cousin—"

A burst of giggles greeted this suggestion, and Arianlyn looked annoyed. Ailia swept on toward a study table, her cheeks burning. It was empty except for one other girl: Lorelyn, the orphan from the Archipelagoes. She was reading a book, gripping its covers with her rather large, strong-fingered hands as though she were wrestling with it. Ailia felt a little pang of sympathy. Lorelyn was a misfit too: tall and awkward, and rather plain but for her magnificent hair, which fell to her knees and made the Island girl ache with envy. It was common knowledge that Lorelyn was here on charity, and she had come in for her share of taunts and jibes (charity pupils apparently being an even lower form of life than scholarship winners). It was said that she had been raised in a Kaanish monastery, and had no idea of how a proper young lady behaved. She did not lower her lashes becomingly when addressed, as Maurainian girls were taught to do, but met everyone's eyes directly with her disconcerting light blue gaze. Nor did she take dainty little steps when walking, but moved in long strides like a man, and had even been seen to run when she was late for a class, her skirts gathered up in one hand to show her bare knees. The nuns all shook their heads over her in despair.

Poor Lorelyn! Ailia thought. *Now, if this were a story it would turn out that she wasn't an orphan at all, but the lost daughter of a nobleman. And when the other girls realized she was a rich heiress they'd be sorry they were so horrid to her.* She sat down next to the girl. "Are you having trouble with your studies?" she asked.

Lorelyn nodded, looking glum. "Books!" she groaned, shoving the volume aside. "How I *loathe* them."

This was nothing short of sacrilege to Ailia. "How can you not like books?" she exclaimed in disbelief. "I think they're wonderful. You learn so much from them."

"That's what Damion says. He's always giving them to me for presents."

Ailia gasped. "*Damion?* You mean Father Damion, the chaplain—you actually *know* him?"

"Yes—quite well, really," replied the other girl.

Ailia gaped at her. She still felt a warm glow of gratitude whenever she remembered her first—and only—meeting with the young priest. It was, she thought, just like the stories of divine beings that disguised themselves and moved among ordinary mortals, blessing and healing with a word or a touch. Every boy raised in the monastery orphanage was given the name of the archangel Athariel in place of a surname, but she felt it suited Damion best. She gazed at him in the Academy chapel, and in the nuns' chapel whenever he officiated there, so lost in admiration that she often forgot to sing the hymns. But to know him—know him *well*—was something she had never dreamt of. "How did you come to be his friend, Lorelyn?" she pursued.

"You haven't heard, then? He helped me escape from the Archipelagoes. He was a missionary on Jana before he became chaplain here."

"Escape!" Ailia breathed, instantly enthralled. "You don't mean—you were actually in *danger?*"

"Oh, yes," replied the other girl, still in a calm matter-of-fact tone. "Damion and I left on the last ship out of Jardjana port. The Zimbourans were right behind us." She pointed to her book. "What's this word here? One of the monks tried to teach me Maurish, back in the cloister—but I don't think he knew it that well. There are still an awful lot of words I don't understand."

Ailia moved her chair closer to the other girl's, all the while looking at her in amazement. What a life she must have lived—like something out of a storybook. And to know Damion Athariel—know him well! She itched to ask Lorelyn more about him, but at the same time felt oddly shy.

"I'm always making mistakes," the big blonde girl went on. "Yesterday I told the girls I'd found a cat living in the ruins with her litter of cattle. They just bellowed with laughter. What *is* the right word, anyway?"

"Kittens," replied Ailia, keeping her own face straight with difficulty. "Never mind them: you can speak *two* languages, after all, which is more than they can do. Just keep on studying. I'll help you if you like."

Lorelyn sighed. "I'm so tired of it all—of being locked away behind walls! I used to climb up onto the outer wall of the monastery sometimes, and look down at the people in the streets below, and watch the ships in the harbor. The monks wouldn't let me go out on my own, and they never left the place themselves. Finally I started stealing out at night when they were all asleep, and going down into the city. I suppose that was wrong, but it just seemed so unfair that I had to stay indoors and not be a part of what was happening outside. When the Zimbourans came I finally got to sail across the sea—but then Father Damion brought me here, and now I'm surrounded by walls again. There's a whole world out there, and I want to go *see* it, not just read about it!"

Ailia felt a twinge of empathy, remembering her own longings on the Island; but she made herself say, "Father Damion meant well, Lorelyn. The world isn't a very safe place, for women especially. We can't travel on our own, and it takes money too."

They had forgotten to lower their voices, and Lusina Field came mincing over to them. "If you two don't stop talking, I'll complain to the librarian," she threatened. "I'm trying to study."

Lorelyn gave an unladylike snort. "Study what? The men?" She jerked her thumb at a table where a group of male students sat grinning and eyeing the girls.

Lusina colored, and turned on Ailia. "I wouldn't have thought even *you* would associate with someone like this, Worm. Goodness knows who her parents were, but I doubt they were respectable."

Lorelyn bridled, though not at the insult to herself. "Worm? Why did you call her that?" she demanded angrily.

"Why, it's short for Bookworm, of course—because she's always reading," replied Lusina, putting on an innocent look.

Lorelyn sprang to her feet. "That's not true—you're pestering her! Now leave her alone!"

Ailia looked up at her in awe. Lorelyn, the nuns often said, seemed to think she had been sent into the world to right all its wrongs. She had once disgraced herself by fighting with a pack of village youths who were tormenting a dog: she returned to the convent with her gown all dirty and torn, but by all accounts she gave as good as she got. Now she towered over the table like a Rialainish warrior maiden: it wanted only a steel breastplate and a spear in her hand to complete the picture. Lusina actually backed away from her. "It was only a joke," she muttered.

"Nobody's laughing."

The head librarian descended on them at this point. He regarded his library as only slightly less sacred than the chapel, and similarly deserving of reverence: it had always been a sore point with him that women were allowed to enter it. "If you *girls* don't want to study, you may leave," he thundered, lowering his bristly brows. "I won't have you distracting the men from their work." Lusina slunk back to her table, and Ailia shrank into her chair, wishing the floor would open beneath her. But Lorelyn met the librarian's eyes with her usual direct gaze.

"I think I'll leave, then," she said. And she turned and strode out of the room, her flaxen braids swinging in defiance.

The librarian scowled after her, then threw a final glare at Ailia and strode back to his desk. The Island girl hastily snatched up the first book on her pile. It was the book with the dragon on its cover, the one she had found on her first day in the library. She had been longing for some time to read it: its intriguing title, printed on the front page, was *Welessan's Wanderyngs: Being an Accounte, by Welessan Dauryn of Mauraynya, of his Travells Through the Worlde and Beyonde.* Small wonder they hadn't tried to get all that on the front cover!

She hesitated as she held it in her hands. She should really be working on her Elensi translations, and she had brought her copy of the *Grammatica Elensia* for that purpose. But something about this little travel book drew her irresistibly. Whatever did the author mean by "the world and *beyond*"? She plunged into the pages. It appeared that this Welessan Dauryn had lived in Raimar a few decades before the Dark Age, and he claimed to have traveled all over the world by land and sea, journeying not only to the Antipodes and the Archipelagoes but to the fabled land of Trynisia as well. His account of the latter place, though obviously a tall tale, was so imaginative that she soon found herself engrossed in it. The author spoke of the marvels of the Fairfolk's homeland, of the glory of the "Faerie Queene's" court, and of making a pilgrimage to the Temple of Heaven:

> If a pylgrym bee goode and worthie, he may passe betwixt the Holie Cherubym that guard the Temple's Portall, and draw nigh unto the Goddesse Elaraynia. For She is the Way and the Door for alle who would seeke the Starre Stone. I speke truly, for I Welessan Dauryn have looked upon it.

Ailia read these words with a sense of having come home. How often, as a child, had she dreamed of this far, fair land—how often gazed on the old maps, where Trynisia was shown at the north of the world, with blank space within its borders and perhaps the legend *Here Dragons Dwell*. She read on:

> Then wyth a Holie Sibyl for my guyde, I did entere into a Trance: and my Spirit did pass from out of my bodie and leve this mortall realme, rysing up unto the Spheere of the Moone that is the First Hevyn, and so up to the Second Hevyn, that is the Spheere of the Mornyng Starre. The Fayre Folke calle this Starre Araynia: wythyn her Spheere there lyeth a Hevynlie Paradis, wherein are many wonderes. The Fontayne of Youthe is there, and precious Gems and Floures of wondrous beaute . . .

Ailia read on, enchanted. The titters and whispers from Lusina's table could no longer reach her: like Welessan, she had left her body behind and was sojourning among the spheres.

* * *

DAMION WAS WITHDRAWN and preoccupied as he climbed the winding road to the top of the escarpment. Kaithan's advice regarding the scroll was reassuring, but the visit with his old friend had disturbed him in a different way. He found that he had less to say to Kaithan with each visit. Their friendship, so strong and precious to him in boyhood, was slowly fading with the years as their personalities and interests diverged. Today he felt more keenly than ever the inevitability of its eventual loss. He had once enjoyed their verbal jousts, but the afternoon's discussion only left him feeling flat and depressed.

"*We're not little boys anymore . . .*"

He glanced behind him, at the sweeping panorama of the old walled city below, the dome of the High Temple gleaming at its exact center like the round boss on a knight's war-shield. He recalled the day of his ordination in the temple, when as part of his formal initiation he had been allowed to pass beyond the portal into the holy of holies, and see at last what lay there: shabby relics in a dim and dusty chamber. No world of wonders had been revealed to him there, and in every temple of the Faith he knew it was the same: old broken things, and dust, and emptiness. At first he had told himself that no doubt all young ordinands went through this brief phase of disillusionment. But the others seemed well content with their vocations, whereas Damion's dissatisfaction only grew with the passage of time.

And then last night the dream had come—a dream so vivid, so profoundly unsettling, that he had ended up mentioning it to Prior Vale in his daily confession. It replayed itself now before his waking eyes, supplanting the view of the city.

In the dream he had stood, it seemed, upon a hill beneath a night sky. Clouds hid the stars, but the veiled moon shone through them and turned them a luminous silver-blue, lighting all the land beneath. He did not recognize the place. There were the lights of a great city below, and beyond lay rolling hills like folds in cloth, smooth and gentle; farther off there were mountains. But such mountains! Never had Damion seen anything like them. They were not the mountains of the Maurainian coastal range—those low, tumescent shapes, worn and round-shouldered with age. These dream-mountains leaped and hung upon the air, great cresting waves of stone. There was something about them that struck him as strange, though he could not at first think what it was. Then he realized that, though they were obviously very much higher than the mountains of the range, they bore no trace of snow upon their sharp summits.

In his dream he turned slowly, surveying the land about him. Then, as he completed his turn, he caught sight of something more wonderful still. Atop the hill on which he stood, ringing its summit like a crown, stood a palace that made the royal residence of King Stefon seem a vulgar hovel. Built of white stone that glimmered in the light of the silver-blue clouds, its walls were topped with a wondrous array of towers and domes. There were round turrets with roofs of pale glinting gold, and great hemispheres of glass glowing from within like lanterns, and tall towers capped with slender cones that imitated the mountains' skyward thrust. And as he watched in fascination, the mighty doors, unprotected by moat or drawbridge, swung open and two figures emerged.

All at once, though he did not move, he found that he

could see those figures as clearly as though they stood next to him. One was a woman, tall and graceful in a hooded blue cloak. By the light that streamed through the doors he saw that she was remarkably beautiful, with eyes the color of her cloak and golden hair that framed a smooth oval face. In her arms was a little girl-child, scarcely more than an infant. The child was fast asleep, her curly blonde head resting on her mother's shoulder. Beside the woman walked a man, also tall and regal in appearance, with dark hair and deep-set eyes.

The two looked at each other, and he could see that they were in the thrall of some deep, shared emotion. Suddenly the man embraced the woman, and they stood together for a time, cradling the child between them as if they would protect her with their own bodies. And then with a swirl of her blue cloak the woman hastened away down the hill, while the man gazed after her with sorrow-filled eyes, but did not follow.

When he recounted this dream to the prior, the latter responded in a pompous tone: "But the meaning of this vision is simple, Brother Damion. The unfortified castle is your soul, which is vulnerable to the assaults of the Evil One—hence the lack of defenses. The lord of the palace is yourself—"

"But then shouldn't he have looked like me—?"

"Don't interrupt! The woman and her daughter are the wife and child you will never have, since you have sworn the vow of celibacy: you see them departing symbolically from your life. You feel some human regret at this, hence the lord's sorrow. The Heavenly Powers wish to convey to you that you have made a holy vow that must not be broken." The prior wagged an admonishing finger.

"Damion, the first few years of a priest's vocation are always the most difficult, as he faces the fact that he cannot live as other men. You in particular have been blessed, or should I say cursed, with looks that make you attractive to women. And you possess a restless, inquiring mind, which can be dangerous if it is not disciplined. We are all of us prone to temptation, but you, Damion, have more reason than any to fear it, and need to fortify yourself against it."

Kaithan had only laughed when Damion mentioned the dream and the prior's interpretation of it. "Dreams have no meaning, Damion. Yours was the product of indigestion, like as not!"

The Royal Academy lay before him, but Damion did not feel ready to go back there just yet. He set off across the fields instead, heading for the old paved road that led to the mountains. A walk in the fresh air was what he needed, he thought, to clear his head.

The flat, cultivated fields with their low stone fences soon gave way to sloping pastureland, the beginnings of the foothills of the coastal range. Sheep wandered here in flocks, or lay taking their ease, scattered about the stubbly meadows like small white boulders. There were shepherds standing watch over them, more than he could ever recall seeing at one time. Presently he saw one figure approach him, crook in hand: a tall man with a face lined and weathered as a crag. "You're not going to the range at this hour, Reverend?" the shepherd called out to him. "Is someone ill in one of the villages there?"

Damion smiled. "No, no, friend: I'm just walking for pleasure."

"I wouldn't if I were you, son—Father, I should say."

The shepherd drew closer, bringing the musky, overpowering odor of sheep with him. "I wouldn't want to be out walking alone in the hills myself—not with it getting dark," he said.

"Oh, it's perfectly safe," Damion reassured him. "I know these mountains well. I used to play on them as a boy."

"That's all very well, but there's strange things happen on them nowadays," the man said, lowering his voice, though there was no one to overhear. "We daren't leave our flocks for a moment. There's somewhat evil afoot—we go out in the mornings and find animals dead or maimed, and all the farmers say the same. They've had hens and cattle stolen or killed, sheds and barns burnt."

"Brigands, I expect," sympathized Damion. "There are bound to be a few hiding in the forest."

"Don't you believe it." The man leaned close. "There've been no brigands here in an age and an age. Witches, that's what it is. Demon-worshippers. There's covens of them up in the mountains. That old woman that lives on the Mistmount—Ana—is one of them, or so I'm told. And the ghost prince has been seen too. He rides along the Old Road of nights on his big black horse, with his visor down and his eyes all afire." He pointed back along the road with his crook.

This was strongly reminiscent of the Academy's current description of its famous specter, and Damion suspected a little friendly rivalry between villagers and students over the legend. As for old Ana, any eccentric elderly woman living alone in these mountains was believed to be a witch. In their lofty isolation, the inhabitants of the range had not yet been caught up in the Age of Reason that was overtaking the rest of the land. It had stopped, like some mighty flood, short of the mountain slopes with their little eyrielike hamlets.

"Thank you for the warning," he said to the shepherd. "I will take a little walk up Selenna and see if I can find this Ana of yours, and have a talk with her." The man turned away and went back to his flock, muttering and shaking his grizzled head.

Damion walked on, picking his way carefully among the broken paving stones. The Great Coastal Road was of Elei make, ancient beyond the reckoning of those who now used it. For hundreds of leagues it followed the coastline of Maurainia in long serpentine curves, then suddenly digressed toward the mountains in a line straight as an arrow's flight. The portion of the road that paralleled the coast had been repaved and carefully maintained, as it was still a valuable trade route; but only the range's few inhabitants used the part that led to the mountains, and its paving stones were those set down by the "Fairfolk" thousands of years ago. Many houses had dotted the mountains' slopes in their day, and castles had crowned the summits. The latter had not been placed there to watch for enemies in the lands below, for they were not fortified: the Elei had built in high places because they wished to be as close as possible to the heavens, and to the gods whom they called their kin. Their old name for the coastal range was the Mari Endori, the Mountains of the Mother, after the chief goddess in their pantheon. But all their houses lay in ruin: no one dwelt on the range now save for the villagers and shepherds.

Damion felt his spirits lift a little as he walked. He knew these old mountains well: knew them in all their moods, when they were veiled with mist and rain, or ermined with snow, or shadowed against the stars. It was not hard to see where they got their name: they rose from the surrounding plain like the swollen udders of some vast beast whose belly was the earth. Just now their rounded peaks and upper slopes were still golden with sun, while the land below lay in evening's creeping shade: islands of light in a dark sea. The tallest was Selenna, "Mist-mantle," its summit nearly always hung with cloud. The villagers were superstitious about Selenna. Alone of all the mountains it bore no ruins on its peak or sides, and though sheep were pastured on its slopes, no one would build a house there. If you spent the night alone up on the Mistmount, it was said, you would be driven mad—if you came back at all, that was, and were not spirited away by the faeries . . .

Years ago, on a dare, a much younger Damion had ventured onto those mystic slopes alone, right up to the legendary Faerie Cave. He still remembered what he had found there: silence, a vast quietude punctuated at first only by birdcalls and the wind. By slow degrees he had become aware of other sounds: the distant bleating of sheep, insect thrummings, the rushing song of a stream somewhere, high up; and this rich tapestry of sound had seemed to him to hang upon the silence as an embroidered banner hangs upon a stark stone wall, not distracting from, but rather calling attention to, the surrounding stillness. In that moment he understood the truth that lay behind the fanciful tales of the Mistmount: the ancients had not feared Selenna, but revered it.

He thought of the Kaans and their sacred island. The western missionaries had disapproved of the pagan custom of assigning dwelling places to deities and had many times tried to discredit it, but Damion could not agree with them. Were not the Faith's own temples believed to be holy ground, filled with the divine Presence? For the Kaans the isle of Medosha was a natural temple; the same might well be said of the Mistmount. Other mountains could be put to practical use, but not this one. Selenna existed for itself alone.

He looked at the Old Road that led up the mountainside, vanishing into the forest, and was glad to walk it again. As he followed its winding course uphill, he felt the anxieties of adulthood slowly receding, giving way to the wonder he had felt in childhood. Oaks and maples roofed these woods with the bronze and gold of autumn, and laid down a floor of fallen leaves: many were centuries old, by their great girth. Beneath their boughs mail-clad knights might once have ridden, pursuing outlaws and wild beasts in days of old when this was the Dark Forest of legend. How he had yearned to be a knight himself when he was a boy! Over his bed in the dormitory he had hung a faded print, bought for a few coppers at a fair, of a Paladin riding to rescue a maiden from a snaky-tailed dragon. Chivalry—how utterly naive it all seemed to him now. As if any wrong could be righted just by waving a sword about. Knights were no longer needed, even here in the wild lands. The outlaws and brigands were long gone, as were the dire wolves and cave bears that once had lurked within the tangled groves. The Dark Forest itself now stood at bay, its hosts of trees forced into retreat by a burgeoning demand for lumber: only here had they been spared. He continued to walk uphill, breathing in the musty earthen smells of autumn, his mind wrapped in thoughts of the distant past.

He came to himself at last with the realization that it was growing cool, and the brighter stars were beginning to pierce the deepening sky above the trees: he recognized the constellation of the Unicorn, and Modrian-Valdur with its red eye. He should head back before it became really dark, he decided, and leave his errand for another day. There was no telling where the old madwoman might be. Damion sat down on a stony outcrop, to rest his legs before making the homeward journey. He was, he saw, about two-thirds of the way up the mountainside now, near the so-called Faerie Cave. There it gaped from the living rock of the mountainside, just a few paces from where he sat: a narrow triangular opening that he would now have to stoop to enter. He often wondered why the locals had not chosen a more impressive cave for the setting of their legends. Here the faeries assembled for midsummer revels, feasting and dancing by the light of the moon: the faeries who were the Elei and their lost gods, reduced to mere figures of folklore in the minds of the mountain people.

Someone else had been here not long ago, he saw, for resting on the ground near the mouth of the cave was a small crude figure formed of dried corn husks and wheat sheaves. He rose from his rock and went to pick the object up, turning it over in his hands. It was a corn doll, such as many farmers made at harvest time, using the last sheaves gleaned from their crops. Most of them had long forgotten that the doll symbolized the old Elei goddess of the earth. But whoever had placed this one here had not forgotten. It could only be a pagan thank-offering: to the goddess, to the faeries, or perhaps to both. Was it true, then, what the shepherd had said about witches meeting in the hills?

A sound intruded into Damion's thoughts: a soft shuffling as of footsteps on stone, coming from behind him. His skin pricking, he dropped the doll and spun around, staring at the Faerie Cave. The hairs on the back of his neck seemed to lift, and he took an involuntary step backwards.

At the mouth of the cave stood a tiny, elfin figure, its pale garments gleaming faintly through the dusk.

AFTER THE FIRST FROZEN instant of disbelief, Damion realized what he was looking at. But his heart was still racing as the gray-clad figure moved out of the cave and came toward him.

Small wonder he had thought, for that brief irrational moment, that he was facing some sort of supernatural being. The old woman might have been a gnome or pixie from a child's faerie-tale book, so tiny and wizened was she. Her little hands were bony as bird claws, her round face crazed with wrinkles. Strangest of all were her eyes: clouded over by a gray film, their color was difficult to discern. He thought at first that she must be blind; and yet she made her way easily toward him, leaning hard upon a knobbly cane but neither groping nor stumbling.

"Good even, Father," she greeted him in a dry, crisp voice.

So she *wasn't* blind, then: she must have partial vision in one or both eyes, enough to detect his white robe in the dusk. Damion released his pent-up breath, almost laughing. Of course: this must be Ana, the local "witch." He made a bow. "How do you do, ma'am."

She paused a couple of paces away and smiled at him, wrinkles forming friendly patterns about her eyes and mouth. "Won't you stay for a bit, Father? I don't often get visitors up here," she offered.

He returned the smile. The tiny woman's manner was kindly; there was certainly nothing sinister about her. "You're—Ana, aren't you? I'm Father Damion Athariel."

"I know," she said unexpectedly. "We have actually met before, though you mayn't remember it." The old woman returned his smile and went back toward the cave's narrow mouth, beckoning to him to follow.

"Have we?" he asked. He was certain he would recall an encounter with such an unusual personage. Curious, he stooped and entered after her, moving through a short passage into a large natural chamber within the rock. He had never gone far inside the cave before, and he looked about him with interest. Its floor was quite level, and it was furnished with a few crates and barrels, a crooked old easel, a threadbare pallet, and a table cluttered with various objects, including bundles of herbs, a mortar and pestle, and a globe of glass or crystal about the size of a man's fist. There were also two battered chairs that looked as though they had been salvaged from a rubbish heap. Natural outcroppings of rock served as shelves, on which a few candles burned, while a circle of stones near the entrance made a primitive hearth. Ana waved him inside, as gracious as any noblewoman inviting a guest into her mansion.

"This is, ah, an unusual place to live," he observed.

"It is my summer home," Ana told him. "I will be moving out soon, before the snow falls."

There were animals everywhere, he noticed. A cat and her litter snuggled together in one of the crates, while other cats watched him warily from their perches on chairs and table. On one of the rock-shelves a starling with a splinted wing reposed in an improvised cage of twigs lashed together with twine—designed, no doubt, to keep the cats at bay. At the back of the cave was a large crevice, leading to a second chamber: a musty stable-smell came from it, and in its gloomy interior he glimpsed a goat, a tiny gray donkey, and some chickens scratching about in piles of straw. Sprawled upon the cave floor was an enormous gray dog, which put back its sharp ears and growled a challenge at Damion, glaring with cold amber eyes. The priest recoiled. He had heard of the mountain people's huge sheepdogs, bred to drive predators away from their flocks; but hearing was one thing, confronting the bristling reality quite another.

"Now, Wolf! Be nice to our guest!" reproved the old woman, and at once the great brute laid his head meekly on his paws. "How about some tea? No magic potions," she said with a smile as she went to the cluttered table. "Just the herbal tea I make myself."

It might, Damion reflected, be a good idea to stay and pump the old woman for more information—just in case she knew anything about the shepherd's vandals. He accepted her offer of tea, and sat looking idly around the cave as Ana placed some kindling within the ring of stones and busied herself lighting it. As she removed her enormous shawl to keep it from the flames he saw that the gray dress beneath it was shapeless and shabby—it resembled nothing so much as an old sack—but her white hair was pulled into a neat, grandmotherly knot. She looked so completely different from the disheveled madwoman he had once imagined that he stared at her for a moment, at a loss for words. Then he glanced about the cave's interior again.

"That's odd . . ." he murmured, frowning.

"What is?" asked Ana, filling a cauldronlike pot with water from a chipped earthenware jug.

"Oh, nothing. It's just that this place seemed familiar to me for a moment—as though I'd been here before. That happens sometimes, doesn't it? A sort of false recognition."

"As a matter of fact," replied Ana, "you *have* been here before. It was so long ago, though, I'm surprised you remember it. You were only an infant at the time."

Damion stared. "What? What are you talking about?"

"You were born here," explained Ana, "in this cave. I found you here, twenty-one years ago."

5

Visions and Apparitions

IN THE LONG PAUSE THAT followed every sound seemed to Damion unnaturally distinct—the hissing whisper of the flames on the makeshift hearth, the wind stirring in the trees outside. The dog had fallen asleep, snoring softly with his gray muzzle on his forepaws.

At last Damion found his voice. "*You?* You found me?"

"Yes." Ana stood watching him, her filmy gray eyes unreadable. "I looked after you for a day or so, then I left you for the monks to find. How very curious that you should have come back here—but then, a salmon returns to the very stream where it was spawned, without knowing how it knows to go there. Ah, the water's boiling," she added. She took the pot from its tripod over the fire and emptied it into a venerable brown teapot, which also looked as though it had been salvaged from a rubbish heap. She tossed in a handful of herbs from the table. "We'll let it steep a bit."

He had recovered from his shock, and looked at her now with suspicion. "Why did you never come to me and tell me about this before?" he asked.

"I didn't want to burden a young boy with the thought that he might have been abandoned by his mother. Don't distress yourself about it, young Damion. It is all in the past now."

He said nothing, but sat for a time staring into the fire. Was Ana telling the truth? Or spinning an imaginative lie, or perhaps suffering from some sort of delusion? Impossible to say. He decided it was time he left, and made as if to rise.

"Oh, do stay! The tea's ready," she said, pouring the honey-colored fluid into a pair of earthenware mugs. "Or do you not want to keep company with a witch?" She smiled.

He remembered the shepherd's warning, and his reason for coming here. Her astonishing claim he must set aside for the moment: there might be more important things to learn here. "Now, Ana—*I* don't believe all that nonsense about your being a witch," he replied in a firm voice, settling back into his chair again and accepting a mug of tea. It smelled of flowers, and had a strong sweet taste with a hint of some unfamiliar spice.

Her cloudy eyes dwelt on him in such a penetrating fashion that he began to doubt her vision was impaired at all. "Well, it all depends on how you define the word, doesn't it? If you believe, like the holy Patriarchs, that witches are servants of the Dark One, then I am not a witch." She went to the starling's cage and, opening its door, reached in and drew out the injured bird. It lay in her hand without struggling as she gently flexed the splinted wing, stretching it to its full span. "Some children brought this poor fellow to me. The villagers know they can come to me with any injured bird or beast they find. I treat their sheep and cattle too." She placed the starling back in its cage, then picked up her own mug and went to sit in a chair opposite Damion. "Nemerei—that was the old word for users of magic."

"You're a white witch, you mean?" asked Damion.

"You might call me that—though it still puts me outside the pale of the Faith, does it not? But the Nemerei do not practice black magic. Nemerei are the servants, Damion, of the power that aligns itself with life. What *is* this life, this joy and energy, but your benevolent God? Are we not really the same, you and I?"

"That's—an interesting idea," he agreed carefully. "But I don't think I will mention it to the Patriarchs just yet."

"No, that wouldn't be very wise. I don't suppose they would entirely approve of us."

"Us?" Damion asked, ears pricking. "You mean there are more witches about?"

"Quite a few, yes—and not all of them of the white persuasion, I'm sorry to say. But most are. My friends and I revere many of the same things you do, for the holy scriptures of the Faith contain some of the old Elei writings that are sacred to us. Stories of old Trynisia, and the Star Stone—like that most interesting scroll you brought from the Archipelagoes. Don't look so surprised! We have heard of it too. Now," said Ana, before he could pursue the subject further, "is there anything else I can offer you? A bite to eat, perhaps?"

He declined, and sat for a moment sipping his tea and looking about him. Several unframed paintings were propped against one rock wall, evidently the work of the cave's resident. Some were exquisitely detailed studies of birds and plants, while others were executed in an odd, dreamlike style: groves of dancing, undulating trees, birds and animals connected to one another by strange luminous lines, stars that scintillated and coruscated, sending whorls of light across the sky. The strangest of all was a flight of sheer fancy: a castle with impossibly tall and top-heavy towers, about which figures were flying—human figures that seemed to have wings in place of arms. In the dark sky were stars and a tremendous exaggerated moon, bright blue in color: yet the sun was up too, shining brightly. When he saw that painting Damion began to wonder if Ana might be a little mad after all.

He looked away from the painting and suddenly caught sight of something even more peculiar and unsettling: a pair of eyes glowing like live coals in the dark space inside one of the crates.

"That's my Greymalkin," said Ana, seeing his look. "Come on out, Malkin dear, we've got company."

A lean gray cat emerged from the crate, stretched and gave a wide pink yawn, sauntered past the nose of the big gray dog (who ignored it completely), and amiably rubbed its furry flank against Damion's ankles, purring all the while like thunder. Its eyes, though they had reflected the light with a red glow, were actually green: they turned up to him with an approving expression as he stroked the cat's back.

"Some of the villagers believe she is a demon," Ana remarked. "My familiar, you know."

"No offense, but I don't believe in spirits either," he told the cat as it nuzzled his hand.

"Tell me, Father Damion, how can you not believe in spirits? What of the beings you call angels, are they not spirits? What of the Dark One?" Ana stroked the gray cat, and it leaped up onto her lap.

"Valdur, you mean?"

"He is called that by the Zimbourans—and by the

Faithful, ever since the Holy War. In days of old he went by the name of Modrian. But it matters little what name you call him by. Evil is always the same."

"I don't think the Faithful really *believe* in Valdur anymore—the educated people, that is," Damion explained. "He's just a personification of evil—as the angels are personifications of good."

"Well, well! A priest who doesn't believe in anything!" she said with a laugh.

"I do believe in something," he replied, piqued.

"And what might that be, may I ask?"

Damion found himself answering, "Justice."

"Interesting!" said Ana. "I should have thought that would be the most difficult thing of all to believe in—seeing there's so little of it in evidence."

Damion's voice was firmer now. "All the more reason to work to create it."

Ana's face lit up, like that of a prospector who has found a nugget of gold. "Aha! An idealist! How delightful. There are so few of you about these days. But back to this business of believing in things unseen," she went on. "You've read Meldegar, of course."

"And you have too?" interrupted Damion, surprised.

"I am acquainted with his writings, yes. It was Meldegar who declared that all reality could be compassed by man's five senses. Now, anyone who has had some acquaintance with animals knows that this cannot be true. A dog, for instance, can hear and smell things a man cannot. A cat may walk with ease through the darkness that causes a man to stumble and lose his way. How then can man be the Measurer?"

"Ana, you should be teaching at the Academy," replied

Damion, covering his astonishment with a light tone. Where in the world had she picked up all of that? She could never have been a student: in her far-off girlhood days no woman would have been allowed to study at the Academy. But he realized, somewhat to his own surprise, that he was enjoying this unexpected conversation. Though he did not concede her point, she argued it well. Learned minds unfettered by orthodoxy were rare in his experience. He leaned forward, as was his habit when debating with Kaithan. "Ah, but the man *understands* that certain things must lie beyond the scope of his senses, and so he makes them a part of his knowledge, all the same."

"My point exactly!" Ana exclaimed. "It is the mind, Damion—the *mind* that is the key. Reason as Meldegar defined it actually limits knowledge by making us depend overmuch on our senses, which are dull and easily deceived. I of all people should know that," she added, waving a hand at her filmy eyes. "The phenomenal world can actually be a barrier to understanding. Once we acknowledge its silent sounds and invisible atomies, we must also acknowledge the possible existence of other, unknown things. The angel, the demon, the faerie—all these are but words for the Other, the immaterial reality. The mind must accept this limit to its *certain* knowledge, and admit that the universe may be stranger than it can know."

Damion's amazement was growing by the minute. He could find no words to refute hers, and a long pause followed as he sat there speechless. It was dark outside the cave mouth now: from somewhere in the distance came an owl's mirthless cackle, and the leaves that had not yet fallen sighed and murmured on their boughs. Again, as in his youth, he became aware of the woven sounds of the mountainside and then sensed beyond them a deeper silence: only now that silence spoke to him of the overarching sky, of its endlessly circling celestial bodies and the black fathomless voids above them. He felt lost suddenly, adrift in that appalling immensity, as the once-vast world of hill and forest seemed to shrink beneath it into insignificance.

After a few moments Ana's voice broke the silence and the spell it cast. "Tell me, Damion, have you ever heard of clairvoyance—the Second Sight, as our Rialainish friends like to call it?"

"Well, yes—but I never believed in it."

"Yet another thing you don't believe in! There seem to be rather a lot of them. Let me see if I can make you change your mind about this one." Ana dislodged the cat from her lap and set her mug down. Going to the table, she picked up the glass globe.

"Look into this," she said, bringing it over to him and placing it in his hand. "Oh, it's not magical. The crystal is only an aid to concentration, like your prayer-mandalas. Look into it, look deep . . ."

Damion set his mug down on the floor and looked at the shining ball. The firelight danced in its depths, and he could see the shapes of the flames burning within the circle of stones, and the passage opening into the cave's mouth beyond . . .

Damion blinked. He knew that objects seen through a globe of glass should be inverted, but the scene he saw was right side up; and he could see a human figure standing by the hearth. He jerked his eyes up: there was no one there. He looked down at the globe, and again he saw the standing figure.

Damion drew in a sharp breath. The figure was slim, fair-haired, female: as he watched she drew near—nearer. She was dressed in a long green robe or gown. He could just make out her face: eyes green as her garment, creamy skin framed by soft curls that tumbled about her shoulders . . .

"How interesting!" said Ana's voice in his ear. She was standing close beside him. "Your mother, it must be—and seen through your own unfocused, infant eyes. A memory from very long ago."

He looked up from the crystal, stared at her. "I don't understand. How did that happen?" he whispered. He held the crystal up, turning it this way and that, peering into the depths that were now clear and empty.

"The image that you saw came from your mind. The crystal served only to focus your thoughts."

"In my mind—" Damion shook his head from side to side. Then he gave a violent start. "But how did *you* know what I saw? I said nothing."

She took the crystal ball from his hand. "You have not heard of the thought-speech—the communion of minds? It was strongest among the Elei sorcerers, who in olden days used it to communicate with one another, even across great distances."

"That's—that's just a faerie tale." His mouth was dry, his hands unsteady. *There must be a reasonable explanation, there must. It's all a trick of some kind* . . . Damion rose with an abrupt motion. His heel struck the earthenware mug and it fell over, its contents streaming across the stone floor.

"My dear Damion, you're not afraid? What is there to fear? You have a gift, a wonderful gift, that's all . . ."

The candles had burned down. The only source of illumination in the cave was now the pulsating fire-glow that cast shifting shadows on the rough rock walls. It played on Ana's figure too: her withered face was half lit, half webbed with darkness, and her eyes were masked. The globe in her hand burned yellow, glutted with captive light. Her shadow loomed up huge behind her. He stared at her, his palms sweating, and the cave seemed to reel around him.

Old Ana . . . Ana, the witch . . .

Without another word he swung away from her and made for the cave mouth.

He heard her call after him, but he paid no heed. A blind unreasoning panic had seized him, and he could think only of returning to the safety of the Academy. In the darkness he could not find the path: twigs clawed at him as he stumbled downhill, and there were scrabbling sounds and strange cries in the underbrush. Around him the forest's aged trees stretched out gnarled limbs and gaped at him with black-mouthed knotholes. A pathetic receding woodland no longer, it had become again the Dark Forest that had struck terror into the hearts of errant knights.

He began to run, feeling his way wildly from tree to tree, like a man possessed.

AILIA SAT BY THE FIREPLACE in the students' common-room, a circle of little girls from the orphanage grouped around her. A goblin-lantern sat atop a nearby table, casting its fiery grimace upon the far wall: its glow, and that of the flames on the hearth, provided the only light in the room. Bedtime had long gone, but it was an evening for ghostly tales, and the orphans had coaxed Ailia to tell the story of the ghost prince. The older girls held aloof, with the exception of Lorelyn, who sat with the children, chin cupped in one hand, listening as eagerly as they.

"Long ago," Ailia recited, "when the old Elei Commonwealth was still great and powerful, a war was waged against the Zimbourans. King Brannar Andarion marched on their capital city with his knights. He was fair of hair and blue of eye, a man of divine beauty" (she was picturing Damion Athariel as she spoke) "for he was the son of a faerie—that is, one of the lesser angels, some of whom still roamed the earth in those days. So he alone was able to fight and slay the Demon King, Gurusha.

"After Brannar Andarion triumphed over his foe, he remained in Zimboura for a time, riding from temple to temple to tear down the idols of Valdur. Entering one of these unholy shrines, he beheld a terrible sight: a beautiful maiden chained to an altar. She was very lovely, with flowing dark hair and ivory skin and eyes like deepest amber. When he freed the maiden from her chains she fell at his feet in gratitude. Her name, she told him, was Moriana, and she was a human sacrifice, sent to the temple as an offering to Valdur in return for victory over the Paladins. She was of a noble and ancient lineage: not only Zimbouran but also Shurkanese and Kaanish blood ran in her veins, and she was descended from the great emperors of old. As proof of this she drew out a ring that she had hidden among her garments: it was a signet ring, bearing the coiled dragon that was the sign of the old imperial house of the Kaans. King Andarion offered to reunite her with her kin. But her family was dead, she said, and she implored him to take her with him to Maurainia. Andarion agreed to this, for from the first moment he laid eyes upon her he had fallen in love with Moriana. And so it happened that, soon after their arrival at Raimar, he offered her his hand in marriage, and she accepted.

"But before a year was out the Maurainians began to be suspicious of their new queen. Word went out that she had lied to the king, only pretending to be a sacrificial victim: in fact she was a priestess of Valdur, and practiced black magic in her private chambers. Andarion, though, would hear no word against his wife, not even from his most trusted councillors.

"One day, when a party of Paladins arrived at the Temple of Heaven in Trynisia to look upon the holy Stone, the Faerie Queen Eliana herself approached them, and said: 'Beware! For the bride of your king is not what she seems. She was never offered for sacrifice: that was but a ruse, so that she might win his sympathy and entrap him. Let the king go to the chamber wherein she performs her secret incantations and he will learn the truth: that she is an evil sorceress.'

"When the Paladins approached him with this counsel Andarion was angered, and said that he would not spy upon his beloved. Yet there must have been some doubt deep within his mind, for one dark night he went to Moriana's private chamber as she had many times asked him not to do. What he saw therein he never revealed to any living soul. But he came forth with a face blanched and haggard; and Moriana fled the castle that very night. She was never seen by anyone in Maurainia again.

"More than ten years later, Queen Eliana appeared at the court of the king; and this time she brought with her a young boy. This, she told Andarion, was his son and Moriana's—"

Arianlyn looked up. "Ailia, I don't think this is a proper story for children."

"Never mind her!" cried Lorelyn as Ailia hesitated. "Go on!"

"Well, the sorceress had died and Eliana had taken in the boy, whose name was Morlyn. 'Watch over him well,' the Faerie Queen warned King Andarion, 'for he was born to be a cruel sorcerer and tyrant. If he is not taught compassion that evil may yet come to pass.' Then she departed, leaving the boy in his father's care.

"Brannar Andarion took his son into his household: and when Morlyn was grown to manhood he joined the Paladin order. Yet there was a dark side to his nature, and his father was afraid of him. When the prince chose for his royal sign the dragon, symbol of his mother's imperial ancestors, Andarion was distressed. And though Prince Morlyn became a knight of great renown, performing many deeds of valor, he was a solitary man with few friends, and never grew close to the father who feared him. After the aging Andarion went to dwell in Trynisia, Morlyn was given the castle of Haldarion and the title of viceregent. But he spent all his days poring over forbidden books of black magic, seeking to understand the powers of Modrian-Valdur's servants and so devise strategies to defeat them. But as he read he became fascinated by the dark arts, and was tempted to make use of them himself.

"Many years after the departure of Andarion to

Trynisia, trouble came again to Maurainia. The land began to be wracked by mysterious cataclysms, floods followed by droughts, tempests on sea and on land. The sibyls of Trynisia told Andarion of these things, warning him that they were not natural occurrences, but rather the result of an evil power loose in his homeland. And they named Viceregent Morlyn as its source.

" 'Nay, that cannot be!' Andarion exclaimed. But the sibyls told him that his son had taken to black sorcery, for over time the Fiend had won him to the ways of darkness. Morlyn it was who ravaged the land with evil spells, for he was an enchanter like his mother before him.

"Andarion was filled with sorrow, but he knew what must be done. With his friend Sir Ingard the Bold and a great force of knights, he set out for Maurainia. He found Haldarion armed against him, and his son would not come forth. They laid siege to the castle, and the forces of the king had the victory. Breaching the inner keep's defenses, Andarion and his men entered. But though they searched the keep from roof to cellar, they could find no trace of the traitorous prince.

"Then Sir Ingard discovered a secret stair, leading down from the deepest of the dungeons into a cavern. Here lay a lake that the sorcerous prince had used as a scrying-glass. And as they gazed in fear upon its dark face, Prince Morlyn came rushing upon them out of the shadows. But his evil magic was of no avail against Andarion, son of a faerie, and he drew his sword instead. They fought, but Andarion held back, and it seemed he must die by the hand of the one foe he could not bear to slay. Then Ingard the Bold leaped forward and fought the prince. Long they struggled, there in the darkness, until at last Ingard struck Morlyn a mortal blow, and the prince fell into the dark lake and arose never again. Thus perished Prince Morlyn the Magician.

"But Ingard too was gravely wounded, and he begged the weeping Andarion to have him carried up to the surface of the earth that he might die gazing on the heavens. And the Paladins did as he bade them, bearing him up out of that dreary place into the warmth and light of the sun, and there as Andarion held him he breathed his last. And thus Andarion was spared the shedding of his own son's blood, and Maurainia was delivered from the sorcerer-prince."

Ailia leaned back, into the leaping shadows flung up by the flames. "Now, the magisters say that Prince Morlyn was a real person, and people just made up these stories about him after he died. There are others, though, who say it is all true—that he really was a sorcerer, and there really *is* an underground lake far below the castle. From its dark depths his spirit rises at times, to wander through the ruins of his home."

The children squealed. "But it's just a story, isn't it, Ailia?" asked one little girl, wide-eyed.

Seeing that they were alarmed, Ailia hastened to reassure them. "Of course it is. Now you had better get ready for bed."

"You'll give them all nightmares, I shouldn't wonder," said Arianlyn in mild reproof as the little girls headed for the door.

"I thought it was terrific!" declared Lorelyn. She gazed into the fireplace, her blue eyes burning with its reflected glow. "I wish I could be a knight, like Ingard."

They all stared at her, and one or two girls laughed. "A knight—but you couldn't," said Belina. "You're a *girl.*"

"What of it?" Lorelyn picked up the poker from the hearth and tried a few experimental swings with it. "I'm sure I could wield a sword as well as any boy. And how wonderful it would be to ride about the country, righting wrongs."

"Knights don't do that sort of thing nowadays," Ailia told her. "Knighthoods are just honorary positions, conferred by the king. And only men can receive them, Lori."

"For goodness' sake put that poker down," implored Arianlyn. "You'll hit someone if you wave it about like that."

"Why, that's odd," said Wenda suddenly, pointing out of the window. "I thought I saw a light just now, in the men's chapel. A funny dim sort of light, moving to and fro."

"The ghost!" shrilled the little girls, halting at the door and clutching each other.

"Nonsense!" said Arianlyn. "Wenda, you ought to be ashamed, frightening the children like that."

"No, she's right," declared Lorelyn. She tossed the poker to the hearth with a clang and bounded over to the window. "There *is* someone there."

"It's probably just one of the monks, looking for something he left in the chapel," said Janeth.

"No, that isn't it. Something's wrong," said Lorelyn. Her eyes seemed unfocused, and she swayed where she stood. "I can feel it . . . It's something . . . *dark*."

"Lorelyn's having one of her spells again," exclaimed Wenda, looking scared. Some of the girls edged away.

"Lorelyn, you're putting it on," said Lusina sharply. "Stop it this minute or I'll tell Reverend Mother."

The tall girl came suddenly out of her trance. "I want to go over there and look around," she said.

"Lorelyn! You can't!" gasped Wenda. "What if it's the—the ghost?"

"What if it is? I've never seen a ghost," replied the other girl. She headed for the door.

"You're not to go out there, Lori," said Arianlyn firmly. "You know we're not allowed to leave the convent after sundown. If it is a ghost then let the men worry about it."

"But someone should tell them about it," replied Lorelyn with determination. And before anyone could stop her she had sped from the room.

"Oh, dear," fretted Ailia, distressed. "Now she'll get herself into trouble. I shouldn't have told that silly story."

"Don't worry," said Arianlyn with a weary look. "The nuns won't let her out of the building at this hour."

"She'll climb out a window. She's done it before. I must go after her: if she gets in trouble it will be my fault." Ailia stood up.

"Sit down, Ailia," ordered the prefect. "There's no use in your getting in trouble as well. You can't be always helping her. She'll just have to learn her lesson the hard way."

DAMION MADE AN EFFORT to study the notes for next day's sermon. But the words kept blurring and drifting before his eyes as his thoughts returned to the day's unsettling events.

His parents . . . He had not given any thought to them of late. As a boy, of course, he had often wondered about them. He was a mere infant when he was abandoned at the monastery gate, and the monks had never glimpsed the one who brought him. At the orphanage being parentless was normal, however, and he had not been greatly troubled by it at first. The burden of the unsolved mystery of his existence had only begun to make itself felt in recent years, as he moved out of the cloister and into the world. Some of his boyhood friends, like Kaithan, had a few dim memories of their parents; others had been able to track them down in time. Not so Damion: the two nameless, faceless figures in his past grew ever dimmer with each passing year, like fading frescoes. He had reconciled himself to the fact that no answer such as romances provided—no dying nursemaid's confession, no ancestral locket concealed among his swaddling—would ever restore his full identity to him.

And then, this evening, had come that disturbing vision in Ana's cave . . .

Vision—what nonsense! he scolded himself. Ana was renowned as a witch and fortune-teller: no doubt she had all manner of tricks up her sleeve. She must have used some form of mesmerism on him, hypnotized him into "seeing" a scene that she described aloud to him. And that tea—who could say what she had put in it?

Far away in the night he saw the yellow flames of a bane-fire rise from some farmer's field—warding off the spirits of the unshriven dead. He recalled Kaithan's words: "*we will be forever panicking at eclipses, or waging wars over sacred pebbles, or believing that a girl with bunged-up ears is a saint.*"

Or believing in a God, he thought suddenly.

He recoiled, but there was no silencing the inner doubt now that it had spoken. He had walked in the Faith, the narrow middle way between two chasms: on the one side gaped the new science and its cosmos void of meaning; on the other superstition, paganism, primitive terror. But for some time now his beliefs had been eroding, the footing becoming more treacherous. And tonight, in fleeing from one pit he had stumbled into the other. His encounter with the old witch-woman had laid bare the lurking doubt by appealing first to his irrational and then his rational side. How easily superstition had taken him, in those fearful moments when he actually believed her mad claims; and how speedily he had sought the comforts of reason. At no time, he realized, had he turned to the Faith for guidance in his extremity. For a priest, a real believer, that should have been his first thought.

With that admission, thoughts he had thrust aside and silenced came clamoring into his mind. How often had he been told that nature was the mirror of its creator, the truest and oldest scripture—that lessons were to be found in flowers and streams and stones? Yet in every grove and meadow and serene-surfaced pool, in the very earth beneath one's feet, countless fangs, stingers, and mandibles were at their gruesome work. Poisons lurked in root and berry, plagues and pestilences waited to burst forth from dank marshes. Hawks dived on screaming hares; ravening wolves carried off helpless lambs; women died in childbirth. The world was no divinely ordered Creation but a chaos born of mindless matter, without plan or purpose, heading only toward a final cataclysm. What could he find, now, to say to the young students gathering in the chapel tomorrow? He did not even know how to counsel himself.

There was a sudden knock at his door.

"Yes?" he called, half irritated and half grateful for the interruption. Who could be disturbing him at *this* hour?

"Pardon me, Father Damion." A servant opened the door and looked in, his face apologetic. "The night porter asked me to tell you there's a young woman at the front entrance, wanting to see you."

He looked at the man in puzzlement. "A *woman?*"

"Name of Lorelyn, Father."

"Oh." Damion rubbed his forehead. "Yes. I did tell her to come to me if she had any problems to discuss—but at this time of night?" He shoved the half-finished sermon aside and rose. "I'm coming."

Lorelyn was in the porter's lodge by the main door, talking in urgent tones to its unsympathetic occupant. She broke off at the sight of Damion and ran toward him. "Father Damion—"

"Lorelyn, you know you're not supposed to leave the convent by yourself, especially after dark," he reproved.

"But Father Damion, we were looking out of the window and we saw a strange light in the chapel, and I thought someone ought to tell you . . ."

Not again, Damion thought. All week long there had been wild rumors circulating among the students: strange lights, apparitions in the ruins. "This isn't more of that ghost nonsense, is it?"

"Some of the girls thought it might be the ghost. But Father, isn't the Jana scroll kept in the chapel?"

Damion stared at her for a second. Then he spun around and set off down the hallway at a hard sprint.

First that unnerving business with old Ana, and now this! If it was a student playing a prank he'd give the young blighter what for. But with the scroll in the sanctum he could take no chances. *Why* hadn't he burned the thing when he had the chance?

Lorelyn joined him unbidden, running at his side with long loping strides like a deerhound. She reached the doors before he did and he put a hand out to restrain her. "Stay back," he cautioned. He pushed open the great oaken doors and entered the chapel.

It was now utterly dark save for the lamplight from the hallway behind him and the moonlight, which fell in faint slanting shafts through the windows. No candle burned, and the Sacred Flame had been removed to the holy of holies. It no longer seemed like the familiar chapel, sacred and safe, but a place withdrawn and mysterious. Above his head in the dim light angels hovered with motionless wings outspread, while the bronze Modrian-Valdur showed as a black shadow, clinging like a monstrous bat to the stone ramparts of the sanctuary. Then, as he watched, the curtains of the sacred portal opened, and for a moment the inner sanctum gaped like a firelit cave. A shadow moved in that dim red glow: a figure in a black monk's robe with the hood drawn up over his head. Only no real monk would slink along like that, with his hood up to hide his face; nor was it at all likely that this was a student. Whoever it was had profaned the sanctum, and there could only be one reason for that. Outrage arose in Damion, thrusting caution aside. He strode forward and shouted, "Who are you?"

The figure turned toward him. For an instant he saw two fiery points of light glowing within the darkness of the cavernous cowl. Behind him he heard Lorelyn's sharp intaken breath. He stood there gaping; and the robed figure headed for the doorway that led down into the chapel crypt, vanishing into the darkness within.

Damion took a firm hold of himself. He was determined not to give way to superstitious fears this time, certainly not in front of Lorelyn: he hesitated only an instant before starting after the figure. The man (for of course it was only a man) would get away if Damion didn't act immediately. Seizing one of the votive candles near at hand, he groped for a tinderbox. It took a long time to light the candle, for his fingers were far from steady, but he knew there was no other exit from the crypt. The intruder had trapped himself.

Candle in hand, he advanced warily down the spiral steps to the chamber below, Lorelyn following. Together they stood in the large stone space, with its squat pillars supporting the low, vaulted roof. The candle-flame showed them nothing but shadows, and the reclining stone images of long-dead knights.

"I don't see anyone," whispered Lorelyn.

"He's hiding," Damion replied.

"Shall we search for him?"

"No." He reached into his pocket and snatched out his copy of the chapel's master key. "Now, back up the stairs." The two of them climbed the steps again, and Damion closed the door, turning the key in the lock. "There—we've got him," he said. "Lorelyn, run and fetch the night porter—quickly!" She looked at him for a moment with wide eyes, then raced off.

His heart pounding, he ran up the central aisle to the sanctum and set his candle down on the floor. There on one of the shelves lay the small wooden ark that contained the scroll. He snatched it up and pulled off the jeweled lid.

It was empty.

He ran out of the sanctum again and back to the door of the crypt. "Whoever you are," he shouted through the door, "you had better come on out of hiding. I know you've got that parchment."

There was nothing but silence from the other side.

"All right, then—we'll see what the night watchman has to say."

He stood waiting by the door. Presently there came a sound of footsteps and the glow of lamplight at the chapel's main doorway, and Lorelyn and the porter entered, the latter gripping his truncheon. Damion unlocked the door again, and the three of them descended the stone stair and shouted, but nothing stirred in the burial chamber of the Paladins. The porter advanced into the crypt, his weapon at the ready. After searching up and down the length of the chamber he turned to Damion and Lorelyn with a raised eyebrow.

"There's no one in here."

"What!"

Damion ran into the crypt and swung his candle around. He saw only bare stone walls, pillars, and stone knights. The robed figure had vanished as though it had never existed.

6
The Doom of the Dance

WINTER CAME TO MAURAINIA, bringing with it one of the east coast's rare snowfalls. For three days the snow fell steadily, settling feather-light upon tree branches and the icy lids of lakes and ponds, laying on every roof a pale thatch and on every doorstep a rounded white loaf. It transformed even the poorest quarters of Raimar, turning middens and rubbish heaps to innocent white mounds, spreading a smooth pavement over broken and dirty cobblestones. At the Royal Academy minor avalanches thundered down the steep roofs, and the gargoyles sported beards of ice and jaunty caps of snow.

On the third snowbound evening Damion, growing restless within the building's confines, went for a long walk in the countryside. He huddled into his heavy priest's cloak as he strolled through the white silence of the wintry fields. So quiet was it that Damion was convinced he could hear a faint sifting sound, made by the large soft flakes as they fell and clumped and clung to every twig until trees and bushes turned to white lace and filigree. Woolly strands of smoke mounted from the chimney pots of distant cottages, but there were few other signs of life, and no one else walked the smooth whiteness where the road had been. He trudged through the floury drifts, deep in thought. Two months had now passed since the strange incident in the chapel, and he was still disturbed by it. Though Lorelyn's account of the ghostly apparition had caused a sensation among her fellow students, only the mildest of upheavals had followed the theft: with its historical veracity in doubt, the scroll was worth little more to scholars than the parchment on which it was written. Nor did the monastery's abbot and prior show any concern whatsoever at its disappearance. Any suggestion that war might result if it ended up in King Khalazar's possession was greeted with the same tolerant amusement that Kaithan had shown.

Damion wished he could know for certain who the thief was. It would be so easy for anyone to search the chapel, disguising himself as the Academy ghost so that anyone seeing him would dismiss him as a student prankster (or even believe he was the famous phantom, if the witness was inclined to be superstitious). How the escape from the crypt had been achieved Damion did not know, but for the moment he set that mystery aside and concentrated instead on the thief's possible identity. He might have been one of the Zimbouran half-breed spies—most likely the half-Moharan man, Jomar, who was the taller of the two. If the Zimbourans had the parchment there was nothing to be done but hope, as Kaithan had suggested, that their ensuing voyage to the northern sea would end in disaster. But perhaps the Zimbourans had not taken the scroll after all. Damion glanced toward Mount Selenna. It had veiled its face again: only its snow-blanched base was visible, the upper slopes vanishing into low-hanging clouds. Old Ana would have left her cave home by now, seeking her winter refuge—wherever that might be. Damion wondered if she and her "Nemerei" friends might have the stolen scroll in their possession. As a document of things they too held sacred it would be of great importance to them. But even if Ana and company were the actual culprits, the Zimbouran spies might yet find their hiding place and seize it from them. He should have followed Kaithan's suggestion and destroyed the wretched piece of parchment when he had the chance. Now it was out of his reach.

The early winter evening had fallen by the time Damion got back to the Academy, and the huge sprawling structure was almost invisible in the dusk, not a window glowing from its walls and towers. The convent too was lightless, and beyond the escarpment's edge, where Raimar's broad sprawling constellation should have glimmered, there was only darkness. Today was the winter solstice, long ago transformed by the Faith from pagan revel to sacred festival. To the Faithful, the lengthening of the hours of daylight after this shortest day suggested the final victory of good over evil. For a week now the city and surrounding towns and villages had been plunged in the gloom of the "Dark Days," when by ancient custom no light must shine by night, nor any lamp be lit unless the windows of the house were heavily draped. Withindoors life went on as usual, hearths glowed and lamps and candles burned, but no ray of light was allowed to escape into the dusky streets. Even the ships in the harbor lay unlit at their moorings. At midnight tonight candles and lanterns would suddenly glow from the windows of every home, in defiance of the dark. And in the countryside an old, old ritual would be performed: a young girl, chosen by lot, would lead a procession through all the houses of the village. Wearing a crown of candles and carrying a star-tipped scepter, the "Queen of the Festival" would drive out bad luck from every home. This curious observance originated in the ancient Elei prophecy of the Tryna Lia, who would one day descend to fight the forces of darkness, and the festival was still named after her: the Trynalia.

Damion entered the main hall of the keep and shook the snow off his cloak. A large Tanaura tree constructed of dead tree branches dominated the entrance hall: from its upper boughs hung lanterns, gilded stars, and angels to symbolize the celestial realm, while on the middle branches hung doll-like figures, beasts and birds, and floral emblems of painted paper. At the very top perched the Elmir, the Bird of Heaven, while at the base of the trunk coiled the figure of Vormir, the Serpent of Chaos. The Tanaura, or Tree of Life, was another old custom dating to the days of the Elei. Damion gave it a thoughtful look as he passed it and climbed the grand central staircase to his room.

He hung up his snow-damp cloak, drew the heavy blackout curtain before lighting his lamp, and then sat down at his writing desk. On it were piled several volumes from the Academy library: books on witchcraft and sorcery.

Though many volumes described such things as scrying, demon-summoning, and spell-casting, it was hard to tell how much of this was genuine Nemerei lore and how much the invention of superstitious peasants. In one book he finally found an entry that caught his interest. Melbryn's *Beliefs of the Ancients* declared the Nemerei to be the adherents of an ancient religion, dating back to

Elei days; they had worshipped the old gods of the Elei pantheon, whom Orendyl later reinterpreted as the subservient "angels." The Nemerei knew these gods as the "El" and believed they dwelt within the land, invisibly inhabiting rivers, mountains, and forests. There were also El of the sky: the sun, moon, and each star and planet had its own indwelling deity.

The Nemerei had also believed in the "Three Planes of Existence": the physical plane and two others "beyond" or "above" it. The Ethereal Plane was not made of earth, water, fire, or air like the mortal realm, but of another, holy element called quintessence, or "pure energy." Beyond and "above" this in turn lay another heavenly realm, the Empyrean. Gods and spirits dwelt on these two "higher" planes, and one who mastered the Nemerei disciplines could communicate with them, or even learn to travel from plane to plane as spirits did. This curious Nemerei lore apparently coexisted quite peacefully with the Faith's teachings in the early days. The "Cult of Angels" was only outlawed at the start of the Dark Age, when the Patriarchs declared that the beings revered by the Nemerei were in fact fallen angels, bent on deceiving and destroying mankind. Many in the knightly order of the Paladins had belonged to the Nemerei religion, and for this reason they were stamped out along with other "witches" during the time of the Inquisitions.

"Some there are," wrote Melbryn, "who claim that secret Nemerei cults still exist, meeting in hidden places at night to practice their arcane rituals. But such claims may safely be dismissed as the folly of the ignorant."

Damion was not so certain. He was inclined to believe

that Ana and her "friends" were members of a small but very real Nemerei coven: either a new attempt to revive the old religion, or perhaps even descendants of a group that survived the inquisitorial purges. He reached for another book, Galdiman's *Daemonologie,* and as he opened it a piece of paper fell out onto the floor.

Damion picked it up and stared at it. It was a letter, addressed to him.

To the Reverend Damion Athariel:

It has come to my attention that you have been seen consorting with a member of the cult of the Nemerei. I need hardly remind you that the company of witches is forbidden to members of your faith, let alone to its priests. It is you, moreover, who furnished the Nemerei—albeit unintentionally—with the scroll you brought out of Zimboura. It should be obvious to you by now that this object is the focus of numerous intrigues. By involving yourself in this affair you have placed many lives in danger, including your own.

You know where your duty lies in this matter. You must report this witch and her cult to the leaders of the Faith in Raimar. If you wish to lead a long and harmonious life, you will do as I advise.

There was no signature.

Damion held the letter under the lamp and scrutinized it closely. It was written in a graceful, flowing hand, and both script and phrasing were strangely antiquated: he was reminded of documents in the Academy archives, dating back a century or more. Who had penned this anonymous note and placed it in his library book? Was there a hint of a threat in that last line?

Damion threw down the letter. *One thing's for certain—my life's been far from "harmonious" ever since I accepted that benighted scroll!*

He turned and strode out of his room. *Ghosts and witches, mysterious letters and magic stones! It's exactly like one of those absurd stories the convent girls love. But there's something else those stories always have—secret passages . . .*

Damion headed for the chapel.

HE SHOULD HAVE THOUGHT of this before. How many tales had he heard of the Paladins' Door, the secret passageway that led to the warren of tunnels beneath the castle? Designed to shelter the inhabitants in times of siege, they were later used by persecuted knights as a refuge from the Inquisition. Damion and the other orphan boys had spent long hours searching for the hidden door in the gloomy vaulted cellars of the Academy: they were certain the monks knew where it lay but would not tell them, for fear they would get lost in the maze of tunnels. They became convinced that it was in the chapel crypt, for this was the one place where they were not allowed to go. Now that he was an ordained priest Damion could enter it whenever he pleased, but he had forgotten his boyhood dreams—until this moment. There were no such things as ghosts; there was no other exit from the crypt; therefore, there must be a hidden door in here somewhere. Damion ran his hands over the stark gray walls of the crypt, pressing every stone that he could reach. He felt foolish, but also determined to find the answer to the mystery.

Even so, he was surprised when one stone in the north wall gave way at his touch.

A gritty, grinding noise came from the wall, and Damion felt a section of it shift beneath his hands. He leaped back, thinking for a confused instant that he had upset some delicate balance and the whole wall was about to cave in on him. In the next moment, he found himself staring at a black gap, man-high, from which breathed a musty smell.

For a brief, exhilarating moment he was a boy again. *I was right!* he exulted. *It* is *the Paladins' Door. The old rumor was true! This is where our "ghost" went—through the tunnel, and down to the catacombs!*

Damion hesitated before the opening. It was pitch-dark inside, and there was something sinister about its appearance. But his curiosity was piqued. Through this dark door hundreds of Paladins had passed, vanishing from history, from the world that persecuted their kind. Had they left any traces of their presence in the silent passages below? He picked up his lantern and approached the entrance. The tunnel was large enough to walk in, though he would have to stoop a little. Fascinated, he entered, and followed where the Paladins had gone before.

The tunnel sloped downward, twisting and turning, for a considerable distance. But of course it would: the castle's inhabitants had wanted to feel completely safe from attacking armies. After he had walked for about three minutes it began to level off, and he emerged into a large echoing space that his lantern could not entirely illuminate. Swinging it to and fro, he saw what seemed to be a labyrinth of stone passageways, walls and barrel-vaulted ceilings of rough gray masonry, crude archways opening onto bleak, empty chambers. He advanced, holding the lantern high. Before its light the shadows retreated, flinching back into archways and tunnel mouths as he approached, stealing out again behind him. To his left he glimpsed a long arcade, with a low wall of stone beyond. He lifted his lantern over the parapet, and saw light spring up from below. It was his lantern's reflection, with his face beside it staring up at him. An expanse of water lay there, black and stone-still beneath the vaulted ceiling. Large cisterns like these would have been needed to sustain the people during sieges; later in time, the hiding Paladins would have depended on them too.

Turning to examine a nearby wall, he saw with rising excitement that it was scratched and scrawled with writing—brief messages in Elensi, from these fugitive people of centuries past, to all who might come after. He leaned close, studying the scribbled phrases.

Then he heard the singing.

High and pure and remote as a star, a woman's soprano voice pierced the silence of the catacombs, singing what sounded like a hymn. The sound echoed through the vaults and shadowy spaces, so that he could not tell from which direction it came.

> Beast and being, star and spirit,
> Circling ever in a trance,
> Know ye not ye tread the measure
> Of the universal dance?
> To its strains celestial moving,
> Every dancer, small or great,
> Passes into light, or shadow;
> Makes its choice, and binds its fate.

Other voices—high and deep, rough and clear—joined in at the final verse, until the catacombs rang with the sound. Damion felt the hairs on the back of his neck rising. They might have been voices of ghosts, of refugees who had fled to this dark warren centuries ago.

Light or dark shall own the victory
When the ageless music dies,
And the tally of our choosing
Shall decide which way it lies.
So the sphere of starry Heaven
Spins upon this thread of chance:
On the choice of every creature
Hangs the doom of all the Dance.

"Who is it?" he burst out, without thinking. "Who's there?"

There was a sudden silence in the maze of catacombs. As he stood there wondering whether it might not be wiser to make a break for it, the searching beams of lanterns appeared up ahead of him, reaching long fingers of light through archways and tunnels. Figures sprang forth, black shadows against the light: all approaching him. And then behind them a fair, slender figure, crowned with light, stepped into view.

She was dressed in the traditional garb of the Festival Queen, or Princess: a white robelike gown and a gilded circlet upon her head into which six lit tapers were set. The flickering candle-flames illuminated her face: recognizing it, he cried out in disbelief.

"*Lorelyn!* What are you doing down here?"

"Father Damion!" she exclaimed. She rushed toward

him, her crown of candles tilting precariously. "I didn't know you'd be here too! They never told me—"

But before she could reach him a burly man strode out of the shadows to one side and confronted Damion. "Who're you, and what are you doing here?"

"I might ask you the same question!" Damion retorted.

From behind the man an elderly woman hastened toward him, her cane clicking on the stone floor. "Father Damion!" she exclaimed. "There, Brais, it's all right, he's a friend. I'm so glad to see you, Damion. I do hope this means you've decided to join us." She turned to Lorelyn. "Put out your candles, dear, before you have an accident."

It was old Ana. Was this her Nemerei coven, then? His first, absurd impression—that these must be descendants of the original Nemerei, still dwelling in the catacombs that had sheltered their ancestors—quickly faded as he swept a glance over the group assembled before him. Most of them looked like common folk, farmers and people from the villages and city. He even recognized one face—Ralf, a village idiot from one of the mountain hamlets, waving his crooked arms and moaning. Ana turned toward him and appeared to listen carefully to his wordless utterances. "Yes, that's right," she said, for all the world as though she understood him. "It was he who found the scroll." She turned back to Damion.

"What are you all doing down here?" he demanded.

"Discussing our plans. We are the Conspiracy against the reign of Valdur," Ana answered. "The Nemerei, the prophets and servants of the Light."

"How did you get into these tunnels? It can't have been through the chapel."

"There are other entrances, well-hidden ones quite far from here," Ana explained. "The designers of these tunnels intended that the castle's residents should be able to escape a besieging army by traveling for some distance underground before coming up to the surface again."

Damion turned to Lorelyn, who had removed her gilded headgear and was blowing out its candles. "Lorelyn, why are you here?"

Before the girl could reply Ana broke in: "Damion, why don't you come apart with me and I'll explain everything?" She turned to Lorelyn. "You had best go back to the chapel now, my dear, and wait for the Academy procession to begin. Janina"—she spoke to one of the younger women—"show her the way back, will you? And take a couple of the men with you, just to be safe."

"I don't understand, Ana," said Damion when the girls and their escort had left. "What is going on here?"

"These are my friends, the other Nemerei I told you of back on Selenna. We are celebrating Trynalia—it's a Nemerei festival too, you know."

"But why down here?"

"Because it is safer, naturally."

Damion scanned the group, looking for a figure tall enough to have been the robed thief in the chapel. "Which one of you played at being the ghost prince?" he demanded accusingly.

A murmur arose among the people in the corridor and then died away again.

"I think I know the person you mean," said Ana at length. "He has been using the catacombs, but he is not one of our number."

"But he *must* be. Wasn't it he who took the scroll for you? I saw him, in the chapel—"

"The scroll? No, we have had the scroll in our keeping since late autumn," Ana told him.

Damion stared at her, and she smiled. "Come with me, Damion."

Stay calm, Damion counseled himself, *she and her friends may be insane but that doesn't mean they're dangerous.* He followed the old woman, and she led him down one of the side tunnels. They passed through a low doorway at its end into a large rectangular chamber. It was full of wooden chairs and benches, and at its far end a wooden table was set up like a crude altar, with a guttering votive candle at each end. Between them lay the parchment scroll.

And before it, head bowed as if in prayer, stood a short stooped figure in the gray robe of a monk. The figure turned toward them as they entered, and Damion saw framed within its cowl the face of Prior Vale.

THERE WAS A LONG SILENCE. Damion started forward, then stopped again. He could not seem to find his voice, and behind him Ana just stood quietly, letting the two men confront each other.

At last the prior gave a cough. "Ahh, Brother Damion," he said. "This is a surprise. I didn't know they'd let you in too. Who sent you?"

"Sent me? I don't understand," the young priest rasped. "What is happening here, Prior?"

The monk glanced from him to Ana and back again. "The abbot didn't tell you, then? He didn't send you here?"

The abbot! Damion thought. "Why would he? Prior Vale, what are you *doing* here?"

"Observing the Nemerei ritual. Our brotherhood has been doing this for years now—centuries," the prior explained, approaching him.

Damion continued to stare. "No one ever told *me* about any of this!" he burst out.

"Well, you see, the location of the Paladins' Door and the catacombs is a very old secret," the monk replied. "The original monks of Saint Athariel swore a sacred vow to protect the Nemerei from the Inquisitors during the Interregnum. Only a few of the most senior monks are allowed to know where the door is—that is part of the vow."

"But Prior—they're witches!"

"We've never called them that. The Faith and the Nemerei teachings aren't so very different. We believe in many of the same things." But the prior looked uneasy as he spoke, as though not quite convinced by his own words.

Damion swept his gaze about the candlelit chamber. The walls were carved with bas-relief designs in the shapes of people, birds and beasts, stars—Elei work, from its delicate intricacy. He was reminded of the carving on the ark of the scroll. The human figures had the perfect—some said idealized—beauty that characterized all Elei sculpture. On the wall behind the table was carved an Elvoron, that most ancient of Elei symbols: it depicted the Elmir bird and the Vormir serpent, each biting the tail of the other, their curved bodies joined to form a circle. Elmir—light, order, spirit, and Vormir—dark, chaos, matter. Together they were a whole, their seeming strife no more than the competing stresses in a stone temple that create stability through counterbalance. Beside them was a female figure: the Queen of Heaven—or possibly her daughter, the Tryna Lia—with the sun and stars above her and an upturned crescent moon beneath her feet.

Ana spoke from the doorway. "I think some of the monks are a bit dubious about the whole business nowadays," she added, watching the prior's face, "but of course it's impossible for them to break a sacred vow made by their predecessors."

"There—you see?" The monk spread his hands helplessly. "Abbot Hill agrees, and he is head of our order. I cannot disobey him."

"Which of the Brothers took the scroll from the sanctum?" Damion pursued, remembering the robed figure.

"Oh, the abbot gave the Nemerei the scroll to guard back in autumn, after your two intruders came to the library," Prior Vale explained. He gestured to the roll of parchment. "Some of the Patriarchs tried to make out that it was a heretical document, too, and wanted it destroyed. So we couldn't leave it where it was. At first we were going to pretend that we had destroyed it. But as it happened there was no need for us to lie, because no one noticed it was gone. Until that night when you opened the ark—but you assumed that fellow masquerading as the ghost had stolen it. The abbot decided to let you and Lorelyn spread the story. It gave us an explanation for the scroll's absence, should anyone come looking for it." He gave a little cough, and fell silent.

"Look here," the young priest said, anger rising in him, "you know this is wrong, Prior. That vow of yours has ended up tangling you in a web of lies! And you still know more than you're telling me, that's plain. Who *was* that man in the monk's robe, and what was he doing? He obviously knows about the catacombs. Ana says he's not one of her crowd, but—"

"He isn't." Ana shook her head. "He is on no one's side but his own."

She offered no further explanation, and Damion appealed again to the prior. "How can you, a man in holy orders, have anything to do with a secret cult like this? There have been terrible things happening in the countryside—crimes the villagers say are witches' work—"

"That is nothing to do with us," said Ana calmly.

"Well, why don't you just practice this—this *religion* openly, if it's so innocent? The Interregnum is long over. There's no danger now."

"Isn't there?" Ana interjected. "We don't wish to be secretive, Father Damion, but the fact is there are still many who would disapprove were we to practice our rites by the light of day."

"All the same, you've got to tell the Patriarchs about this, Prior."

"And break our solemn vow?" exclaimed the Prior. "I'm sorry, Damion, but the abbot won't allow it. He will swear you to silence as well."

"But—"

"You must settle this later, gentlemen," Ana interjected firmly. "We have other matters to discuss tonight."

"Such as?" Damion demanded.

"The signs that are now appearing—the signs that mean the prophecy has begun to unfold. The sun has hidden her face at noon, and those who have the gift have begun to prophesy and have visions. Before long a new star will appear in the sky, shining even by day."

"You believe the Apocalypse is near," Damion said, recognizing the signs from the scroll. He threw a sidelong glance at the prior. Many a sect throughout history had come to believe that the last battle was at hand, and been left looking foolish when nothing happened. "So that's why you wanted the scroll. But why is Lorelyn here? How did *she* learn about this, if it's so secret?"

The prior looked even more uncomfortable. "I—" he began, fumbling for words.

"We asked to see her," Ana said. "And the prior brought her here. He did not tell her the real reason until they were in the Chapel of the Paladins."

Damion turned on Prior Vale, incredulous. "You *lied* to Lorelyn?"

Vale's face flushed. "It wasn't lying exactly," he replied. "The abbot—"

"The abbot asked the nuns to choose Lorelyn to lead the Procession of Light through the chapel this evening," Ana intervened. "Naturally she assumed she was going to receive some final instruction before the event: it was not necessary for the good prior to lie."

"What do you want with her?" Damion demanded.

"She is a Nemerei, like us. A very powerful one, gifted from an early age. The 'voices' she claims to hear are the mental voices of other Nemerei, communing mind to mind. She needs to be trained to use her gift properly. And she may prove to be central to our plans. Come, sit down and I will explain it all to you both."

Ana turned and gestured toward the doorway: Damion saw Ralf and Brais standing there, with many more figures behind them. At her signal they filed into the chamber in silence and seated themselves on the chairs and benches. Vale followed suit. Damion stood for a moment, his hands clenched tightly at his sides. Then he took a seat beside the prior.

Ana went and stood in front of the table-altar. "My dear friends, and brethren of Saint Athariel," she said, changing to a more formal tone of voice, "the time has come for us to discuss our plans. The day that we have long awaited draws near. First I must decipher the visions some of you have seen."

"You mean the palace?" called a woman's wondering voice from the back of the room. "The one with the walls of white marble, and towers—"

"I saw it, I had that dream too!" a man exclaimed excitedly. "The palace stood on a hill, in a place where there were mountains—I saw a lady standing before it in a blue cloak, with a little child in her arms."

Damion tried to speak, but could only manage a small strangled sound.

"My dream was different," said another woman. "I saw a lady sitting in a chair, rocking her child in her arms. In *my* dream it was still a tiny babe—such a beautiful child, with great eyes as blue as its mother's, blue as the sky."

More voices were raised, and Ana lifted her hand to calm the gathering.

"How can this be possible? How can we all have had the same dreams?" demanded Brais.

"Because they were not dreams, my friend," she answered. "They were visions. To some the gift of the Second Sight is given, and at this time all those with that gift will have glimpses of what has been, and of what is yet to come. I realize that some of you here tonight are new to our circle, and I will try to explain all I can.

"As I told you before, many of us here can communicate with one another across distances, without using the spoken word. Most live here in Maurainia, though we have touched minds in other lands."

"But this vision of the palace," the first woman called out. "Who was that lady? And what country was that, with the high mountains? Marakor perhaps, or Shurkana—?"

"No, the Marakites are dark and so are the Shurkas," the second woman corrected. "This woman and her baby were fair, with blue eyes. What became of her, Ana, and the child?"

"I am sorry," said Ana firmly, "but I cannot answer all your questions yet. Some because I do not know the answers, others because the knowledge I give you could prove dangerous. We are living in perilous times. Remember that you are not to speak to anyone outside this assembly of what you have seen. This only can I say with certainty: that the child of your visions is the one for whom generations have waited, the Holy Child, the Tryna Lia. The time of her earthly reign has come."

"Wait, wait!" interrupted Brais, waving his hands impatiently. "Don't the clergy say that the Tryna Lia is just a symbol—that she stands for the Faith?" He turned to Damion and the prior.

"The old writings do not say so," replied Ana before monk or priest could speak. "It is said there that she is the daughter of the Morning Star."

"Yes, yes," said Brais, "and the Elei said she would

come down out of the sky, so they must have meant she was an angel or spirit of some kind. How can you say she's a human child?"

"It may seem strange to some of you," Ana admitted, "but among the Nemerei it has always been taught that the Tryna Lia will assume a mortal form when she enters our world.

"How can the Tryna Lia be human? Have you never seen a shooting star fall to the earth? In the heights it blazes brilliantly, but when it reaches the ground its fires are spent. Anyone who comes upon it then will think it an ordinary stone among the stones of the earth, and never guess that it once shone amid the stars. So it is with the Tryna Lia, the Child of Earth and Heaven. She left the celestial realm to be born as a mortal, and to dwell among mortals."

"Where is she now, then?" Brais demanded, folding his arms across his chest.

"I do not know for certain. I can tell you, though, that the visions you have all had are of a distant past. The heavenly powers will not reveal her incarnation until she is of an age to defend herself from her enemies. She must now be grown to womanhood, though she likely knows nothing of her true identity. But I believe," said Ana, lowering her voice, "I may know who she is."

There was a breathless hush. Then the woman at the back of the crowd cried out again. "It's that girl Lorelyn—isn't it? The orphan the Kaanish monks found. *She's* the Tryna Lia!"

"No!" Damion shouted. He leaped up, ignoring the prior, who tried to take him by the arm. "Leave her alone! She's got nothing to do with you and your coven."

Vale caught at his sleeve again, and Damion shook him off. "And as for that bit about the palace—was that supposed to impress me? To make me think I was one of you, sharing your visions? You got that from Prior Vale!"

"Damion! What are you saying?" remonstrated the prior.

"*I* had that dream about a palace and a woman with a child. I told you about it, and you've gone and told them!"

"How can you say that?" Vale protested, his face reddening.

"The prior did no such thing," denied Ana in her quiet voice.

Damion took up his lantern again and started to head for the door. Ana called after him. "Damion! I know you must find this hard to accept. But I believe that you are one of us. Why else should you have come here, at this time? It cannot be coincidence. Something led you here tonight. You are a Nemerei."

"Listen to me!" said Damion, turning and giving her a fierce look. "I'll keep your vow, on my honor as a priest: but on one condition. You're to leave Lorelyn alone from now on, and not breathe a word to her of this Tryna Lia nonsense."

"I had no intention of telling her," Ana replied. "In fact the knowledge would endanger her: and I am not yet certain. If this truly is her destiny, she will learn of it soon enough."

"Just let her be!" Damion shouted over his shoulder as he left the room. "Or I promise you I'll go straight to the Supreme Patriarch about this, vow or no vow!"

"Brother Damion, wait!" Prior Vale called after him.

Their voices followed him as he hastened away down the tunnels, echoing throughout the dark and ancient spaces: but there were no sounds of pursuit. To Damion it all seemed unreal. Surely all this would turn out to be a nightmare—he would wake in a moment, in his room in the monastery, and heave a sigh of relief. But no, it was all too real, and it was his fault. For bringing that cursed scroll to Maurainia when he knew well the harm it could bring to gullible minds, for failing to destroy it when he could have done so. And now Lorelyn was being drawn into this business as well . . .

As he passed one of the gaping archways, the shadows in it appeared to stir, and he saw, with a start, eyes reflecting the glow of his lantern—like an animal's, but at the height of a man's head.

Damion broke into a run, his lantern swinging wildly, sprinting up the slanting tunnel that led to the crypt above. When he reached the secret door he dropped the lantern, letting it roll upon the floor while his hands swept over the stones. Which portion of the wall made the door close again—was it here, or over there . . . ? It was no use; he couldn't find the spot. And now from the tunnel below came a rustling, stealthy sound. Farther down its length the eyes appeared again: discs of luminous yellow, the fiery eyes of a fiend.

He snatched up the lantern again, ran out through the crypt and up the spiral stair. Footsteps followed him. He tore through the door into the main chapel, preparing to yell for help, when the sound of chanting came from the far end of the aisle, and a blossoming of light.

* * *

AILIA WALKED ALONG in the train of taper-bearing students, monks, and nuns, chanting with them the words of the ancient hymn. Lorelyn walked at the front: she looked unexpectedly magnificent in the white ceremonial dress and crown of candles, with her unbraided, knee-length hair streaming down her back in a golden cascade. The nuns probably chose her for her lovely hair, and also because she was so tall. She seemed ill at ease in her finery, though, holding her star-tipped wand at an awkward angle and forgetting to wave it about as she'd been told to do. A *real* princess, Ailia could not help thinking, would be much more dignified.

Just then Father Damion came hurrying out of the door to the Paladins' crypt, a lantern in his hand. (Why a lantern, instead of the traditional candle?) He stopped in his tracks at the sight of the procession, and stood staring at Lorelyn—admiring her in her festive garb, no doubt. Ailia felt a sudden twinge, almost of jealousy: the young man's gaze was so fixed, so intense. She longed for him look at *her* in that same way.

As the light from Lorelyn's candle-crown and the handheld tapers drew near, shadows went flitting into corners like fleeing phantoms. One dark shade that hung in the doorway behind Damion looked for a moment quite eerily like a man's cloaked form, looming over the priest: it was not Damion's own shadow, for that lay to his right. With the light's coming this black shade too withdrew, slipping back into the stairwell that led to the crypt; really it looked almost exactly like a man retreating down the stair, and she was reminded with a shiver of Lorelyn's wild story about the cowled ghost in the chapel. But when the procession passed Damion, sweeping him into its flow, Ailia glanced through the doorway at the stairwell and saw no one there.

7

Star of Omen

AILIA STIRRED IN HER BED with a sigh. Though dawn was near, she hung still between sleep and waking, like a swimmer suspended between the sea's dark depths and its sunlit surface. She had been dreaming, but only a few fragmentary images remained in her conscious mind: a dream-debris, slowly sinking back into the deeps from which she had just come. It must have been an interesting dream, for it had left her with an afterglow of enchantment, the sensation of having sojourned in some wondrous magical place. She struggled to secure its fading memory, to bring it back with her, like sunken treasure, into the waking world.

There had been something about a woman in it—*a beautiful woman, wearing a golden crown . . . or no, it wasn't a crown, it was her hair, lovely thick braids of golden hair like Lorelyn's, wound about her head.* And yet the impression of royalty still remained in Ailia's memory of the woman. *How do I know she was a queen?*

Somehow I'm sure she was one. And that glorious hair! She unpinned the braids, I remember: they fell loose like golden ropes, right down to the floor, and she sat there unbraiding them, until her hair flowed all about her, rippling and shining. Ailia ached with longing at the vision. *What I'd give to have hair like that! And how beautiful her face was, with such blue eyes—but now I come to think of it, she didn't look very happy. Worried, I think. Yes—that was when her husband—I think it was her husband, the man with the dark hair and solemn-looking face—came in, and they talked together. I can hear their voices yet—they said something about an enemy coming, and having to protect—was it their daughter? Yes, their daughter, and her name was . . . what? El . . . El-something—*

A damp washcloth hit her on the cheek, and the rest of the dream vanished at once beyond recall. "Get up, Worm," called Lusina's voice. "Morning bell's rung."

Ailia sat up with a groan. *What a shame! I've never had such a vivid dream before. I'm sure it would have made a splendid story to tell, and now most of it's gone forever . . .* It was curious how often one forgot the details of dreams, she reflected as she joined the queue for the washbasin. And what of those you never even knew you'd had? It was as though you were not one person but two, and one kept secrets from the other.

Lusina kept looking at her and sniggering, but Ailia ignored her; the girl's malice was now the exception rather than the rule. Lorelyn's staunch defense of the Island girl might have had something to do with it: Lusina and the others had by now learned not to criticize Ailia in her presence. Indeed, now that final examinations were not far off, a few of them had even approached Ailia for help with their studies.

"The nerve of them!" Lorelyn exclaimed in indignation. "Picking your brains—and after they were so horrid to you, too!"

"Oh, I don't mind," Ailia replied. "They look so sheepish when they come to me, it's rather funny. I don't feel angry with them anymore."

She glanced out the dormitory window. Only a few pathetic rags of snow lingered, lying under bushes and in little dints and hollows in the ground: winter was truly over. She had thought at first that it must be an early thaw, until she spied green shoots tonguing up through the earth, and flowers beginning to unfurl their petals: snowdrops, crocuses. *In winter!* thought Ailia, amazed, for back on the Island flowers would not appear for at least another month. Tree branches that a few weeks ago had been black and barren as charred sticks in a hearth now showed countless little pregnant swellings; widening mirrors of meltwater reflected the softened blue of the sky, and the grass beneath their still surfaces grew green as seaweeds in a tidepool. The winds were warmer and brought the moist organic smells of spring in through the window, now opened at the bottom to let in the fresh air.

With the vernal equinox the year began anew, in the festival of Tarmalia, the Kindling of the Stars, which celebrated the Creation. Last night they had attended the midnight service in the Chapel of the Paladins. Its cavernous interior was lit with hundreds of candles to symbolize the new-made stars, and Father Damion presided, wearing over his robe the golden festal mantle that was the gift of the nuns to the chapel, embroidered on the back with the figure of Saint Athariel subduing the dragon. Ailia could not take her eyes from him. He was so beautiful that it hurt her; she had never in all her life striven so hard to commit detail to memory. As she waited for her turn to wash, sunlight bannered through the dormitory windows; but Ailia saw only the chapel's weave of shadow and fire, and at its center the man who seemed made of light.

She was troubled at the increasing oddness of her behavior around Damion. Once content with worshipping him shyly from afar, she had of late taken greater pains with her appearance whenever she knew he would be near. Last night she had added ribands to her hair and arranged it in a new style, braided at the temples, in the hope that his gaze might light and linger on her for a moment. It was foolish and she knew it: she was nothing to the priest, and never could be. But for a mere instant she had half persuaded herself that he had indeed looked her way briefly, and at the close of the service she had walked out in a daze of bliss.

A voice spoke in the line behind her. "Wasn't Father Damion *magnificent* last night?" Belina exclaimed.

Ailia gave a little guilty start to hear her own thoughts so exactly echoed. "The chaplain?" she murmured, feigning surprise.

"Oh, *Ailia!*" cried Belina, turning on her. "Your head's always in the clouds. I don't believe you've even noticed Damion—and him so handsome! We're *all* in love with him."

"Belina, Damion's a priest!" reproved Arianlyn. "Really, you're all being a bit silly about him, girls. He's taken a vow of celibacy, remember."

"I know," said Belina regretfully. "What a waste of such a comely man!" Several girls sighed along with her.

Hearing her classmates discuss Damion gave Ailia a strange jealous feeling. She, who had never minded sharing anything before, felt resentful that they too should enjoy her angel-priest's beauty. And they spoke of him in such a crude, common way—as though he were just an ordinary man! Nevertheless, she found herself listening hungrily to their conversation as they walked downstairs to breakfast, hoping she might learn something interesting.

"Cheer up, you lot," said Janeth in her most ironic voice. "The word around the Academy is that he's struggling with his faith. He's been to see the abbot and prior several times over the past few months: they're his confessors, you know. Maybe he'll leave the priesthood altogether, and marry one of you."

Ailia almost choked. Damion *married*! This was worse than the thought of him leaving the Academy. She felt a sudden, irrational spasm of hate for the hypothetical wife.

"I think he's got a lady love already," declared Lusina.

"Oh no!" Belina gasped.

"He's always going off for long walks through the countryside—visiting some country lass in her cottage, I'll wager."

"Lusina!" exclaimed Arianlyn, appalled. "You mustn't say such things!"

Lusina tossed her dark head. "You'll see—there's a woman at the bottom of this. Faith struggle, indeed! There's only one reason a man like that leaves the priesthood!"

Ailia could not bear to hear any more of this. She lagged behind the others, her face flushing with annoyance, until their chattering voices were far ahead of her.

Lorelyn too walked at the rear of the procession, and her face was long—though for a different reason, Ailia knew. Mother Abbess had summoned Lorelyn to her office in the cloister the day before, no doubt to give her a reprimand of some sort. The tall blonde girl had looked dejected ever since. Ailia glanced at her, feeling a vague sense of guilt. Ever since the Trynalia service she had kept a slight distance from Lorelyn. The envy she had felt for the other girl then, fleeting as it had been, alarmed her. She had examined her conscience, worried that she was cultivating Lorelyn not out of real friendship, but only from a desire to get closer to Father Damion. And so she had withdrawn from her a little in the last few months.

But there was such an air of misery in Lorelyn's drooping posture and downcast gaze that Ailia, who had intended to slip quietly behind her, hesitated and then walked at the girl's side instead. "Are you all right, Lori?" she inquired.

"No," Lorelyn replied, her tone morose. "I'm all wrong." She raised her head and looked straight at Ailia, who as usual found it rather difficult to meet her eyes. They were such a pale, clear blue, at once ethereal and piercing. Sometimes they seemed to Ailia like an angel's eyes, and at other times like a child's. Under the burning purity of their gaze she always felt somehow abashed, though there was neither accusation nor reproach in them.

"What do you mean?" she asked. "Did Reverend Mother scold you about something?"

Lorelyn shook her head, looking doleful. "Scold me? I only wish she had! No, she sent for me to tell me that I ought to think of taking the veil. I told her I don't want to be a nun, but she says I ought to give it some thought. The nuns will look after me, feed and clothe and shelter me if I go to live with them. I know she meant to be kind, Ailia, and really there isn't much else for me to do. I'm an orphan, and poor as a temple mouse. But I just can't bear the thought of it: changing my name to something dreary like Prudence or Piety, and trailing about in heavy robes and veil for the rest of my life."

Ailia tried a cheery tone. "It isn't such a terrible thing to be a nun. I've been thinking about it myself."

Lorelyn's pale eyes stared. "You *want* to go into the cloister?"

"Why not?" Ailia returned, with some force. "Why is it so much worse to enter a convent than to marry and have babies until you're ready to die of exhaustion? If I were a nun I could go on studying all my life—read histories and dissertations, perhaps even write a few of my own—" She stopped short, a little taken aback by her own vehemence.

"Well, you're clever after all," agreed Lorelyn, "so I suppose you wouldn't mind it. But I'd feel like a prisoner in there." She looked out a window at the high barred gate of the inner cloister, revulsion plain in her face.

"The convent isn't a prison," Ailia began.

"It certainly looks like one. And I thought a nun had to have a—what-d'you-call-it?—a vacation."

"*Vo*cation," Ailia corrected. "Well, perhaps you have one and don't realize it yet."

Lorelyn said nothing for a moment. "There *is* something

I should be doing," she stated presently, "but it hasn't anything to do with the cloister. And if they shut me up in there, I'll never be able to do it."

Ailia was puzzled. "But what exactly is it you want to do?"

Lorelyn's face fell. "That's the trouble. I don't *know*—it's just a feeling. Do you remember that evening when I talked about being a knight? I felt I'd come close to learning what I'm here for." She stood still, gazing off into space. "I'm meant to fight—to protect something. If only I knew what it was!"

"I don't understand."

The other girl sighed. "Neither do I. That's the worst of it. And no one can help me."

Ailia searched for more words of comfort, but she could find nothing to say. After a moment Lorelyn turned on her heel and strode off, her shoulders hunched and unhappy.

I CANNOT ACCEPT IT, Father," Damion told the abbot. "The whole business is quite mad."

The two men stood alone in the empty, sunlit chapel. The elderly abbot wore a worried frown on his thin, lined face. "That's what some of the monks say," he replied. "Those who know, that is. A secret like this one is bound to be a burden. But a sacred vow is . . . well, sacred. The Brothers have kept the location of the catacombs secret for centuries, even when there were no Paladins or Nemerei to hide in them. We must continue to honor our promise."

Damion turned to face him. "And the sanctity of the confessional? Is that not to be honored too?"

"You don't still believe the good prior broke it?"

Damion turned away again. "I don't *want* to believe that he did. He swore, on everything sacred, that he didn't. But confound it all, Father—what other explanation is there? The only person I told about it aside from the prior was Kaithan Athariel, and *he* would never have anything to do with these people!"

"The Second Sight," murmured the abbot. "That's what we call it in my homeland, in Rialain. There's many a Rialainish man and woman born with the Sight. We consider it a gift from God."

Damion stared at him. "Some say it's the opposite—the work of the Fiend."

"True enough, but I never could see any harm in it. In Rialain those with the Sight use it to help others—search for missing children, and so on. My own mother, bless her, often had premonitions. And weren't the holy prophets themselves given visions of the future? How can the Sight be evil, then?"

But Damion did not want to talk to someone who believed in clairvoyance. He wanted desperately to be told that it was all nonsense, that Ana and her followers were frauds, that none of this had anything at all to do with him . . . Why *was* he so anxious not to believe in it himself?

Because it changes everything, he thought in a sudden instant of clarity. *I wanted to be like Kaithan: to believe in a God who was only another word for justice, a Faith that was only another word for discipline, an orderly universe obedient to Reason . . . If I let myself believe in clairvoyance, I'll end up believing in it all—magic and miracles, an absolute Good . . . an absolute Evil.* He shivered.

He had dreamed again in the night—a dream both beautiful and troubling.

The abbot watched him with a pensive eye. "The Nemerei are our brethren, Damion: I've observed their rites for years now, and they've no more to do with black magic or demon-worship than ours. But there are still some who would like to see them rounded up and imprisoned. Patriarch Norvyn Winter at the High Temple, for one—*he'd* start up the whole Inquisition again, if he could. He's always looking for heretics these days. He's taken to riding about the countryside with a group of Zimbouran men for his personal guard—"

Damion froze. "Did you say Zimbourans?"

"Yes. They're converts to our faith, who fled King Khalazar's reign—or so they claim."

"Converts my foot! Spies, more likely. They might even be here to find the scroll for their king!"

"That is true. It would not be his first attempt. But Patriarch Winter won't be separated from his guard. He has his eye on the Supreme Patriarch's throne, it's said, now that the Holy Father has become so frail. It looks well for him to be seen with heathen converts walking tamely at his heels. People might think he converted them himself." The old man walked away down the aisle, shaking his head. "If he becomes Supreme Patriarch, we'll see troubled times indeed."

Damion frowned. Concerns about witches and clairvoyance faded, replaced by this real and immediate threat. He stood for a few moments struggling with himself. Then he lit a candle, and opened the door that led to the crypt and the catacombs beyond.

* * *

THE VAST DIM WARREN of tunnels was empty, but Damion heard distant echoing voices and followed them into the scroll room, where he found Ana sitting in a chair beside the makeshift altar. Before her squatted Ralf the village idiot, uttering his mournful seagull sounds and tossing his head about. She listened attentively, nodding her head from time to time or making comments of her own, for all the world as if this were a normal conversation. At Damion's approach Ralf turned and howled, showing a bruised cheek and black eye.

Ana smiled at Damion. "This seems to be my day for visitors," she observed. "I will be with you in a moment, Father." She took Ralf's left forearm in her hands. There was, Damion saw, a seeping wound just above the elbow, and the hand was bandaged.

As he waited for Ana to finish her ministrations, he glanced around the room. The back of its dim candlelit interior was cluttered with objects he had not noticed on his first visit: now he recognized them as the crates and other crude furnishings from Ana's cave home. Wolf lay on the floor not far away, and Greymalkin sat at her feet; seeing Damion, the big dog growled low in its throat, but the cat rose and headed straight for the priest, winding her lean gray body in and out of the young man's ankles. Damion walked over to look at the wound on Ralf's arm: it was large and jagged, purplish round the edges, and in the center was a whitish mass. He uttered an oath and recoiled in disgust, his hand to his mouth. There was a clump of pale, writhing maggots in the open wound.

Ana ran a finger around the lips of the wound, then nodded. "Good. That's healing very nicely, Ralf."

The man made another baying sound and flapped his

free hand. Damion stared, swallowing revulsion. Could she not see? "Ana—his wound, it's full of worms—"

"I know," she cut him off. "I put them there."

"*Put* them there?"

"To clean it." Calmly she took a maggot between her thumb and forefinger, plucking it from the wound. Opening a small wooden box that sat beside her chair, she dropped the worm in. "They eat away dead tissue, and their presence also halts infection. They've done their work, Ralf. And now for the hand." She twitched the last worm from the wound and placed it in the box, then took Ralf's left hand in her own and unwrapped the bandages. The palm was scarred and the thumb swollen and purple; crude stitches held torn skin together at its base.

"His thumb was almost severed, you see: it was quite a task for me to sew it back on again. But the blood is still not flowing properly through it; it's clotting up. You'll need a leech or two," she told Ralf.

Sickened but too fascinated to look away, Damion watched as she fetched a pail from the far corner of the room and plunged her hand into it. There were several dark shapes floating in the water within the pail. She drew out one, a slimy green sluglike shape with red streaks along its back. He felt compelled to protest: "No one uses leeches nowadays, Ana!"

"I do," was her quiet reply. "The creatures have been misused in the past by ignorant physicians, but they can do a great deal of good when used properly." She held the leech up to the bloated thumb until its suckerlike mouth took a firm hold. "No pain, Ralf?" she asked. The man made no reply, but his bruised face was placid. "Good. It shouldn't hurt," she explained to

Damion. "Leeches secrete a fluid from their mouths that deadens pain—that is how they are able to attach themselves without your noticing . . . There, it's drawing out the blood now." The leech's green body began to swell. "You see, Father Damion, how a creature maligned by man can actually do him good? You may go home now, Ralf. Take care you don't knock the leech off until it has had its fill. Those tissues must be drained, and the blood set to flowing freely again. When you remove the leech, wash the wound well, and come back to see me again in a day or two."

The injured man rose and shuffled out of the room, still moaning and gesticulating with his free hand. Damion stared after Ralf's retreating back. "How was he hurt?" he asked Ana.

"He was set upon by some very unpleasant men in an alley of the city. He is only alive because his attackers thought he would not be able tell the authorities who hurt him. But he *could* tell me." She got up and walked over to the scroll table. "You came about this, didn't you? You are quite right about the danger it poses, Father Damion. But the scroll of Bereborn is safe in our keeping, I promise."

"Is it?" he challenged. "I just learned there might be more Zimbouran spies here in Maurainia. I think they may be posing as converts."

"I know all about them. It was they who attacked poor Ralf."

"*They* did!" He stared. "But why would they harm Ralf?"

"He has been spying on them for us. We thought they would never suspect him because everyone believes he is simple, and he could always pretend that he only wanted to beg from them. But when the Zimbouran men saw him following them through the back alleys they beat him and slashed him with knives. It would appear they take no chances." Her tone was bland.

"It's outrageous." Damion turned hot with anger. "They can't do such things here, to our people. I'll complain to the Patriarch, and the magistrates. I'll see that Ralf has justice—"

"No use, I'm afraid. Ralf cannot speak, so he cannot testify in court. And I could not speak on his behalf: no magistrate would believe that I can understand him."

"And can you?" he asked.

"We speak the wordless language, Ralf and I," she answered, returning the pail and box to the far side of the room. "The language of thought. Words are so often a distortion or concealment of thought rather than its true expression. When Ralf and I talk together, we may speak aloud from time to time out of habit, but we really communicate with our minds, not our mouths." Ana shook her head. "Poor Ralf! There is nothing at all wrong with his mind, but an inborn condition deprives him of speech. He is *not* an idiot—such an unpleasant word!"

"It's a Nemerei ability, then, this wordless language?"

"It is." She smiled. "The heart of our conspiracy."

Damion stared into the withered old face. Who *was* this woman? No one seemed to know where she had come from, how long she had lived in this land, how old she was. The villagers told many tales about her. She had, it was said, an almost magical influence on animals. Birds, rabbits, deer—none of these, they said, showed any fear of old Ana, but would come right up to her, even allow her to touch them. She had been seen taking some honey from a hive in an old oak tree—"and the wild bees didn't sting her," the astounded witness reported. Some people, Damion knew, had a natural way with wild animals, and were able to calm them with slow gentle movements and a soft tone of voice. But the villagers believed that Ana possessed sorcerous powers.

And did she?

Damion met her veiled gaze. "Tell me what I'm thinking right now, Ana."

She shook her head. "No, Damion," she answered gently. "It doesn't work that way. Nemerei cannot read minds. We may share what we wish, but our thoughts are our own. It is rather like the monastery at the Academy: in the corridors, chapel, and refectory the monks gather together, yet at night when they go to their cells and close their doors, each monk is alone. We Nemerei can open the doors of our minds to one another, but none may enter without leave; and if we venture into the communal place where minds can meet, it is always by choice. If you were to *project* a thought toward me, though—concentrate on something, and *will* me to see it—then I could share it."

Damion closed his eyes. Into his mind sprang the dream he'd had the night before: the dream of the golden-haired woman from his first vision. She was seated in a chair, he recalled, clad in a robe of royal blue, her hair bound atop her head in shining braids. Her daughter was in her arms: not a child in this scene but an infant, tiny in a white gown that hung to the floor, her hair only a few golden wisps on her head. Her great eyes, blue as her mother's, were wide open and wondering, seeming to gaze straight into his own. On waking he had told himself that the Nemerei at their meeting in the catacombs described dreams similar to this one, so it was perhaps unsurprising that his overtaxed mind conjured the same image. But it still seemed so vivid, so real . . . With all his might he concentrated on the scene.

"Ah—the little Tryna Lia with her mother," said Ana's voice softly. "She cannot have been a week old at the time . . ."

Damion's eyes snapped open. He stared at her, shaken. "How can you—*do* that?"

"It is a gift—an ability you and I both possess. Your mother had the Sight too: it is often passed down from parents to their children."

"My mother had it? How can you know that?"

"I recognized her, in the vision we both shared in the cave." Ana sat down on a bench, and her cat leaped up beside her: she stroked it absently as she talked. "I would have told you, but you left in such a hurry. Ah, yes, I remember her . . . Her name was Elthina. She lived alone in the mountains: a free spirit you might call her. I used to meet with her now and again, and we also communed with our minds. But she left the mountains many years ago. There was a man of the city, Arthon, a man who had dreams of one day restoring the Paladin order . . . She loved him very much. They used to meet in the woods on Selenna. But then he died, with all his ambitions unfulfilled, and she could not bear to return to the place. When I found you in my cave I was quite certain it was Elthina who placed you there, and the vision that you and I later shared confirmed it. Back then I thought of raising you myself, as she plainly desired. But I decided it would be better for you to live among children your own age, and so I took you to the monks."

Damion turned away from her, pondering all this, still not quite wanting to believe her but having no reason now to doubt her word. A Nemerei mother, a father fascinated by knights and chivalry . . . it would explain so much about his own life. But he could not speak of it, not yet. Instead he said, still without turning around, "You and your friends could abuse this . . . power. Even if you can't read minds, you could be plotting and scheming together all the time, and the rest of the world would never know it."

A trace of sadness entered Ana's voice. "I won't say that no Nemerei has ever misused the gift, Damion. It has happened more than once in our history. But most of us use it responsibly, to help and not to harm. We would never use it to plot against others."

He turned and faced her again. "Then why do you call yourselves 'conspirators'?"

"There really isn't any Maurish word for what we are. *Conspirators*—'many who think as one'—comes the closest. That is what 'Nemerei' means, literally: 'those who think together.' "

"I thought it translated as 'sorcerer.' "

"Again, the Maurish term isn't quite accurate. There is far more to so-called sorcery than the more dramatic magical feats, though in the old Academy of Andarion's day many of these skills were taught—scrying, for instance, seeking visions by gazing at some reflecting surface; and *glaumerie,* the creation of harmless illusions; and ethereal projection. Many Paladins learned these skills: that is why they were executed for witchcraft during the time of the Inquisition. But only the White Magic was ever taught at Andarion's Academy.

"It all ended in the year 2497 with the Day of Disaster." Her face was solemn. "On that day hundreds of shooting stars fell to the earth, and destroyed all they touched. Clouds of dust and the smoke of burning cities filled the skies and lingered for months afterwards, withering crops and giving the name Dark Age to the centuries that followed. But those early days were a time of figurative darkness too. Many of the Faithful believed the Disaster was a divine punishment, that the users of magic had incurred the Lord Aan's wrath. To make matters worse, Brannar Andarion left no heir to rule Maurainia, and Trynisia, the seat of the old Commonwealth, was laid waste. So the holy Patriarchs moved to fill the void."

"They brought order to the kingdom," interrupted Damion. "And they crowned a new king in time."

"That is true. But in the early days of the Interregnum fear of magic filled the people's hearts, and so the Patriarchs appointed Inquisitors to purge all Nemerei from the land. Of course they could not hope to harm the great sorcerers, who could use their powers to escape. But many innocents were mistaken for Nemerei and punished or slain. The Paladins' Academy was denounced and destroyed; ignorance and terror gripped the countries that once had been part of an orderly Commonwealth." Ana sighed as she spoke.

"But we must do something about these Zimbouran men!" urged Damion, steering her back to his main concern. "I know why they're here in Maurainia. Their king wants that piece of parchment, there on your table."

"I know it," she replied. "Khalazar sent an embassy to King Stefon last month, offering him a treaty of peace in exchange for one thing—a parchment scroll, containing some ancient writings sacred to Zimbourans. The Royal Academy had possession of this document, it was said, but had no right to it. Stefon sent some men to retrieve it, only to learn it had apparently been stolen." She gave a little smile. "The embassy then left Maurainia—except for several Zimbourans who remained behind, claiming sanctuary, and asking to be allowed to remain in the country."

Damion nearly stopped breathing. The shock of the shared vision, the tale of his parentage—all receded in importance. If this account was true, then all his deepest anxieties were confirmed. He looked again at the double roll of parchment, old and crumbling, seemingly innocuous. "It ought to be destroyed, Ana. What if they find it? It may be worthless in itself, but if their king is ready to go to war for it—"

"Is that your worst fear?" said Ana. "The Zimbourans are only the least part of what we have to face, Damion. They are tools of the dark power, of Modrian-Valdur: instruments of his will. But he has other weapons, older and greater, to use against us." Greymalkin suddenly hissed and arched her back, reacting to her mistress's tone of voice, perhaps. "It is these great powers and principalities we have to fear, not the Zimbouran people," she added, her face solemn. "Khalazar is a deluded man: I doubt the enemy's true incarnation has come yet. That is not to say that Khalazar is *no* danger. Through him, and other tyrants like him, Valdur seeks to pervert and destroy the world. It is always the same pattern, the same tale told again and again: the face of our foe is but the mask of Valdur."

"You Nemerei have some dangerous enemies, haven't you?"

"I would hardly want them for friends," she replied lightly. She went back to the makeshift altar, gazing down at the scroll. "My most pressing need is for a ship to take me to the far north. I must seek out Trynisia, and the Stone. So, you see, I cannot destroy the scroll. I need the sea chart and the sacred writings. And to make a copy is no solution, for it too can fall into the wrong hands."

"Ana, you'll never get any sea captain to go to the arctic ocean. Too many expeditions have never returned."

She nodded. "It is a serious problem, indeed. But I must get there somehow."

"You're afraid the Zimbourans might get to the Star Stone first, aren't you?" he asked, voicing his own worry. "That Khalazar will find it and take it home—and then try to conquer the world?"

"The Zimbourans will be seeking it, yes: but they at least do not know where it is. They have never seen the scroll. Our other enemies—the great powers—also desire it: and they know full well where it lies. I must go to Trynisia. The Tryna Lia's time is come."

"You mean Lorelyn, don't you? You can't really believe that girl is the . . . the—"

"Lorelyn," Ana said, "is only an adoptive name, given her by the Jana monks. She may well have another. The true name of the Tryna Lia is Elmiria." The filmy eyes were unreadable in the candlelight. "The name given her by her mother."

"And who *was* her mother? A goddess—or a mortal woman?"

"I would say she was both, in a manner of speaking."

Damion groaned. "More riddles!"

Ana looked thoughtful. "One day, perhaps, I may be able to give you a straight answer," she said. "The truth is that I do not know everything yet. In the meantime, I must ask you to keep your promise and say nothing of this to anyone—anyone at all. If those Zimbouran spies should learn about this—that Lorelyn is our prophesied leader, our Princess—you know what they will do."

He stared at her in growing horror as her words sank in. The Tryna Lia was to battle the Dark Prince, the incarnation of Valdur: and King Khalazar claimed to be that incarnation. If Lorelyn were identified with that other prophetic figure . . .

"Yes." Ana, watching his face, nodded her white head. "They will kill her, Damion."

THAT EVENING AILIA and her classmates were allowed to go to the Spring Fair in Raimar, accompanied by two of the novice nuns. Lorelyn did not join the party. She had been withdrawn and remote all day, not answering right away when spoken to: it was as though she were not attuned to the real world at all, but inhabited some other realm where no one could follow. When Lorelyn announced that she would not go with the others on their excursion, Ailia felt disquieted, though she could not say quite what it was that troubled her. But she thrust the feeling aside, and joined the others with their chaperons.

As they descended the steep path to the city they could see that the festival was already in full swing. People danced in the streets below, and strains of merry music came wafting up to them. Hanging stars of silver and gold paper turned, glittering, in the breeze, and rows of brightly colored lanterns glowed in the trees that lined the wider avenues. The fair itself was held in the central marketplace of the city. Ailia had never seen an open-air market before: Great Island's buying and bartering took place in large, fusty, fish-smelling halls, owing to the usually inclement weather. Nor had she ever seen such a bewildering variety of goods as that which now greeted her eyes. There were sweetmeats of every imaginable kind in these stalls, and jewelry, and embroidery, and woodcarvings; there were sculptures carved from huge blocks of butter, and strange exotic fruits and spices brought from Marakor. And everywhere she looked there were eggs, the symbol of Creation: real eggs with painted and gilded shells, others that were confections of sugar, or fashioned from glass or porcelain. It was customary at Tarmalia to give gifts in this shape. Small children, waking to find the festival eggs their parents set beside their beds, believed the magic Elmir bird had laid them.

Watched over by Sister Serenity and Sister Hope, the girls went from stall to stall, buying cheap trinkets and sweets and painted eggs, skirting jugglers and street minstrels and revelers in masquerade costume. Walking around one booth, Ailia came face to face with a princess of olden days, the sleeves of her ivory-colored gown hanging almost to her ankles, her flowing dark hair crowned with gilt and glass gems. A man strode by on stilts, trailed by shouting children. Most wonderful of all was a knight in very real-looking armor, riding through the market on a huge black horse in full jousting panoply.

His visor was down, and there was a steel crown upon his helmet surmounted by a spread-winged dragon. There was also the device of a red dragon rampant on his shield and tabard, and on the flowing black caparison of his horse. *Of course—Prince Morlyn,* she thought in delight as the figure rode majestically past. *What a pity Lorelyn didn't come: she would have enjoyed seeing that!*

Turning back toward the stalls, she suddenly caught sight of her cousin Jaimon: she was on the point of hailing him when she noticed that he was not alone. With him was a young flaxen-haired girl in peasant attire, and Ailia could not help noticing how close together they stood, with shoulders nearly touching. Even as she watched them, she saw Jaimon slip his arm through the girl's, who made no objection. The two walked on, then paused to watch a group of young people dancing around a small tree, its still-bare boughs hung with Tanaura decorations. The dancers' bodies were liberally bedecked with garlands, twigs from shrubs and fruit trees that they had cut and forced into early flower; they laughed and sang in lusty voices as they capered to a lively tune played by a lad on a wooden flute.

Something deep within Ailia stirred at that music; it beat in her blood like a pulse, like the waking impatience of spring itself. She stared at her cousin and his girl. It was not jealousy, rather a sudden understanding that now burst upon her. She rejected it at once in utter dismay.

I am not *in love,* she told herself firmly. *I'm not!*

She had always been determined not to fall in love: it led, she knew, inevitably to marriage and the heavy burdens of home and children. Romantic tales and ballads were all very well, but reality was a different matter. Her own life, Ailia resolved, would be dedicated to reading and learning. She gazed now at the laughing blonde girl, her plump bare arm about Jaimon's shoulders, and she was disturbed to feel a little flutter beneath her own boned bodice. She would not have exchanged places with the girl: she felt for her cousin only the same warm affection she had known since their earliest childhood.

But what, said a voice within her, *if he were Damion Athariel?*

Her heart leaped even as her mind recoiled. No, it was too stupid: it put her on a level with Belina and the others. But recalling what the other girls had said about Damion also made her remember, with alarm, the fierce possessiveness she felt whenever they spoke of him. She turned away from the dancers, her face flushing. Jaimon and his girl also moved on, to watch an open-air Creation play. A man dressed as God in gold robe and mask was reciting a speech to some actors dressed as animals. It looked interesting, but Ailia did not want to be seen by her cousin now. He might think she was tagging after him, and he likely wanted to be alone with his lady friend. She looked around for the other girls, and saw them standing by a complex of tents that dominated the eastern end of the market square. One housed a rather raucous puppet show, while in front of another a conjuror entertained onlookers with sleight-of-hand tricks. The convent girls had gathered to watch him, but a smaller tent caught Ailia's eye. Its sign, decorated with silver stars, read FORTUNES. Curious, she went up to the tent and looked in.

A little old woman sat in the dim interior before a small table, clad in a gauzy gray gown. A gray silk scarf, patterned with stars, was wound about her head and shoulders. Before her on the table lay a globe of clear glass or crystal into which she appeared at first to be gazing. Then as she turned toward Ailia the girl saw that the old woman's eyes were faded and filmy. She must be blind.

"Hello?" called the old woman. "Who is it? Do you wish to learn of your future?"

Ailia did not believe in astrology, but the old woman sounded so hopeful that it seemed a shame to disappoint her. Everyone else was watching the magician, who had just turned a bouquet of flowers into a scarf and pulled a live pigeon from it. She fished in her pocket for a coin. "I'd like to hear my fortune, please," she said.

"Ah," said the old woman, smiling. "Very well!"

It was all in fun, thought Ailia defensively, as she sat down opposite the old woman. A gray cat rose from its cushion in the corner and rubbed its sides against her ankles. She reached down to pet it and the animal purred loudly.

"That is Greymalkin," said the old woman. "So: you come from the convent." The girl looked at her in surprise, wondering if she were blind after all: she had obviously seen the white gown. The woman smiled. "I do not see only with my eyes, but with the inner Sight. I'm a witch: old Ana, they call me."

Old Ana. Ailia seemed to recall hearing about this woman from her year-mates. She was supposed to be insane, wasn't she? The girl studied the old, faded face opposite her, but it seemed to her placid and gentle. Ailia found herself thinking suddenly, *She was beautiful once.*

"So, my dear," Ana said, "you wish to know your future."

"Yes, please," she answered. "My name's Ailia Shipwright, by the way."

The old woman smiled. "How do you do. Well, then, let us see what the Fates have in store." She might have been a kindly grandmother offering a cup of tea. "There's nothing at all to be frightened of, you know. Some people of the Faith are a little alarmed by fortune-telling—they say it's the work of the Evil One, but it isn't really. All you must do is sit there and think—all about yourself, your life, and everything that matters to you, and I will see what I can read in it." She sat very still as Ailia thought, then she said in clear precise tones, "You have traveled a great distance over water."

"Yes," admitted Ailia. It was, of course, a stock phrase of fortune-tellers, but the coincidence was a bit startling.

"You will travel over water again," Ana continued, "on a journey that you will share with others. I see many lives touching yours. But I see also a path that you must walk alone. It is a dark path, but at its end I see a light."

Her strange filmy eyes opened, and she seemed to look right at Ailia for a moment—at, through, and beyond her. There was a brief silence, during which the faint pulse of the dance music could be heard through the tent's thin walls.

"Is that all?" asked Ailia at last, feeling rather disappointed.

"That is all," said Ana. "I do not, like some fortune-tellers, pretend to know all the future. I merely detect patterns of probability, projections that have their roots in the present. The future is not graven in stone, you know; we are not like those players out in the square, following a script already written for us. There is always free will. It is the way of the Tanaura, the Tree of Life.

"To the Elei the universe was like a great tree, in whose boughs all living things dwelt. They were right, as mythmakers so often are. The universe of space and time has the form of a tree, with many branches forever growing and dividing. When one of us pursues a certain course of action, it creates a consequential chain of events—like a new twig sprouting from its parent limb. You hesitated just a little before entering my tent, didn't you? If you hadn't come in, we should not now be having this conversation, and whatever small change it may make in you would never have taken place. The cosmos itself would have followed a different path. But you did come in, and we are talking, and so a new branch grows upon the Tree of Being. Who can say what fruit it will bear?"

"But . . . I'm just an ordinary person," said Ailia, puzzled. "How can I change the cosmos?"

"The future of all things great is bound up in all things small. You are a part of the pattern, and more important than you realize." Ana smiled.

"But you mentioned the Fates," said Ailia.

"I wasn't speaking of predestination. I used an old word: Fates, or *Fays*: the ancient powers of earth and sea and sky, and of the celestial bodies." Ana indicated the stars embroidered upon her scarf. "Naturally, they too have some influence on the pattern. "From the old word *Fay* comes the term faerie: it was once *Fayerie,* the power of the *Fays.*"

"I used to believe in faeries," said Ailia wistfully, "when I was small."

"But not anymore? What a pity! You must be thinking of all the strange fancies that have arisen over the ages. To you faeries are quaint little people who live in flowers and under toadstools. The Elei knew better: to them the inhabitants of the higher realms were powers, forces for good—and for evil."

"Higher realms?"

Ana nodded. "There are other planes beside this one, and worlds beyond the world. I know them all. I see only imperfectly—like the sibyls of old, who veiled their faces to shut out the material world—and so I must rely on the mind's vision, not the eye's. Such a person can behold the inner world: the Hamadryad in the tree, the Salamander in the flame, the spirit in the shell of the body. The higher planes lie beyond the world that we know with our eyes and ears and other senses. You come from Great Island, do you not?"

"Why—yes," replied Ailia, surprised anew. Had the old woman recognized her accent?

"Think of your island as the world. It is bounded on all sides by the sea, a limited space, and those who live on it know it well—or so they think. For you Islanders are mountain-dwellers, though you do not know it: your home is in fact the summit of a mighty sea-mount, thrusting up through the surface of the ocean. And far down in the murky deeps the slopes of that mountain are inhabited by many other things—strange sea-denizens, beasts and fish of which no Islander will ever catch a glimpse. Our universe is the same. The physical realm, the world we know, is but a small part of it. It has other dimensions—depths you cannot plumb, inhabitants you cannot see."

Ailia had listened to all of this with growing fascination, and now for the merest of instants she entertained the thought, *Suppose she is right.* What if the reality she had always believed in was nothing more than a false perception: if this "world" was only a small part of some other, larger realm? It was no stranger than many of the things she had learned in her philosophy classes.

Then the brief, thrilling instant passed and was replaced all at once with guilty fear. *She said she was a witch! Is she trying to make a witch of me, too?* Ailia sprang to her feet, almost knocking over her chair. "I must go," she exclaimed.

"You are frightened," remarked Ana. "I am sorry." She sounded as though she meant it, and Ailia felt a twinge of compunction.

"It's time I went back to join the other girls, that's all," she amended hastily. "I don't want them to think I'm lost. Thank you for everything." She put her coin down on the table, but Ana did not reach for it.

"Goodbye, Ailia," the old woman said quietly. "I think we will meet again. But you're quite right, you'd better go now: the Sisters will be looking for you."

Ailia all but bolted out of the tent. She looked around her for the other Academy girls as she reentered the square, then gave a little start.

The man in the knight's costume had ridden his great caparisoned steed right into the market square and halted directly opposite Ana's tent. Something in his posture suggested hostility, even malevolence; and though his eyes were invisible behind the slits of his steel visor, she had the unnerving impression that he was looking straight at her.

* * *

HOURS LATER, AS THE TIRED schoolgirls climbed the road to the convent, Ailia told Arianlyn about her unsettling encounter with old Ana.

"Astrology is a lot of nonsense," Janeth declared, overhearing. "The stars are just big sparks left over from the Primordial Fire that formed the cosmos, and the planets are embers that are nearly burnt out. That's what the astronomy magister says. But you still find people who think they're quick-tempered because they were born under Arkurion."

"Why Arkurion?" Arianlyn asked.

"It was the Choleric Star," Ailia explained. "Each of the planets was supposed to correspond to an element. Arkurion was the Planet of Fire, Talandria the Water Planet, Valdys the Earth Planet, Iantha the Planet of Air, and Arainia the Planet of Quintessence, the holy element. A man named Welessan wrote about them. He said that they move about in the sky because they're set into spinning crystal spheres, each one bigger than the last like sections of an onion, with Mera—the world—at the center. Welessan said that each of these spheres was a separate Heaven, inhabited by angels and other spirits. He saw them himself, in a sort of vision he had in the temple at Liamar. He and a sibyl journeyed in spirit to the moon, where they stood and looked down at the world. Then they went on to the Second Heaven, the sphere of the Morning Star, which held a beautiful paradise. In the Third Heaven Welessan saw a burning plain with rivers of fire, and Salamanders living there: fire-elementals, that is, not the little newt-things."

"What were the other spheres like?" asked Janeth, curious in spite of herself.

"The Fourth Heaven was the sphere of the Sun, ruled by the Sun Goddess. The Fifth Sphere belonged to Talandria, and was full of water: the Undines, a kind of mermaid, lived there. In Valdys the Earth Gnomes lived, and in Iantha Welessan saw winged Sylphs flying through banks of cloud. After they left the Seventh Heaven the sibyl took him up to the Starry Sphere, and he saw all of Lesser Heaven below him—'as it were a turning wheel,' he says. Then he went on to a Ninth Sphere called Mid Heaven, which was the home of angels and filled with a glorious light, but the last sphere, High Heaven, was too holy for him to enter and the sibyl had to take him back to his body. I just love the way Welessan wrote about the spheres: you'd think they were real places he'd actually visited."

"What a fraud!" snorted Janeth. "And what fools people were in those days. It's the *sun* that is at the center of the universe, not the world. And if there really were giant crystal spheres up there, they would have been smashed to pieces by *that.*" She pointed out to them the great comet whose recent appearance in the celestial landscape had caused such excitement among the learned and the superstitious alike. Ailia felt a thrill whenever she saw it—this celestial visitor making its regal processional through the stars, its luminous train sweeping behind it.

"You can even see it in the daytime, if you know where to look," Janeth told them.

"The star that shines by day," said Arianlyn suddenly. "The Jana scroll said that was the Tryna Lia's sign, didn't it?"

"That's a comet, not a star," Janeth corrected.

Wenda gave a squeal at that. "I forgot—I must take my comet pills!"

"Your what?" asked Janeth.

Wenda emptied out some small tablets from a glass vial. "Comet pills—they protect against the poisonous vapors and evil influences of comets. I bought them from a peddler at the fair."

"Nonsense!" said Janeth. "Comets don't give off vapors, you little silly. As for being omens, that's ridiculous."

"The Tryna Lia story isn't scriptural, Arianlyn," agreed Sister Serenity. "And even in the Apocrypha the passages about her are obviously meant to be symbolism. You don't talk about real people being born in Heaven to goddesses, do you—or fighting dragons?"

"Of course the dragon's just a symbol for Valdur," conceded Arianlyn, "and the part about the Tryna Lia being throned on the moon and so on is just symbolism. But I believe the Princess herself is real. She mayn't be an ordinary person like you and me, but she's real, and she may be coming soon."

"I always wanted to believe in her," Ailia remarked. "It would be so comforting to feel that someone's going to come and set all to rights here on the earth. And really, the sooner the better. Look at the terrible things that are happening: the Zimbourans, and their tyrant king—"

Several exclamations interrupted her. A shooting star, cast out of the heavens by the passing comet, traced a brief arc of light across the western sky. Its trail of shimmering dust lingered for a fraction of a second after its fiery head vanished from view.

Ailia gasped. "Isn't it beautiful? I never saw such a sky! On nights like this I always wish I could fly. I've dreamt of it so often—skimming through the air. It always seems so real. When I wake up I could just cry with disappointment."

"Someday we'll learn to fly," Janeth opined with confidence. "If a bird can do it, so can a man. One of the magisters has drawn some diagrams for a flying vehicle, like a huge kite with a seat inside and canvas wings that can be made to flap up and down."

"Oh, he has *designed* it," snorted Lusina. "That's not to say it will *work.*"

"Something will work, one day. We'll conquer the skies the way we've conquered the seas."

"I don't know about that," Sister Hope admonished, looking prim. "I think if God had intended us to fly, He would have created us with that ability."

"But why?" asked Ailia, uncharacteristically rebellious. "Why would He give us souls and not wings?" She gazed skyward with yearning eyes. "And even if we do learn to fly we'll never get to the stars. I suppose that's why we've so many stories about stars coming down to *us*—the Morning Star Goddess, and the Star Stone—"

"Why, who's that out in the fields?" interjected Belina.

Ailia came reluctantly back down to earth and looked in the direction Belina was pointing. There were two white-clad figures walking there in the darkness like drifting ghosts. As they drew nearer the girls saw that these were novice nuns, like Serenity and Hope, with shoulder-length veils and postulants' gowns instead of full monastic robes.

Sister Hope held her lantern higher. "It's Sister Faith," she exclaimed, "and that is Sister Angelica with her. Is anything wrong, Sisters?"

"We hope not. Is Lorelyn with you?" one of the novices asked, moving into the lantern's circle of light.

"No," Sister Hope answered. "She decided not to go to the fair, Angelica. I thought you knew."

"We'd hoped that perhaps she had changed her mind, and joined you in the city." The young novice's face was pale, and she sounded as though she were close to tears. "We've looked everywhere, but we can't find her. She's run away."

8
The Black Knight

DAMION SAT AT HIS WRITING desk with his chin propped on his hands, staring out the window.

In front of him lay two notes. The first, written in an awkward childish hand, read: "I'm sorry but I was never meant to be a nun. Please don't look for me." It was signed simply "Lorelyn." The other was penned in the same graceful old-fashioned hand as the letter that had appeared so mysteriously in his library book. The nuns had given him Lorelyn's note; he had found the second earlier in the day when he returned from his visit with Ana in the catacombs. It was lying in plain sight on his writing desk. Though he made inquiries of all the servants and the scholars who lived on this floor, no one had seen or heard anyone go into his room. He glared down at the note in frustration.

To the Reverend Damion Athariel:

I can see that my previous letter has not had its desired effect. I give you fair warning: you are treading on dangerous ground, violating the rules of the Faith you profess to serve, and also (which is far more serious) trying my patience to its limit.

One more word of warning, then: denounce the monks and expose the Nemerei cult, or I will do so in your stead—and condemn you along with them.

Who *was* this anonymous writer—someone from the Academy, he wondered, a monk or magister or even a student who knew of the Nemerei and did not approve of the ancient vow? But why threaten him in this oblique fashion, instead of confronting him openly? And why only him? The abbot and prior had received no such letters. Why hadn't this person gone straight to the Supreme Patriarch with his information, if he was so annoyed about it? Why expect Damion to take all the responsibility instead?

His head ached at the temples. How he longed to talk to Kaithan Athariel about this matter! But his vow to the monks and the Nemerei bound him to silence. Perhaps he ought simply to distance himself from the entire affair. There was nothing more that he could do: the matter was out of his hands now, together with the scroll. As for

Lorelyn, he was certain that she had gone to the catacombs again, and was with the Nemerei even now. He felt a pang of compunction. She was his responsibility. He had brought her here in the first place, and he had also known what the Nemerei believed her to be.

"*I'm sorry, but I was never meant to be a nun.*" Did that mean Lorelyn had somehow learned of her "destiny" as their messianic leader? In that case, Ana and the other Nemerei had broken their half of the pact. They might have decided her danger was too great for her to be left in ignorance, and summoned her back to the catacombs for her protection. But she could hardly stay down there indefinitely. Should *he* have taken her someplace else when there was still time? But where? He hadn't the money to pay anyone to care for her. And what if she had not wanted to leave? He could hardly have dragged her away against her will. But he had promised Shan that he would keep the girl and the parchment safe, and he had failed in the latter trust: that this was not entirely his fault gave him little consolation. He must not fail again.

The Nemerei would not be able keep her safe. One person already knew about the tunnel gatherings—the writer of the anonymous letters. And if he grew impatient waiting for Damion to take action, he would surely carry through on his threat to expose the Nemerei himself. Then the high Patriarchs would learn about Lorelyn, about the Nemerei's beliefs concerning her—and Patriarch Norvyn Winter's Zimbouran followers would learn of her too.

"*They will kill her,*" Ana had said. Recalling the savage injuries the Zimbouran men had inflicted on Ralf, he did not doubt her words. If they could treat a harmless beggar so, what would they do to a girl they believed to be their God-king's adversary?

Damion paced the floor. What to do? He must save the girl; only he could do so, for outside of coven and cloister he alone knew of her danger. But how was it to be done? Should he follow the letter writer's advice and go straight to the high Patriarchs himself, telling them of the hidden tunnels and the cult, and the peril in which Lorelyn had been placed? He could beg them not to tell Norvyn and his Zimbouran underlings about her. But in order to tell the Patriarchs these things he would have to betray the monks—to break the sacred vow he had sworn to them, as a priest of the True Faith, not to disclose the location of the Nemerei refuge. His promise had held him so far, and he had no real proof that the Nemerei had broken theirs. In Maurainia a man's worth was measured by his fidelity to his sworn word. A priest was held to standards higher still: sacred vows were even more binding than secular oaths. The penalty for breaking such a vow, for any reason, was dismissal from the priesthood. He might save Lorelyn by breaking his word, but the personal cost to him would be high. Unless . . .

Unless he first asked the Patriarchs to release him from the priesthood, since it was on his priestly honor that he had sworn.

Damion ceased his pacing, arrested by this sudden thought. It was, he saw in an instant of utter clarity, the best possible solution. He would not be able to remain in orders in any case: at least by formally renouncing his vocation first he could leave the priesthood with some shred of dignity intact. Returning to his desk, he tossed the two notes aside and, taking up paper and quill, began to pen one of his own—to Abbot Hill.

It took several drafts to get it exactly right, and when he had finished he penned another to the office of the Supreme Patriarch. More than an hour passed before he set his quill down again and stood, stretching his aching shoulders. He felt as exhausted as though he had been fighting a physical foe. But it was over: with the act of writing these letters, he had ended the most important chapter of his life. No matter that the messages had not yet been delivered, his vows not yet formally renounced. The decision had been made in his mind. Like the isle of Jana, dwindling in the wake of the fleeing ship, the world of the priesthood—with its aura of dignity and sanctity and antiquity, its glorious trappings of robe and ritual—had already retreated from him. The Faith would still be there, its comfort still offered, its temples still open to him. But the institution that had sheltered and succored him since infancy would do so no longer. He was a waif once more, with no blood kin nor any place to call home; cast out now to make his own way in the world. The safe and comforting future that had lain before him was gone, changed to a waste of bleak uncertainty.

But Lorelyn would be safe. In the end, he told himself, that was all that truly mattered: not his future, not his vocation, but the human life that hung now in the balance.

He gazed down dull-eyed at his letters, then went to his wardrobe. There, alongside his spare robes and his winter cloak, hung the civilian clothes that every priest was required to keep, in case his superiors chose to defrock and dismiss him. The coarse white linen shirt and trousers were a constant reminder of the penalty for disobedience: expulsion into the world. Damion fingered the rough fabrics, then on an impulse he pulled off his robe and donned the forbidden garments. They felt strange to him after nearly two years in the loose and comfortable cassock. But he would grow used to that.

In the room's close confinement he suddenly felt as though he were suffocating. He opened the door, still clad in his nonclerical attire, and walked along the empty hall with its rows of closed doors. Down the great stone staircase he went, and on through the front vestibule to the outer doors. On the threshold he paused, holding one door ajar so he could breathe in the evening air with its overtones of spring. The night was calm and mild: a half-moon rode the deep blue sky like a wind-bellied sail, and overhead the stars shone with large, hazy halos, as though they had swelled in the moist atmosphere. In their midst the Great Comet spread its long gauzy tail. After sunrise it would continue to gleam through the daylight sky, a point of light visible to the naked eye.

A new star will appear in the sky, shining even by day . . .

A shooting star traced a fiery, evanescent trail across the sky above him, recalling Ana's words: "*Have you never seen a shooting star fall to the earth? In the heights it blazes brilliantly, but when it reaches the ground its fires are spent. Anyone who comes upon it then will think it an ordinary stone among the stones of the earth, and never guess that it once shone amid the stars. So it is with the Tryna Lia, the Child of Earth and Heaven.*"

The very heavens appeared to be joined in one vast conspiracy with the Nemerei: each sign had come in its turn, like a celestial clockwork. But was that so very strange? The ancients had possessed a detailed knowledge of the heavenly bodies and their movements. There was a geometrical pattern, a symmetry to their orbits and transits, that a skilled astronomer might be able to predict for centuries to come . . . None of which explained the scroll's foretold appearance, or the unnerving powers of the Nemerei. They could not be dismissed as coincidence.

As he stood there it suddenly struck him as strange that, after all these months of growing doubt, he should abandon the priesthood when at last the universe had begun to show traces of intelligent design.

He descended the steps and walked away across the fields.

LORELYN TOO WAS WALKING alone beneath that luminous sky. After much thought, she had decided she would be less likely to be found in the countryside than in the city, where too many people would see her and identify her later. Her plan was to cross the mountains and seek work in the farm country beyond, and so she had left the convent by the Old Road that led to the range. It would be a pleasure, she thought to herself as she walked, to work on a farm: to milk cows or cradle young lambs in her arms, surrounded only by the drafty wooden sides of some rustic byre. In such a place she could come and go as she willed. "Yes, that's the life for me," she said to herself as she walked. "Lots of freedom—and no more walls!" And maybe someday, when she had earned enough money, she might even travel the land searching for her family and parents. There could not be very many western folk who had traveled to the Archipelagoes to live. There might possibly be someone who could tell her who they were, and where they came from. And perhaps—she thought this with a sharp stab of longing—she would also find the answer to the most important question of all: why she felt deep within her the burning certainty that there was something she must do, that she existed for a *reason.* The Purpose that drew her might lie somewhere in lands unknown, or it might even find her. But she knew that it could not come to her within the walls of the nunnery. She set out with high hopes, therefore, her heart growing lighter with every step she took away from the convent grounds. Over her shoulder she had slung a satchel containing a spare gown and undergarments, a little food, and a few other necessities.

Only one thing gave her pause. Lorelyn kept thinking of Ailia Shipwright, of her gentle voice and sympathetic eyes. The Island girl was as close to a real friend as she had ever known, and for a moment her footsteps faltered, her resolve turned to misgiving, as she thought of the worry that Ailia must surely be feeling by now. Should she perhaps have left another note just for her, explaining why she had left? And what if the other girls began tormenting Ailia again? "They will give her a rough time, I shouldn't wonder, now that I'm not there," Lorelyn said, talking out loud again. "She's the sort that never fights back, and they know it—the bullies!" She halted for a moment, debating with herself, and looking back in the direction of the convent. But then she thought once again of spending the rest of her life in its confines, and she made herself go on, though she braced her shoulders as if she walked into a wind.

When she reached the first foothills of the range she

heard hoofbeats clattering along the road behind her. It might only be some villager on an errand, she thought, but it could be someone the nuns had sent to find her and fetch her back. It was too late to hide: the rider must see her there on the moonlit road. She stood where she was, arms crossed in defiance, waiting for him to approach. Whoever he was, she decided, if he thought she was going to let him force her to go back to the convent, he had better think again.

The dark shape of horse and rider drew rapidly nearer, limned by the light of moon and stars. She gave a sudden gasp as that shape became distinct, and then stood transfixed for several moments before it occurred to her—much too late—to run.

DAMION COULD NOT SAY why he went to the ruins. Something called to him: a yearning, formless yet insistent, directed his steps. Ahead of him lay the bleak broken walls and exposed foundations overgrown with vines, and an evocative scent of greenery and old damp stone blew toward him on the night breeze. He halted, breathing it in. As a boy he had come here to play, pretending to be a knight riding to challenge an evil warlord, or rescue a damsel in distress. All the lost desires of childhood returned to him on that cool, vernal air. He thought of his father, and wondered if he had cherished similar dreams as a boy—dreams that had endured into adulthood, if old Ana's guess about his paternity was correct. He stepped through a crumbling archway, onto grass-grown paving stones. Weathered walls and the shell of a tower rose before him into the night; the figure of a stone dragon perching on the battlements snarled down upon him with its broken fangs. This old boyhood haunt should feel safe and familiar, but in the darkness it took on an inexplicable menace. As he stood there he heard a sound that made him pause, suddenly alert: a horse's hooves clopping on stone. It came from the old Elei road.

Some extra sense, newly awakened, warned him in time. He dodged swiftly out of sight behind a collapsed wall.

From the shadows beyond the broken curtain wall came the horse and its rider. Both were a strange sight. The horse was arrayed like a war-steed of olden times, with flowing dark caparison and armor of steel, so that only its black neck and legs and its long streaming tail showed. The rider was also armored, in greaves and gauntlets and cuirass of steel under a black surcoat. Emblazoned on surcoat and shield was the device of a dragon rampant.

The ghost prince! Damion thought, astonished. *Someone is impersonating him again. But what is that white thing he's carrying?*

It looked like a half-unraveled bolt of white cloth, trailing over the horse's flank. Then as rider and mount drew nearer Damion saw the limp figure of a girl draped over the saddle's pommel, her white postulant's dress shining faintly in the moonlight. Her torso was propped against the knight's chest. Long braids of fair hair hung from her lolling head.

"Lorelyn!" Damion cried. Abandoning all caution, he sprang to his feet. The horse snorted and shied. Its rider pulled it to a halt, and man and mount in their archaic armor stood still for a moment, gleaming and impossible under the moon and stars.

With a yell Damion ran at the rider and seized hold of Lorelyn's dangling arm. She showed no sign of life at his shout or touch. Was she in a faint—or dead? "Let go of her!" Damion shouted as he struggled to pull the limp body from the other man's grip. Whatever else he might be, he was no insubstantial spirit: Damion could not break the hold of the metal-clad arms. He glared up at the faceless head and the moon's light, probing the eye-slits of the knight's visor, reflected back from two pale, glowing eyes.

Damion recoiled, his rash fury turned to fear—too late. A heavy gauntleted arm came down on the back of his head even as he tried to swerve away. There was a burst of light behind his eyes, and then a darkness that came rushing up to meet him.

HE REVIVED WITH A THROBBING pain in the back of his head. Groaning, he stirred, feeling hard stone beneath him. His eyes flickered open. He was lying on the ground, in some vast, dark space where red light threw shadows on walls of rough-hewn stone. The light came from leaping tongues of flame, before which dark demonic silhouettes bustled to and fro. The air was acrid and thick with smoke, and his bleary eyes smarted as he gazed about him.

He never had believed *literally* in the Pit of Perdition . . .

At the sound of his groans one of the figures approached him, kicking him in the ribs with a booted foot that felt all too real. "Get up," the demon ordered.

Damion grunted in pain and struggled to his feet. His senses cleared, and he saw that he was in a large, tunnel-like chamber with walls of coarse masonry. The infernal bonfires resolved themselves into the flames of torches bracketed to the walls. *The catacombs?* As he stood, clutching his aching ribs, two men came forward, pinioned his arms behind him, and dragged him toward the back of the chamber, where other figures milled about. He saw about a dozen men and women, their faces half shadowed in the fitful torchlight. Were these Nemerei?

"Let me go," he rasped. They ignored him.

He recalled his struggle with the armored man, wondering for a moment if it had been a nightmare. It was all impossible—absurd: a scene out of boyhood fantasies. The evil knight riding into the castle keep; the damsel in distress. And himself, like one of the youthful heroes in the faerie tales, straying into the midst of a perilous adventure . . . But his head still throbbed where the knight had struck him. "Where is she? Where's Lorelyn?"

The large man who had kicked him answered: "Mandrake has her."

"Mandrake? Who's he? I want to see Ana," he said.

Jeering laughter greeted this demand. "Small chance of that," chortled one shadowy figure.

"She knows me. Tell her I want to speak with her!"

"And why would we go to Ana?"

"She's your leader, isn't she?"

The man snorted. "That old hag? We've naught to do with her."

He stared. "Then you're *not* Nemerei?"

"The Nemerei? They're no friends of ours."

"Who *are* you?" he croaked.

Another man approached, thin and unkempt, and

smirked at Damion. The smirk shifted into a laugh, showing yellowed and rotting teeth. Suddenly Damion understood. "*You*—you're the ones who have been burning the farmers' barns, attacking their livestock. But *why?*" he cried. There was no reply from the shadowy figures, but no denial either. Damion fought to keep his voice steady. "Look here. I'm a priest of the Faith, I've nothing to do with you people."

"Oh, haven't you?" returned the thin man implacably. "Wasn't it you who brought the scroll out of the Archipelagoes? And then gave it to old Ana? And what were you doing wandering about the ruins in the early hours, eh? Looking for your precious Lorelyn?" He thrust his face close to Damion's, laughing. The breath from the gap-toothed mouth was foul.

"You'd better let her go, and me too, or you'll be in trouble with the authorities." He tried hard to force a stern note into his voice.

The man shook his shaggy head. "Oh, no—you've seen our gathering place now. You know too much."

Damion opened his mouth to protest, then shut it again. These people were utterly mad; there was no point in attempting to reason with them. Someone would surely come looking for him when he was found to be missing . . . Then with a sickening lurch of the heart he recalled his letters to Abbot Hill and the Patriarch, still lying on his desk in plain sight: the letters in which he declared his intention of leaving the Academy and his vocation. Would the abbot, on reading them, assume that his wayward chaplain had simply run off as Lorelyn had done, leaving the letters there for him to find?

Damion's brief burst of confidence wilted. All he

could hope was that Ana and her Nemerei might find out about his capture, and alert the abbot. Until then, he must wait—and hope his captors did not decide to turn their savage impulses on him.

Hours passed as he sat there, head on knees, half dozing. All the night, and perhaps most of the following day, dragged past. In time his eyes grew accustomed to the dim light. By the flickering glow of the torches Damion could see that he was in a long tunnel-like chamber with curved roof and walls, vanishing at either end into darkness. On the nearer wall a crude symbol was daubed in black paint: a crowned dragon, curled into a circle with its tail in its mouth. The Vormir was sometimes represented this way, as the *uroboros* serpent whose circular body symbolized infinity. But it was not usually shown with a crown. This must be the emblem of Modrian-Valdur, the self-consuming Dragon.

He stared at it as if mesmerized. The books on sorcery he'd read touched upon the cult of Modrian. Some scholars held that the fallen archangel, the traitorous "Fiend" of the Faith, was once a god of the ancients. But then his worship was banned for its cruel rituals, and Modrian was struck from the old pantheon. This, the scholars suggested, was the origin for Modrian's mythical "expulsion from Heaven." In the Antipodes Modrian became closely linked to the Zimbouran god Valdur, whose rites were similar: hence the later belief that the two gods were one. If a Nemerei coven still existed in modern-day Maurainia, then why not a Modrianist one? It was not impossible. If this were such a coven, its followers and Ana's would be bitter enemies. For both believed in the Tryna Lia: to the Nemerei she was a messiah figure, but to the Modrianists their worst foe, the adversary of their own dark god. Certainly both groups would be interested in the scroll, which spoke of the Star Stone's supposed location and the powers it would bestow on either Princess or dark Prince. And what of the Zimbourans—were they allied with the Modrianists, or did they view them as rivals for the prize, or did they not know of them at all . . . ?

Presently he became aware that his captors were holding an urgent debate, trying to decide what should be done with him. He wondered if there was any point in trying to run for it, and quickly dismissed the idea. He listened anxiously. It appeared that the witches, or Modrianists, or whatever they were, had to leave the tunnels in a hurry: someone had found out about them. The word "Patriarch" was mentioned several times, though he could not catch all of what was said. At last the large brutish man said, "There's only one thing to be done, and you know it. The priest can't go with us. Mandrake must take him."

"He's still out on his rounds," said another man.

"He'll be back before long. Put the priest down the hole: Mandrake will find him soon enough."

Mandrake again. Who is Mandrake? Damion wondered as two large ruffians seized hold of his arms and dragged him bodily down a passage leading from the main chamber. *And what's "the hole"?*

The catacombs were far more extensive than he had realized. It was like walking in an immense rabbit warren or mole-burrow, with tunnel after tunnel opening out of one another. As they left the paved passages behind and descended a narrow rough-sided one gouged from living rock, Damion began to feel something akin to panic. All that intolerable weight of earth and stone seemed precariously poised above his head, pressing down upon him. The flames of the men's torches burned low in the still, sepulchral air. It might have been some pagan netherworld in which they walked, far removed from the lands of the living.

At last they entered a large, cavelike space, in whose rock floor gaped a hole large enough to cast a man into. His captors led Damion toward its black mouth. "In there," one of them ordered, shoving him in the back.

He shrank from the pit's edge. "What's down there?" he asked.

Without further ado they grabbed his arms and hurled him into the hole. He yelled: but the drop was not as far as he feared, and he landed safely on his hands and feet. For a moment he saw the torchlit faces of the two men above him, peering down through the mouth of the hole. Then they made off in the direction from which they had come—in haste, almost as though they were afraid. The light of their guttering torches dwindled and vanished, leaving him in pitch darkness. He could not even see his hand when he raised it before his face.

The floor of his oubliette was apparently of natural rock, rough and uneven. In the distance he could hear water-droplets falling into some hidden pool, the hollow echo conveying to him the impression of a vast space, broader and higher than he had at first thought. He started walking forward, slowly, and barked his shin on a tall upright stone. His grunt of pain and surprise reverberated through the cavern. He stood still then, afraid to move lest he stumble upon some crevasse in the floor and fall in. Horror filled him—horror of the dark, with its treacherous concealment of dangers: pits, precipices, lurking beasts. Horror of the dark itself, blinding, enfolding, pitiless.

Carefully he sat down again on the hard ground and, with his back against another tall upright rock, rested his still-throbbing head on his knees.

What have I gotten myself into? And where is Lorelyn?

SOMEONE WAS CALLING HER NAME.

The voice that was not a voice summoned her insistently, through the dark space that lay behind her thoughts. It was not vague and muffled like all the mind-voices she had previously known, but clear and precise: every word came to her as distinctly as if it were uttered close to her ear. She moaned, stirred, felt the softness of a bed beneath her.

Lorelyn, the voice called.

Lorelyn opened her eyes. A web of yellow light glowed before her, coalesced, resolved itself into the flickering flames of several candles. They were distributed about the interior of a large room, resting in candlesticks on tables or burning in wall-sconces. She lay on a bed with a heavy red-curtained canopy, looking out through a gap in the hangings. She thrust them aside and leaped to her feet. The room was cluttered with objects: painted screens, vases with coiling dragons on them, chests of brass or carved wood. The walls were built of great blocks of stone, and hung with tapestries. There were no windows. Her satchel lay on the floor, next to the bed. There was no one else in the room with her, yet still she felt a presence.

"Where am I?" Lorelyn demanded, out loud.

And the voice answered her. *Do not be afraid,* it said—or rather, thought—in her mind.

But for perhaps the first time in her life, Lorelyn was truly afraid. She rubbed her temples, trying hard for a moment to remember. Then she recalled the black knight on horseback, and looked wildly about the dim-lit room. "You . . . you're the same person Father Damion and I saw in the chapel."

It was I. Yes.

The ghost prince. Her voice dropped to a whisper. "You're a spirit, aren't you?"

No. I am real—as real as you are. There is no ghost, and never was. That was only a hearth-tale. I disguised myself as a ghost to make people fear me.

"But why?" She spun around, staring into the shadows beyond the candles. "Who are you? *Where* are you? I don't see you."

Because I am not in the room with you. But I am not far away. I am coming: before long you will see me.

"What is this place? Where am I?"

For your own safety, I cannot answer that.

"Let me go."

Not yet. You are in danger, Lorelyn. Because of your special abilities there are many people who will wish to do you harm, and others who will try to make use of you. But have no fear: as long as you stay with me you will be safe. I will be your protector, your friend. Now, I have left you a meal: you see the covered dishes, there on the table? Trust me: I will provide for all your needs.

She raised her chin, trying to feel brave. "I won't stay here. I'll not be shut up again. Why is everyone always trying to keep me locked away? I won't stand for it, I tell you—I'll escape!" she shouted at the darkness.

The voice seemed amused and indulgent rather than angry. *You may try if you wish. But you will find it impossible.*

9

Jomar

AILIA STARED OUT THE common-room window, feeling utterly miserable. It was midafternoon, but the day was so dark that it seemed much later: a mist had come down from the mountains, blotting out the sun and the countryside. She could not even see the Academy or the ruins from here. It was like looking out on a blank gray void.

"Has there been no word yet?" she asked anxiously as Arianlyn entered the room.

"I'm afraid not."

"They'll never find her in this," said Janeth. "They'll have to wait for it to clear."

"But it's been foggy all day. Who knows when it will clear? And she might be lying somewhere in the fields, hurt—" Ailia's voice cracked with worry.

"Oh, stop twittering, Ailia!" said Janeth irritably. "They would have found Lorelyn by now if she had been hurt. She's far away from here, I'm sure. Remember what her note said."

Sister Faith had shown them all the little piece of paper with its untidy scrawl when she questioned them about Lorelyn last night. The pathetic words were still seared upon Ailia's mind, deep as a brand. "I knew she wasn't happy, but I never believed she would actually run away," Ailia moaned. "Poor Lorelyn. Where in the world could she have gone?"

Lusina laughed without humor. "The question isn't *where* she's gone, Worm. It's *with whom.*"

"What do you mean?" Ailia demanded.

"Think! Who else is missing from the Academy?"

Belina's usually rosy face had gone very pale. "Father Damion."

It was true: Damion had not been in chapel that morning. One of the village priests had taken the service in his place.

"Is that why Patriarch Norvyn is here at the Academy?" asked Arianlyn. "But why has he brought all those men with him?"

"That I couldn't tell you. But I know Damion left the Academy last night," declared Lusina. "There's a rumor going round the men's dormitory: they say he just ran off, leaving a note for the abbot. The monks and magisters are all being very close-mouthed about it, but the boys have heard things. He's been unhappy in his vocation for some time now, they say, and he's given up on it at last. He's left for good."

"I don't believe it!" Belina cried in dismay.

"No?" Lusina grinned. "Ferrell Woods told me he actually saw Father Damion walking away over the fields last night. *And he was dressed in a shirt and trousers.* Now, where was he going so late, dressed like that, and why didn't he return?" she demanded.

"Maybe he was searching for Lorelyn," Ailia suggested, trying to quell the growing dismay in her heart. "And it was too hard to walk the countryside in a long robe."

"Or maybe he ran off to join her." Lusina sniggered. She aimed her words at the tearful Belina, deliberately tormenting her, and did not see Ailia's stricken expression. "They must have been planning this for some time, he and Lorelyn. He's in love with her, of course: the young maiden he saved from the perilous Archipelagoes! Now he's going to save her from the cloister and the veil. How romantic!" She leered at Belina. " 'I'm sorry, but I was never meant to be a nun!' " From her mocking mouth the words were odiously suggestive.

Ailia rose from the window seat and left the room.

She took her cloak from its nail in the front hall and opened the door. Pale wisps of fog drifted in, and the air outside was damp and chill, but it was a welcome change from the stuffy calefactory. She stood on the threshold, gazing out into the grayness. The paved drive seemed to wind away into nothingness: only the first few pairs of trees in the long avenue were visible, their dark boughs teared with trembling mist-drops.

Where could Lorelyn have gone? *If only I'd been a friend to her!* Ailia thought guiltily. *She might have confided in me, told me her plans. I might even have talked her out of running away.*

Ailia walked out across the sodden field until the curtain walls suddenly emerged before her, materializing out of the mist. Lorelyn had often retreated to the ruin when she was unhappy, finding temporary refuge within its empty chambers. It was quite possible that she was hiding here, in one of the hidden dungeons perhaps: waiting for the inevitable searches to end before striking out on her own. The castle ruins covered acres, so she would feel quite safe. Ailia walked on, picking her way carefully through stone passages and roofless guardrooms where creepers spread questing tendrils through glassless windows, covering outer and inner walls alike.

"Lorelyn! Lorelyn, are you there?" she called. "I won't tell anyone you're here, Lori—just answer me, please!" She held her breath, longing for a reply. There was a silence as the echo died—then an eerie, wailing cry.

She swung around in alarm, certain that the voice was Lorelyn's and she was lying injured somewhere in the ruins. But in the next moment the voice was joined by several others in a wordless, inhuman chorus. *Whatever can it be?* wondered Ailia, trembling. It sounded like a conclave of witches, or like all the ghosts of the castle mourning together . . . Then she saw the small huddled shapes sitting beneath a broken arch a few paces away. As she stared at them, one of the tiny figures raised its head and uttered a high wavering cry. The others joined in, making a chorus.

It was only the feral cats that lived in the ruin! She thought she recognized old Ana's gray cat among them, sitting in the center of the group. Relieved, she called to them, holding out her hand, but at the sound of her voice they slunk off into the mists, no doubt to continue their wild madrigals elsewhere. Ailia walked on.

There was no sign of Lorelyn anywhere. Doubt filled her, little poison-pangs of suspicion. What if those spiteful remarks of Lusina's were true? Had Damion been lured away from the priesthood by his feelings for Lorelyn, and had they run off together? Ailia was desperate to believe it impossible, but . . . the more horrid something was, she thought miserably, the more likely it was to be the truth.

Horrid? You hypocrite! The simple fact is, you're jealous. Admit it: you wish you *were the one he'd eloped with.*

"No," she whispered in horror, as though speaking aloud would banish the taunting inner voice and the realization it brought her.

She was in love—she had accepted it at last; in love like Lady Liria, like all the heroines of the old stories. For a brief, exhilarating instant she understood the great romantic tales as never before, felt the joy and the yearning in them—and the heartbreak too. She tried to see her situation as tragic and romantic. But it was no use. The wound ran too deep, for once, to be salved with imaginings. "Oh, why didn't you even try to talk to him?" she reproached herself in a whisper. "You might have made friends with him at least—had some happy memories to take away with you. But no—all you ever did was gawk at him, you ninny; and now he's gone, gone forever!" She paused, then added another "Forever," torturing herself. The ancient walls threw the word back at her.

She gazed at them, despondent: monuments to a bygone age, every stone steeped in antiquity. Going up to one, she touched its cold rough surface with her fingertips; then laid her cheek against it. This wall was also a bridge, she thought: a bridge through time, spanning a gulf of centuries. On the far side of that time-gulf were the people who had long ago occupied this castle and—she saw in a sudden flash of understanding—had been as real and alive as she. In her mind's vision she saw them, not as stiff stylized figures in illuminated texts, but as human beings: lords and ladies in their fine attire, knights and monks, humble servants. Had King Andarion paced those battlements, his brow furrowed and weighted with the responsibilities of his reign? And his son, the unhappy and traitorous Prince Morlyn—might he have paused once, wrapped in dark thoughts, upon the very patch of pavement where she now stood? By coming to this place she had become one with them all, was incorporated with them into the great flowing stream that was Haldarion in all its long ages of existence. How many had lived out their lives within these walls, felt love and longing, seen wars and plagues and famines come and go? What was her own misery compared to the sum of all their sufferings? A droplet in an ocean—a fleeting second in an eternity. How many more would come after her, to suffer and sorrow in their turn?

But this new perspective, instead of reducing her pain, only intensified it. She thought of Great Island now, plain and rustic and untroubled by the great turmoils of history, and her heart suddenly hungered for it. Her mother and aunt had visited her a few days ago, talking of sailing back to Great Island and their men now that winter was over and no war had come, and it was plain that they expected her to accompany them. She had been dismayed and unwilling then. But now the thought of leaving the Royal Academy could no longer sadden her, for what was the Academy with Damion gone—without the possibility of coming across him in hallway or library, or of glimpsing him at the lamplit window of his room? Ailia stood, fighting the lump in her throat. She would rejoin her family: go back to her home and village, to her little room with the porthole window. *But what life would I have there? How would I live? I'd end up marrying someone I didn't love, just out of necessity—for how could I love anyone after Damion? And it's that or become an old maid, a burden on my relatives, a person for everyone else to pity.* It did not bear thinking about. *I might stay here and become a nun, join the Holy Sisters in the cloister. The nuns would let me study and write treatises, and teach the postulants. I would be too busy to feel lonely, and perhaps Jaim could visit me sometimes, when he's here on shore leave.* Again she sought to reassure herself. *I never really wanted to fall in love: perhaps it's just as well that when I did I chose someone I could never, ever have. Now I can reconcile myself to the thought of never marrying.* But she felt a restlessness, as if something within her had stirred and come near to waking: something that must sleep now forever. She seemed to hear the gate of the convent clanging shut upon her, closing out the world, hemming her in, and she knew a brief sensation of panic. A woman with a true vocation, she knew, would not feel this way. She would go to the cloister as if to a loving embrace.

What was it Lorelyn had said? *"I'm so tired of being locked away behind walls!"*

The voice in her memory was yearning, forlorn. The girl had been so unhappy. Perhaps if Ailia had not held back, if she had really tried to be Lorelyn's friend, none of this would have happened. Lorelyn would have stayed at the Academy, comforted by her friendship; she might even have become reconciled to life as a nun if she and Ailia could take the veil together. And perhaps Damion would still be here, too. *It's all my doing—I brought this on myself.* She buried her face in her hands for a moment, rocking to and fro.

Then she raised her head and looked around the ruin, and called out, one more time, in the faint hope that she might yet hear a reply: "Lorelyn! Can you hear me? It's Ailia, Lori. Please, please answer me!"

No answer. Ailia walked on through the rubble.

Inside one of the ruinous watchtowers she paused, looking about her. In the vine-hung wall to her right she now noticed an opening, one she could have sworn had not been there before: a little low doorway giving onto a passage whose stone ceiling slanted downward into darkness. The thick ivy curtained it, and so, she assumed, she must always have overlooked it; yet now it was perfectly plain to be seen, as though it had appeared by magic. As she stared, wondering where it led and whether it would be safe to go in, a sound of footsteps came from within its dark mouth. Someone was coming up a flight of steps inside.

"Lorelyn!" The footsteps paused, then began to climb again, more quickly. Relief filled her. "Oh, Lorelyn—thank goodness! I knew you were here—"

But when the figure appeared, it was not Lorelyn but a tall monk, clad in a black robe with the cowl drawn over his face. He stooped under the low lintel and walked out into the open, straightening to his full height.

Ailia stared at him in confusion. The Brothers of Saint Athariel all wore pale gray habits. Whoever could this man be? Even as she thought this the fantastic answer came, in Belina's high fretful voice: "*He wears the robes of a monk, with the hood up hiding his face.*" No, ridiculous! But, as long, white, thin-fingered hands emerged from the sleeves and began to draw back the cowl, Ailia's imagination told her that that death's-hood would reveal some ghoulish, supernatural horror. She watched in a kind of fascination, unable to speak or stir.

So it was with a shock of surprise that she saw that the face beneath the hood was human—and beautiful as well. Loyalty would not let her admit that he was as handsome as Damion, but he was undeniably comely. His face was lean and narrow-featured, its eyes set somewhat aslant beneath dark, well-marked brows, the nose almost aquiline and the cheekbones high. His complexion was unnaturally white, the color of skin that seldom sees the sun. But the hair that fell in long loose waves to his shoulders was a rich vibrant hue: gold with a touch of red in it, like a lion's mane. So relieved was she to find he was a man and not a specter that she did not stop to think that this made him rather more dangerous.

"You must be either extraordinarily brave or most uncommonly foolish," the man said. His voice too was beautiful, deep and resonant.

"I beg your pardon?" she stammered.

"I recognize you. I saw you with old Ana, the night of the fair. You are one of hers, aren't you? Did she send you here?"

"Send me?" she repeated, backing away. "I don't understand. I haven't the slightest idea what you're talking about."

The man raised an eloquent eyebrow. "Oh, you haven't, have you?" His eyes narrowed, and he took another step toward her. Too late, she now realized her danger: she was alone in the wild ruin with a sinister stranger, and no one was near her to call on for help. The man was furious, for some reason she could not fathom: his eyes held a cold and savage light. There was something wrong with those eyes . . . As he approached her she saw them more clearly, and her blood seemed to freeze in her veins. They were unlike any eyes that she had ever seen in a human face. They were not blue or gray, green or brown; they were yellow, a clear pale gold like the eyes of a wild animal. And the pupils were not round but *slit*, cleaving the irises vertically like the pupils of a cat.

Ailia could not cry out, could not stir a limb; as in a nightmare, she could only stand and watch helplessly. There was a roaring in her ears, and a seething grayness swam before her eyes. She collapsed, enfolded in a soft smothering darkness, and knew nothing more.

DAMION WANDERED THROUGH endless, winding tunnels, far down in the bowels of the earth. Through vast chambers he went, each one larger than the last: immense spaces whose far corners no light could reach, steeped in never-ending night. Stone archways yawned before him, black as the mouths of mines. Something about these deep silent places of the earth filled him with dread, a feeling that had nothing to do with prosaic fears of becoming lost or injured. There was no end to it, no sign of daylight—only chamber after chamber after chamber, stretching on into infinity. His footsteps raised forlorn echoes from distant walls. He stopped in despair. But though he stood motionless, the echoes continued—ghostly footfalls. The sounds were not coming from his own feet after all. He whirled, and saw in the darkness behind him two glowing eyes.

"Who are you?" he cried, and the reply came in a rasping whisper that woke more echoes from the unseen walls: *"Mandrake . . . Mandrake."*

Damion woke with a start.

He had nodded off from sheer exhaustion, lying on the cave floor; in the total darkness he did not know at first where he was. Then he felt the hard clammy stone beneath him, the pain in his shin and the ache at the back of his head, and he remembered. Had hours passed while he drowsed, or mere minutes? And was it only his imagination, or did he still hear footsteps? With an effort he sat up, chilled and shivering. And it was then that he saw the light.

At first, with a leap of the heart, he thought it was daylight, seeping in through some far-off chink in the rock walls. Then he saw that it was in motion: the yellow glow of a candle. As it progressed through the darkness another light sprang up beneath it. A reflection. There must be an underground lake or pool nearby. Someone, still invisible in the darkness, was walking along its opposite shore.

He rose and walked forward, drawn to the light like a mesmerized animal, until he stood on the edge of a large body of water. He could just make out the line of the shore from the candle's glow, and followed it around to the other side—the light all the while glowing like a beacon before him. Everywhere it went, beauty sprang to meet it. From out of the darkness appeared graceful fluted columns, chandeliers of glittering crystal, strange draperies that hung in rich, patterned folds dyed in soft hues, greens and blues and rose-reds.

The sound of footsteps ceased; the light paused. "Who is it? Who's there?" called a woman's voice.

He hesitated, uncertain whether to risk calling out: this must be another of the Modrian-worshippers. But the light darted toward him, quick as a firefly. "There *is* someone there—I know there is! Show yourself!" cried the voice. It sounded familiar.

He stepped forward into the light, saw that the light-bearer was a tall young woman dressed in white, her braids of fair hair hanging to her knees. A bag or satchel of some kind was slung over her left shoulder, and in her right hand was a candle in a brass holder. "Lorelyn!" he cried. "Is that you? Where in the Seven Heavens are we?"

"Damion—Father Damion!" she gasped.

She set down the candle so hurriedly that it fell over and nearly went out. Rushing toward him, she seized him by the arms.

"I can't believe it's you!" she exclaimed. "How did you find me? Did you come to look for me?"

"No, they've been holding me prisoner too," he replied. "The Modrian followers—they threw me down into this cave." He glanced around him in wonderment.

"It all looks so strange—I felt as though I'd wandered into a sort of faerie-land." A slight tremor went through her.

He reached out and touched a fold of the hanging

drapery above them: it was made not of cloth, but of a stone as hard as marble, tinted in delicate shades of rose and pale green. A drop of water splashed onto his hand; looking up, he saw a fringe of what appeared to be icicles on the ceiling above him, droplets welling from their points. "It's beautiful," he breathed, reaching up to touch one of the icicles. It, like the curtain, was opaque and made of solid stone. On the rock floor beneath, little conical shapes jutted upward, as though built up over time by the falling drops. Some had met the ceiling formations, creating slender columns. "It looks as though it all formed naturally, by water dripping down over rock." How long, he pondered, had it taken for the trickling moisture to contrive these wondrous shapes out of the slowly yielding stone? Centuries, perhaps even eons?

Lorelyn interrupted his thoughts, her voice urgent. "I haven't been able to find a way out, anywhere. He wouldn't have left the door unlocked, of course, if there'd been a way to escape."

"He?" Damion turned. "Who's *he?* And what door do you mean? Didn't they throw you down the hole too?"

"What hole? I got in here through a doorway."

He took her by the arm. "We'd better start from the beginning, Lorelyn. What happened to you?"

She looked at her feet. "I ran away from the convent when the others were in town, at the fair. I knew I could never be a nun, and I couldn't go on taking charity from the Sisters. It just didn't feel right."

"You might have come to me."

"I thought, being a priest, you'd be bound to agree with Reverend Mother. And then there were the monks' friends, Ana and her crowd: but if I joined them I might have to hide in the tunnels as they do, and I couldn't stand that either. I wanted to get right away—make a new start. I thought I might even travel and find out who my parents were, where they came from."

He could find nothing to say to that: it struck too strong a chord within his own mind. She went on: "But I hadn't gone far when I heard a rider coming up behind me on the road. He wore armor like a knight. And his eyes—do you remember that man, or whatever he was, in the chapel that night?" She shuddered.

"Go on," he prompted gently.

"I tried to run, but he—*it* rode after me, and I felt a hand reach down and grab me, and then there was something over my mouth that had a sickly sort of smell, and I think I fainted. I woke up later in a room I've never seen before, and *he* was there. At least, he was there but he wasn't there. It was just his voice."

"You mean he hid in the room somewhere?"

"No—his voice was in my head. Like those other voices I've heard before, only his was so much clearer: I could hear every word. He told me he would come to see me soon. I said I planned to escape, and he just laughed and then he wasn't there anymore. I found a hallway outside, and lots of doors, but some were locked and none of them led outside. Then I felt hungry, so I went back to the room, and ate some of the food he'd left for me there, and after that I felt tired so I lay down again. I fell asleep; and when I woke again Mandrake was there."

"Mandrake?" said Damion sharply.

"That's his name. He stood by the bed looking down at me. I wasn't afraid—he was really quite gentle, for all he looked so strange."

"Strange? In what way?"

"Well, his eyes, for one thing. They were yellow, and looked rather like a cat's—not *human* at all. He stepped closer, and then he spoke to me, but without talking."

"How's that?"

"His mouth never moved. He spoke right into my mind—I felt a sort of kindness and understanding flowing from him, with a warm, comfortable sort of feeling. 'Are you a magician?' I said. 'How did you do that?' He told me yes, he was a magician—a very ancient kind of magician called a Nemerei. 'Like Ana and her friends,' I said—forgetting that I wasn't supposed to talk about them. But he told me they—Ana and the others—weren't proper Nemerei but wicked witches who want to use me, use my powers; and he said if I let them do that my life would always be in danger, from some other people who meant me harm. Unless I stayed with him. He would take care of me, take me far away where they couldn't find me. Finally he left me, and I looked again for a way out. I found a door that led me down a flight of stairs and into this cave-place." Lorelyn took up her candle again and caught his hand. "Come on, you must help me escape! I haven't yet managed to find a way out of the cave, it just goes on and on; but there's one door at the end of the passage—I'm sure it must lead out of the building. It's locked, but the two of us together might be able to knock it down."

"Lead on, then!" he said.

Damion would never forget that walk through the caves. On their way to Lorelyn's prison they passed through scenes of otherworldly beauty, half-familiar and half-strange. There were groves of graceful sylvan shapes, stone cataracts like winter-frozen waterfalls, or like the falling fronds of weeping willows. From the floor rose delicate many-branched corals that might have grown in a southern sea, tinted with pale colors. Glassy strands dangled overhead like crystalline cobwebs. Damion felt an unexpected lift of the heart. Even here, in the earth's dark and stifling depths, there was beauty. This place was a temple, raised by the earth to itself.

And then, as a sleeper passes from one dream to another, Damion and Lorelyn passed into another cavern, larger and loftier than the one that had preceded it. Its floor was covered in small flowerlike formations, blue and rose and mauve: and in and out of these a small stream ran. Over it arched a stone bridge. Damion looked at the latter in amazement. It looked for all the world like a real, man-made bridge, not a natural formation. Yes, certainly that bridge had been made by human hands: he saw now that there was a path leading toward it, winding in and out of the limestone flowerets. And at the path's end was a doorway—an arched doorway improbably set into the cavern wall, half hidden by a fringe of stone icicles.

Lorelyn led him on impatiently, along the path and over the bridge to the doorway. She pushed open the heavy oaken door and urged him on, through a narrow passage whose walls and roof were of rough-hewn rock, then up a spiral stair and through another doorway into a long stone hallway lined with wooden doors. Between the doors stood silent figures, gleaming with plate armor. Their visors were lowered, and they clutched swords and battleaxes in their gauntleted fists.

"What's the matter?" asked Lorelyn, puzzled, as Damion leaped back with an involuntary yell.

Damion laughed at himself, feeling shaky: he had thought, for an instant, that the suits of armor were living men-at-arms. There were about ten complete mounted suits—Paladins' armor, it looked like. He had seen similar ones in the Academy museum.

"Here's where I was kept. Look." Lorelyn opened one of the doors and showed him inside.

On the threshold Damion halted, staring. Even the royal apartments in the palace at Raimar could not be more sumptuously furnished than the chamber before him. Huge tapestries hung on the stone walls, and the great bed at the end of the room had a red-and-gold-curtained canopy and ornate carved bedposts. In an open wardrobe hung about half a dozen gowns, each fit for a queen: brocade, velvet, samite. The rich red carpet underfoot was intricately patterned with gold and had piles so thick that his feet sank into it as if into moss. There were vases of crystal and fine porcelain, silver candelabra. In one corner a small lacquered chest overflowed with gem-encrusted necklaces, bracelets, and rings.

This Mandrake, Damion thought, must travel extensively. The tapestries were Marakite work, the chest Kaanish, and the carpet was Shurkanese. The larger pieces of furniture were Maurainian by the look of them, and these also were of the finest make: marble-topped tables and cabinets of mahogany. And the jewelry, and the sculpture—some of that was surely Elei in origin. Lorelyn's captor was a man of immense, secret wealth. Damion doubted it was honestly earned.

He picked up a candelabrum, went back to the door,

and looked down the corridor. "Where does that door at the far end of the hall lead to?" he asked Lorelyn.

"I don't know. It's locked. I tried—" Lorelyn suddenly stopped in midsentence and went very still, her head cocked at a listening angle, her blue eyes unfocused.

"What is it?" Damion asked nervously. He had heard nothing.

"Yes . . . very well, I'll do as you say," said the girl. Her words were not addressed to him, he realized with a creeping sensation, but to some other person whom he could neither see nor hear. "I've no choice, have I?" She turned to Damion, her eyes wide. "It's Mandrake! He's coming back here, he says. And he's bringing someone with him. Someone to be company for me, he said. He's going to take us both away somewhere."

He seized her hand. "Lorelyn—we must go now. At once!"

"I won't argue with that!" she replied. "Come on!" And she ran out into the passage.

Damion followed her. Stopping at one of the suits of armor, he wrenched the halberd from its steely grasp and hefted it. Then he attacked the door. The blade of the axe bit deep into the ancient wood; gasping with the strain, he jerked it free and swung it again. At each blow he turned, half expecting Lorelyn's abductor to come raging down the passage. When he tired, Lorelyn took the weapon from him and chopped at the door. She was remarkably strong for a girl, he thought in amazement. After what seemed an age, taking turns with the halberd and panting and groaning with the effort, they succeeded in hacking the lock away. The mutilated door opened inward, showing a stone staircase beyond. "We've done it!" Lorelyn cried in triumph, and before he could say anything she had seized him in a tight embrace.

It was only a childlike demonstration of affection, spontaneous and exuberant. Yet Damion nearly reeled from it, and not merely because she was a tall, strong girl and the hug an energetic one. He was aware, all at once, of her warmth, the pressure of her encircling arms, the faint scent that seemed to hang about her flaxen hair. When she released him he stumbled backwards, feeling dazed and a little disturbed.

"Now, up the stairs!" she said, taking up her candle again.

"Just a moment." Damion went to another of the suits of armor and dismantled it, putting on the breastplate, gauntlets, and helmet. As an afterthought he slung on the sword-belt as well. Goodness only knew what awaited them beyond those stairs—this Mandrake person could well have set guards in the ruin. "I'll go first," he said, taking the candle from her.

He hurried up the stone steps, almost forgetting Lorelyn in his own driving need to be above ground once more. The stair ended in another archway, which led to still another large chamber. Damion stared around it, blinking: this room was an empty unadorned space, its walls of worn and aged masonry. It was floored with straw, and as he entered it two horses lifted their heads and stared at him. One was a massive, night-black animal, the other its mirror opposite, a white palfrey with cream-colored mane and tail. Hanging on the wall were their harnesses, including the antique armor he had seen on the black horse—was it really only the night before?

One mount for Mandrake and one for Lorelyn, Damion thought grimly. He looked about the ancient, crumbling chamber, realizing at last where he was, what part of the castle ruin he had been held in. Lorelyn's underground prison had been, appropriately enough, one of the castle dungeons.

She stood behind him. "What do we do now, Damion? There's no way out."

"Yes," he said, "there is. Look!"

Before him in the gray wall was the faint but unmistakable outline of a door—a stone door with no handle. Damion groped among the stones for the one that would give way, as in the wall of the Paladins' chapel. A few minutes' search set off the hidden mechanism. He rushed through the open door, on down another passage. At the end was another set of stairs, of more recent make: the steps were very broad and shallow to accommodate the stride of a horse. They led upward at a gentle slope, and there was the outline of yet another door. Another stone pressed, another gaping hole opened up—and they were through, running out into the overgrown wilderness of the castle ruin.

Damion was first to halt. He pulled off the heavy helmet and stood panting, listening to the sound of birdsong, the wind shushing in the trees. The pale daylight, at first dazzling after the darkness of the dungeon, seemed to wane as he watched: a heavy mist hung about the castle towers and trailed through the trees beyond. He filled his lungs with the damp, fresh air, and opened his mouth to call out to Lorelyn.

"Stop right there," commanded a voice.

* * *

DAMION FROZE, THEN TURNED SLOWLY. Several paces away stood a horse, this one black with a white blaze on its forehead and one white foot; on its back sat a dark-skinned man. With a sinking heart he recognized Jomar, the half-Mohara man who served the Zimbourans. He was clad all in black leather with a breastplate of steel, and he wore a curved Zimbouran sword at his side.

"I know you," the man growled, scowling down at him. "You're that meddling priest, aren't you? The one who started it all, back on Jana. And now you've gone and joined those fools in the tunnels."

"What do you know about them?" demanded Damion.

"Patriarch Norvyn's been getting anonymous notes about them. He ignored them at first, but we talked him into taking action. He set me and the rest of his guardsmen to search the ruins for your little bolt-holes: we knew one of you would have to come up for air, sooner or later."

"I'm not a *member* of the cult. I'm escaping from them." Even to Damion this protest sounded feeble and unconvincing.

"Really," Jomar sneered.

"You don't work for the Patriarch, do you?" Damion challenged. He took a step forward. "You serve the Zimbourans."

"Where's the rest of your witch-coven—*Father?*" The Mohara man countered, with a sneering emphasis on the title.

Damion made no reply. He spun around and ran—and crashed full-tilt into Lorelyn, who was right behind him. They stumbled, clutching at each other, and fell in a heap of flailing limbs.

"*Run,* Lorelyn!" Damion cried, scrambling to his feet again and hauling her up.

"Lorelyn!" the Mohara repeated. A glint of interest came into his eyes, and he spurred his horse closer. "So: you're *that* girl. The one the notes mentioned—the one the witches call the Tryna Lia—"

"Tryna Lia?" echoed Lorelyn. "What do you mean?"

Damion grabbed her arm and pulled her away through the ruin. As they fled they heard a loud clatter of hooves: the rider was close behind. *We'll never outrun him,* Damion thought. But the black horse stumbled on the broken paving stones and fell to its knees, neighing in alarm. With an oath the Mohara man sprang off its back and continued the chase on foot. There was a harsh scraping of steel as his sword slid out of its scabbard.

Despite their lead he overtook them with ease, seizing Lorelyn by her right arm. Pointing the sword threateningly at Damion, he backed away with the protesting girl in his grip.

"Ow! Let go!" she cried indignantly, trying to wrench herself free. "That hurts!"

"It'll hurt more if you don't come along quietly," the man snapped.

Still holding the girl by her arm, and ignoring the blows she rained on him with the other, the Mohara man made for his steed, which was still on its knees in the courtyard. He forced Lorelyn at sword-point onto its back, then vaulted into the saddle behind her and kicked the horse's flanks. Snorting, it struggled to all fours and stood shuddering and tossing its head. Lorelyn's struggles alarmed it: she shouted and thrashed about, inadvertently kicking Damion in the face as he ran to pull her off.

He collapsed onto the cracked pavement. The Mohara held his sword at the girl's throat and grabbed for the reins with his free hand, jerking his mount's head around and urging it toward the nearest of the moat-bridges. The noise of hooves and Lorelyn's yells receded down the stone road.

Damion, rubbing his smarting cheek, scrambled to his feet and started to run after them, then realized it was futile and stopped short in despair.

I try to rescue her, and all I do is place her right in the Zimbourans' hands!

A slight sound from behind made him turn. The white palfrey had come up the steps on its own and now stood looking out of the doorway in the curtain wall, an expression of mild inquiry in its large dark eyes. It whinnied softly as he stared at it.

Damion winced. He hadn't ridden in years, and there was no time to put on the saddle and reins. But there was nothing else to do; he ran to the horse. It was a good-tempered animal, superbly trained: as soon as it saw that he wished to mount, it bent one foreleg in a "bow," enabling him to clamber onto its bare back. Gripping a handful of mane, he urged it forward. It obeyed him at once. In a moment they were thudding across the grass of the outer bailey, then cantering along the broken cobbles and across the wooden bridge.

Lorelyn and her captor had not gone very far: the Mohara man had pulled up his mount, and was struggling with the girl. Damion thumped his own horse's flanks with his heels, but apparently it had been trained to go no faster than a canter. As he watched, Lorelyn and Jomar fell off the horse's back and continued to wrestle on the ground, rolling over and over on the turf. They both looked up at his approach. The Mohara man stared, then laughed. "First he thinks he's a warrior, now he thinks he can ride. Be careful, priest," the dark man added with a sneer as Damion unsheathed his short sword and held it out uncertainly. "You could cut yourself with that." He sprang back into the saddle.

Damion, grim and silent, continued to ride toward him. The other man wheeled his mount about, raised his own sword, and stood waiting. The horses seemed to have become infected by their riders' antagonism: as they drew together they rolled their eyes, snorted, and snapped at each other. The Mohara man lashed out with his own weapon and Damion somehow caught the blade's edge with his own, parrying successfully, though the shock of the blow sprang up his arms and into his chest. Again the two swords rose and met. Jomar struck Damion's weapon from his hand; but as he leaned over to deliver the blow the priest seized his opponent's sword arm. Jomar lost his balance and tumbled to the ground, dragging Damion with him.

The Mohara man was the first to regain his feet. Furious, he clouted Damion in the face, not bothering to use his blade. The priest fell back gasping and holding his cheek: it was the same one Lorelyn's foot had struck. As the frothing horses fled the scene, Jomar turned on the girl.

"You're coming with me now," he snarled. He strode forward and grabbed her by the arm. "They'll kill me if I lose you now. You're coming whether you want to or not."

Without another word Lorelyn drew back her free arm, made a fist, and punched him in the jaw.

The man gave a startled grunt, stumbled backwards, and fell. At the same time the girl yelped and sprang back, nursing her wrist.

Damion lurched to his feet again. "Jomar!" he shouted. At the use of his name the other man whirled to face him.

"How can you do this?" Damion continued. "I know who your real masters are! How can you serve the Zimbourans, after all they've done to the Moharas—"

"Shut up!" shouted the dark man furiously. "You don't know what you're talking about. You don't know anything."

He advanced with his sword, but Damion walked toward Jomar with his own empty hands held out. The Mohara man stood still. "Jomar—listen! You're in Maurainia now. You can go free, anytime you want. Leave the Zimbourans! Stay here, with us."

"Leave!" A wild look had come into Jomar's eyes. "What do you expect me to do—go off to the city perhaps, or some nice small village? I'd blend in perfectly, wouldn't I?" He waved a hand at his dark-skinned face. "They'd track me down. They'd kill me. Don't you see? I know too much now—"

"We'll hide you," Damion promised. "In the catacombs, where the Zimbourans will never find you. We'll smuggle you to another country."

He was within a couple of paces of the other man now, within reach of his blade. The point lifted, but did not strike.

"Jomar—they'll kill her if you take her to them," he said in a low pleading voice, pitched for Jomar's ears alone.

The dark man looked at him, then at Lorelyn standing

not far off, her face distressed and alarmed. He stared, as if seeing her properly for the first time. A spasm of something like pain crossed his own face, and his head sagged forward, as if in defeat: the sword's blade fell, the hilt slipped from his hand. A silence fell over the three figures, standing there by the Old Road. It deepened, became a part of the larger silence that hung with the mist over the land beyond.

In the meadow the white horse and the black one stood side by side, still snorting and blowing with exertion. Then they lowered their heads and began to graze.

10

Mandrake

AILIA YAWNED, STRETCHED, and stirred into wakefulness.

She had been having another dream: a strange dark dream of being carried in someone's arms through long tunnels, where dim figures came and went; of a cave that was filled with groves of stone trees, and a lake like a sheet of shadow stretching into emptiness. The lake: that came from the old legend, didn't it? The underground lake beneath the castle, the scrying-glass of the sorcerous Prince Morlyn and his final resting place . . .

Ailia was dimly aware of two voices conversing somewhere in the darkness. She often heard voices while she lay at the indeterminate border between sleeping and waking, and knew that they were a common phenomenon of the somnolent state: sound-phantoms conjured by the drowsing brain. But the ones she heard were not usually so distinct. One was a man's voice, she realized, and the other belonged to a woman: both were naggingly familiar, but if they were in fact real she could not find the faces that went with them.

"Very well," the male voice said, "if she is not one of yours then what was she doing there? How did she know Lorelyn was here?"

"Are you certain that she did know?" asked the woman's voice.

"Don't play games! I saw her go into your tent, and I know how long it took for her to come out again. She's one of yours—your conspiracy!"

"I only told her about the old beliefs. She knows nothing of the Nemerei."

"No matter. Even if you haven't corrupted her yet, you were likely planning to do so."

"You used to trust me once. I wish you would again." This was said with a sigh. "Please don't let it come to a fight between us. I am not your enemy. I saved your life, remember—"

"Of course I remember! There's no danger of my ever forgetting, is there, when you remind me of it on every possible occasion? Very well! Keep that worthless scrap of parchment, for all the good it will do you. But as for the girl—I advise you to leave her alone, or I'll not be responsible for what happens to her."

"You mean Lorelyn? All I want is for her to go free—and the young priest too. Where are they now?"

"The truth is, I don't know. When I came back she was gone, and the door to the stairs has been hacked to pieces with an axe. I put that down to your usual meddling."

"I assure you, my Nemerei and I had nothing whatsoever to do with it."

Ailia's eyes fluttered open. Through a gap in thick red draperies she glimpsed an elegant furnished room, lit only by candles. She closed her eyes again. Yes, clearly she dreamed still: this room could not be real.

"I wondered what you were up to here," said the woman's voice. "Dressing up in armor and pretending to be a ghost. I couldn't imagine what it all meant."

"Perhaps I merely find it amusing."

"It also draws unfriendly attention from the villagers, doesn't it? You want to frighten them into having the whole place exorcised, and so expose the catacombs and the Nemerei. But why hide Lorelyn here, then?"

"She was only to stay here temporarily, until I found a better hiding place."

"And this poor child?"

"Company for Lorelyn, of course. So she won't have to face her lifetime of captivity alone. You see, I can be thoughtful." The man spoke with deliberate irony.

There was a sound of footsteps, and the speakers moved into the narrow field of vision afforded by the gap in the curtains. The woman, who was very short and slight, stood with her back to Ailia, her head and shoulders swathed in a gray shawl. Before her the man paced to and fro, restless as an animal: it was the man with the strange yellow eyes. He was clad now in what looked like the apparel of a knight from elder days, steel plate armor and a long dark surcoat. "But release her if it pleases you: I can always find another to take her place. I'm going to go search the countryside for Lorelyn now, and you had better be gone when I get back—or I might just forget my debt to you." The man in armor faced the shawled woman as he spoke these words, and the light of the candles was reflected in his feline eyes, turning them to discs of yellow flame.

Ailia tried to sit up, but there was a dull rush of noise in her ears and she fell back again, sinking into the twilight place from which she had come.

SOMETIME LATER SHE REVIVED again. But when she tentatively opened her eyelids, the strange room was still there. She shut her eyes, willing it all away. Sometimes this happened: one would fancy oneself awake two or three times before really waking up. In a moment she would come to full consciousness, and the strong sunlight of early spring would be streaming through the dormitory windows, while Arianlyn—always the first to rise—called out to the other girls, "Wake up, sleepyheads! It's a lovely day!" She smiled, and opened her eyes again.

But the red-curtained bed and the room were still there.

What's wrong with me? she thought, the smile dropping from her face. She sat bolt upright, looking around her in alarm. She reached out to the bed-curtain, closing her hand upon its drooping folds. "It *feels* real," she said aloud as she ran her fingers over the coarse red fabric. "It isn't—like—a dream."

At the same instant she heard soft footsteps on the carpet. She looked around sharply, to see the slight shawl-clad woman approaching her, leaning on a knobby cane. She seemed familiar.

"Hello, my dear," said the old woman. "So you're back with us again."

Of course: it was old Ana, from the fair. "I don't understand," said Ailia, standing unsteadily. "What happened? How did I get—here?"

"A case of mistaken identity, it appears," Ana explained. "But everything has been cleared up, don't worry."

Ailia put a hand to her own temple. Her head was swimming, and everything seemed dreamlike still.

"Perhaps I had better accompany you," said Ana thoughtfully. "You don't look well. I expect he drugged you."

"Drugged?" Ailia murmured. She rose, took a step forward, and the carpeted floor seemed to heave beneath her feet, like the deck of a ship when a wave rolls beneath it. Before she could fall Ana took her by the arm, supporting the girl as well as she could while leaning on her own prop.

"Now then," she soothed. "This way."

Slowly and awkwardly the two of them progressed across the room and out the door, along a grand corridor lined with suits of armor, and then—with even greater difficulty—up a long staircase and through several more empty stone rooms. At last they passed through an archway overgrown with ivy, and were outside: and Ailia recognized the castle ruin, a wilderness of broken walls and weed-sprouting pavements stretching before her. It was evening, and a shredding mist still trailed through the ruins.

There was a sound of padding feet ahead of them, and a great gray animal came bounding out of the darkness to greet the old woman—a dog, bigger than any Ailia had ever seen. Ana placed a small withered hand on its head. "Hello there, Wolf!" she said. "Is Greymalkin here too?" She turned to Ailia. "Don't be afraid, my dear. I won't let him harm you."

But Ailia felt no fear. Everything was remote and unreal: her mind felt disconnected from her body, watching as if from a distance. The waxing moon had risen above the mists, but it was hard to see where she was going. The ground still seemed to move about under her feet and she stumbled, almost pulling Ana down with her. The dog followed, whining. In the distance, through a gap in the broken walls, Ailia caught a glimpse of a long line of reddish lights like torches, streaming from the Academy toward the ruin. It seemed far away, and nothing to do with her. But Ana drew in a sharp breath and turned around. "We must go the other way, I think, dear," she whispered. "It wouldn't do for you to be seen here with me."

Ailia thought of asking why, but it seemed too much of an effort. She went obediently along in the new direction. They were about halfway across the outer bailey when a voice called out, from somewhere near at hand.

"Ana! Ana, is that you?"

Ailia stared as a rider came trotting out of the ruined keep on a white horse. He wore a Paladin's silver breastplate, gleaming in the moon, and she could see that he was a young man, with a handsome face—rather like

Damion Athariel's. Her head began to spin again; she had a foolish desire to laugh. *Damion—a knight in shining armor! It's too extraordinary, even for a dream.* For a dream it surely was. There was a figure behind him on the horse—a white-gowned girl with long braids of blonde hair, like Lorelyn's. A man on another horse followed them. He had a strange dark face that even the moon could not illuminate. She was reminded of the silent Mohara man she had seen in the library on her first day at the Academy.

The man who looked like Damion commanded his horse to halt, and swung himself down from the saddle. He started to move toward her and Ana, and seemed about to speak. But what he meant to say she never learned.

"I knew it!" shouted another voice, in angry triumph.

They turned as one. There in the bailey behind them was another man on horseback, this one clad in full armor under a dark surcoat. Ailia's head spun again and she slipped from Ana's loosened grip, sitting down abruptly on the ground.

The Mohara man recovered first. "Who are you, and what do you want?" he shouted.

The figure rode its warhorse closer, and took off its helmet. Long tawny hair tumbled free, and through its loose locks a pair of eyes glittered in the moonlight, cold as frost. Of course—it was the strange, lynx-eyed man Ana had been talking to, the one who wore the armor of a knight.

"I said, what do you want?" the Mohara man shouted again.

"I want the girl," the other man replied in a cold,

controlled voice. "Now." Ana's big dog growled at him, making his warhorse snort and pound the turf with its great hooves.

"Wolf," Ana said sharply. "Stop!"

Ailia watched and listened in complete bewilderment. Turning her head from one figure to the other, she tried to make sense of the scene, but all this accomplished was to make her feel giddy again.

"She isn't going anywhere," Damion said to the lynx-eyed man, "except back to the convent."

The man ignored him, continued to gaze at Ana. Wolf snarled again. Only Ana's hand on his ruff seemed to restrain him from lunging toward the man—no mean feat, thought Ailia, as the animal must weigh as much as Ana did. The lynx-eyed man rode his horse over to the white one and seized its bridle in an armored fist. His voice rang out commandingly as he addressed the girl still sitting on its back. "Come with me, Lorelyn. Ana is not your friend. I told you she wants only to use you."

So it is *Lorelyn!* thought Ailia, fascinated by the turn her "dream" had taken. *I* must *remember all of this one—it's too marvelous. Lorelyn—Damion—old Ana—that Mohara man from the library . . . Curious, how people one has met end up in one's dreams.* Her head spun again, and she felt an urge to laugh.

"Well, Ana and her friends never held me against my will!" Lorelyn countered, slipping off the horse's back and running over to the old woman. "I'm not going anywhere with you!"

"You hear, Mandrake?" said Ana. "You cannot keep her, nor prevent her from fulfilling her destiny."

"Then her death is on your hands," he snarled. He set

his heels to his mount's flanks, making the huge armored creature charge forward. They scattered in haste as horse and rider plunged between them, tearing the mist to tatters, then raced at a full gallop through one of the gaps in the curtain walls. There was a silence after the pounding hoofbeats faded into the distance.

"Wonderful!" murmured Ailia indistinctly, and fell backwards on the grass in a swoon.

DAMION HURRIED OVER to Ailia's side, stooping over the unconscious girl. "Is she all right? Who is she, Ana? She looks familiar—"

"That's Ailia Shipwright," Lorelyn told them. "I know her."

"Mandrake mistook her for one of my Nemerei and abducted her," explained Ana. "I think he has drugged her."

"I'll carry her back to the convent. Lorelyn, you come with me too." He gathered Ailia in his arms and stood, jerking his head toward the Mohara man, who still sat on his horse in silence. "Ana, this is Jomar: he's a refugee from Zimboura. If you and the other Nemerei could give him temporary shelter in the catacombs, I'm sure he'd be much obliged."

"He says I'm the Tryna Lia," Lorelyn told Ana.

Jomar snorted. "I said those fools *think* you are," he scoffed, dismounting and walking over to join them.

She ignored him. "Is it true, Ana?" she demanded. "Am I what he says?"

"I'm afraid, my dear, that it very much looks as though you are," said the old woman gently. "I did not tell you before, because I did not know for certain."

"*Come,* Lorelyn." Damion spoke sharply. "Ana, I asked you not to tell her about that."

"It appears she already knows about it, and not from me," the old woman replied. "It is no use hiding the truth from her any longer."

"We had an agreement—" he began and then broke off, remembering with discomfort his own decision to break his word. But Ana was not paying any attention to him. She was standing very still, with her white head cocked at an angle, as though listening to something in the distance. And then he heard it too: a low and ominous sound, like a river rising in flood. Human voices, many of them, raised in anger. The broken fragments of the curtain walls glowed yellow, tinted with torchlight. The glow moved toward them through the ruin, along with a gathering din of voices and trampling feet.

A great, bellowing voice called through the night. "We know you're hiding in there!" it roared. "You're surrounded. Come on out, the lot of you!" A large crowd of people began to stream through the outer bailey. They looked to Damion like villagers from the countryside. Their clothing was plain and coarse, and though a few women of robust appearance were with them, the majority were men. They had a tumbrel with them, drawn by a large, hairy-hocked dray horse, in which several torch-bearing youths were riding.

Ana walked calmly forward to meet them, and a hush fell over the crowd, as though they were disconcerted at having their prey face them openly. A few who stood at the front backed away, their right hands outheld with fingers splayed in the sign to ward off evil. To the rear of the crowd Damion glimpsed several figures standing apart, including some men on horseback. These were not villagers: the mounted men had the pallid complexions and black hair of Zimbourans; another man, stout and middle-aged, wore the white robes of a Patriarch of the Faith. Standing with him were two gray-robed monks.

Damion expelled a long breath. The monks were Abbot Hill and Prior Vale.

Into the sudden quiet Ana's voice rang out clear and unafraid. "I am Ana. What is it you want with me?"

A village man moved toward her, brandishing his torch. "We want you out of here, witch!" he shouted. "You and all the others who meet here in the ruins! You'll meddle no more with us!"

"Why, what have I done?" she asked.

"What haven't you done! Barns burned, livestock found killed and maimed! It's you that's done all this—you and your cursed coven!" He glared in suspicion at Damion and the others. "You've no right to dwell here among decent folk!" He took another step forward and Wolf growled, his hackles rising.

"Mind the dog," warned Damion.

"Dog!" the man gave a harsh laugh. "That's no dog! That's a *wolf!*"

The big gray beast growled again, torchlight reflecting back from his fangs and amber eyes as he strained forward. "Nonsense," said Damion uneasily.

"Think I don't know a timber wolf when I see one—living in the mountains all my life? She's a witch, I tell you. A beast-charmer." He turned to face the mob. "And that isn't all her mischief. Didn't we see the ghost prince just now, riding out of the ruin? *She* summoned him. This place is cursed!"

An angry murmur arose from the villagers. But when Ana spoke again they fell silent. "There is no ghost: it was a living man you saw ride from the ruin. As for your barns and your beasts, it is not my people who have done those things, but the black witches, the worshippers of Modrian. I have warned you about them before."

The high-ranking cleric strode forward, and Damion recognized his thick brows and short graying beard with a sinking sensation. It was Patriarch Norvyn Winter, from the High Temple. The Patriarch spoke in a stern voice. "Woman, you stand accused by these people of witchcraft, demon-worship, spell-casting, and necromancy. You have been suffered by men of God to live here and practice your black arts, when it is the duty of all God-fearing people to report your kind to the ecclesiastical authorities." He glared at the two monks. "When the deputation from the villages came to me, I hoped that their reports of witchcraft were merely fanciful rumors. But when I summoned the prior and abbot of the cloister and placed them under holy oath they could no longer deny their role in this obscene conspiracy. A scroll that presumes to *add* to the holy scriptures is blasphemy enough, and had I only had my way the document would long ago have been destroyed. But to give it to avowed witches! And when I come here to perform the ritual of exorcism upon the ruins, what do I find but a company of witches hiding in their midst—one of them in a sorcerous trance!" He made an angry gesture at the unconscious Ailia, hanging limp in Damion's arms.

Abbot Hill walked forward through the crowd, accompanied by Prior Vale. "I'm sorry about all this, Ana.

I can't say how it came about—I'll swear the Brothers said nothing before tonight—"

The prior, who looked both nervous and sheepish, cleared his throat and added, "It might be best if you left this place, Ana."

"No!" One of the Patriarch's aides spurred his horse forward, and in the torchlight Damion recognized his face. It was the dark-haired, thickset man who had intruded on the Academy library with Jomar. The man bawled, "You must not let her get away! She must be punished!"

"She will be, Hyron," the Patriarch assured him grimly. "And all the other witches as well."

With a sickening shock Damion suddenly realized what a sight he must present, standing there in the ruins—decked in bits of Paladin armor—an unconscious young maiden in his arms—a self-confessed witch standing at his side. Quelling an urge to laugh that would have proved disastrous, he set Ailia down on the ground again and began to pull off the armor. "We're not witches, Your Reverence. I just freed Lorelyn and this other girl. They were being held captive here in the ruins—"

"You hear? It's *she*—the girl Lorelyn, the source of the heresy! She was named in the letters you received. We must take her now, and the priest too," snapped the man called Hyron.

Damion approached the monks, but Abbot Hill stared at the ground. "I am sorry, Damion," he said.

"This is Damion Athariel?" The Patriarch's eyes were cold. "Come aside with me. I wish to speak with you."

Reluctant, Damion obeyed. They walked a few paces apart from the others through the firelit ruins.

"It grieves me, my son, to see you thus attired," observed Patriarch Winter. "You know, of course, that you have committed a grave offense in donning layman's garb without leave, let alone taking up a weapon."

Damion looked down at the sword-belt, still around his waist. "I—" he began, but the Patriarch cut him off.

"I have read the letters you left in your room, asking that you be released from your priestly vows. I am glad that you at least had the honor to set your holy vocation aside before engaging in this dubious affair—no, do not interrupt me—unlike the monks who committed their offenses while still wearing the cloth of their order. When I first heard of your role in bringing the scroll here to Maurainia, I believed you meant no harm and had merely been used by others. No, do *not* interrupt! You may yet be pardoned. You have been beguiled, perhaps, by this young woman, this Lorelyn, into joining her and her coven—"

"I've no part in any of it, Your Reverence, I will swear to that under any oath! And neither has Lorelyn. We were both held captive here, in the dungeons of the ruin, and helped each other escape. I was planning to return her to the Sisters—"

"It is too late for that now, I fear," said the older man, shaking his head. "A heresy such as this one is like a contagion, hard to fight once it has taken hold in people's minds, and apt to spread to others. If Lorelyn returns to the convent she may pass the heresy on to the other girls. As for you, your vocation is beyond hope, though perhaps your soul is not."

"My soul!" Suddenly Damion was angry. "What about those Zimbouran men you're riding with, who worship Valdur?"

"They do nothing of the kind. They have renounced their heathen god, and turned to our faith."

"Have they? That aide of yours, that Hyron man—I've seen him before. I found him prying about the library, asking after the scroll. You might ask him why he wanted it!"

The Patriarch was unruffled. "To remove its evil influence from your midst, of course. Medalar Hyron is a good man: I have come to trust him completely."

"He's a spy!" Damion almost shouted. "A spy for King Khalazar."

Patriarch Winter flushed, then composed himself with an effort, resuming his grave expression. "Do not raise your voice, my son, or presume to contradict me. You are not yet released from your vows, including the vow of obedience. I will give you one last chance to redeem yourself. Help me to stamp out this heresy before it goes any further. Reveal to me the location of this coven's hiding place, and of the scroll of false scriptures that you gave them."

Damion looked back at the armed Zimbourans, saw that they wore expressions of smug satisfaction. "What will you . . . do to them?" he asked.

"What must be done. It is not only that they look to this young woman for salvation, rather than to the Faith. They have committed serious crimes, which they will have to answer for."

Damion hesitated. The Modrian followers deserved punishment, but to his knowledge Ana's people had hurt no one, and to reveal the hiding place of the one group was to betray the other. Might they be unjustly blamed and punished for the crimes of others?

After waiting a few moments the Patriarch shrugged, an eloquent gesture. "I have given you every chance, but you seem determined to condemn yourself. Say no more, then; what you speak here may be used against you at your trial."

"Trial?" echoed Damion. "You can't mean . . . not an Inquisition?"

"Don't be foolish. This is a matter for the secular authorities, and to them you will all be delivered."

"But all that nonsense about demons—it belongs to the Dark Age!"

"These village folk still live in the Dark Age," replied the older man. His voice had altered, become almost confiding. "Superstition cannot always be quelled with reason. You may think it nonsense, but it is real to them. These people came to me believing that I can deliver them from their fears, and I must be seen to do so, even if that requires some pretense on my part. I owe them no less."

Damion looked at the bland-faced man before him, chilled. At last he understood. He, Ana, Lorelyn, the monks, and the Nemerei were all to be used by this man as his Zimbouran "converts" had been used, to serve his own end of self-advancement. No argument Damion might make could sway him. His plans were already laid.

As they walked back to the others Damion sought, and met, the eyes of Abbot Hill. The old man looked worried and miserable. "Your Reverence—can't we—"

"Silence, monk!" said Norvyn Winter in a loud and carrying voice. "You and your prior have allowed these Nemerei witches to practice their black arts and persecute the good people of this region. Only a corrupt shepherd permits wolves to roam near his flock. You were also the keepers of the scroll that was the source of the heresy. Come back to the Academy with me now, and show to me the lurking-place of the witches."

The half-Zimbouran man made a signal to Jomar to follow him: apparently he did not as yet suspect any treachery on the part of his slave. Jomar obeyed with his head lowered, not looking toward Damion and the others: his eyes had returned to black extinguished embers. Hyron drew a rolled-up document from his saddlebag, which he waved in front of Damion with a smirk. "This is a letter from the Supreme Patriarch himself, signed and sealed by him, to the effect that the Brothers of the Holy Order of Saint Athariel stand accused of violating their vows by consorting with witches. The coven leader, Ana, must be punished for her crimes against man and God, and with her all of her followers, as well as her demonic familiars which have possessed the bodies of a gray cat and a wolf . . ." Damion could see in his mind the shaky handwriting of the senile old man. What other tales had Norvyn Winter told him? "The possessed animals must be destroyed, and a rite of exorcism must be performed on the ruin to rid it of its ghost. But Ana's sentence will be lessened should she provide a full confession and reveal the names of all her coven-members. Signed, His Eminence Pious IX, Supreme Patriarch of—"

At that same moment there was an eerie yowl, and Damion turned to see the cat Greymalkin perched on the firelit battlement above like a gargoyle, glaring down at the crowd. At least a dozen other cats were ranged alongside her. Their eyes reflected the glow of the torches to uncanny effect.

"The demons! The demons!" someone screamed.

Wolf slipped away from Ana and charged into the crowd, snapping and snarling at those who threatened his mistress. Panic broke out as people began to flee in several directions. But the Patriarch, the monks, and the Zimbourans remained where they were, as did Ana and the young people gathered round her.

"You, Abbot and Prior, come with me," said Winter again. "I will get to the bottom of this conspiracy of yours if it is the last thing I do. Hyron, you are in charge of the accused witches. Take them to the city and place them in prison. I will deal with them when my work here is finished." He and the two monks began to walk back toward the Academy, leaving Ana and the others with the Zimbourans.

"You will come with us now," the man Hyron said. He and the other men moved their horses to hem the prisoners in.

"No!" Lorelyn shouted. "I haven't done anything wrong! None of us has."

Hyron made no reply but laid a hand upon his sword-hilt. Desperate, Damion stood in front of Lorelyn and drew his own sword. As the men dismounted and advanced upon him, he swung the weapon at them in a whistling arc, and they halted in surprise. Evidently they had expected no resistance. He had little hope of winning against such odds, but at least he could hold off the moment of capture as long as possible. He swung the sword again, and as he heard the blade cleave the air it went like wine to his head. He was not powerless. He would not give way without a fight—

"Stop it, you fool," growled Jomar morosely. "Can't you see you're outnumbered?"

"Disarm him," ordered Hyron. Three of the men came on with swords drawn. Damion stood irresolute for an instant, his blood still surging fiercely in his veins. Then as the men moved to ring him he lowered his blade. Contemptuous, the lead man swung his own weapon and struck the sword from Damion's grip.

Ana stepped forward into the circle of men, laid a hand upon Damion's arm. It rested there light as a leaf, yet the touch stilled him. Ana turned and confronted Hyron. "There is no need for violence. We will come with you."

There was another yowl from above, and Greymalkin leaped down from her perch, ran over to Ana, and sprang up into her arms.

"Her familiar!" shouted one of the Zimbourans, raising his sword.

Hyron snorted. "You fool. You did not believe that nonsense their dotard of a high priest wrote? It is a mangy old cat, nothing more. Now, you prisoners: move!"

They carried Ailia to the tumbrel, which stood abandoned near at hand, and dumped her limp body in it. Ana, still carrying her cat, and Lorelyn were then forced to get in, followed by Damion. The tailboard was closed and fastened. One man went to the dray horse's head and, laying hold of the harness, began to lead it. The others, including Jomar, remounted and moved off, leading their companion's horse and also the white palfrey, which the Zimbourans seemed to consider a spoil of war.

They traveled in dismal silence for what felt like leagues. Presently Damion, who had been watching the road, spoke to their captors. "Where are you taking us?" he demanded. "This isn't the road into the city!"

"We go to the sea," responded Hyron, turning in his saddle and leering at the prisoners.

Damion stared at him. "The sea! What do you mean? Your orders were to take us to prison."

Hyron cawed with laughter. "Prison? You should be so fortunate. No, it is to the king that you are going."

"Why would King Stefon—"

The captain's lips curved in a thin smile. "King Khalazar. He awaits us in a ship off the coast."

Ana stood up and peered over the wooden side of the tumbrel. "Captain," she said in her quiet voice, "you only need me. To find what you seek, you will need my help. I have what you require here—" She reached into a deep pocket of her dress and pulled out the parchment scroll. There were a few involuntary gasps from the onlooking Zimbourans, and from Damion as well. Hyron gave a shout in Zimbouran, and the procession halted. He rode up to the cart and snatched the parchment from the little gnarled hand.

"Yes, it is the document you seek," said the old woman, "the scroll with the sea chart, showing the way to Trynisia. And I know, also, what the chart does not show: the exact spot where the Star Stone lies in the land of Trynisia. Release these young people, and I will be your guide. I will cooperate with you fully."

The half-breed spy gave another raucous laugh. "Oh, you'll cooperate, all right! I'll see to that, old hag. But your precious Princess"—he gestured to Lorelyn—"comes too. Do you think we of Zimboura don't know the prophecies as well as you? Khalazar is not going to let his rival out of his sight." He signed to the man at the dray horse's head to move forward again.

"She has nothing to do with any of this, nor has the other girl," said Ana. She pointed with her cane at the still-unconscious Ailia sprawled on the floor of the tumbrel. "Nor has the priest. They are not of my coven."

"You expect me to believe that, witch? They were here, with you. They'll come with us too—unless you would prefer that we killed them? I see they are of value to you, or you would not try to bargain for their freedom. You will lie to us if it is only your own life at stake, but if *their* lives depend upon it—that is another story, is it not? For every false turn you take as our guide, for every 'mistake' that you pretend to make, we will kill one of them. And if you anger us, we will make you choose which one shall die."

The tumbrel rolled on with its armed escort, down a long earthen path that led to the sea. Soon the air reeked of brine, and they moved on sand, which at its sea-wet edge had the gleam of dulled silver. And there among the black rocks there lay, as if cast up out of the depths by the surf, long dark low-hulled boats crewed by silent figures. The Zimbourans dismounted and passed their horses to a couple of men, who stood holding their reins. But the white palfrey's rough halter of rope was made fast to the stern of one of the boats: it appeared the men intended it to swim out to sea with them. The tumbrel was brought to a halt, and the prisoners were led out of it at sword's point—all but Ailia, who had not revived and had to be carried—down the beach to the boats. The soldiers and the boatmen exchanged no words. Once they were all aboard, the silent crews began to row—away from the shore, away from Maurainia to the dim horizon where the galleons waited. The captives could see them approaching under sail, looming shapes of shadow under pale canvas, eyed with small red lights.

AILIA AWAKENED TO A NEW NIGHTMARE. She lay on a hard wooden floor in a cramped and fusty room, so dark that she could see nothing of its interior. Her head had cleared, yet still the room seemed to her to be rocking and swaying to and fro. "Where am I?" she cried aloud, staggering to her feet and feeling about her in the darkness. There was a wooden wall to her left, but it seemed to slant crazily and she could not steady herself.

"They think we're witches," said Lorelyn's voice from off to her left. "Well, you two are: I'm the Tryna Lia. According to them, that is."

Ailia was relieved at the familiar voice, but could make no sense of what it said. Her legs folded up underneath her and she collapsed in a heap on the rocking floor. "Witches?" she said aloud. "I *am* dreaming still, I must be. I know I was dreaming before, Lori, about you and Father Damion, and old Ana of all people—"

"I am sorry, Ailia," came Ana's voice out of the dark, "but it is all quite true."

Ailia reeled. "Ana—you *are* here? Then—where—"

"The Zimbourans have taken us prisoner."

"The *Zimbourans*—?"

Lorelyn's voice spoke again. "Oh, of course: you fainted before the villagers arrived, and the Patriarch and—"

Heavy booted feet thumped across the ceiling, and shouts rang out. The room plunged and rolled, and there was a sound of water slapping and gurgling against the walls.

"We're on a ship!" gasped Ailia.

"A Zimbouran galleon. And by the sound of it," said Ana's tranquil voice, "I'd say we are under way."

Part Two

THE STONE OF HEAVEN

11

"To the World's End"

DAMION HAD GROWN USED TO the monotonous motion that at first made him ill. Even the stifling and noisome air no longer sickened him, and the continuous creaking and sighing of stressed wood did not keep him awake. Sometimes he felt as though there had never been anything but this rolling, heaving ship's interior: the rest of his life receded into a dreamlike realm lost beyond recall. How long had they been at sea? It could not be the eternity it seemed, but it must be weeks—a month at least—since they had first set sail. Yet in all that time the Zimbouran vessel had not made landfall.

Now once again he awakened to see the same dreary scene that had become his world. There were cabins on the Zimbouran vessel for officers, but no quarters for soldiers or sailors—or for unwilling passengers: only this large open space running the length of the lower deck, that the sailors and soldiers shared. The horses and other livestock were stabled on the same level, and their presence did not improve the atmosphere. Crates and barrels of supplies took up all the rest of the space. Some of the men had slung makeshift hammocks from the beams above; most slept on the floor, using sacks or bundles of rags for pillows. There were no portholes on this level, so night was indistinguishable from day, and Damion could not even guess what part of the Greater Ocean they might be in; though it seemed to him that the air grew ever cooler with the passage of time.

They were going north, then, into oceans not yet freed of winter ice. Not far away must lie those bleak lands whose thinning forests gave way to treeless barrens, and finally the white wastes where nothing grew. Accounts of doomed arctic expeditions had been found in recovered logs: melancholy tales of men sailing into seas of jagged ice, then escaping onto floes when their ships' hulls were crushed like nuts between grinding bergs. Those men had learned at terrible cost that nothing was to be found in the far north but eternal and unrelenting winter. Yet all the stories of Trynisia described it as warm and verdant! Were they all going to perish, as the luckless explorers had, on a fool's errand? The Zimbourans had the sea chart, which they believed showed the fabled island's position; and they were driven by their God-king and their own unreasoning zeal. No doubt they would persist long past the point where the other explorers had given in—until at last their vessels yielded to the gnawing ice and the cold deeps consumed them.

Damion stood up, fighting for balance. His captors no longer bound his feet, or even troubled to post a guard. Where could he go? He now had the run of the lower deck, so long as he kept his distance from the sailors. Most were slaves, their bodies bearing the signs of brutal abuse: whip wheals that had left permanent scars, broken noses that had healed askew. Some bore slave-collars of iron, and still-festering wounds showed on their ankles and wrists where shackles and manacles had rubbed the skin raw. Many sported bruises and other injuries that were fresh, apparently inflicted during their duties above decks. They were as much prisoners as Damion and the women were. Even if he could talk to them, he did not speak their language. He had made one attempt, offering his daily ration of soaked biscuit to another man when he himself felt too seasick to eat. A guard with a leather whip descended on them both, screaming in his native tongue and lashing them both about their backs and shoulders. Damion fled, then watched in horror as the other man was flogged, wailing and cowering beneath the blows that tore his already ragged clothing to tatters. The guard stopped only when his victim lost consciousness. Damion's own untreated wheals throbbed like burns for some time afterwards, preventing sleep and adding to his nausea. He put the guard's savage attack down to pure malice at first. It only occurred to him later that the officers might fear a mutiny, being so greatly outnumbered by their unwilling thralls.

He brooded over his fate and that of the captive women, of whom he had seen little since the ship first set out; he worried, too, about his friends in Maurainia. What explanation, if any, had been offered them for his sudden disappearance? Would the Patriarch say that Damion and the others must have fled, resisting arrest? He would have to explain the disappearance of his "converts," too, in a way that avoided embarrassment. One thing was certain: Kaithan Athariel would never believe the charges made against his friend. Witchcraft! He could almost hear Kaith's contemptuous laughter. But Kaithan could do nothing, and neither could anyone else. The abbot and prior were probably in prison by now, and Ana's followers routed out and punished. *They'll never know what really happened to me or the women,* he thought. *Perhaps they all think we're dead. And before long we may well be.*

He searched for ways to distract himself from these hideous thoughts. The Mohara man Jomar was also on the ship, though Damion saw very little of him. Jomar kept apart from the other men whenever possible. Perhaps their Zimbouran prejudice would not let them accept him as one of them, or perhaps Jomar himself did not care for their company. While the Zimbouran soldiers and seamen passed the time with dice games or wrestling matches, the Mohara man held aloof, taking long drafts from a tin flask he kept in a pocket. He had found a dark corner behind some ration barrels, not far from the stabling area, for these drinking bouts: the area was ill-lit, redolent of moldy straw and dung, and most of the other men avoided it. After what felt like an age without speaking to another living soul, Damion finally risked stealing over to the spot and engaging the Mohara man in furtive, whispered conversation. The priest had no doubt about the contents of the flask: after several drinks Jomar became less reserved and his tongue loosened. No doubt he had been raiding one of the rum kegs. Sometimes in his inebriated state he forgot to lower his voice, and spoke in his full booming baritone, much to the priest's alarm. But the Zimbourans never came to investigate—they were accustomed, no doubt, to Jomar's little bouts. By approaching him when he was in these tipsily expansive moods, Damion was able to piece the man's past together, like assembling the fragments of an old mosaic. The completed picture was not a pleasant one. Jomar, after repeatedly refusing to divulge his age, finally revealed that he did not know it. His father was a high-ranking Zimbouran who had risked an illicit liaison with a Mohara woman. Angry Valdur-clerics, on learning of the miscegenation, had raided the house when Jomar was still unborn, arrested his father, and dispatched the unlucky mother and her infant to a labor camp. Damion had heard fearful rumors of these places, of the squalor and brutality that took place in them.

"How did you get out of it?" he asked.

Jomar's eyes grew deep with memory. "When I was big enough I was sent out with a work party, building a road in the desert for King Zedekara. Hot as blazes by day, cold at night as . . . as a Zimbouran's heart." He glanced around, evidently hoping this had been overheard, but either none of the Zimbourans was within earshot or they did not understand Maurish. "We had no tents or anything to sleep in at night," he continued. "We had to lie on the ground, in groups for safety, with a fire for protection if we were lucky. Wild animals used to come right up to our camps after dark. Now and then a lion or leopard would drag someone off. We'd hear screams in the night, maybe find some blood on the sand next day.

"One night a lion attacked my camp, grabbed a man lying right next to me. I ran at the brute—all I had was this big rock-pick for digging. I must have been out of my mind. Next thing I knew the lion was lying dead at my feet, with the pick in its skull."

"You killed a lion with a *pick?*" repeated Damion. He believed the story: there was something in Jomar's terse unadorned narrative that gave the ring of truth. "That's . . . amazing."

"It was stupid," corrected the Mohara man, turning morose. He took a swig from his flask. "The Zimbourans heard all about it, and before I knew what was happening I was sent back to the city—to the Royal Arena. They called me the Mulatto, and they made me fight lions and Shurkanese saber-tooths. Gladiators, too. I was a challenge—they threw everything they had at me, hoping to kill me. They couldn't. The Mulatto won every time." Jomar gave a fierce grin.

Damion smiled too. "Ah! I thought you were holding back when you fought with me, back there in Maurainia. But tell me, how did you get out of the arena?"

"One of their generals bought me—thought he'd put my strength to some use."

He had seen action in the uprising against King Zedekara, he said. He had been happy to oppose the forces of that hated monarch, fighting so well that, had it not been for his skin color, he would have been rewarded after Khalazar's triumph. Instead they had used him as a spy in foreign countries—first Shurkana, then the Archipelagoes and Maurainia. It was a role he detested, and had undertaken only in the hope that he might somehow manage to escape while in one of these foreign lands. But as a highly valued slave he was kept under close guard. His partner in many of these missions was the man called Medalar Hyron, whose real name was Zefron Shezzek.

"He's a brute," Jomar growled. "Rotten to the core.

They say his mother was a Maurainian woman who was snatched off a ship by pirates and sold to a Zimbouran noble. Half-breeds aren't accepted in Zimboura, so he's spent his entire life trying to claw his way up through the ranks. He managed to convince Khalazar's generals that he'd make a good spy since he doesn't look Zimbouran. They agreed, and they've kept him busy ever since."

"Why is he being sent up north then? There surely can't be much spying to do there."

Jomar shrugged. "Don't know. But Shezzek's a little too good at what he does. Khalazar likes to keep his more dangerous servants far from home, and out of his rivals' hands." A little silence fell; then Jomar looked at Damion again. "I knew you were in that trash heap in the alley, back on Jana. You couldn't have gone anywhere else in that short a time. I could have told the Zimbourans where you were."

Damion looked at him, startled. "Why didn't you?"

"I never help them more than I have to. When General Mazur bought me, he said he would kill one Mohara slave for every time I disobeyed him, or if I ran away. I believed he would do it. That threat held me for years. My own people thought I was a traitor, a collaborator: if I rode by a slave camp they would spit at me, and there was no way I could explain it to them. I found little ways of defying the Zims—but they had to be secret ways."

Damion nodded in sudden understanding. "When you realized Lorelyn would be killed, you had to choose one life over another."

Jomar took a long swig from his flask, and made no reply. Damion reflected with rising anger that it likely had amused the Zimbourans to see Jomar reviled as a traitor when in truth he was saving Mohara lives. How wounding it must have been, and how it would have twisted the man's mind over the years. If only fate had let him remain in Maurainia, and not doomed him to this hopeless voyage. Damion's concerns for himself faded, thrust aside by the poignant shade of a Jomar that might have been.

DURING THIS TIME the three women were locked away in one of the lower stern cabins, a windowless prison of a room. There were two bunk beds with thin dirty mattresses, and a third mattress flung down on the floor. An oil lamp dangled from the ceiling on a chain. Beyond the sloping walls they could hear the roar and thud of the waves, and through the locked door came the bellowing of Zimbouran voices. Three times a day the door was unlocked, and they were allowed into the main part of the lower deck, where they were given the same rations as the sailors and slaves: ship's biscuit soaked in a pail to make it soft enough to eat, sometimes with salt fish or leathery preserved meat. A small water barrel in one corner of their cabin supplied their only drink. It was replenished at times, but not as often as any of them would have liked, and they were often maddened by thirst.

Some clothing was provided for them, loose, rough robes of the sort Zimbouran men wore, as two of them had only the dresses they were wearing when they were caught. These were not particularly clean. Lorelyn shared the other contents of her satchel, which she had managed to keep with her. A bucket of seawater was occasionally provided to them for washing.

It did not help that much of Lorelyn's and Ana's story was fantastical, the stuff of faerie tales. Lorelyn's talk of hearing other people's voices in her head was quite incredible, and Ana's calm acceptance of that claim even more disturbing. Indeed, the old woman claimed to possess a similar power. "I see all that I need to see," she explained, gesturing to her filmy eyes. "Light—and darkness. The rest I am content to perceive with my inner eye." Ailia felt sometimes that she was shut in a madhouse, sometimes that she herself was going mad.

"They . . . kidnapped me," she said out loud, as if trying to convince herself that all of this was actually happening. It was so like something from one of her own stories or daydreams that even now it seemed unreal. "They took me because they thought I was a *witch*—" She broke off and drew up her feet as a rat scuttled across the floorboards.

Ana turned to her with a kindly expression. "I know it's all very tiresome for you," she said, addressing both girls. "And for poor Damion too. I am truly sorry about what happened. But for my part, I can't complain. I wanted to go north, and I couldn't find any sea captain willing to go there. Now here I am, well on my way—it's positively providential." She broke off a piece of ship's biscuit and held it out to the rat, which took it tamely from her fingers and darted away again.

"Ana—" Ailia protested.

"The conditions aren't all one could wish for, it's true," the elderly woman added, "but I can hardly complain, as I'm getting free passage—"

"But Ana—you're a prisoner. We're all prisoners!" Ailia almost screamed.

"For the time being. We'll part company with our disagreeable hosts when we arrive at our destination."

Ailia relapsed into a despairing silence. She wondered what story the Patriarch had told her family. They would never believe she had participated in witchcraft! But even if they didn't believe the tale, what could they do? They didn't even know where the Zimbourans had taken her. She shifted about, trying to get comfortable. Her legs were growing stiff. She tried to stand up, but the rocking motion of the ship defeated her, and she lay back again groaning. *Go away, don't be real,* she urged the wooden walls. But they stubbornly persisted. "None of this is happening, I *must* be dreaming it all."

"Ailia, it's been days—weeks. You *can't* have been dreaming all that time," pointed out Lorelyn with ruthless logic.

"Perhaps I've got a fever and I'm delirious," Ailia suggested hopefully. "I'm not really here, but safe in bed in the sanatorium having fever-dreams—Ow!" she yelped as Lorelyn leaned over and pinched her arm. "What did you do that for?"

"Did it hurt?"

"Of course it hurt!"

"Well, then you're not dreaming." Lorelyn turned back to Ana. "So you think you were somehow *meant* to end up on this ship? But what about the rest of us? Why am *I* here, and what has it all got to do with me? I wish you would tell me what this is all about."

"Yes, I suppose I should. I did not want to frighten you, but it is certainly time you knew. You are the focus of all this, the nexus," said Ana. "In a way, we are all here because of you. The man Jomar was told by both of his masters to find you; Damion tried to take you from Mandrake; Ailia went into the ruin to find and comfort you. And I, too, went to look for you when I heard that you were gone. For despite the note you left, I thought Mandrake might well have something to do with your disappearance. You—or the Fates—have brought us all together for some common destiny."

"My Purpose," the girl breathed.

"I told you about the Tryna Lia," Ana began.

"Yes, but I still don't understand. I thought she wasn't supposed to be a real person," Lorelyn persisted.

"In western tradition she became a symbol, the personification of the Faith," Ana explained. "But the original Elei lore spoke of her as a real, living being. The coming of the Tryna Lia was foretold by the queen of Trynisia more than two thousand years ago. The Elei believed that a time of great evil and suffering would come, when the world would fall under the rule of a wicked tyrant. But they also believed that another great leader would be born, a woman who would bear the title of Tryna Lia—Princess of the Stars. She would be born human, but her true nature would be divine. According to Elei beliefs, you see, the gods vowed never again to intervene directly in the lives of mortals unless they were explicitly asked to do so by the mortals themselves. And they were not to take corporeal form anymore unless they became incarnate—born into human form, assuming not only flesh but the vulnerable nature that goes with it. So the Elei looked for their divine Princess to be born as one of them."

"And you think she's *me*," said Lorelyn. "Who were my parents then? I would have to be the daughter of a king, wouldn't I, to be a princess?"

"Not necessarily. The word is merely the feminine form of 'prince,' which can mean any high-ranking ruler."

Ailia looked hard at Lorelyn, frowning. She didn't believe for a moment all this nonsense about her classmate being . . . that person. *She's just an ordinary person—like me, like anybody else!* She recalled her glimpse of Princess Paisia riding in majesty through the streets in her carriage. Now that was true royalty. *Princess* Lorelyn? Impossible! And as for her being divine . . . It was all too ridiculous. But the Zimbourans, it appeared, believed otherwise.

"I have strange dreams sometimes," said Lorelyn slowly, "or at least I think they are dreams. I see pictures in my head just as I'm falling asleep: places I've never been to, faces of people I've never met."

"A white palace, perhaps, with many towers?" Ana prompted. "And a woman with long golden hair?"

Lorelyn started, a look of wonder on her face. "How did you know about *that*?" she asked in a low voice. "I've had that dream for years, but I never told anyone."

"Because I have had the same visions, many a time. And so have the other Nemerei. Lorelyn, that woman may have been your mother."

"Mother . . ." Lorelyn spoke the word softly. "When I was very young I thought I could just remember . . . arms that held me, and a gentle voice. But the face was never there, I couldn't find it—I didn't think of it being the golden-haired lady in my dream. I didn't think she was real. If she *is* my mother, then what became of her?"

"That I do not know."

"Was she an Elei? Am I?" demanded Lorelyn.

"I believe so. You have a look of the Elei, certainly: like them you're uncommonly tall, and then there are your special abilities."

"Ailia told me the Elei died out ages ago."

"They did," put in Ailia from her corner.

Ana smiled. "Perhaps not."

Ailia stared at her, and at the long-limbed, fair-haired girl. A living Elei! Could it be? No—more nonsense! But something deep within her quickened at the thought.

"If I am this leader of theirs, what exactly is it I'm supposed to do?" pursued Lorelyn.

"The task of the Tryna Lia is to unite Earth and Heaven: that is, institute a new era of peace and justice to make the earthly realm more like the heavenly one. But to do this she must first conquer the Dark Prince."

"And who is *he*?"

"Ah, if only we knew that, we might rest more easily! We would be able to trace his movements then, and not always wonder from what quarter the attack will come. The Dark Prince is our enemy's champion, a mighty warlord who will rise up in obedience to the commands of the Fiend. The Nemerei say this man will lose his soul and become only an empty vessel for the Fiend's dark will, and so our ancient enemy will escape the bottomless Pit to which he was imprisoned long ago. But the Zimbourans say the Prince will *be* Valdur incarnate. King Khalazar believes this, and that he is the one foretold; and your life has been spared for that reason. The prophecy of the scroll clearly states that the Prince and the Tryna Lia will battle over the Star Stone, but also that she will come to it first. Remember, the king is a very superstitious man, and takes the prophecies quite literally. Though he fears and hates you, he has not attempted to murder you because he also believes a doom cannot be denied. You must go to Trynisia, for so it is written: you must take up the Stone, and only then can he seize it from you. He cannot slay you unless the Stone is present, nor can he take the Stone unless you find it first. I know it seems odd, but in Zimboura even the gods are believed to be bound by fate. And let us be thankful for those beliefs, because so far they have kept you alive."

"But only for now. He'll kill me later," said Lorelyn. Her voice was flat and toneless, but her blue eyes were wide as they looked into Ana's.

Ailia gasped, and Ana reached out to lay her withered hand on Lorelyn's. "No, my dear. I will not let him do that."

"But how can you stop him? Especially if he's that Prince you mentioned—"

"He believes he is; I do not. I doubt that Modrian-Valdur would show his hand to us so soon. He will conceal the identity of his lieutenant from the Nemerei as long as he can, the better to take us unawares. I think the true Prince must know his own identity by now, though, and what his mission is. And he would not believe in dooms. He may have tried to destroy you, Lorelyn, when you were only an infant; and so your mother hid you away. The monks kept you safe. Thanks to them, you lived and have now grown old enough to confront him. You will have to be very brave, my dear." Her hand tightened on the young girl's.

"I know, Ana," said Lorelyn quietly. "I'm not frightened. I've always known somehow that I was born to do something important. I believe I'm meant to be . . . a fighter."

"But you deserve at least to know why it is that you fight. It is to protect others, to save the weak from the strong." Ana's pale eyes seemed to search Lorelyn's. "Would you really be prepared to risk your life to save the life of another? This is important, Lorelyn. You must accept your mission freely."

"I do accept it, Ana—now that I know everything at last."

"Perhaps not everything, dear, but that will do for the present." The old woman smiled and released her hold on Lorelyn's hand, seeming to relax. "If we are to have peace, the Tryna Lia must conquer the Prince and his followers—but I hope that will be many years from now."

"I'll fight him whenever he wants," declared Lorelyn. "Whoever he is, I'll see that he's put paid to. Especially if he murdered my mother and father!" Her lower lip trembled slightly.

"We don't know that he did, dear. But I'm afraid it is a possibility."

Lorelyn laid her head on her knees for a moment. "It's all my fault," she said in a muffled voice. "If my parents are dead, it's because of me—who I am. And Abbot Shan and the monks in Jardjana: they protected me, and now I suppose they're dead too."

"Lorelyn, dear—"

The girl raised her head again; her freckled face was white, but tearless. "It's all right, Ana. Thinking about it just makes me feel even more like fighting."

At that moment the door was opened by a guard. Ailia recognized the dark-skinned Mohara man she had first seen in the Academy library, so long ago. "Dinner," he announced in a glum voice, waving them through the doorway.

"Jomar," Lorelyn began, but he cut her off.

"Don't talk to me," he said, curt and sullen, and turned his back on her.

As they approached the doorway something gray and swift darted in through it. Ailia recoiled, thinking for an instant that it was an enormous rat. But a second glance showed her it was Ana's cat, Greymalkin. "Ah, there you are, my dear!" Ana greeted her pet. It sprang up onto a barrel and gazed at them, purring. "And what have you been up to?"

"Hunting rats, I hope," remarked Ailia. "She had better be careful. If the Zimbourans catch her they might throw her overboard."

"I'll throw *them* overboard if they try it," cried Lorelyn, putting her arms around the cat. It nuzzled her face.

Ana led the girls out into the main section of the lower deck. Ailia supposed she should be grateful to get out of that claustrophobic cell of a cabin, but the main room was not much better. The smell of it was terrible, all sweat and unwashed bodies, and she did not much like the way some of the men looked at her and Lorelyn. Most averted their eyes, however. Either they feared the girls really were witches, or else they dared not touch their tyrant king's rightful prey.

One man stood out, his fair hair conspicuous among all those dark heads. Ailia stared at him, as she always did. If there was one thing in all this strangeness she could not accept, one thing that made her feel she *must* indeed be dreaming, it was the presence of Damion Athariel. She had listened to Lorelyn's story of the scroll he had brought from the Archipelagoes, and Ana's account of his meeting with the Nemerei, and they were so like the fanciful tales she loved reading that it was easy to believe they originated in her own befuddled head. The young priest entered into so many of her dreams; surely this must merely be another of them? She gazed at him as she lined up for her share of the thin and watery gruel that was today's main meal. He *looked* like the Damion she had known at the Academy. Though his chin was now covered in a stubbly beard and his eyes were shadowed with weariness, those eyes were still the same intense blue, the untidy hair as golden-blond as she remembered.

He glanced up at that moment, and the blue eyes met hers.

"I'm sorry about this, Ailia," he said in a soft voice, moving toward her. "I should have known better than to get involved in this affair. But you had nothing to do with it—"

"You! Prisoner!" barked a soldier. "No talk to women."

The young man raised his hands to her in a gesture of helplessness, then turned away again.

A DEEP VOICE BROKE into Damion's gloom some time later.

"Get up, priest," it said. He looked up bleary-eyed, and saw that it was Jomar addressing him. The Mohara man now wore a full-length fur coat and carried another on his arm.

"You're to come up on deck." He held out the coat and said, "Put this on." His tone was brusque.

"But why—"

"Don't talk to me!" snapped the Mohara.

Damion could see that he was sober, and therefore in a bad mood. He donned the coat, then followed his surly guide up the wooden ladder leading to the deck. Were the Zimbourans going to pitch him overboard to the sharks? But in that case they would hardly have provided him with a coat.

Up on deck the cold struck him like a blow, and he gasped. The wind was bitter, sea and sky the same leaden color. Spring had not come to the northern ocean: Damion could see his own breath steaming on the air. Sailors and soldiers stood about, indistinguishable from one another, inhuman-looking figures in bulky furs. Gray waves webbed with foam heaved and surged around the ship's hull, and the deck pitched constantly, sometimes sloping as steeply as the roof of a house. To keep his balance, Damion had to sway and wave his arms wildly, as though performing a ritual dance. There were ice floes riding the wild swell, he saw, and two more ships plunged through the waves to starboard. They were not oared, lateen-rigged galleys like the one Damion had seen in the Archipelagoes, but galleons like this vessel in which he rode: huge ships designed to sail before the wind, square-rigged like the ships of the west with only one three-cornered sail at the stern.

One ship, he saw—with a shiver that had nothing to do with the cold—flew the royal sun-standard of Zimboura. Why would the God-king choose to undertake such a dangerous voyage, leaving his kingdom vulnerable to usurpers in his absence? *But of course he believes it's his destiny—that he will return in triumph with the Star Stone, and no one will be able to stand against him then . . .*

There was distant land in sight to port, a few snow-mottled mountains and a gray, barren shore, but the ship was not heading toward it. There was nothing but ice ahead of them: the remnants of the polar pack, no doubt, that must only recently have begun to break up. Icebergs drifted perilously past, sculpted by wind and sea into strange abstract forms: as he watched, their galleon passed quite close to one tremendous ice-mass, the size of the High Temple of Raimar. It even had the appearance of a temple, Damion thought, gazing at it in fascination—smooth and white as finest marble, with two huge sea-carved columns framing an opening that gave onto a dim, blue interior. The other men seemed as awed as he, staring up at the vast white shape that dwarfed the vessels moving past it.

He glanced at Jomar, but the Mohara man was gazing listlessly out to sea. Pity stirred in Damion at the sight of that exotic dark profile, so out of place against the background of bleak gray sea and ice. It belonged to a different world—verdant jungle or sun-baked desert, he thought.

The captain of the vessel strolled toward him, thrusting his broad black-bearded face close to Damion's. The priest waited apprehensively. Then the captain laughed, foul breath blowing past broken teeth into the young man's face.

"Time you help out a little on deck, boy," he said in harshly accented Maurish. "This not pleasure trip." He glanced up at the empty crow's nest, swaying with the mast, and grinned. "Maybe we try you up there—yes?" He shouted something to the other Zimbourans in their own language, and they all guffawed. "Yes—you be lookout! Up mast now!"

Damion winced. But there was nothing for it but to obey: some of the soldiers fingered their weapons, hoping no doubt that he would put up a struggle and give them an excuse to injure him. Jomar continued to stare moodily out to sea. Damion approached the mast, waving his arms for balance, and laid his hands on a rung of the rope ladder. His fingers were already numb with cold, and the ladder seemed to stretch above him into infinity, vanishing into clouds of bellying canvas. Slowly and painfully he climbed, long-disused muscles protesting, hands clumsy with cold, fumbling for a proper grip. Occasionally he was obliged to stop, clinging to a rough wooden rung and trying very hard not to look down. Once, his foot slipped and he found himself dangling precariously by his cramped hands, terror jolting through his frame as he kicked about for a foothold. The men below watched, with amusement, he knew, wishing he would lose his grip and plummet to the deck. He gritted his chattering teeth, determined not to give them that satisfaction.

Up and up, hand over hand . . . The wind shrilled in his ears, freezing their lobes, while the sails swelled and flapped like flags all around him. The crow's nest was just above him, bobbing and swaying with the ship's movements—within reach . . .

Hours later—so it seemed to him—he clambered up into the basket-shaped structure, gasping and shivering violently, thrusting his frozen hands into the sleeves of his coat. Now he could look down at the deck, spread out beneath him and seeming very far away, at the little knots of men watching him in disappointment. Well, he wasn't going back down—not until he'd rested, at any rate. If they wanted him, they would just have to come up here and get him.

Damion huddled in the bottom of the basket, blowing on his hands. He could see farther from this height, but all that was revealed to him was more floating ice. His chilled ears throbbed, and he cupped his hands over them. It began to snow, sea and sky vanishing into a gray-blue void of falling flakes. Soon the flakes obscured the shapes of the other galleons like a thick fog. Damion could only see for a bowshot in any direction: there was nothing but the white-crested waves, roaring out of a blank grayness. The sea was even rougher than before. As he clutched the wooden rim of the crow's nest the wind abruptly shifted direction, blowing full in his face. He gave a start.

The wind was warm.

Warm, and moist, like a breeze out of the tropics. He must be imagining it . . . No—there it was again. An intermittent gust of hot, sultry air alternating with the colder wind from the sea. It smote his numbed face like a blast from an oven, made him reel.

And it came from the *north.*

The snow was damp and fell more rapidly now, like sleet. No—that was rain falling on him, out of the louring clouds. The gray blankness ahead was not flurries, but a bank of thick fog. Through the occasional gap in its swirling mass he caught glimpses of the ocean, heaving and hummocked with foaming waves. There was a flicker of lightning through the mists, an answering rumble of thunder. The ship bucked like a frightened horse. The crow's nest swooped and wove wide circles in the air, while the sails with their spidery black stars billowed beneath him, the canvas cracking in the gusts until the sound rivaled the thunderclaps from above. Damion clutched the edge of the wooden basket, but it was slick with rain and he could not get a firm grip.

Through the driving rain he saw sailors in the rigging below him, trying desperately to trim the sails and regain control of the vessel. The man at the wheel could not steer a straight course, for the ship was plunging about so much that the rudder must be as often in the air as in the water. Damion dropped to his knees and flung both arms around the mast, terrified that he would fall over the side of the crow's nest. He would likely plunge into the sea as the ship rocked hard on its keel—though a fall to the deck would kill him too. He crouched low and clung with all his might, staring about him as thunder cracked again, seemingly right above his head. The lightning bolts would hit him first, he knew, up here in this airy perch . . . He glanced skyward, and gasped. The storm clouds hung low over the sea, and like the water beneath them they were filled with swirling, churning motion. In the ragged gray underside of one a great bulge formed, revolving as though it were caught in an airy maelstrom. He released his death-grip on the mast and peered over the rim of the crow's nest. The men down there had seen the rotating cloud too: they yelled and pointed where they stood, ignoring the swamping waves. Out of the ominous gray swag a shape grew, long and pale and sinuous; it snaked downward, blindly seeking the sea. And the sea rose to meet it, swelling up into a tremendous wave, a watery hill capped with foam. Cloud and water came together, joined, and formed a gray, bowed pillar linking sky and ocean. Lightning flashed again, illuminating one side of the vaporous funnel, and Damion saw it undulate all along its length like a living thing.

A waterspout. His teeth chattered as the great gray shape advanced. It was heading in their direction. Would it strike the ship? If it did they would all die: no vessel could survive the tearing winds of a water-cyclone—

"Down!" Two large hands gripped the side of the crow's nest, followed by the head of a Zimbouran, his thick black beard and hair streaming in the rain. "Down," he ordered again, heaving himself over the rim. Damion was crushed to one side by the man's bulky frame.

"But—"

"Down, or I throw you down."

Without further protest Damion hastily swung himself over and grabbed the ladder, clinging for his life to the slick sodden rungs as the wind whipped it back and forth, flinging him against the mast. He looked down. The deck was all churning foam and debris: it would be madness to go down to it and risk being swept overboard. Men scurried about amid the flying spray, up to their waists in water, screaming at one another. One of them yelled something, pointing toward the masts.

Damion looked up. A strange phosphorescence leaped and danced about the rigging: every rope, every spar was haloed with green, flickering, phantom fire. The men moaned and gibbered with fear below. *Sailors' fire,* thought Damion as he clung to the swinging ladder. It would not harm him, he knew. He had seen this phenomenon once before, on a ship in southern seas: the Kaanish sailors had told him they believed it was the spirits of drowned sailors. These Zimbourans must have seen it before too: were they also superstitious about it?

But even as he thought this he saw that the ghostly luminosity had begun to fade from the air, and the energy of the storm appeared to be ebbing. There was no more lightning or thunder. To his relief he saw that the writhing column of the waterspout had broken off from its watery base, and he watched it slowly retract into the cloud layer. As suddenly as it had begun, the sea-tempest had ended.

As he began to make his way down the ladder, there came a shout from the lookout above.

AILIA LOOKED ANXIOUSLY at Ana: the old woman had not eaten all day, but had sat in a corner with her cat in her lap, looking very pale and drawn. When the girls spoke to her she appeared not to hear them. Waves thudded against the hull, boards creaked, ropes groaned, while in the distance the terrified livestock contributed to the cacophony with a din of their own: yet Ana showed no reaction. There was a slight frown on her face, her lips moved yet no sound came from them, and her hands were restless in her lap: their knobbed rheumatic fingers flexed continually. Ailia wondered if she might be praying, and to what gods her petitions would be addressed. For her own part, she tried very hard not to think of all the shipwreck stories she had heard. There had been a terrible one off Great Island's southern coast, many years ago. Ailia herself had been far too young at the time to be able to recall it, yet the villagers *still* spoke of it in hushed tones . . . She watched the wild orbits of the oil lamp, swinging from the ceiling above their heads, and sent up a silent prayer of her own.

"Is it my imagination," ventured Lorelyn presently from her corner, "or is the storm dying down a bit?"

They sat very still, listening intently to the sounds of wind and water. It was true: the fury of both had abated somewhat.

"And have you noticed how much warmer it is?" Lorelyn added.

Ana's eyes opened. "I believe," she murmured, "we are nearing our destination."

"Are you all right, Ana?" Ailia asked, turning to the old woman in concern.

Ana still looked pale, but she nodded at the girl and smiled. "Perfectly all right, thank you."

"Ana, I've been thinking," said Lorelyn, also going over to the old woman. "What would happen if the Zimbourans *were* to find the Star Stone? What would they do?"

"We must see that they do not get it," replied Ana. Her manner was as confident as ever.

"But they're holding us prisoner, aren't they?"

"Not for long, I promise you," the old woman replied. "We must go to the mountains in Trynisia, and seek out the Guardians."

"The what?" inquired Lorelyn.

"The Guardians are votaries of the Star Stone," Ana explained. "Long ago, their order was entrusted with the task of watching over the sacred gem until the time came to relinquish it to the Tryna Lia, even should her coming take ten thousand years. They also promised to give her, and anyone who came with her, any sort of assistance that should be required. Bereborn told the Jana monks that the Guardians remained in Trynisia after the Disaster. They hid themselves among the northern mountains, to keep watch over the Stone for all time. It was a vow that was binding not only on them but on all their descendants to come."

"I don't remember anything about that in the stories," Ailia remarked.

"The order was a secret one. Few in Trynisia knew of it."

Heavy boots pounded along the deck above, and a babel of bellowing voices rose. Ailia's relief at the storm's passing vanished. What new danger threatened them?

DAMION GAZED ABOUT him in wonder.

The rain had ceased and the sea was calmer now. A few ice floes were scattered on the rolling waves, the largest no bigger than a rowboat. The air was mild, even balmy: the sailors had shed their heavy coats. He saw Jomar standing not far off and staggered toward him. Without speaking, the Mohara man proffered his tin flask. Damion took a quick swig of the contents, which burned in his throat.

"What happened?" he rasped, handing the flask back. "Where *are* we?" Jomar merely shrugged.

The Zimbouran captain and his underlings were in the middle of a vociferous conference.

"What are they saying?" Damion asked.

Jomar frowned. "The captain says all the ship's compasses have stopped working. It must be the storms: lightning can do that to lodestones. But some of the sailors think it's magic. They're terrified." He snorted. "Idiots."

"They can't sail by the sun, either—not with all this cloud."

"Wouldn't make any difference if they could see it. You haven't noticed, being belowdecks, but the sun's been doing strange things lately too."

"What?"

There was a shout from the crow's nest, and all the sailors on deck looked toward the bows. Damion looked too. The sky above the sails was still overcast, but far ahead, on the northern horizon, a gap had opened, win-dowlike, in the clouds. Through it he could see the sun shining in a far-off blue sky, and below it lay some darker shapes that seemed to sit upon the sea like icebergs. Clouds? As Damion stared the wide arching gap slowly shifted its shape, but the darker forms beneath did not change: they looked solid, and seemed to be nearer than before. Mountains—the profile of a distant land?

He studied the shapes with interest as the ships sailed on—saw them resolve themselves into a blue distant coast. *Could* it be Trynisia? If it was, then they had suc-ceeded where no other explorer had . . . A warm breeze off the water caressed his face, which only minutes ago had tingled with cold. How it was that this place should have a separate climate he could not understand, but he was ignorant of geography, so he did not waste his time on speculation. This could indeed be Trynisia—the "warm and verdant" land of the north. In spite of himself, he was excited.

There were a few rocks protruding above the water, not large enough to be called islands: others lurked below like sea monsters, shadowy and dangerous. As he stared over the side into the blue-green depths to starboard, the surface broke in a trail of white spray about a stone's throw from the hull, and something gray and gleaming came and went, so quickly that for a moment he half wondered if he had imagined it. Then he saw it again—a long lithe shape, keeping pace with the ship's progress through the waves. It might have been an enormous fish, longer than a man is tall, but its sleek, streaked sides bore no scales, and the fin that divided the water above it was a smooth sickle-shape rather than a fish's fin of webbed spines. A dolphin! How often had he watched these graceful creatures swimming in the Kaanish seas? He had thought they only liked the warm waters of the south.

The dolphin raised its head above the water, revealing long beaklike jaws full of small pearly teeth, and a large eye that looked up at him. Damion marveled at the gaze of that great dark eye, so unlike a fish's. It seemed to gleam with intelligence—as though the ocean, having thus far endured his inquisitive regard, now inspected him in its turn. Damion stared at the dolphin, and it stared at him, and something moved between them: the creature's toothy grin widened, and it uttered a merry chirruping sound.

In a moment Damion regretted his prolonged scrutiny of the dolphin, for one of the soldiers noticed it, and, rushing into the cabin, reappeared with a spear in one hand, hefting it like a harpoon. At the last moment, however, one of the sailors saw and ran toward the man, seizing the butt-end of the spear and screaming at him in Zimbouran. The soldier's face darkened: he clouted the sailor across the face, sending the man spinning to the deck. But he lowered the spear and turned away from the railing.

"What was all *that* about?" Damion asked Jomar.

Jomar's lip curled. "More superstition. The sailor said the Elei were friends with dolphins and could speak their language. He thinks that if we kill it the Elei gods will get angry and cause another storm, and our ships will be wrecked."

"The Kaans had a sort of reverence for dolphins too, now that I come to think of it," Damion remarked. "They would never harm one, even if they were hungry." Superstition aside, the ship's occupants were soon glad that they had not killed the dolphin. It resurfaced in front of them, riding the bow-wave, and it became apparent that the creature, for reasons of its own, was guiding them through the perilous rocks. Had these animals some ancestral memory of swimming before Elei ships?

Damion, gazing after the creature, could not dismiss the thought that within its dark gleaming eye he had seen a soul.

THE THREE WOMEN LOOKED up as heavy footsteps approached their door. It was flung open, and Ailia cringed; but the two Zimbouran men did not enter. They merely stood and gestured to the women to come out.

Ana rose, leaning heavily upon a barrel. The two girls rushed to help her. "If you would hand me my cane, my dears?"

Ailia passed the stick to her and the old woman stood, a trifle unsteadily but with determination. Lorelyn slipped her own strong young arm under Ana's, supporting her.

Ailia stooped to pick up the gray cat, which was mewing anxiously.

"What's all this about?" Lorelyn wondered out loud as she helped Ana across the lower deck and—with more difficulty—up the ladder. There could be no doubt about it: the wind blowing through the hatch above *was* warm. As she ascended the ladder behind Lorelyn, Ailia heard the other girl shout: "Land!"

Ailia scrambled up through the hatchway in her turn, hampered by the cat, which she held in her left arm. She passed the animal to Ana, then stood staring across the water.

There it was—a sloping sandy shore, lush verdure above it, and a range of green misty hills.

"We have come to the end of our journey," said Ana. "But not of our mission."

She looked much better now, Ailia noted. It must be the fresh air. All her own fear and misery had vanished in the glow of wonderment. "Welessan was right!" she exulted. "About there being a warm land in the north." The sea chart on the scroll had been real, after all. It had led their captors safely to their goal. "It is, it must be . . . "

"Trynisia," said Damion's voice behind them. "They have found Trynisia."

12

At the Back of the North Wind

THE PRISONERS HUDDLED together on the beach in a little silent knot, watching the noisy jubilant groups of soldiers and sailors. No more boats were coming ashore: King Khalazar apparently had decided to remain safe aboard his galleon until the soldiers had scouted the unknown land for hostile inhabitants and other dangers. The God-king's ship lay apart from the others, its heavily gilded and ornamented aftercastle gleaming in the light of the setting sun. The flag of Zimboura, a black star on a red field, hung from the rigging: above it there streamed a banner with a man's face in a golden sunburst. The royal standard.

"Just think," said Ailia, shivering. "*He's* on board that ship. So close!"

"I'd prefer not to think about it," Damion muttered.

Sailors on the ships were engaged in lowering the live-stock in canvas slings to large raftlike boats waiting be-neath. At the shore, goats, sheep, and horses were herded from the rafts into the shallows, from which they emerged panting and dripping. Mandrake's white palfrey came ashore in a spray of foam, snorting and tossing its sodden mane. Several vicious-looking guard dogs were also brought over from the ships: Damion recognized the big black-and-white animals as a fearsome Zimbouran breed, half boarhound and half mastiff. Their great jaws were bound with leather muzzles, and even their handlers treated them with respect. The Zimbourans, it seemed, were taking no chances in this alien land.

Ahead of them rose low, sandy bluffs, and beyond these steep green hills, almost high enough to be called mountains, with summits lost in heavy hanging mists. Presently the sun disappeared behind them and its saffron-colored afterglow faded from the sky. In the gathering dusk a group of officers stood poring over the scroll by the light of a driftwood campfire, arguing and gesticulating. Then Zefron Shezzek tossed the ancient parchment into the flames, and the soldiers laughed and jeered as the once-precious document blackened and shriveled to ash. One of them thrust his sword-point down in the sand, and shouted something. Damion took it at first for a display of temper, then realized the man was probably enacting a ritual—claiming the land for Zimboura. The crescent of cliffs flung back echoes of his voice, as if in mockery.

Not far away a scout party had assembled, saddling some horses and laying heavy packs on others. Damion wished he could understand Zimbouran: there was a great torrent of conversation, much of it sounding quite heated. After some time had passed Shezzek approached the captives and spoke to them in Maurish.

"You are all to come with us. Do as you are told and no one will be hurt." He then added something in Zimbouran to Jomar. The Mohara man grunted a reply, then watched with resentful eyes as Shezzek strode back to the scout party.

"What did he say?" asked Lorelyn.

"I'm going to be their tracker," said Jomar. "They must be afraid of wild animals."

Ana stooped to pick up Greymalkin, but when she carried the cat toward the horses Shezzek stepped forward shouting and waving his arms threateningly. The gray cat hissed at him, then sprang from her mistress's arms and fled across the beach. Ailia and Lorelyn cried out.

"No! She'll die in the wild!" protested Lorelyn.

The half-breed turned on her, scowling, and Ana placed a restraining hand on Lorelyn's arm. "Greymalkin can take care of herself, dear. She has lived in the wilderness before."

"It's cruel." Lorelyn glared at Shezzek, but he had already turned his back on her, shouting orders at the soldiers.

The captives were forced to mount horses, Zimbouran riders taking the reins of their mounts and leading them. Lorelyn was placed on the white palfrey. Damion found something vaguely disturbing in that choice of mount; then he remembered that in ancient Zimboura human sacrifices had been led to the altar on white horses. There were a dozen mounted soldiers, including Jomar, and a couple of dog-handlers with several muzzled guard dogs on long leads. Shezzek snapped a command in Zimbouran, and the party rode farther down the beach to a place where the bluffs became a gentle sandy slope. Beyond and above this lay a steeper slope, coarse meadow-grass giving way farther up to thick-forested hills. Between the nearest two lay a wide pass, through which nothing at all could be seen but the grayness of trailing mists. The dusk did not deepen as they rode uphill: in fact, it seemed to Ailia as they rode into the woods that the misty twilight under the trees was lightening. *But that's not possible,* she thought. *The sun only set a couple of hours ago . . .* She glanced through the tree trunks to the northeast. That was the dawn, streaking the sky with yellow and crimson!

A line from an old story came to her. "*In Trynisia the sun never set all summer long, nor rose in wintertime.*"

As they rode up the slope toward the pass, the blazing limb of the sun rose from behind the hills, only a short distance from the place where it had gone down.

AS THEY RODE with their captors down the far side of the range Damion emerged from his worried thoughts and noticed his surroundings. A vast valley lay below them, through which a river wound from east to west in long shining coils: on its far side were more hills, and far beyond them lay true mountains, taller than those of the Maurainian coastal range, with jutting peaks of ribbed rock capped by ice. As the party rode slowly downhill the pines and firs gave way to a leafy forest even thicker than the aged groves of Selenna. There were great, centuries-old oaks and elms, wide around as temple columns, mottled with moss and frilled with fungi. Most of the trees were in early green leaf, and some were in flower: though Damion was no better versed in botany than geography, he recognized the white and rose-pink garlands of wild cherry and apple trees, and flowering almonds still in bud, and hawthorn bloom like drifts of blowing snow. Presently his gaze fastened on one clump of ancient trees, with trunks so gray and gnarled that they looked more like rocky outcrops than living wood.

Surely those were olive trees, such as he had seen growing in the Archipelagoes of Kaan? And climbing the trunk and limbs of one huge cedar, right up to its towering crown, were great tangled skeins of what looked to him very much like grapevines run wild. He had seen many such vines, pruned and tamed, growing in neat rows in Maurainian vineyards. But how could they grow and thrive here, where the winter must be infinitely harsher?

Through the trees blazed a gold-orange brilliance, like a fire burning among the boughs: the glow of the already returning sun. Here was yet another oddity. What was this place, that it should have not only an unnaturally warm climate but so brief a night as well? Damion seemed to recall reading of northern lands where for half the year the sun never went down at all—where night never came for months on end. Not understanding how this could be possible, he had always dismissed it as fancy. Now it seemed that this old fable, too, had some basis in fact.

There was a shout from up ahead: their captors had called a halt. Some of the soldiers dismounted, apparently to examine something on the forest floor. The dogs snuffled at it and whined excitedly through their bound jaws. It appeared to be the spoor of a large animal. Jomar, after studying the prints with the intensity of an experienced tracker, said he could not identify the creature that had made them.

"It's a cat—but not a lion or a leopard," the puzzled Mohara declared as they moved on. "It looks almost like a cross between the two."

"A libbard," said Ailia.

"A *what?*" Jomar stared at her.

"A libbard: a lion-leopard. I read about them in Welessan's travel book. Libbards were supposed to be mythical creatures, like unicorns and dragons. But perhaps they're real."

"They sound dangerous to me. I hope this one isn't lurking in the bushes somewhere," remarked Damion.

Jomar shook his head. "It's an old track."

Shezzek turned in his saddle and barked, "No talking!" Jomar fell back sullen-faced, and Damion looked warily around him. Trynisia, he reflected, as an isolated continent might well have its own unique fauna. He thought of the giant flightless birds and other peculiar animals that haunted the Outer Isles, far away in the Lesser Ocean. The trees of this land might be familiar, but who could say what strange creatures might dwell among them?

As they moved deeper into the forest they soon began to glimpse its animal life. In one glade they surprised a young hind at the edge of a stream and saw her leap away, all grace and fear; in another a whole flock of wild pigeons whirred up from the grass at their approach, the sudden loud applause of their wings startling the horses. And once, in the distance, they spied a whole herd of what seemed to be hornless, dapple-gray beasts of the antelope kind: but when these bounded in alarm from the shelter of the trees into full sun, the color of their coats showed a soft bluish-purple, spattered with white spots like stars.

"Pantheons!" exclaimed Ailia, forgetting that she was not allowed to speak. *The star-beasts! Welessan wrote about them too. They lived in Elarainia's country, Eldimia; but the Fairfolk brought a few to Trynisia.* As they rode on Ailia tried to remember what else she had read in the book of Welessan the Wanderer. "*Trynysia, that som calle the Londe at the Back of the Northe Wynd, lyeth farre to the northe, where ben the Ocean of Ice. In that londe the sun setteth not all sommer longe, ne riseth in wynter-time. Therein dwellen the Elei, the Chyldren of Fayerie, wyth the Spirits of the Woodes and Wateres, and Beestes passyng straunge: gryphons, unicornes, grete wormes, and the lyke . . .*" Then was this really Trynisia? If so, Welessan had not been a complete fraud, after all. There were no such things as gryphons or "great worms," and his fabulous "vision of the spheres" might be dismissed as a flight of fancy, but that was not to say that his descriptions of Trynisia itself were unreliable. The warm and verdant island in the north existed, exactly as he had described it.

After a few hours they entered a clearing, a wide grassy expanse scattered with pale rocks and surrounded by more gray-trunked olive trees. Here Shezzek called a halt, and they all dismounted. Ana and the others were herded together at spear-point, while the Zimbourans gathered kindling and made two rings of pieces of loose rock to set campfires in. Once the flames were burning high and strong, two huge iron pots were set up over them, to cook a sort of soup made with dry salted meat from the ship's stores. The prisoners were not offered any. Jomar, who had volunteered to stand watch over them, was not allowed to eat either until he was relieved. Damion guessed that the Mohara man preferred to be their guard since he could then wait for his meal and eat it alone, rather than join the Zimbourans by the campfires.

Ailia, Damion, and Lorelyn sat down wearily on the ground, but Ana approached the cook-fires, offering amiable advice to the men stirring the pots. It was ill received, and at an angry shout from Shezzek she shrugged and returned to the others. They were all growing hungry, trying hard not to look at the pots or smell the aroma of their simmering contents. Ailia leaned back against one of the larger stones rising from the meadow-grass. It was flat on top, but had a rounded shape; her fingers, running idly over its chalk-white surface, encountered grooves too regular in shape to be natural. She looked at them sharply, then at the other pale fragments strewn across the clearing. She saw, now, the fallen stone columns that had been indistinguishable at first from the trunks of rotting trees, so heavily covered were they in lichens and creeping vines. Getting up, her weariness forgotten, she examined one more closely. Its marble sides bore lines of carving in bas-relief, a pattern of leaves and flowers. Worn and weathered as it was, its delicate intricacy was unmistakable.

"Look," she whispered to the others. They all turned and stared at the stone.

Damion whistled softly through his teeth. "I wondered if this land was once inhabited. So many of the trees and plants here are the sort that people cultivate: fruit trees and so on. Orchards and vineyards must have been planted here long ago, and run wild over the centuries."

"Who planted the trees? The Elei?" Ailia asked.

Ana nodded. "This must be the remnant of one of their great houses," she said, gesturing to the tumbled stones.

"Five centuries have passed since it fell, but it was most likely built long before that: a thousand years ago, or more."

The Elei. Ailia had always thought of them half-consciously as faerie-tale figures, half-mortal children of minor angels: majestic beings in flowing robes with faces of unearthly beauty. But of course they had been real people, real as any that lived today . . . And they had lived here, on this island. *Trynisia—we are in Trynisia.* Like an exhausted swimmer who no longer fights the waves but floats with them limp and unresisting, Ailia found herself surrendering to the events that had befallen her, no longer questioning, but simply accepting the strange new reality around her. Surrounded by uncertainty and unnumbered fears, she found herself thinking not of them but of the Elei, wondering what it must have been like to dwell in this land when the old Commonwealth was alive, and Trynisia the world's great center of culture and learning.

"If the Elei were really here," she said out loud, "then their holy city must have been real too. Liamar." They all looked toward the dim blue mountains in the north. "And—the Star Stone!"

"Yes. Chance, fate, providence," mused Ana, "whatever you choose to call it, has placed us all here in the land of the Stone. The question is, what are we going to do about it?"

"*Do* about it?" echoed Lorelyn.

"*Us?*" said Ailia faintly.

"Us," repeated Ana, her tone calm and firm. "There is no one else."

Damion stared at Ana. "You mean," he said slowly,

"that we should try and take the Stone away from the Zimbourans?"

"Or find it before they do!" exclaimed Lorelyn, her expression turning eager.

Ailia looked at her in alarm. "But to do that we would have to escape!"

"And so we must. But I cannot tell you exactly where the resting place of the Stone is," Ana said, "for if we are recaptured you can be made to tell all you know. I will guide you there instead, if you will trust me."

Ailia trembled at those words. She knew where the Stone lay: Welessan had described the sacred shrine of the Stone in his book. If she were caught and tortured, would she tell? She opened her mouth, then closed it again. If knowledge was dangerous, perhaps her companions should not even know that she knew. "How can we escape?" she asked instead. "Would Jomar help us? Didn't he try to leave the Zimbourans before, Father Damion?"

"Yes—but things are a little different now. We can't offer him freedom and safety, as we did in Maurainia."

"Couldn't you ask, all the same? He might say yes."

Damion stood up, took a few sidling steps closer to their guard, and spoke to him in a low voice. "Jomar—listen to me."

Jomar continued to gaze blank-faced into the distance. "Stoop over, as if you're looking at something on the ground," he hissed out of the corner of his mouth.

Damion did so, pretending to examine a broken capital.

"All right," said Jomar after a moment. "One of the officers was watching us, but he's gone. What exactly did you want?"

"To escape," Damion whispered back.

"Is that all?" Jomar snorted. "Have you noticed we're on an island? In case you don't know, that's a piece of land surrounded by *water.* Were you planning to swim home?"

"I thought perhaps we might get back to the ships somehow, talk the slaves into a mutiny, or . . . or"—Damion dropped his eyes before Jomar's incredulous stare—"I was hoping you might have an idea."

"Why am I listening to you?" grumbled Jomar, glowering at the ground. "Back in Maurainia we had a chance, but now—what's the use? This place is uninhabited. Even if we could get away from the Zims, we'd be marooned here—"

"Not uninhabited," corrected Ana, also speaking in a low voice. "The Guardians still live here."

"The what?" asked Jomar and Damion together. Ana explained.

"If the Guardians have experienced the same visions the Maurainian Nemerei have," she concluded, "they will already be on the alert for our coming. When we arrive on Mount Elendor, they will wait and watch. If they are satisfied that Lorelyn is indeed the one foretold in the prophecies, they will give her the jewel as promised."

"And then?" prompted Damion.

"And then they will assist her and her companions to leave Trynisia, if we ask it of them. They will even convey us to Eldimia if we wish."

"Eldimia is a real place too, then?" asked Lorelyn with interest.

"It is."

"It wasn't on the sea chart," added Damion. "Where is it?"

"Ever since the Disaster its location has been kept secret," Ana answered. "But the Guardians know where it lies."

"In the old stories Eldimia was in a sort of faerie place, the Otherworld," Lorelyn commented.

"That's true," said Ailia. "But some of the stories called Eldimia the Land Beyond the World's End. As though it were a real country you could travel to, if you only went far enough."

"But *where* was it exactly?" asked Damion.

"East of the sun and west of the moon," replied Ailia, looking apologetic. "Those are the only directions they ever gave."

"*That's* a lot of help," snorted Jomar.

There was a pause; then Damion spoke again. "What if the Guardians of the Stone are *not* satisfied that Lorelyn is the one they're waiting for?"

"Then," said Ana placidly, "we will be on our own."

"But—they wouldn't let the Zimbourans take the Stone!" exclaimed Lorelyn.

"Yes, I am afraid they would. It was stolen once before, you know, and later returned to its rightful place. The Guardians were commanded not to take any action at all until the Tryna Lia herself appeared, and required their aid. That was their sacred vow, and they will hold to it no matter what happens. They believe that she is destined to take the Stone, and that no earthly agency can prevent her coming. So they would accept its theft by the Zimbourans as just another turn of fate: after all, Zimbourans stole it once before, and it was brought back to Liamar. They would bide their time, waiting for fate to return the Stone again, and for the Tryna Lia to come."

"Well, the Tryna Lia *has* come," said Lorelyn. "If you're right about me, that is."

"Tryna Lia!" Jomar snorted, turning on her. "You don't actually believe all that falderal? You're no more a princess than I'm king of Zimboura."

"The Tryna Lia isn't that sort of princess," Lorelyn explained earnestly. "It just means 'leader.' "

"Well, you're not leading *me* anywhere—and definitely not on a wild-goose chase in the wilderness. I'm better off with the Zims."

"Please, Jomar," Ailia implored. "We need your help. And don't you want to be free again?"

"You still haven't come up with a *plan*," the Mohara man pointed out, exasperated. "How are we going to escape from this camp? Just walk away?"

"No, we will ride," old Ana replied, her face and tone perfectly serious. "We'll take some of their horses, and some supplies too. There are packhorses already laden. But first we must wait for the Zimbourans to go to sleep."

"They're not all going to go to sleep at the same time!" retorted Jomar, beginning to lose his temper.

"They will, once the sleeping-potion I slipped into their stewpots takes effect."

The young people stopped arguing and looked about them. The camp *did* seem unusually still. One man nodded over his bowl. Others lay sprawled on the grass, and there was a sound of snoring.

"They really should have searched me when they first apprehended me," said Ana with a shake of her white head. "I always carry my herbs about with me, never knowing when I might be called upon to heal someone. I put a couple of bags of the herbs I use for sleeping-drafts up my sleeves, and poured in the contents when the cooks weren't looking. Well, Jomar, what do you say now?" she went on. "Will you come with us, and help us? We may have need of you."

"Come with you!" A broad white grin suddenly spread across the man's dusky face, like the sun breaking through cloud. He unsheathed his sword, tossed it in the air, and caught it again by the hilt. "Valdur's teeth!" he crowed. "To cheat the Zims out of their treasure—what wouldn't I give for that?"

"Then it's decided," said Ana. "And we must be quick: the herb I gave the Zimbourans will only make them sleep lightly, for an hour or so. If we delay, they will begin to rouse."

Jomar strode across the camp to stand over the slumbering Shezzek, who lay sprawled on his back, snoring. The Mohara man's mouth worked, and he fingered his sword-hilt: the weapon was still loose in his hand. Behind him Ana spoke in a neutral tone, as if to the air. "Mohara warriors do not kill sleeping foes."

Jomar sheathed his sword. "Another time," he muttered.

They hastened to where the horses were tethered, walking as quietly as they could, but none of their captors stirred. Ailia looked down in terror at a dozing soldier's flushed face. "If they wake—"

"Don't think about it. Just move," hissed Jomar.

"Take all the weapons, but leave them some food. And untether all of the horses," Ana directed them. "That will delay any organized pursuit."

Jomar reached for the bridle of Shezzek's big black

stallion. "Could it be this easy?" he murmured. Even as he spoke there came a loud growl from behind them.

"The dogs!" hissed Damion. "*They're* not drugged!"

Ana turned to face the guard dogs, which advanced in a pack over the supine bodies of their handlers, bristling and snarling. Their muzzles had been removed to allow them to eat, and their lips were peeled back to show their fangs. Raising one hand, Ana spoke in a soft low voice. The brutes halted, their ears pricked as if in astonishment, their hackles lowering. The lead dog approached the old woman, and as the other travelers watched in amazement it licked her hand tentatively. She smiled, laid a hand on the great black-and-white head.

Jomar muttered something in his native tongue. "She really *is* a witch," he added in Maurish.

"Animals aren't so difficult to deal with, really," Ana observed, scratching the dog's ears. "I only wish humans were so easy to manage." She turned to the smallest of the sturdy pack-ponies. "If someone would give me a leg up, we can be on our way."

Lorelyn rode pillion with Damion, while Ailia clambered up behind Jomar on the black stallion—"And don't you *dare* fall off," he warned her fiercely—and Ana followed on her small sturdy mount, leading two other well-laden packhorses. All the remaining horses followed them too: obeying a herd instinct, perhaps, or else Ana's mysterious influence on animals had something to do with it. In haste the companions rode away from the camp, with many nervous backward glances. Together they plunged into the depths of the forest, heading for the cloud-hung mountains beyond.

* * *

THEY MADE GOOD PROGRESS at first, fear speeding their flight. After a few minutes the riderless horses began to stray and fall back, tearing up wild grasses or stopping to drink at small forest streams. The dogs also trailed them for a time, like a pack of tame wolves, until some scent or other caught their attention and they all made off through the trees baying furiously.

Jomar was pleased. "It'll be hard for the Zims to follow us now, without any mounts, or dogs to follow our scent."

"They'll find the animals eventually, though, won't they?" worried Ailia, who was starting to have second thoughts. "And then they'll be after us—and they'll be so angry—"

"We'll be long gone by then—but," added Jomar, turning to Ana, "you had *better* be right about those Guardians, or we're all dead." Ana said nothing in reply: she was apparently concentrating hard on staying in the saddle, as well as ensuring that their provisioned pack-beasts stayed with them. She led them without a rope, turning from time to time and calling to them softly.

After an hour's hard riding, with no sound of pursuit from behind, they came upon the river. In its midst lay the ruined piles of a long-fallen bridge, but the water was shallow enough for horses to ford. The mountain that was their destination lay on the far side.

"We had best cross the river here," declared Ana. "Farther up it will be swifter, and deeper, as it comes down from the mountains." As they headed down the bank there was a sudden rustling in the bushes a few paces away, and Ailia turned to look. A gray-furred animal emerged from the greenery and strolled unconcernedly toward them. For a moment she thought it was a lynx. Then she called out in amazement.

"Why, it's *Greymalkin!*" she exclaimed, pointing. "However did she find us? I thought the poor thing was lost in the wilderness forever." Lorelyn sprang down from her horse with a cry of delight and snatched up the cat, which purred loudly and rubbed its head against her cheek.

Ana did not look in the least surprised. "Cats are very good at trailing their owners. And Greymalkin is better than most—aren't you, my dear?"

Lorelyn held the cat up to Ana, who took it in her arms. "And she's caught up with us just in time, clever thing. A little longer and there'd have been a river between us. You wouldn't have liked the water much, puss!"

The only answer Greymalkin gave to that was a superior look, and a contented thrumming from her throat. Ana set the cat on the pommel of her saddle, and they rode on.

It was not a difficult crossing. At its deepest point the water was up to the horses' chests, and the legs of the riders were soaked from the knees down, but the river's bottom was flat and even and its flow sluggish. Once they were on the far bank Ana suggested it would be safe to call a brief halt, and after following the bank for about a hundred yards they all dismounted, stretched their stiff muscles, and let the horses have a long drink from the river. The sun still had not risen by many degrees, choosing instead to circle the horizon of this strange hyperborean land. As they rested Ana explained to them all the natural phenomenon of the Midnight Sun: how for months in summer the daylight never faded from the sky here in the far north, due to the canted axis of the great sphere that was the world, and its position in its long orbit around the sun. In midwinter the effect was reversed, and the spinning north pole never saw the light of day. But still it seemed like magic to Ailia—as though here in Trynisia the natural laws that governed the rest of the world were somehow held in abeyance.

"Here in the northlands high summer was one long day, untouched by the shades of evening," Ana said, "but still its inhabitants loved the winter dark. Though it bound their land in night and bitter cold for months on end, the Elei always rejoiced to see the stars again. For from the Celestial Empire their divine ancestors came long ago."

"How is it that there are trees and vines growing here," Damion asked presently, "when the only other land I saw from the ship was icy and barren? How could there *be* a country like this, here in the far north?"

Lorelyn answered him. "In the stories Ailia told, it was the gods who made Trynisia the way it is. In the beginning the island was covered in ice, but they made it warm and filled it with all sorts of trees and animals. They could grow anything they wanted here."

"But that's just a myth," said Damion. "I was wondering what the *real* explanation was." No one had any suggestions to make.

Ana found some skin-bottles in one of the packs and knelt by the river to dip up some water. "We must boil it before drinking, I'm afraid," she cautioned. "And that will mean building a fire. But we must take care the smoke doesn't give us away; and we must hide the fire-pit afterwards, as well as we can."

"We shouldn't rest here too long," Jomar advised. "The Zims may already be after us. I know Shezzek: he doesn't give up easily."

"I shouldn't be surprised if they were afraid to follow us," commented Damion. "Zimbourans are a superstitious lot, aren't they? It will be terrifying for them to wake up, as if from an enchanted sleep, and find that not only we but all their beasts and even their weapons have vanished! Maybe they'll think Ana put a witch-spell on them!"

"They're terrified of Khalazar too, though," Jomar told him. "Some of them believe he's a god, remember. They'd rather hunt for us, even without horses and dogs and swords, than go back and tell him they lost us. And they can always send a messenger to get reinforcements."

Ailia sat in silence, listening to their talk. Again and again her eyes strayed to Damion's face. At the Academy Ailia had held many imaginary conversations with the priest, all of them sparkling (she liked to think) with intelligence and wit; now, in his real presence, and in these strange and awesome surroundings, she felt tongue-tied. At last she ventured to give voice to her thoughts. "I wonder what we will find on Elendor," she said. "Do you know, I'm almost afraid to see the Star Stone. I don't want it to be just a bit of ugly black meteor-iron. I so want it to be just as it was in the stories—a beautiful, magical gem."

"I know what you mean," said Damion. "But the Stone was an important symbol—like the Sacred Flame of the Faith—and symbols are very powerful. In the old wars between Maurainia and Marakor our soldiers used to carry torches lit from the Flame—and they used them to burn whole towns and villages."

Ailia stared at him in shock. The Sacred Flame of Orendyl used to harm, to destroy . . . "I didn't know."

Damion gazed at the far-off peaks. "To the Elei, the Stone was the symbol of all they valued: beauty and purity and the generosity of their gods. But to the Zimbourans it would be a sign that the time has come for their nation to rise and conquer the world. Whether that's true or not doesn't matter: they will *think* it is, and act accordingly. If we don't find the Stone first, King Khalazar's men will—and the whole world could end up being at war just because of a piece of stone."

"How horrible!" Ailia remarked. "And how awful to think that so much depends on *us!*"

"We'll just have to do what we can," he said.

With that the conversation ceased. Jomar waded into the river, to try and catch some trout he had spied there: he fished with a bow and arrow, Mohara-fashion. Ana, Damion, and Lorelyn sat together on the bank. The horses drank from the shallows or rested near the water's edge. Ailia sat down with her back against the trunk of a tree and stretched out her legs: their muscles still ached from gripping the horse's sides. The circling arctic sun shed a soft slanted light like that of late afternoon. It gave to the lower reaches of the sky a dusty, aureate cast that reminded her of the dim golden backgrounds in old oil paintings. The landscape before her might have been a pastoral scene from just such a painting, and created the same sense of tranquillity. Trees, earth, river: everything the rich mellow light fell upon was subtly transformed. It beat through the young green leaves on the boughs above her head, so that their finest venous traceries, their most delicate maculations, were minutely shadowed forth; it streamed through the translucent bodies of the mayflies hovering over the water, turning them to motes of dancing fire; it turned the droplets in the reeds at the river's edge to prisms at whose rainbow-vivid, inconstant colors she stared half-mesmerized. With the light came a languor that stole upon her like sleep, calm and easeful. Bullfrogs sounded their bass notes among the reeds, and farther up the riverbank a blue heron stood still as a sentry, watching the water. The soporific scene combined with her fatigue to lull Ailia almost into a doze, and she gave a start when the heron rose in sharp, sudden flight, flapping away along the bank.

She looked anxiously about, but saw nothing on either bank of the river. The others had not noticed the heron's flight. Perhaps she was just feeling edgy. She settled back among the rushes again. And then she realized that the bullfrogs had all fallen silent.

She sat up a second time, glancing around her. The river flowed on, deep and lucid, its gliding surface smooth as glass. But she saw the water near the far bank ripple, bending the reflections of the overhanging trees. The river was opaque from this angle, reflecting the gold-tinted sky above; but still the impression remained of a large body moving just beneath the surface. Were there crocodiles here? she wondered. She doubted this climate was hot enough for them. But no fish could be large enough to make a ripple like that. Unless perhaps she had imagined it—

The water stirred again, an eddy foamed and swirled

in the midst of the current, and something dark and glistening—like a rock, only where no rock had been before—broke the surface briefly and vanished again.

"Jomar!" she yelled.

The Mohara man lowered his bow and glared at her. "What is it? You'll scare off all the fish, shouting like that."

"There's something in the river—something big!"

Jomar swung around. There could be no mistaking it now—he, too could see the undefined shape moving beneath the water, a shattered shadow like a passing figure seen through dimpled glass.

"Is it a crocodile?" asked Ailia as Jomar splashed hurriedly ashore and joined the others standing among the reeds.

"If it is," answered the Mohara, "it's bigger then any croc I ever—"

Foam swirled once more, and the gleaming rocklike thing reappeared. As they watched it thrust high into the air on a long sinuous neck that swung to and fro, dripping. Neck and head were covered in gray-green scales that gleamed dully in the sun. A black, cloven tongue flickered at the end of the blunt snout. The horses began to snort and pull at their tethers.

"It's some sort of giant water snake," declared Jomar, raising his bow.

"There's another!" exclaimed Lorelyn as a second dark scaly head thrust up out of the water not far from the first.

"And another—over there, look," added Damion, pointing.

The water was churning like a pot on the boil. Jomar

stared, lowered his bow again. "The whole river's *swarming* with them—"

"Back away from the water—slowly," said Ana in a low voice, stooping to pick up the growling Greymalkin.

They obeyed in silence, retreating toward the nervous horses and loosing their tethers. The long, glaucous necks—there were several of them now—dipped and swung and intertwined in midcurrent, forked tongues darting in rhythm: then as one the serpents' heads all turned toward the travelers, and sent up a manifold hiss.

"We've been seen," said Ana as Damion helped her into her saddle. "Ride away—as fast as you can!" There was more urgency in her voice than they had ever heard before.

The horses were as eager as they to leave. They fled the bank and were soon riding among trees again, the river left far behind.

"So your magic animal-charming skills don't extend to snakes, Ana?" remarked Jomar caustically when at last the companions had pulled their sweating mounts to a halt.

"Would they have attacked us?" asked Ailia.

"Not *they,*" said Ana, holding her still-bristling cat with one hand and patting her pony's neck with the other. "*It.* There was but one body for all those heads. It was a single creature."

They all stared at her. "What do you mean? What *was* it?" demanded Lorelyn.

"A hydra. They always have more than one head—sometimes as many as seven or nine."

Jomar snorted. But Ailia recalled the large, dark body she had seen moving just below the river's surface;

remembered also the odd synchronous movements of the serpent heads, as though they were all linked by one dominating will.

"And they're dangerous?" asked Lorelyn. "Will that one chase us?"

Ana's face was grave. "I think not. Hydras are not swift runners. They do not need to be. They are venomous, but their poison is not in their fangs like an adder's: they breathe it out, in the form of a deadly vapor that can travel nearly as fast and as far as an arrow. And they are very hard to kill. If you cut off one of a hydra's heads, *two* more will eventually grow in its place. It is said that they are not natural creatures, but were created by servants of Valdur who released them in the countries of their foes, to poison all the rivers and lakes. The Elei's enemies must have loosed a few when they attacked the island, and the creatures have lived and bred here ever since. Had I known that hydras dwelt here I would not have allowed any of you so near the river."

"And we were *in* the water," said Ailia, shuddering. "It's a good thing the hydra wasn't there when we crossed the river."

"If the Zimbourans do follow our trail," said Damion, "they'll have to cross the river too. They're riding into more danger than they know."

"Good," grunted Jomar.

Ana looked solemn. "Perhaps. But we have been fortunate, and they may be as well. We cannot count on their being delayed at the river. Let us ride on!"

13

The Lost Land

THEY WERE ALL ANXIOUS to make as much progress as possible before their former captors came after them. The snowcapped mountain range was at least two days' ride away, according to Jomar's estimate.

"This fair weather will not last, either," said Ana. "There will be storms before we reach the mountains." She spoke with the air of one making a definite statement of fact, though the day was perfectly clear with scarcely a cloud in the sky. Perhaps, having lived out of doors so much, she had become adept at reading weather signs invisible to others.

Jomar was also a very useful addition to their group. When they paused for a rest he taught them how to respond to a warning whistle, imitating a bird's call, which he would make whenever he suspected there was danger near at hand. On hearing it, they were all to halt whatever they were doing and run for the nearest available cover. He also taught Damion some swordplay with their stolen weapons, demonstrating lunges and feints and parries in case the Zimbourans should attack them and they had to defend themselves. Lorelyn, watching this, was eager to learn swordsmanship too, but Jomar at first dismissed her pleas for a lesson.

"She ought to learn to defend herself," said Damion,

concerned. "The Zimbourans want to kill her. She's in more danger than the rest of us," he argued.

Ailia shivered a little at that. Before now she had never been exposed to any real danger in all her short life: her greatest adventures had all taken place within the covers of books. Quests like these were for the strong and courageous, she thought in dismay, and not timid weaklings like her. But she did not voice any of her fears to the others. For a sight of Liamar and the Star Stone, she resolved, she would risk anything. And there was the urgency of their errand as well.

Jomar grudgingly showed Lorelyn how to use a sword. The moment he placed the hilt in her hand the girl's pale eyes glowed. She swung the long steel blade to and fro, staring at it as if fascinated. "This feels . . . right," she murmured when the exercises were finished. "As though I'd held a sword before. Of course I haven't, but somehow it feels almost . . . familiar. I can't explain it." She relinquished the blade with reluctance.

It was strange to see a girl holding a sword in her hands, especially when she was clad in rough trousers and a tunic. The men had found some Zimbouran clothing folded away among the packhorses' supplies, and had changed into it; Lorelyn had also taken some, being tall enough to wear male attire. The other women had to make do with Lorelyn's small supply of spare garments: but her gowns were large for Ailia, even with a rope tied about them for a belt, and they did not fit Ana at all.

The brief night fell again as they journeyed on—little more than a dim blue curtain, pierced only by the very brightest stars. There were still no sounds of pursuit in the forest behind them, and as they were all exhausted Ana suggested that they encamp for a few hours. Two flimsy canvas tents were also among the supplies on the packhorses, and Jomar and Lorelyn set them up while Ana tethered and fed the animals.

"He's a wonderful mount," said Damion to Ana as he stroked the palfrey's neck. "A horse in a thousand, aren't you, Artagon?" Ailia had named the palfrey and Jomar's black stallion after the famous steeds of Andarion and Ingard. Kaligon was a temperamental mount and sometimes bucked, though the Mohara man was a match for him; but Artagon was always docile and well- mannered. He stood snorting gently as Damion petted him, and when Ana's cat wandered up he dropped his head to touch her small pink nose with his.

"I'm sure Mandrake would be furious about this," Damion remarked. "Imagine his prize palfrey ending up here in the far north!"

Ana smiled, laying her hand on the hard bone between the horse's eyes. "Knowing Mandrake, I doubt he came by the horse honestly. And in a way, you might say Artagon has come home. The thoroughbred horses of Maurainia are all descended from three famous Elei stallions—faerie-horses, as the breed was then called—brought out of Trynisia in days long past."

Ailia looked up with interest. "The faerie-horses turn up in a lot of the old tales. They were supposed to be one of the three kinds of animal that could see spirits: the others were faerie-hounds and cats."

Ana smiled. "Perhaps this fellow's ancestors were steeds of the Fairfolk in days of old, and carried ladies and lords."

Jomar, declaring that he could not stomach another

meal of ship supplies, took his bow and quiver and went off hunting. He returned in about half an hour with a brace of rabbits. Ailia and Lorelyn, gazing appalled at the furry corpses, were certain they could never eat them, but the smell of the sweet tender meat roasting over the flames weakened their resolve. Ana did not partake of the meat, but ate only some dried fruit from the saddlebags. Greymalkin was offered some by Lorelyn, but turned up her nose at the cooked flesh with catly disdain. She sauntered away through the meadow, no doubt to find another meal more to her liking.

Throughout the meal Damion wore a troubled look, his thoughts on other matters. "Ana," he said abruptly as they finished, "what about Mandrake? He seemed a dangerous sort of man to me, and he's still running around loose in Maurainia. Aren't you concerned about him? Who is he, really?"

There was a pause before Ana answered. "Mandrake," she said slowly, "is an extremely powerful and dangerous Nemerei. I first met him in the land of Zimboura, many years ago."

"*You've* been to Zimboura?" exclaimed Ailia in amazement.

"Many years ago," she repeated. Her face took on a faraway expression, her voice dropped nearly to a whisper: she might almost have been talking to herself and not to them at all. "Mandrake was an orphan: his mother died giving birth to him, and owing to his . . . deformity the Zimbourans thought he was the child of a demon. Some priests of Valdur cared for him a while, believing him to be a creature of their dark god. But the people of the surrounding villages attacked them, and drove out the child and flung stones at him whenever he dared to show his face. He was almost feral when I found him, cowering in a cave, terrified of other human beings. I won his trust and took him away with me, for though he was only a child I sensed his Nemerei gifts at once. I knew that, given his background of hate and persecution, there was a possibility that he would grow up to misuse those powers. And so I did what I thought best: took him to live with other Nemerei, and taught him everything I knew." She sighed deeply. "I still wonder sometimes if I did the right thing. He fell out with me and the other Nemerei, long ago, and left us. I have seen very little of him since."

"You're afraid of him," said Jomar accusingly.

"No—though I am afraid of what he might do." Ana gazed into the fire. "And I am afraid *for* him."

"I don't believe in sorcery," Jomar stated. "Or miracles, or anything like that. You witches and sorcerers and priests, you're all the same. Always claiming to have special powers."

"Sorcery runs strong in your race, Jomar. The Mohara shamans are famous." Ana turned, appeared to be appraising him. "Perhaps you have the talent—I could try a test or two—"

"Oh no you don't." Jomar backed away. "You're not doing anything to *me.*"

Ana smiled. "But I thought you didn't believe in sorcery?"

"How do I know what witch-tricks you've got up your sleeve?" Jomar returned.

Ana looked at him. "You've come this far with me. I do think you might trust me a little." The Mohara man looked away. Ana's face softened; she seemed to look right through the man before her. "Oh, Jomar—I am sorry," she said.

He stared at her for a long moment. "What do you mean? How do you know?" he whispered at last.

"You told me yourself. Your tone, your expression. It didn't require any sorcery for me to understand. You lost someone, didn't you—a friend, a member of your family? The shamans could do nothing, and you were angry with them . . ."

Jomar was silent, but they all saw, now, the fleeting look of pain in his eyes. He got up without a word and walked away from the fire.

Ailia stared at Ana's firelit face. Like Jomar, she found it hard to believe the old woman was really a sorceress, but . . . Ana *was* uncanny. The girl recalled the disturbing session in the fortune-telling booth, how for a moment she had almost believed the woman to be a witch. She looked around her—at the sinuous limbs of the trees, at the mountains in the dusky distance. This was Trynisia, the motherland of myths. Anything, she thought, might happen here: anything at all . . . Something touched her leg, and she jumped with a little shriek before realizing that it was only Greymalkin.

"I think it's time to retire," said Ana.

"I'll take the first watch," said Jomar. "We'll all take turns keeping an eye out for the Zims."

Ailia went to the tent the women shared, followed by Lorelyn. But she found herself tossing and turning, tormented by her own unquiet mind.

"Can't you sleep either?" asked Lorelyn presently.

"No," Ailia said. "I keep on thinking of things—our journey, what's ahead of us . . ."

"Why don't you tell a story?" Lorelyn suggested.

Ailia complied. She told what she could remember of Welessan's journey to this land, and of his vision of the Celestial Spheres: ". . . Welessan and the Sibyl stood in the presence of the Moon Goddess, who dwelt in a palace of pearl, attended by the faerie-folk of the Moon. They looked like beautiful men and women, wearing feathered mantles upon their shoulders that enabled them to fly like birds. 'But what are these shapes of fire I see, darting about the vault of Heaven?' asked Welessan, pointing through a high arched window at the sky. And the Holy Sibyl sighed, shaking her head. 'Alas! It is the war of the Celestial Empire that you see. Now you know why men make strife on earth: can there be peace below when the heavens are at war? The great lords of the Spheres and their armies are even now fighting the enemy in the fields of the sky. They are led by the forces of the Queen of Night . . .' "Ailia's voice trailed away.

"Go on," urged Lorelyn. "What happened next?"

"I—I'm a little tired. I'll have to finish later," Ailia murmured.

She lay still, wondering who this girl who listened so intently to the old tale really was—wondering where the Zimbourans were—wondering what her family back in Great Island and Maurainia must be thinking, and wondering also what would become of their little group even if they did find what they sought. And when she drifted off to sleep at last, it was to dream that she and the others were being pursued by shadowy figures through a forest grown vast and dark and filled with menace.

* * *

SHE WOKE TO FIND the sun shining again, its rays beating through the sides of the tent and making a delicate sketch in shadow on the canvas wall of the fern-fronds and blades of grass outside. Opening the tent's entrance, she peeped out, startling a plump gray rabbit, which bounded away through the trees as she guiltily averted her eyes. There was a slight ground mist, but the sky was clear overhead. Greymalkin glided through the long grass a short distance away, her tail twitching: perhaps she smelled the rabbit. At the edge of the little clearing Artagon and Kaligon grazed placidly in the company of Ana's pony and the sturdy brown packhorses. Ana was feeding one of the horses with oats out of a small sack, while Damion rummaged through the saddlebags of another, whistling to himself.

"Will you stop that blasted whistling!" exclaimed Jomar in irritation, thrusting his tousled head out of the tent-flap. "It's driving me out of my mind." Damion promptly ceased whistling and began to hum instead. Jomar looked at him with dislike. "I *hate* people who are cheerful in the mornings," he grumbled and pulled his head back in again, like an irritated tortoise.

"Nobody asked me to do a watch," commented Ailia. "Or Lorelyn either. She'd have wakened me if she'd crawled over me to get out the tent-flap."

"I decided to let you two rest, and complete the watch myself," replied Ana.

Ailia and Damion stared. "But—aren't you terribly tired?" Ailia asked.

Ana smiled, shaking her head. "I am old, child, and the old sleep very little. Only young things like you need their rest. And how did you sleep, once I relieved you?" she asked Damion.

"Not a wink," replied Damion, packing up the saddle-bags again. "Jomar snores like a boar. You must have heard him: it's a wonder he doesn't wake himself up."

"Well, *you* talk in your sleep," retorted Jomar, crawling out of the tent-flap again. "Natter, natter, natter, for hours on end."

"How can I talk in my sleep when I don't get any?" demanded Damion.

"I'm sorry, gentlemen," said Ana, "but as there's no other sleeping arrangement that doesn't offend propriety, you'll just have to get used to each other."

Lorelyn came out of the tent behind her, gave a vast uninhibited yawn, and stretched her arms skyward. "What on earth's happened to the weather?" she asked, puzzled.

The wind had risen: a cold wind, coming down out of the north. Thunder rumbled in the distance, and the trees were uneasy. Never had Lorelyn seen such a swift change in the weather. Hurriedly they helped themselves to a sketchy breakfast, canteens of boiled water from one of the streams they had passed and some ship's biscuit they had set to soak in a pan. As they packed up and rode on, they saw that the north had become one vast maw of dark gray cloud, its upper edge swelling into bulbous shapes. It advanced in a solid mass, dwarfing the mountains, swallowing the blue sky over their heads with amazing speed.

"You were right about the weather, Ana," said Damion. "How did you know?"

"I don't like it," remarked Ailia aloud. "It's almost . . . alive."

"It's wrong, this storm," declared Lorelyn. That

peculiar unfocused look had come into her eyes again. "All wrong—it shouldn't *be*."

In less time than they would have believed possible the dark cloud mass completely swallowed the sky, blotting out the soft hazy light and creating a twilight of its own. They reined in their horses, staring up at it in consternation. "Did you ever see anything like it?" asked Damion, awed.

"Looks as though it's going to rain hellfire," was Jomar's comment.

There was a blinding, blue-white flash, and a grinding roar came from the depths of the thunderhead. The horses neighed, straining at their bits. Lightning illumined random sections of the sky. Huge cloudy chasms gaped out of the dark. Cumular ridges stood out black and solid-seeming as mountain ranges. The trees tossed and roared above their heads, and debris danced in the air. Gazing up fearfully, they saw blue bolts arcing from cloud to cloud, and for an instant Ailia thought she glimpsed something else—a flying flicker of greenish fire, that darted through the clouds with the same wild, leaping motion as the thunderbolts. She blinked: there was nothing there, only a cloud canopy dark as smoke, blue-veined with lightning. *I must have imagined it,* she thought.

And now the rain came, in lashing torrents that soon drenched them to the skin.

"We've got to find a cave or something," yelled Jomar. He turned in the saddle to glare at Ana. "I don't suppose Madam would care to use her magic powers and find us one?"

"I'm afraid not." Ana, as always, responded to Jomar's jibe by taking it seriously. "I cannot make conspicuous use of my powers here without drawing unfriendly attention." In her arms Greymalkin mewed plaintively, and the old woman tucked her travel-cloak about the cat.

They rode on, drawing the hoods of their cloaks down over their faces to keep out the rain, trying to soothe their snorting and skittish mounts. Thunder boomed again overhead, a loud rending report as though the heavens had split, and a huge lightning bolt fissured the sky directly ahead of them. This one did not move between the clouds, but reached down to the earth. There came the sound of a loud detonation, and an acrid smell.

Greymalkin screamed; the horses reared and halted. Ana drew in the reins of her mount and sat absolutely still. Ailia, glancing at her, saw with concern that she was very pale, her face as haggard as it had been when their galleon passed through the storms. Slowly Ana raised one hand, her lips moving soundlessly.

"It's stopping!" exclaimed Lorelyn.

The clouds began to shred like wool and break up, though the sky was still an ominous sight. Ana sighed and motioned to the others to continue riding. The eastern sky was a ghastly hue—a vivid, violent yellow, its lurid light filling all the inverted valleys and hollows of the cloud layer. Then the sun reemerged, and there behind them hung a colossal rainbow, seeming to bridge the world from end to end with its vivid hues.

"Look—isn't that smoke?" called Lorelyn presently. "Up ahead."

"Lightning strikes, probably," suggested Damion.

But when they approached the mounting columns of smoke, they saw that they issued not from burning trees but from holes in the ground. Damion peered into one. He thought he could see a red glow deep in the earth below. Fumaroles? Was there volcanism in Trynisia? Perhaps that was the explanation for the island's warm climate.

"Hob-holes," murmured Ana absently. "They're the chimneys of hobgoblins' underground dwellings."

"More likely some kind of volcano," opined Jomar, echoing Damion's thoughts.

They rode on for some time in silence. "I'm afraid I must have a rest now," said Ana at length when they reached a secluded grove. Her face was deathly pale. "If you don't mind stopping too, and waiting for me."

They all dismounted again, looking at her with concern as she seated herself on a fallen tree trunk, drawing deep breaths. Greymalkin went to sit at her feet, grooming her wet fur. The air was damp, the trees still dripping from the storm, and the four younger people were in exceedingly low spirits. Jomar and Lorelyn could not agree on whether the rain had really finished, or if it was just a lull: neither would give way, and the disagreement became a heated argument. Lorelyn had picked up a good deal of colorful language from the Mohara man, not knowing what any of it meant, and Ailia blanched at the obscenities that fell from the girl's innocent lips.

"You had better all have a rest too," interjected Ana at last. "And light a fire if you can find any dry wood. Everyone's feeling a little edgy and overwrought, I think."

"There's nothing wrong with *me,*" returned Jomar. He turned to Damion. "Will you stop that!"

"Stop what?" asked Damion.

"Kicking me—like that." He gave Damion a swift kick in the ankle and the other man leaped up in pain.

"I never touched you!" he said, wincing.

"Well, somebody did."

"Whoever it was, it wasn't I." He rubbed his ankle tenderly. "There's no need to cripple me."

"Well, if it wasn't you, who was it?"

"Jomar, I think you must be mad," said Lorelyn, staring.

At that moment there was a rustling in the bushes around them, and a series of high-pitched cries that sounded eerily like human laughter. Ana stood, leaning on her cane. "We must leave at once," she said. "They do not wish us to remain here."

"Who *are* they?" Lorelyn exclaimed, springing up.

"One of the Hobgoblin races."

"Goblins!" Ailia gasped, paling.

"*Hob*goblins," Ana corrected. "A different creature altogether. Goblins are evil and malicious creatures, but Hobgoblins—Hobs as they always used to be called—are merely playful. They are humanity's closest kin, and not really dangerous; but I think we had best not linger in their territory, or they may do us some minor mischief or other."

"I'd like to see them try," growled Jomar. There was a chorus of titters from the underbrush. Snatching up a small stone from the ground, he lobbed it into the bush. It came back promptly, whizzing a finger's length past his head.

"Don't provoke them, Jomar," advised Ana. "Let's get our gear and be off."

They packed up again and rode away from the spot.

They heard no more laughter, though occasionally a stick or stone was cast at them out of the branches of the trees high above. Ailia, glancing up, caught a fleeting glimpse of a face. The hairs on the nape of her neck rose at the sight of it. She was reminded of a tame monkey that she had once seen, perched on a sailor's shoulder: the tiny visage in the tree bore that same eldritch and half-mocking resemblance to a human face. The little round head, no larger than a year-old infant's, had ears and eyes proportionately larger than a human's, and the nose was almost flat. The skin was unnaturally pale, almost mushroom-white, the scalp topped with a fuzz of fine hair like dandelion-down. Seeing her looking, the creature dodged out of sight, and a furious chattering came from the trees along with more sticks and stones. The travelers were pelted for some time as they rode on in haste through the wood; only Ana was spared. Perhaps, Ailia speculated, the creatures did not find the old woman threatening, owing to her diminutive size.

The trees thinned, and the twilight beneath their boughs lightened: the missiles ceased, along with the chattering. The Hobs did not wish to pursue them into the open, it appeared. As they rode out of the wood the sun shone overhead again, but the sky over the mountains was clotted with the curds of cloud that promised rain.

NOW THAT THE FOREST was left behind, the exposed land showed a surface scarred by the passage of glaciers in ancient times. Great boulders strewed the fields, and where the earth's granitic foundations were bared long gashes and striations were revealed even in the rock, like the marks of gnawing teeth in old bones. The dwindling of the trees exposed another feature, not natural in origin: an old paved road, much like the old Elei road in Maurainia. They guided their horses onto its cracked and grass-grown stones. It ran straight toward a great double-peaked mountain that stood a little forward of the vast blue range. "Elendor," said Ana. "We are only a day or so away."

As they rode they began to see that not all the land's wounds came from vanished ice. The meadows were pocked with many deep pits and basin-shaped craters, some with pools of water lying at the bottom. Ana said these were gouged into the earth by the Great Disaster: the graves of fallen stars. Some were more than fifty feet deep, and surrounded by scattered boulders of great size. One had obliterated part of the ancient road, and they had to make a detour around it. As they rode on the number of craters increased, until the travelers felt as though they were journeying on the moon. But though trees no longer grew here, there was still an abundance of plant life, mainly of arctic varieties: wild grasses and sedges and low-growing, shrubby heaths clothed the land. Even the bleak boulders rising from the ground bore bright lichens like splashes of gray-green, yellow, or vermilion paint. And the land thronged with wild fowls that had flown across stormy northern seas to this island sanctuary: wild geese and sea-ducks massed in little fleets on the calm pools and meres, and rose up crying as the travelers passed.

Within a few hours the level ground began to climb toward the rolling foothills, and the road rose with it. Elendor loomed in the sky before them. Though it was not as high as the mountains behind it—perhaps seven thousand feet from foot to summit—its proximity made it seem larger.

"We're almost there," said Ailia, with a lift of the heart, as they paused on one of the foothills to rest. Lorelyn opened a sack of feed for the horses, while Jomar took out his bow and arrow again.

"We should get a good supply of meat while we can," he said. "Game's plentiful here, but it may not be when we reach the mountains."

"Must you kill something?" reproached Lorelyn. "We don't really need it, we've plenty of supplies."

"Ship's biscuit and meal! And the biscuit has to be soaked before it's edible. You didn't mind eating the rabbits, I noticed."

"I know, and I wish now I hadn't, if you're going to be casting it up to me from now on. I won't eat anything else you kill, so there."

"Please yourself."

They had seen a number of pantheons on the plain earlier, the odd alien coloring of their violet-blue coats and their pale constellations of spots making them highly visible against the monotonous hues of the tundra. But none was in sight at the moment. Apart from a few hovering hawks, and the flies that rose in whining clouds from the long grasses, no living thing was to be seen.

"I should have shot some ducks when I had the chance," grumbled Jomar, his eyes searching the land.

Damion knelt by a small pond at the roadside, using the shallows for a mirror. He had found a bar of tallow soap and lathered his chin with it, grimacing as he tried to shave with a Zimbouran dagger.

"Why bother?" the Mohara man asked him. He ran a hand over his own bristly beard, grown during his time on the ship.

"It itches," Damion complained. "I'm not used to whiskers. And I think something's living in it."

Ailia stared at him. As the soft yellow hair hiding his cheeks and chin was cut away, a more familiar face emerged: the young priest from the Royal Academy, the Damion Athariel she had known there. Somewhat to her own surprise she felt a familiar pang beneath her breast, and she averted her gaze. *But how ridiculous!* she thought. *So much has happened—so much has changed. How can I feel like this about him still, just as though we were back at the Academy and everything was perfectly safe and normal?*

Her thoughts were interrupted by a great flurry and a bellow, followed by a shout from Jomar. As the others turned in alarm the heath in front of the Mohara man's feet seemed to burst asunder, and out of it there sprang a creature like a huge snow-white antelope. It snorted through flared nostrils and trumpeted again, tossing a head crowned with arching horns. Jomar, too startled for the moment to make use of his bow, gaped as the animal galloped away across the heath, still lowing.

Their horses snorted and whinnied in alarm, and Damion and Lorelyn rushed to keep them from bolting. Jomar, recovering his wits, raised his bow. But before he could shoot, the meadow all around the travelers erupted with a dozen more of the tall ibex-like creatures, rearing up seemingly out of the earth itself. And now the travelers saw that other recumbent shapes, which they had at first taken for hummocks in the ground or glacial rocks, were in fact antelopes: those lying on the heath were green-gold in color, an exact match for its verdure, and those huddled amid the boulders were stone-gray. As they sprang to their feet their hue changed to pure white, as though they blanched with fear. The whole herd made off along the sloping ground in a thunder of pounding hooves.

Jomar overcame his stupefaction and aimed an arrow at one of the fleeing creatures.

"You're not going to shoot one!" cried Lorelyn, catching hold of his arm. The swan-white beasts were so majestic, so beautiful in flight.

"Why not?" He drew the string back.

"Jomar, please don't!" pleaded Ailia. "Not for us. There's no need."

Jomar stood for a long moment looking along the shaft of his arrow. Then finally he lowered his bow with the bolt unspent. He looked at the others, cleared his throat, and looked away again. "Too much meat to carry with us," he muttered. "It'd only spoil."

THE RUINOUS ROAD NOW snaked into the hills in long loops and meanders, but it still led toward the two-peaked mountain. Soon there were many ruins of buildings as well. Some had a few broken walls still standing; most were mere outlines of foundations littered with rubble and overgrown with grass. Hollowed-out shells of towers stood on the tops of hills, their windows filled with sky. They looked rather forlorn, Ailia thought.

"What were those creatures back there, Ailia?" Damion asked her when they paused again for a meager meal. "Do you know?"

"I think that was a *parandrus* herd. Welessan wrote

about them, and Bendulus too. They're like a cross between chameleons and antelopes." Ailia spoke absently, looking up with longing at the tall ranges rising in endless rows, their dim blue blending with that of the sky beyond. "The Numiendori, the Mountains of the Moon. And Elendor is so close now."

Her voice trembled a little, and of its own, her hand went suddenly to his, seeking reassurance. He closed his fingers upon it, applying a comforting pressure, and she looked down at his hand on hers—it was slender, with long sensitive fingers, and where the arm emerged from the sleeve of his coarse linen shirt she saw small blond hairs glint like gold wires. She looked up then, at the face she had never imagined would be so close to her own: at the sky-colored eyes with their dark lashes and well-marked brows, the straight-bridged nose, the firm mouth and chin no longer hidden by the blond beard. He smiled at her, and she returned the smile.

"Time to go," called Jomar behind them. "Be careful to pick everything up—we don't want to leave any more traces behind than we can help. And find that blasted cat!"

The clouds above the range grew gray and dense as they rode on, rolling down from the heights to meet them. Before long it was raining again—not a violent tempest this time, but a steady, spiteful drizzle that soon soaked through their clothes and got into their packs and saddlebags. The clouds blotted out the sun, and the mountain peaks were lost behind a pall of gray vapor. They entered another stretch of woodland, but the trees with their sparse spring foliage gave little shelter. Ailia had lost all her enthusiasm for quests. Faerie tales and romantic ballads, she reflected, never mentioned riding in the rain, nor had they anything to say about having to sleep in one's clothes or wash in cold brook-water, nor what it was like to share a small stuffy tent with other people. Ailia huddled into her heavy Zimbouran cloak, pulling the hood down over her face. Jomar, too, was in one of his sullen monosyllabic moods: shortly after setting out he discovered that Kaligon had played the old equine trick of blowing himself up with air while his girth was tightened, then slowly letting it out again so that the saddle slipped. Jomar made Ailia dismount while he fixed the girth, cursing in three languages. When he remounted, Kaligon reared and threw him into a bush. Ailia was nervous about riding the black horse after that. Why couldn't Damion let her ride with him on the white horse occasionally? Sometimes he even let Lorelyn ride in front and hold the reins. And how nice it would be to hold on to his waist . . .

"Don't mind Jomar," Damion had told her. "He's like a volcano, he just has to erupt once in a while. The volcano doesn't mean any offense and neither does Jomar. He's had a hard life, remember."

Ailia understood, and never quarreled with the Mohara man. He and Lorelyn, however, had already had a number of heated exchanges. Their worst tiff occurred late in the day, when the mizzling rain gave way to a dense fog that hid the mountains from view altogether. Lorelyn suggested they keep going.

"What, in this? I can't see two paces in front of me," argued Jomar. "I say we should stop here and wait for it to lift. The horses need a rest anyway." He began trying to build a campfire, since the fog would safely mask its smoke: but the damp tinder would not light.

"But what if the Zimbourans come? We'd never see

them in this fog until it was too late," she persisted. "It's a much better idea to keep going."

"Don't boss me," he snapped. "You may think you're some kind of royalty, but I—"

"Who's bossing? I just said it would be a good idea," returned Lorelyn, indignant.

Ailia, after one or two unsuccessful attempts to mediate, walked away—she hated scenes—and stood gazing into the trees. Presently she glimpsed, through the trailing mist and the mass of foliage that had at first shielded it from her view, a large dark form—a boulder it must be, big as a horse. But there was something curious about its shape: it was oddly symmetrical, its surface smoother than any rock she had seen, and black as cast iron. An odd pattern of furrows and indentations crossed its front. They looked almost like . . . Ailia gasped.

There could be no doubt about it: the "boulder" had teeth. They were huge: she could just see them through the screen of leaves, jagged lines that resolved themselves into the spaces between jutting black tusks. The "rock" was the tip of a giant snout. Ailia gave a cry and the others came running, the men drawing their swords.

"What is it?" exclaimed Damion, catching hold of her shoulder.

"Now what?" Jomar demanded at the same time.

Ailia pointed wordlessly. It took them all a moment to see the thing behind its screen of leaves. For an instant they all stood motionless, staring.

"It's just a lot of old bones!" Lorelyn said. "Whatever it was, it's long dead."

"I know," Ailia replied.

"Why did you yell like that, then?"

"But don't you see what it *is?*" exclaimed Ailia in excitement.

They all walked toward the dark shape. Behind the huge skull the rest of the creature's skeleton lay sprawled across the forest floor. These bones were black too, and immense. There were leg bones big as an elephant's, but ending in claws like scythes; the rib cage arched over their heads like a beached whale's. Trees had grown up between the ribs, and the limbs were festooned with vines. Greymalkin leaped up onto the bony muzzle and peered into a cavernous eye-socket: a wood pigeon that had been nesting inside came whirring out.

"It's got wing bones, look!" noted Ailia, pointing to two long shapes like the trunks of toppled trees, half-buried in the underbrush. "Like a bird, or a bat."

"They can't be *wings,* not on something that size—" began Damion. And then he fell silent.

"You see?" cried Ailia. "They were real, Damion—real!"

"You are right. It is the skeleton of a firedrake," said Ana, speaking what was in all their minds now. "A fire-breathing dragon."

Jomar snorted. "Can't be. There are no such things as dragons. Nothing could breathe fire. It'd burn *itself.*"

"Oh, firedrakes were well protected, outside and in," said Ana. "Their bellies were like great furnaces, full of burning gases. It took great courage for a knight to confront one." She ran her hand over a giant mossy rib, looking solemn.

"Men *fought* these things?" asked Jomar incredulously, waving a hand at the skeleton. "How could you fight something that size?"

"They fought because they had no choice. The creatures were servants of Valdur: corrupted offspring of the true dragons, the Loänan."

"Are—are there *still* firedrakes in Trynisia?" asked Ailia, her excitement giving way to apprehension.

"Oh, no. Their kind is long gone from the earth. For that we can thank the Paladins."

"It's been here for ages," declared Jomar. "Look at those trees growing up around the bones."

Damion stared at the tumbled ruin of the monster, the staggering size of it, the gruesome architecture of the jaws and limbs. *Dragons.* They truly had existed, then, outside the faerie tales. Here in Trynisia, where so many other unique creatures yet lived, the giant flying reptiles that cast their shadows over the ballads and romances and myths of men had once soared through the skies, and menaced towns, and lain coiled in caverns until brave knights came to do battle with them. What eyes had once stared from those empty sockets—what ghastly, scaly flesh had clad these monstrous bones? Damion recalled the picture he had hung over his bed in boyhood, the print of a mounted knight spearing a dragon. He had always thought the monster disappointingly small: the artist was so concerned with the heroic stature of knight and steed that by contrast the dragon looked no larger than a dog, and had seemed to Damion to be in as much danger from the horse's trampling hooves as from the spear. But to face *this* . . . how could anyone have summoned the courage?

"Imagine what it would have been like to look up and see a creature as big as this flying through the skies!" he said aloud. "We'll never know, but it must have been terrifying." Damion walked alongside the skeleton, following the massive backbone as it tapered into the long sweep of the tail. "There are hind legs too," he noted. "Four legs—*and* wings. Whoever heard of an animal with six limbs? And how could anything as big as that fly? You'd think it would be too heavy."

"Firedrakes were magical creatures, able to levitate," Ana explained. "Their wings carried only part of their weight. As to their shape, you must remember that according to tradition dragons are not of this world at all."

"But that's just a faerie tale," objected Jomar.

"Did they really keep hoards of gold and jewels?" Lorelyn asked curiously. "Or is that a faerie tale too?"

Ana smiled at her. "They really did keep hoards."

"What would an animal want with gold and jewels?" scoffed Jomar.

"Dragons were attracted to precious stones because there are powers within them, what the Elei used to call the 'spirits' of the gems. Each ruby or emerald or amethyst was said by the ancients to have an indwelling spirit—hence all our tales of fateful diamonds, and genii that live in jeweled rings, and so on. In fact, natural crystals are filled with earth-magic—a sort of power, like the force within a lodestone. Dragons can feel this, being sorcerous creatures and sensitive to any kind of power. As for gold, it is a very potent metal, filled with star-magic."

"Star-magic?" repeated Lorelyn.

"Long ago, it's said, when our world was still forming, the stuff of the stars fell into her sphere and was incorporated into it. When some stars come to the ends of their lives, you see, they burst like seedpods, scattering their inner fires across the heavens. That star-stuff is present throughout our world of Mera, in the stones and the earth we walk upon—even in ourselves. But its purest, strongest form is in the metals, gold and silver and iron and so on. Alchemists have tried for centuries to make gold, but in vain: it is born only in the fiery hearts of stars. Deep within it lies the star-magic that is the oldest magic in our universe, and so the dragons loved it. Lying for days upon a hoard of gold and silver augmented a dragon's own powers, giving it the ability to fly and to use sorcery. Dragons did not care for iron, however. Iron is too potent a star-metal: the magic in it is so concentrated that it overwhelms and negates any other sorcery. That is why cold iron was used against witches and faeries in days of old."

"More hearth-tales," grumbled Jomar.

"Well, we needn't linger. I don't think the hoard would be anywhere near here, and I expect the dracontias has been plundered." She peered into the eye-socket the pigeon had vacated.

"Dracontias?" Damion inquired.

This time it was Ailia who answered. "Dragons had precious stones that grew inside their heads," she said. "Dracontias-stones, they were called. They looked like gems, and had all sorts of magic properties—rather like the alicorn, the horn of a unicorn. People would do anything to get hold of dracontias-stones, even mount dragon-slaying expeditions. We should take it, if it's still here—"

"It is gone. And a firedrake's dracontias could only be put to evil uses, child," Ana told her.

"That's true," Ailia admitted. "I know a story—"

Suddenly Jomar went rigid. "Quiet, you lot!" he hissed. "Don't anyone move!"

"What is it?" asked Ailia, her heart beginning to hammer.

Jomar spun around, his sword already in his hand. "There! Did you hear that? Just to the east of us."

Damion whirled, his hand on his own sword-hilt. Footsteps—heavy ones. Not hobgoblins, then. "Men," he said grimly. "Coming this way."

"The Zimbourans!" exclaimed Lorelyn. "Hadn't we better run?"

"Too late!" Jomar crouched, ready for battle.

There were crashing noises in the underbrush. Ana seized Lorelyn by the wrist in a surprisingly strong grip, forcing her to back away as several large shapes plunged through the fog about twenty paces away. Damion counted at least ten tall, thickset men, apparently wearing grotesque masks. Not Zimbourans, then—

Behind him he heard Ailia cry out. "Monsters! They're *monsters!*"

And then he saw that the hideous faces were not masks at all.

14

The Holy Mountain

DAMION STARED IN SHOCK at their attackers. They were not Zimbouran soldiers—were not *men* at all. Their bodies were squat and ungainly, with heavy hunched shoulders and massive torsos. One had no nose, just snakelike slits for nostrils; another had tusks jutting through his lips. All were crudely clad in animal furs and leather, and their massive hands were clenched upon weapons—clubs, maces, rusty swords.

The creatures returned the travelers' disbelieving stares for the space of a heartbeat. Then they charged, brandishing their weapons. Cursing savagely, Jomar leaped to meet them. Stooping as he ran, he caught up a now-blazing log from the campfire, swinging it in one hand and his sword in the other. The beast-men squealed and yelped in fear at the sight of the flames thrusting toward them, and their noise redoubled as he rushed on two of them, setting their fur cloaks alight. Bellowing, the burning ones rolled over and over in the rain-wet grass, while their comrades recoiled, snarling with rage like animals.

Damion ran to stand at Jomar's side. Behind them Ana moved in front of the two girls.

Suddenly the largest of the creatures, a burly brute clad in primitive leather armor, lunged forward feinting, and then swung his great spiked club at the makeshift torch in Jomar's hand, smashing it in two. Red sparks flew through the air and died hissing in the grass.

And then it was all confusion and noise as the warriors engaged in the fog, swords and clubs whistling in the air as they struck out blindly. Jomar thrust out with his sword and killed a man more by accident than by design; Damion slashed the arm of another and it dropped its cudgel, howling with an inhuman voice. The two men kept shouting to each other, lest they attack each other by mistake in the mist.

"Damion! Blast it, Damion, where are you?"

"Over here—"

The women could not see what was happening. They backed away slowly from the noises of combat, feeling their way through the trees. When they were a safe distance away Ana told them to stay put.

"I am going back to help them," she said.

"I want to go too!" cried Lorelyn.

But Ana had already slipped away into the mist, moving through its gray opacity with impossible ease. The tall blonde girl gazed after her for a moment, then made as if to follow her.

"What are you doing?" cried Ailia, plucking at her arm. "You can't fight, Lori—you don't know how!"

Lorelyn glanced toward the faint shapes of the horses, still tied to the trees a short distance away. Her face brightened, and before Ailia could stop her she ran to the white horse and loosed his tether. "Toss me a sword," she said.

"But—"

The girl snatched a weapon from a horse's pack and vaulted into the palfrey's saddle.

"Lori—you *can't!*" Ailia called after her desperately. But the other girl galloped off through the fog unheeding.

Damion spun, his curved Zimbouran blade whirring, trying to defend himself on all sides at once. He called out to Jomar but received no answer. A shadow moved in front of him, and uttered a rumbling growl. He thrust, missed as the monster dodged him with surprising agility, and something struck him a glancing blow on the temple. He staggered sideways a couple of steps, dazed and momentarily blinded with his own blood. The attacker pressed his advantage, bringing his club down on Damion's sword with a ring of steel on steel.

Steel—it was the spiked club. Only the leader, the big bristly warrior, had a spiked club. Damion dashed his left arm over his face, trying to wipe the blood back from his eye. The ground was rain-wet and slippery, treacherous under his feet.

"Jomar!" he gasped.

No answer—was the Mohara man unconscious? Was he, Damion, all that stood between these monsters and the women?

The women! Damion saw the great shadow loom up before him again, the shape of the club being raised. He lifted his sword, the faces of Ana, Lorelyn, and Ailia floating before him in his mind's vision. *They musn't get to the women—*

The giant shape lunged. So did Damion. He felt the club strike his sword with a clashing shock, pulled back the blade, and then thrust out with it as the leader raised his club once more. In the same instant there came a screaming neigh and a white form charged up out of the mist: the palfrey, with Lorelyn crouching in its saddle.

She brandished a sword and yelled something at the warrior, who half turned at the sound.

Damion seized the moment to attack, felt his blade make contact with the other's body—felt the thrill of that contact run up the sword into his arm. There was a hoarse howl of agony.

A light blazed out behind him: in its glow he saw the leader impaled on the end of his sword, the blade embedded in the man's upper chest under the raised arm. He risked a glance over his shoulder. Ana stood there, a burning branch in one hand. Across the clearing he saw Jomar rise from the ground, covered in mud and blood, while the white horse reared and plunged a few paces away, Lorelyn by some miracle managing to keep her seat on its back. A man lay dead at the Mohara's feet. The others fled into the mist.

The leader backed off Damion's blade, wheezing. Then he stumbled backwards with a grunt, fell to the ground, and lay still.

AILIA STOOD MOTIONLESS, listening. The noises of battle ceased. She watched as the mist trailed away, turning thinner and losing its opacity, leaving behind it only a scattering of droplets on twig and leaf. Sunlight slowly redefined the forest, shaping the trees and underbrush around her. Somewhere in the distance a bird twittered, and was joined by another, and soon a whole chorus rang out around her. As the air cleared she saw to her amazement that the slopes and mighty double peak of Elendor now filled the northern sky. They had arrived at their goal in the mist, unknowing. She murmured a silent prayer there in the woods. *Please don't let any of them be in-*

jured. And please, please don't let anything happen to Damion.

As she stared into the forest depths she saw Greymalkin coming toward her through the undergrowth. The cat's tail was fluffed to twice its usual size, but she showed no sign of panic, and when Ailia called her softly she went to the girl and rubbed against her ankles. The feel of the thick soft fur was somehow reassuring: Ailia reached down and stroked it.

And then she heard voices coming from the direction of the clearing where the fight had taken place. With relief she identified these as the voices of her companions. Ana, Jomar, and Damion came toward her, and Lorelyn was with them, riding the white horse, which still snorted and tossed its head.

They're all right! They're safe!

She ran forward, then halted with a gasp at the sight of Damion's face: the injury to his temple, though not serious, had bled copiously in the manner of facial wounds. She flew to him. "Damion! Damion, are you all right?"

He nodded, too weary to speak.

"Damion! What about *me?*" said Jomar. Ailia turned to him and started.

"Jomar! You're covered in blood!"

"Yes, but it isn't mine," he replied in a tone of satisfaction. Ailia paled and backed away slightly.

"Ailia my dear, why don't you boil up the last of the water from the bottles?" suggested Ana. "Lorelyn, you can help me tend their injuries."

Neither of the men was seriously hurt, and after ministering to them for a few minutes Ana pronounced them to be in no danger of infection or any other complications.

Still, her face wore a worried expression when she looked at Damion. The young man was very silent: when Greymalkin rubbed her head against his hand he ignored her, and when Jomar congratulated him on his victory over the monsters' leader he looked away. "I'd rather not talk about it, if you don't mind."

"What's eating him?" said Jomar, watching Damion as he rose and walked off through the woods.

"I think he needs to be alone for a little," Ana answered.

"What were those things, anyway?" asked Jomar. "They didn't look anything like the hobs."

"They are one of the old Morugei races," Ana said. "The Demonspawn. This particular race is known as the Anthropophagi. They are human, but badly deformed. You may have noticed that some had more than the normal number of fingers, or had oddly-shaped feet."

"I've read about the Morugei," said Ailia in a low voice. "The stories said their ancestors used to be human, but they—they took demons for mates, so all their descendants were ugly and cruel. The Anthropophagi are cannibals." She shuddered.

"They do practice cannibalism, it's true," Ana conceded, "but mainly on one another. They believe that the strength of a dead man enters into those who consume his flesh. No doubt they will feast on the remains of their fallen comrades this day, and feel they honor them thereby. The other Morugei races were far more dangerous than the Anthropophagi—the Trolls, the Ogres, and the Goblins. Fortunately they, like the firedrakes, have now vanished completely from the earth. And the Anthropophagi are a dwindling race."

"Huh! Not hard to see why, if they eat each other," commented Jomar. He turned to Lorelyn. "Why in the world did you come galloping into the fight like that, girl? Are you out of your mind?"

"Well, there's gratitude!" remarked Lorelyn. "I came to help you—and I did."

"I didn't need any help: I was doing all right without you."

"But when I came, they all ran away," the girl pointed out.

"That is true," said Ana. "They did flee at her approach, Jomar. I don't believe they've ever seen a horse before. Lorelyn's intervention may well have saved you both."

Ailia felt a pang of envy. She could still see, in her mind's vision, Lorelyn on the plunging white horse, riding boldly to the men's aid. To be so brave! As for Lorelyn, she seemed quite unperturbed by her brush with danger. Her face was flushed with excitement. "When I was on the horse, I felt as though—as though I'd *grown,* somehow," she said to Ana. "As though he were a part of me. I could *feel* him—not just under me, but in my mind too . . . somehow. It's hard to explain."

"You are an Elei. Your ancestors had many curious abilities, among them the gift of bonding with beasts. Even wild animals loved the Elei. The dolphins that lived along Trynisia's coast came right into the shallows to play with their children, and swam before the bows of their ships."

"Well, perhaps you're part Elei yourself, then," suggested Lorelyn. "You don't really look it, if you don't mind my saying so, but you're certainly a wonder with animals."

"Will the what-d'you-call-'ems come back here?" Jomar interrupted, wincing as he flexed his sword arm.

"No," Ana replied. "Anthropophagi are cowardly creatures, for all their frightening looks. They won't dare return to this spot."

"Thanks to the horse!" said Lorelyn with a laugh.

Ailia scrambled to her feet and walked away from the camp.

DAMION STOOD AT THE SITE of the battle, looking at the bloodstained and trampled ground. The bodies of the fallen Anthropophagi were gone already, and the sight gave Damion a pang. It was a reminder that their adversaries had been not monsters or beasts, but human beings. They had taken their dead away with them.

And I *killed one,* thought Damion, *or gave him his death-wound at least, which is the same thing: he'll likely die. I've killed a man.* A melancholy descended on him which even the returning rays of the sun could not dispel. Did soldiers feel this way after their first kill—this sense of irrevocable loss, of permanent transformation? He paced about the clearing. The great black skull of the firedrake appeared to mock him with its grinning jaws: its eyeless gaze held his own.

So this is what comes of your priestly Vows and your precious Reason, it seemed to say. *They are only a gloss, a pleasing pattern on the surface. Your first desire was for the sword, as was your father's—how long did it take for your hand to grasp a weapon? What lies beneath is the same in man and beast both, and leads always to the same end: struggle and pain and blood, victim and victor. The sword is but an echo of the talon and the fang. Call yourself man if you will, as if that were something unique and holy; but you are a beast as I am, and ever will be.*

"No," he whispered. But the unspoken accusation hung on the air, with the lingering reek of blood.

"Damion?" He turned to see Ailia standing there, eyeing him curiously. "Damion, what is the matter?"

Ailia was filled with admiration. In her eyes Damion was a hero, fit to stand with Andarion and Ingard the Bold: he had risked his life to save her and the other women from the terrible onslaught of the Anthropophagi, even sustained injury on their behalf. In her mind the scar upon his temple became a grievous wound, nobly borne with the fortitude of a Paladin. Why then was he looking at her with this troubled, almost guilty expression, as though he wanted her forgiveness? "You were very brave, Damion," she told him. "As brave as any knight!"

He looked at the young girl standing before him in her convent gown, her eyes large and wide open, her innocence like a reproach; she seemed to him suddenly like a being from another world, a world from which he had forever alienated himself.

"You don't understand," he said. "I've killed someone. A man."

Ailia was startled into stillness by his words. She did not like, of course, to think of Damion killing anyone—not even an Anthropophagus. Now she understood his distress. "But, Damion," she said, her tone earnest, "you and Jomar had to fight. They would have killed us if you hadn't." She added, "Brannar Andarion and his Paladins killed people."

Damion looked straight at her, his anguish showing in his eyes. "Andarion wasn't a priest," he said.

"The Paladins were—they took holy vows."

"Not the same vows as I did. I swore never to harm anyone—ever—as long as I lived. Never to fight in a war, never to bear arms against another human being. And until the Supreme Patriarch summons me into his presence and formally releases me from those vows, I'm still bound by them."

Ailia stood twisting her hands, longing to say something that would comfort him, to repay in part the debt she owed him, but the words she wanted were not there. Finally she slipped quietly away and left him to his despondency.

Why am I here? she asked herself miserably. *I can't help him, or any of them—I can't even find the right words to say. I'm no use to the others at all, I'm just an extra body for them to protect. I wish I was brave, like Lorelyn. Then I might be of some use.*

She wandered on, feeling wretched. Presently she saw ahead of her more broken masonry. Two stone dragons crouched on square plinths: like the statue on Haldarion's rampart they were badly weathered, their batlike wings broken off and the scales upon their winding coils almost obliterated by wind and rain. Behind them a double line of broken pillar-stumps and crumbling walls flanked a narrow lane greened over with moss. They led to a lone arch, beyond which lay more fallen pillars and a glint of water.

Then she saw the stone posts of the door they had once guarded standing behind the dragons: they were broken to knee height, and reached by three low stone steps. She caught her breath. She knew this place, though she had never been here before. It had been a temple once, covered over by a roof. She mounted the steps and began to walk up the green aisle.

Climbing vines spread great mats of lapping leaves over broken walls where elaborate tapestries must once have hung; in the cracked floor beneath, where floral arrangements would once have been placed, hardy wild-flowers now offered their own bright blooms. The fog had cleared: above the broken walls, where the roof's arching vaults had once been, spread the sky, blue and serene as the surface of an untroubled sea, flecked here and there with a spume of clouds. All temples should be like this, she decided—roofless and open to the heavens, with unglazed windows to let the wind and the birds in. Rain would be a problem, she admitted. And there could be no services in wintertime. But on a clear day, such as this, how easy it would be to worship!

As in the ruins of Haldarion, she felt the past as an almost tangible presence. Thousands upon thousands of people had come here before her, walked this same path from the dragon-guarded door to the pool at the end of the aisle. It was, she knew, no natural pond. She walked over the pavement of cracked and ancient stone about its marble rim, heavily grown over with grass and moss, and stood staring down at the water. Its surface was utterly still, reflecting the tree branches and the sky above, white clouds drifting against blue infinity—a mirror to Heaven. Her reflection looked up at her, eyes wide and filled with awe. She knelt, dipped her hands in, splashed the cool water onto her face. Then she kicked off her shoes and lowered herself into the pool, gown and all.

* * *

"WHAT'S THE MATTER with you?" Jomar's brusque voice came from behind Damion suddenly, making him jump.

"Leave me alone," he said without turning around.

Jomar expelled his breath in an exasperated noise. "Damion, we've got to get up the mountain. The Zims may come at any moment. Let's go get that stone of yours and leave."

"And afterwards?" Damion asked, facing him. "What will we do then? Will we kill a few Zimbourans, too, before we're done? I wonder, Jomar, how many people have killed for that bit of stone up on the mountain, and how many believed they were justified. *I* won't kill for the Stone, or for anything else."

"You'll kill for self-defense, same as me."

"But I'm an ordained priest. Don't you see? For me to—"

"I see all right. I see that you're no different from the rest of us," Jomar snapped. "*I've* killed men—I did it because I had to, because they would have killed me if I hadn't fought back. But it's all right for *me,* isn't it? I'm no priest, I'm—what do you call people like me? *Sinners?*" His black eyes blazed with anger. "That's the trouble with you priests and shamans, you pure-and-holy types—you think you're better than anyone else. Then you find out you aren't, and it really bothers you, doesn't it? Well, it doesn't bother *me* because I don't expect it, see? I've got blood on my hands, yes—and I'll probably get more on them before this is over. And you know, I don't care what that makes you think of me."

Damion stared at him, stricken. "Jo—I didn't mean—"

"I know what you meant. And don't call me Jo. I'm going now. I'm going to go on up that mountain, and get that stupid stone, and Heaven help anyone who tries to stop me. How many *more* people will die if the Zims take it away from this island? Think about that. You can join me or not—as you please." He strode off. Damion stood for a moment, white-faced, hands clenched at his sides. Then he rushed after Jomar.

Ana looked relieved when the two men reentered the camp, but her expression quickly changed to one of concern. "Isn't Ailia with you?"

"Ailia?" Damion looked blank. "She came and spoke to me, and then left again—I thought she was heading back to camp."

"She hasn't come back," said Lorelyn.

"What is it with that girl?" exclaimed Jomar in disgust. "Every few minutes she's wandering off. Do I have to hobble her like the horses?"

Damion groaned, struck his own forehead. "This is my fault. She came after me. Jomar, we've got to find her."

They rose in a body and set off through the wood.

DAMION WAS THE FIRST to find the temple ruin. He walked up the mossy aisle, then stopped short at the sight of the pool, staring as the head of a woman rose from behind the marble rim. The ends of her hair drifted upon the water, but the rest was dry and the sunlight streamed through its nebulous mass, tinting it with gold like a sunset cloud. Her cheeks wore a faint rose flush, her skin seemed almost pellucid, alabaster-white and warmly luminous; one ear, caught in a sunbeam, had the pink translucency of a shell. Around her the skirts of a white gown spread flat, floating like the pad of a water lily.

An Elei it must be, some descendant of a surviving

tribe of Fairfolk . . . Then with a little shock he recognized her.

"Ailia?" he said uncertainly.

It must be some curious trick of the light, he thought. He had thought her fairly pretty, but now she was transformed in some incomprehensible way: the face she turned on him was radiant, ecstatic, just as he had always imagined the face of a saint would look. Her gray eyes had a tinge of purple in them, the color of wild violets. She gave him a rapturous glance from those altered eyes as she swam toward the brink of the pool.

"What happened, Ailia?" he asked, helping her out of the pool. "Did you fall in?"

She shook her head as she climbed out, hampered by her sodden skirts. Jomar, coming up behind with the others, began to lecture her for wandering away, but for once the girl cut him off. "The pool—we must all bathe in it."

"Are you joking?" Jomar was taken aback at her intense expression. "There might be anything in there—leeches or water snakes—"

"The water looks clean enough to me, Jomar," said Damion, scanning the surface.

"You can't see right to the bottom, though," said Jomar disapprovingly. "It looks deep. I'm not getting in there."

"I would, if I were you," suggested Damion, who was downwind of Jomar at that moment.

The Mohara man glanced at the dried mud and blood still clinging to his skin and clothes, and shrugged. "It'll wear off."

Ana and Lorelyn were examining the ruin. The stone dragons' heads had been recently anointed with what looked like dried blood, dark crusted runnels flowing down their jaws and necks. Greymalkin reared on her hind legs to sniff at it.

"The Anthropophagi have been here," Ana observed. "They have made idols of these old statues: it looks as though they sacrifice to them."

"They didn't make them, though, did they?" asked Damion, joining her and Lorelyn.

"No!" Ailia replied. "These dragons were the temple guardians. They're meant to look frightening, to remind you that this is a holy place. You had to conquer all your fears first before you were allowed to come in here."

Ana nodded. "Yes, this was the temple of purification. It was dedicated to a Trynoloänan, a celestial Dragon King. Such places were always built with pools enclosed, or placed near lakes or rivers, since true dragons love the water.

"There were two kinds of dragon, you see: the fire-drakes, which were evil, and another kind that were not fearsome monsters but spiritual beings like gods or faeries. The Loänan they were called, the 'Lords of Wind and Water,' for theirs was the power of the sky, of wind and water; they could send down rain or return a flooded river to its banks. Nor were these their only powers. The celestial dragons could change their shapes at will, becoming anything they wished—bird, beast, or human being."

"The Kaans believed in something similar," said Damion, remembering.

"They learned it from the Elei. The Kaanish emperors used to claim that Loänan in human form had mated with their ancestors, and that the emperors of olden days were able to assume draconic form."

"But whyever would the Anthropophagi worship them?" asked Lorelyn.

"Perhaps they believe that these are images of Modrian-Valdur in dragon form, or perhaps they still fear the Trynoloänan and make offerings to stay his wrath at their intrusion. Small wonder they attacked us—we came too close to their holy place."

"Hadn't we better leave, then?" said Damion.

Ana shook her head. "They will not dare to return."

Ailia walked to the stone rim of the pool. "This is the Pool of Purification."

"You're quite right," Ana affirmed.

"In the old days, when pilgrims came from all over the world to see the Stone, they had to be prepared first," Ailia explained to the others. "Welessan said there were three levels to the mountain. First you bathed or washed in this pool by the Dragon Temple: it was a purification ritual. When you came out you were given a green robe, and went on to the next level—the Level of Beasts it was called. It was about halfway up the mountainside. By the time you'd gotten there you were to have mastered the bestial side of your nature, and if you had you were given a red robe by a Nemerei sage and could go higher up, to the Level of Men. There you learned to master your mind: control your emotions and so on. And if you did well at that, you were given a white robe and could go all the way up to the holy city and see the Stone. Some pilgrims took weeks to climb the mountain—or months, or even years. They had to be spiritually ready, you see."

Jomar expressed his opinion of pilgrims and their methods of mountain climbing in a loud snort. "Well, I'm not taking that long, I can tell you. And I'm not going for a swim, either."

Damion peered at the pool's surface with an intent expression. "In there—I saw something move!" he shouted.

"What did I tell you?" Jomar sauntered over to the poolside. "Where? I don't see any—"

Damion gave him a heave and in he went, with a tremendous splash. "You, you—" he spluttered, surfacing, and then the rest was lost as his mouth filled with water.

"That's for kicking me on the ankle," Damion explained. "Well, how's the water?"

"Full of leeches. Hop in."

"Now, Jo. No hard feelings, I hope?" said Damion.

Jomar swam toward the pool's edge and gripped it with one hand, holding up the other. "No. Here, give me a hand."

"Oh no you don't. I'm not falling for *that* old trick."

Jomar gave him a broad white grin. "I seem to recall that priests are supposed to help anyone who asks them. Give me a hand now, Reverend."

Damion sighed and did, and joined Jomar in the pool.

"Children, children!" clucked Ana.

The water was cool and silver-smooth against the skin. Damion began to swim in long, slow strokes, the blue cloud-reflecting surface rippling around him. It was like drifting through the sky itself. An inexplicable calm came over him—more a kind of glad, embracing euphoria. He felt at once soothed and sanctified.

"Come on in, girls," he shouted happily. "Last one in's a rotten egg."

Laughing, both girls plunged in simultaneously. They splashed the men, who retaliated, and in a moment a fine water-fight was in progress. There were no sides: they all splashed one another indiscriminately, laughing and shrieking.

Ana did not join in their play, but merely stooped to bathe her hands and face, and then went and sat on a stone block in the ruined temple, resting her aching feet.

"How you have changed."

The voice came from behind her. She continued to sit still, showing no surprise, and did not turn her head as a tall cloaked figure emerged from behind the dragon statue and stood beside her. Mandrake gazed down at her, his golden eyes intent in his dead-white face. The young people played on in the pool, oblivious.

"So have you," she remarked quietly.

"Not like you. Look at you! Old, feeble—withered like a leaf! How can you endure it? When I think of what you once were!" There was a touch of sadness in his voice.

"When one gets to a certain age," said Ana, "one comes to realize that a body is only an encumbrance. I would just as soon pass on and leave the business of living to others."

"I have no desire to live forever," replied Mandrake. "I was not speaking of death but of old age: life's last jest at our expense."

"I cannot believe you have come all this way just to discuss such matters," said Ana.

The golden eyes narrowed thoughtfully. "Perhaps, after all, you haven't changed so much. But it is no longer as it once was between us, Ana. You were right when you said *I* have changed."

How well she knew it. His aura blazed in her mind's vision, yet there was a shadow in it, like a spot upon the sun: a blighted brightness. A shiver of foreknowledge passed through her, a chill wind from the future.

"I want you to know what to expect from me," Mandrake continued. "You must not suppose that I am on the side of your enemies. I have no more love for the Zimbourans—or, for that matter, any followers of Valdur—than you. The Modrian cult in Maurainia was a temporary convenience for me, nothing more: I was never a part of it. But neither am I on your side. When I assist one party, it's to thwart the other. I don't want *either* of you to succeed in this quest. How like you, to make use of those Zimbouran fools!" A touch of amusement entered his voice, but it soon passed, was replaced by harshness. "The sea-storms were intended as a warning, and the thunderstorm too. I can conjure far worse, as you well know. And your powers are waning, Ana. You can't keep this up for much longer."

He paused again, but Ana still said nothing. From the direction of the pool came a glorious noise: the young people had discovered that they were admirably equipped to sing in four-part harmony, and Ailia's soft soprano, Lorelyn's husky contralto, Damion's clear tenor, and Jomar's magnificent baritone were now raised in a spirited rendition of a popular folk song.

"It's true you saved my life," Mandrake said. "Well, I intend to pay that debt by sparing yours, and the lives of your young friends. Yes, even Lorelyn's. But expect no more from me. I will continue to do all that I can to hinder you." He stepped back, into the shadows of the trees, and was gone.

The young people came out of the pool, still singing and laughing, playfully cuffing Jomar, who had substituted his own ribald lyrics for the song's traditional ones. The pool had performed its age-old work of ablution—of absolution. They emerged from it reborn, the stresses and strains that hindered their relationships washed away. There was no magic in it, and never had been; it held nothing but the pleasure of water, of being made clean. The young people came up to Ana in a noisy cheerful group, wringing out their sodden garments.

"Well, we've bathed *and* done our washing, all at once."

"That should do me for another month."

"Jomar! That's disgusting!"

Ana sat composed and still. The temple lay empty behind her.

THEY COMMENCED THE ASCENT of the mountain in high spirits, having changed their clothes and dried the drenched ones over the fire. *All of this,* Ailia thought, *is going to make a wonderful story, someday. I can hardly wait to tell it.* And the best part of it all—the climax, in fact—still lay ahead of her, on the mountain's summit.

Much of Ailia's good humor stemmed from the fact that she was riding with Damion. Ana had suggested the change, and Ailia, sitting high on the back of the white palfrey and clasping Damion's lean waist, welcomed it wholeheartedly.

It was a pleasant journey at first, the slope gentle, the ancient road that wound up the mountain's side still in remarkably good condition. Presently they spied the two gigantic stone lions, one lying on each side of the road, that formed the gate to the mystical Level of Beasts. So weathered and worn were they that they resembled not so much lions as rocks with a leonine shape: there was only a hint of their heavy maned heads, the powerful flanks and folded limbs, now daubed with many-colored lichens. *How incredibly old they must be,* Ailia thought as the group rode past them. *Older than anything we can imagine.* Beyond the statues lay a region of dense forest, but Ailia had no thought for danger just then. This was a sacred place, this Holymount, exalted in scripture and faerie-lore alike. No Anthropophagus, she was certain, would ever dare to come here.

After riding for an hour or so they paused to rest in a sheltered place, a stand of trees near an igneous outcrop with a mountain torrent coursing nearby, a white veil of water suspended from a shelf of stone. The horses drank deep, while Ana refilled the water bottles. A wind blew off the ice fields of some higher peaks to their right. Jomar shivered and grumbled about the cold, pulling his cloak closer about him, but the rest were glad of the fresh and bracing air and drew it deep into their lungs. While they rested, the Mohara man went and stood on the outcrop, his bow and arrows at the ready, scanning the hillside for any signs of pursuit. He looked, in his dark garb, like a statue carved out of onyx. Seeing him standing there, so strong and confident, Ailia was grateful that he had joined them. Jomar might be alarming at times, but he was exactly the sort of person one wanted to have along in times of danger.

For now, though, there was no danger, and she walked a little farther up the slanting alp, among the wildflowers that thrust their bright heads through the grass: slim yellow glacier lilies, mountain anemones with bluish-purple blooms like crocuses. In her lightened mood she no longer worried about being a burden to the group. Perhaps, just perhaps, she was the fated chronicler of these extraordinary events. In a burst of excitement she realized what that meant. She would be an author: like Welessan the Wanderer or Elonius or the Bard of Blyssion himself, an author with published volumes, her name listed in catalogs, her works studied by scholars. *"My Journey to Trynisia, by Ailia Shipwright," "The Faerie Isle: A Legend Come True," "A Trynisian Bestiary: Flora and Fauna of a Forgotten Land," "Voyage to the End of the Earth: My Role in the Greatest Adventure of Our Time."* She ran the titles over in her mind, savoring them, like a miser fingering jewels.

She no longer felt any envy of Lorelyn either. She sensed a return of the compassion she had once felt for the odd, waifish woman-child. Lorelyn was only a girl, not a goddess, whatever the Nemerei or the Zimbourans might think. Ailia remembered, with a little shiver, what the Zimbourans would do to Lorelyn if they should recapture her.

Damion too was concerned. He walked over to Jomar's rock. "I'm worried about the women, Jo," he said quietly.

Jomar looked at them too and shrugged. "Women are tougher than you'd think."

"Not these women," Damion corrected. "Ailia isn't strong, and Lorelyn is a little too bold for her own good. I don't believe she really knows what *danger* means. Ana's looking poorly, too: that's not to be wondered at, considering her age. We must look after them."

"We can't pamper them either," returned Jomar, "if we want to get to the summit before the Zims. If I know them they'll already be on our trail, with reinforcements. When they want something they don't give up easily."

Ana overheard this. "Neither do I," she said, giving them a sudden impish smile.

"Oh? What are you planning to do, beat the Zims off with your cane?" Jomar inquired. "Or will you sic your attack-cat on them?"

"No dear, Malkin doesn't like fighting," she replied, grave-faced.

"Forget it," he growled. "Let's get on up this mountain. We're wasting time."

They labored on uphill, leading the tired horses by their reins as the slope grew ever steeper. Softwood trees began to give way to hardwoods. Once they saw a wild mountain-antelope with long, straight, backward-slanting horns, perching on a pedestal of rock. As they drew closer, they saw the animal's horns move, swinging around like the mobile "horns" of a snail to slant forward, the sharp tips facing them defensively.

"It's a yale," declared Ailia in delight. "They were supposed to be fabulous too. Bendulus wrote about them—he said they point their horns forward if they have to fight, and put them back when they're at rest."

"Better give it a wide berth," advised Jomar. "It might charge us."

They continued their climb, walking and leading the horses. Only Ana remained on her mount, since she was too weary to walk. Ailia had never been this close to a mountain: she had never had a chance to explore the coastal range in Maurainia. She gazed in wonderment at the cataracts ribboning down steep stone cliff-faces; at the wisps of cloud that webbed the tops of the pine trees like gossamers in grass. It really seemed as though they drew nearer to Heaven, she thought in awe. Earth and sky met here.

Damion was not interested in the scenery; he gazed worriedly at Ana. She looked exhausted, her white head bowed low over her pony's neck. She no longer tried to carry her cat, who now lay curled up in a saddlebag. Looking at her drawn, lined face, he wondered what they would do if she fell ill. Apart from her small store of healing herbs, they had no medicinal supplies with them.

At this stage of the journey it was Jomar who led them. With his military training, he knew that it is indeed possible to go on even when one's feet and back ache, and he bullied them uphill relentlessly. Though some of them resented it at the time, they also knew that they might well be grateful to him later on. As they stumbled forward, two huge shapes came into view ahead. A pair of equestrian statues, forming a gateway.

"Riders on horses," noted Ana, raising her head. "The Elei ideal: man over nature, mind over matter, the intellect curbing and controlling bestial nature. We have reached the Level of Men." But her voice was faint.

They turned back to look out over the valley. They had concentrated so much on the climb ahead of them that they had not bothered with the view behind. Now they realized how far up they were. The lands below were indigo-hued with the haze of distance, the river reduced to a shimmering strand, and they could see the paler blue of the ocean far beyond. The sky was clear but for a few frayed cotton-tufts of cloud, looking so close that Ailia felt she could reach out and touch them: they were, in fact, almost on the same level as the mountaintop. Their black shadows blotched the land below.

Ana frowned. "Is something wrong?" Ailia asked her, nervous.

"That cloud," Ana said. "It is moving against the wind."

They all stared. One fleecy cumulus, gray beneath and snow-white above, was moving in their direction with disconcerting speed, trailing long wispy streamers from its underside. Flashes of blue-white light flickered inside its misty depths, and there was a soft low rumble from within it like an animal's growl.

"A storm cloud?" queried Damion. "But it's not a thunderhead—it's too small. And the rest of the sky's perfectly clear."

Ailia recalled the great storm in the valley. This strange, lone, swift-moving cloud gave her the same eerie feeling. *It's alive,* she thought. *Or something* inside *of it is . . .*

They all turned by sudden unspoken consensus, and began to hasten up the slope once more. The horses too were ill at ease, sensing the storm's approach. Ailia glanced back over her shoulder, and saw with a prickle of fear the great gray shape bearing down on them, looming now over most of the sky. It was going to collide with the mountain's summit, enfold it and them in its muffling depths. There was nowhere to run, or to hide.

The sunlight was cut off, as if a lamp had been blown out; the huge shadow swept over them, swift as a racing horse, and then the cloud's first grasping tendrils reached down. Soon it flowed all around them, dense as a fog bank and clammy on their skin. They were lost in a smoke-dark, vaporous void.

Ana slipped off her pony's back, looking grim. "Be very still and quiet, all of you!"

They dismounted, the men holding the heads of the horses, which were snorting and rolling their eyes. A branching thunderbolt struck one of the mountain's peaks, silhouetting it for a fraction of a second. Then all was gray darkness and noise as the thunder rolled through the stony spaces high above. The horses neighed shrilly, and Greymalkin gave a long yowl.

It's more than the thunder, thought Damion, seeing the horse's flared nostrils. *The animals sense something we don't . . .* There was a rushing noise followed by a tremendous gust, a moving wall of wind like the wake of displaced air from some huge, hurtling object. He clung to Artagon's bridle, but the white horse reared, hooves beating at the air as the lightning flashed again. The mountainside sprang into view: trees, statues, a jutting rock pinnacle beyond them that had a peculiar shape . . . Damion stared. No, that shape was not all rock.

Crouching atop the pinnacle was a demon.

In the lightning-glow he saw it, with perfect clarity: a monstrous shape with two great shadowy wings half-furled at its sides—a huge horned head—eyes that burned like fire. It glared down at them from its stony perch. *The Fiend . . . It's the Fiend himself . . .* Darkness descended, and the apparition was gone.

"Jo—Ana—did you see? Did you see it?" he shouted, pointing. Once again a searing flash lit up the mountainside, and this time they all glimpsed the thing on the pinnacle. It had shifted its position, so that Damion could now see it stood upon four clawed legs, and the great horned head, turned sideways, showed the elongated muzzle of a beast.

No demon this; he was looking at—

"A dragon!" Lorelyn yelled.

15

Here Be Dragons

"ALL OF YOU!" Ana called through the dark. "Gather round me quickly!"

They complied at once, Jomar included—something in her strained, urgent voice demanded obedience. A series of flashes showed them one another's anxious faces and lit up the mountainside. The two equestrian statues leaped at them out of the mist. The belly of the cloud that had engulfed them was alternately gray-black and filled with a brilliant, blue-white luminosity. The horses screamed and bolted in all directions.

The dragon was gone from its rock.

"Do not move!" cried Ana as darkness descended again. "Stay close to me!"

Thunder rolled about the heights and hollows above

them. As it dwindled to silence again they heard another sound, like the cracking of canvas in a gale, directly overhead. They peered up in terror as the dragon passed over them, invisible in the gray cloud, the trees thrashing in the wind from its wings. Then it was gone, and they heard only the hissing patter of rain beginning to fall.

"To the guesthouse—there, do you see it?" As lightning flickered again Ana pointed to an oblong shape about thirty paces beyond the statues. "Run!"

They fled toward the ruin as the rain poured down around them. When they arrived at its doorway they found that it was roofless and missing two walls, but there was a set of steps leading down into a cellarlike subterranean room. They tore down the steps, then turned and looked back up at the entrance.

Ailia gasped. "Where are Ana and Damion?"

Jomar cursed, and started up the steps again. But then there was a noise, a scraping slithering sound: the square of dull gray that marked the cellar's entrance was replaced by a solid darkness. A low rumbling came from it, and a snuffling sound. The dragon was there, lurking, like a cat at a mousehole.

The door is too small—it can't get in, a terrified Ailia tried to reassure herself as she backed toward the far wall. *It can't get in—*

The dark thing shifted, letting in a little light and showing its glistening armor of rain-wet scales. Then an eye looked in at them. It was huge, the pupil black as pitch and circled by a thin yellow ring of iris. Jomar backed away and snatched his bow off his shoulder with unsteady hands. The eye withdrew, and in its place a wet, scaly snout was thrust into the hole. Black slits of nostrils at its tip snuffed and flared wide, drawing in their scent.

Jomar's first arrow struck the lower jaw and bounced off it as though it were plated with steel. The snout became a black pit edged with gleaming tusks, and a grating roar filled the little room, reverberating in their chests and throats and heads like an earth-tremor. The jaws pulled back, and a limb came groping through the opening. It was rust-colored and shaped like a gigantic cockerel's, with a scaly foot tipped by three grasping talons in front and one behind.

"Look out!" shouted Lorelyn.

Jomar, in the very act of drawing his sword, leaped aside as the claw opened and made a snatch at him. The talons closed on air. But he stumbled in his haste and sprawled backwards, his sword falling with a clatter to the stone floor. The clawed limb flailed, trying to reach him as he scrabbled away.

"No!" Lorelyn cried.

She dived for the sword, gripped the hilt in both hands, and swung it vigourously at the scaly leg. Another roar shook them all to the bone. The leg drew away slightly, then the claw opened once more and lashed out, knocking the weapon from Lorelyn's hands and sending the girl reeling against the wall even as Jomar sprang to his feet again.

"Back," he yelled, grabbing for Lorelyn's arm. "Get *back!*"

He shoved her against the wall. But the sword lay on the floor where it had fallen, out of reach beneath the flailing claw. Ailia screamed.

* * *

"ANA! NO!" YELLED DAMION through the driving rain.

Lightning flashed again above him, and by its brief glow he saw a gigantic shape. It crouched upon the shell of the guesthouse like a monstrous bat, the membranous tent of its half-folded wings completely engulfing the ruin. Its body gleamed like wet metal: it seemed to be reddish in color, though it was difficult to tell by the lightning-flashes. Ana stood a short distance away from him, facing the creature. The air all around them was alive with a glowing green discharge, flaring from tree-tops and the points of standing rocks, just as it had hung about the ship's masts during the storm. Ana lifted up her wooden cane, and as its head rose it too flared green-white, blazing like a ghostly torch. The dragon reared up on its haunches: its horned head was at once swathed in the green radiance as well, so that the creature seemed to wear a crown of fire.

"*Il marien lithai, Trynoloänan!*" cried Ana in Elensi.

The dragon roared back at her, echoing the thunder. Then it leaped into the air as the lightning flashed again, and Damion caught a glimpse of vast venous wings, billowing out like wind-swollen sails; a copper-colored body with huge clawed limbs drawn up underneath; a long, serpentine tail. Darkness descended again, but he could still see the dragon, for as it rose skyward the airy luminescence enveloped it completely and it blazed like a shooting star. It plunged into the low-hanging clouds, became a green glow flickering through gauzy layers of vapor. Then it vanished from his sight.

At the same instant Ana, who had been standing perfectly still, arms raised, eyes shut, lips moving as if in prayer, gave a weak cry and fell forward. Damion ran and knelt by her side, turning her over. Her eyes were closed, her face haggard: she made no response, even when he shook her gently by the shoulders. His three companions rushed out of the guesthouse, colliding with one another in the narrow doorway.

"Get back inside," he bawled at them, trying to make himself heard above the storm. Gathering Ana in his arms, he followed them into the guesthouse. "Ana, Ana—" He spoke urgently in her ear as he laid her down on the stone floor. "Ana, can you hear me?" But Ana made no sound: she lay motionless, as if in a deep swoon.

"Oh, Damion, what's wrong with her?" asked Ailia. "Did the dragon hurt her?"

He shook his head, feeling helpless. "No. She was just standing there, shouting at the dragon—"

"Shouting at it?" Jomar echoed.

He nodded. "And then—she just fell to the ground."

"Heart attack?" suggested the Mohara man.

"I don't know."

They stood in a silent circle around the supine woman. They could not light a fire: they had no fuel, and the trees outside were rain-soaked. The supplies were gone with the horses. They had no blankets to put over Ana. Damion wrapped her in her cloak and put his over her as well, and Lorelyn folded hers and put it under Ana's head. Ailia realized her legs were shaking like a frightened animal's: she gave up trying to stand and sank down onto the stone floor, tucking her legs underneath her, but even that could not still their trembling. For a long time no one spoke: they sat or stood in dismal silence, gazing helplessly at Ana. Presently there was a yowl and Greymalkin darted down the cellar steps out of the rain, shaking her damp fur. When she saw Ana she fell silent, then went and curled up beside her mistress with her ears flat against her skull and her tail twitching.

At each gust of wind and growl of thunder they stiffened, fearing the dragon had returned. Still Greymalkin remained by Ana's side, curled up in a gray ball and staring at her with anxious green eyes. Was it true that pets kept deathwatches over their ailing owners? Lorelyn reached over and stroked her ears gently. "What is it, puss?" she whispered. "What's wrong with her?" The cat nuzzled her hand briefly, then continued her silent vigil.

"If only Ana had told us where the Stone is!" sighed Lorelyn. "She said she knew exactly where it lay. How will we find it if she . . . doesn't get well?"

"I know where it is," said Ailia in a small voice.

"*You* know?" Jomar exclaimed, swinging around to stare at her.

"Yes—I read all about it, in that book. *Welessan's Wanderyngs*. He saw where the Stone was kept in the temple."

"Why didn't you say so before?" asked Lorelyn, astonished.

"I was afraid to. Ana said it wasn't safe to know, and—oh, what does it matter now anyway?"

Another silence fell, broken only by thunderclaps. At last, to their enormous relief, Ana stirred. Her pale eyes opened and seemed to stare up at them. Then as Damion knelt beside her she sat up and put the cloaks aside. "My body has recovered, but not my powers," she murmured. "He has deliberately weakened me with many challenges, and now there is not enough strength left in me."

"He? Whom do you mean, Ana?" Damion asked.

"There is another power in this land," she said. She held out an arm, and he helped her to her feet. "A very strong one. It is behind all these attacks against us. First the hydra, then the storm, the Anthropophagi, and now this . . . Did you think these things were mere coincidence? They were weapons, all wielded by one hand. We have a foe who does not wish our mission to succeed. And I am the focus of his wrath. He feels my power wherever we go, and he responds to it."

The young people exchanged glances, and Jomar tapped the side of his head.

"No, Jomar, I am not mad. But I cannot tell you more," Ana said in weary tones. "I told you before that knowledge can be dangerous, and this is one of those times. But this you must know: you are all in grave danger as long as I am with you. I must go apart for a while; I must leave you."

"Leave us!" cried Ailia. "But—you can't! Where would you go?"

"Where does not matter. As long as I am not in your midst, you will be safe—as safe as you can be, I should say, for there are other perils here. But those you can face. This one, this adversary, you cannot. I will draw him away from you if I can. Go on uphill: complete the mission. This storm cloud is a part of his sorcery, but you can use it against him: it will hide you from his sight, and he will not know for some time where you have gone. I will go in a different direction, back down the side of the mountain, and he will follow me thinking that you are with me, that we are giving up our quest. I will be like a mother bird, feigning a broken wing to draw the fox away from her nestlings."

"No." Lorelyn spoke in a more forceful voice than the others had ever heard her use. "I won't let you go off by yourself like that, into danger!"

Ana went to her and laid her small, withered hand on the girl's forearm. "My dear child! I will not let myself be a danger to *you.* I will rejoin you as soon as I can, but that may not be for some time. And if this is fated to be, if you really are the one, then the Stone will come to you whether I am with you or not. Remember what I told you about the Guardians!" She hobbled up the stone stairs, leaning against the wall as she went. Her cat followed her, and after a moment the rest of them did as well.

Outside the sky was still lost in cloud. There was no sign of the horses, though a quick search by Damion and Jomar turned up a few bags lying on the ground, their contents scattered. There were blankets and candles and some other supplies, but very little food, and much of that was rain-soaked. They gathered it all up, as well as some kindling for fires. Ana picked up her stick from the ground and turned to face the others. "One more thing: will you take my cat with you?" Without a word, Lorelyn went and picked Greymalkin up. The cat gave a mournful wail, but allowed the girl to carry her. "There," Ana said. "Now, the cloud is thinning. We are wasting time, and that is becoming precious. Go now, all of you: take the path up to the city, and wait for me there."

They obeyed with great reluctance: Ana looked so very small and old and weary, leaning on her cane. More than one of them wondered if they would ever see her again—if they were not now abandoning her to her death. But it was plain in any case that she would not be able to make the climb up to the mountaintop. And so they turned to continue on the upward path, though not without many backward glances. The last they saw of Ana was her bowed form descending into the vapors: gray vanishing in gray.

AS THEY MADE THEIR OWN way uphill the cloud began to shred and disperse, admitting the waning daylight. Looking back down the path, they saw the gray mass of the storm below them, descending the mountainside. They stood for a moment watching it, the hems of their cloaks lifting in the waning turbulence of its wake, before turning again and marching on. Before long they left the trees behind them and toiled up a slope sparsely scattered with small bushes and covered in rough meadow-grass. To one side a scree slope fell away to blue-tinged depths; above them jagged pinnacles soared. Of Liamar itself they could see nothing, as the heavy knitted brows of the crags above hid it from view. They felt uneasy at being out in the open without the cover of cloud, exposed to the view of sky-roving dragons. But they saw none: the sky above them was empty and clear.

"Do you suppose it's true, what Ana said?" Ailia asked the others. "About a sort of power fighting against her?"

"No," said Jomar. "The truth is that this is a race, us against Khalazar's men. She was slowing us down, and deep down she knew it. That's why she stayed behind. We will go faster without her."

"Jo, how can you say that?" exclaimed Lorelyn, turning to him in reproach. "She may be in terrible danger down there, with dragons about, and the Zimbourans too. One of us should have stayed with her." She looked down the mountain path. "I've half a mind to go back."

"She wouldn't want that," said Damion. "She was right, Lorelyn—you are in worse danger than any of us where the Zimbourans are concerned. I will go back. Jomar can protect you."

"No, Damion." Ailia stepped forward. "Lorelyn needs both of you. Let me go instead."

"But you're not a fighter, Ailia. And you know where the Stone is," said Damion.

"I can tell you that," said Ailia. "It's in the temple of Heaven, of course, the biggest building in the city. It's in a shrine right at the very center." She turned with a heavy heart to descend the path again, down toward the cloud that swirled about the mountainside. She longed to see the city on the summit, and she was filled with terror at the thought of dragons and Zimbourans lurking in the mists below. But her guilt and anxiety over Ana were stronger. She remembered the old woman's calm and comforting presence during the long weeks of the ocean voyage. How could they abandon her? "Lorelyn is right. We should never have left her. She looked as if she were afraid, and trying to hide it. What were we all thinking? You don't need me, and I can keep Ana company. We'll find a place to hide together."

As she walked downhill she was aware of footsteps behind her. Damion and Lorelyn were following at her heels. Behind them Jomar called out in frustration. "What do you all think you're doing? I told you, we have to get to the top. And you'll never find the old woman in all that mist."

"You go, Jomar," Ailia called back. "You're the strongest. And I know how important it is to you to stop the Zimbourans. But we just can't go without Ana."

"She's right," Damion agreed. "No one must be left behind. If need be, I will carry Ana all the way uphill."

They continued to walk down the path. After a moment Jomar followed them. "None of you knows how to fight," he said tersely as they turned to look at him. "If we're doing this, we're doing it together."

They continued the descent in silence, gazing at the cloud below. It still flickered with lightning, but it was beginning to shred about the edges. It was almost, Ailia thought with a prickle of fear, as if some great battle of opposing forces was being waged within.

Suddenly Jomar stiffened and stood still. "Look—over there to the right, on the mountainside. I thought I saw someone!"

They halted. "Didn't Ana say the Anthropophagi never came up here?" said Damion.

"Perhaps it's the Zimbourans," Ailia whispered. What else could possibly happen to them now?

A dark figure was striding down the path toward them. It did not look like a Zimbouran soldier or an Anthropophagus: it was a tall man in a hooded black cloak. As they stood stupefied, gaping up at him, he called down to them.

"What on earth do the lot of you think you're doing?" the man demanded.

The voice was Mandrake's! As they stared at him in disbelief he threw back the voluminous hood, shaking his long mane of hair free. "What are you doing up here?" he repeated, continuing to walk toward them. "Why isn't Ana with you?"

"Lorelyn was the first to recover her voice. "She

stayed behind," she replied. "But we're going back to get her. To help her."

"The dragon," choked Ailia. "There was a dragon—"

"Of course. Didn't you know this mountain was dragon territory?"

"But what are *you* doing here?" Lorelyn exclaimed. "I thought you were still in Maurainia."

"I followed you here," Mandrake replied. "I know the way, from my wanderings: I have traveled here many times before. In fact, I have a home here."

"Who *are* you?" shouted Jomar, stepping toward him in an aggressive manner.

"You may call me Mandrake." He made a slight, ironic bow.

"What kind of a name is that?" retorted Jomar.

"I didn't say it was my name," the other replied coolly. "I said it was what you might call me." Though his speech was courteous, the tone was condescending. He smiled, showing all his teeth: the canines and incisors, Ailia noticed, were unusually long and sharp.

As he drew near, Greymalkin went rigid in Lorelyn's arms. The cat flattened her ears and hissed. "She doesn't like you," Jomar commented to Mandrake.

"The feeling," Mandrake replied, giving the cat glare for glare, "is mutual." His yellow eyes turned back to them. "Why did you leave Ana?"

"Why do you want to know?" returned Jomar belligerently.

"She was . . . tired," Damion explained, choosing his words with slow care. "There was a hard climb ahead, and possibly danger. This journey has been too much for her."

"Too much?" snapped Mandrake. "If it hadn't been for Ana none of you would have survived this long." He glared at them. "It was Ana who saved you from the dragon, Ana who freed you from the Zimbourans, Ana who brought you all safe to shore with her sorcery when the sea-storms would have capsized the galleons. Her powers have saved your lives, time and time again. She has taxed herself to the limit for you. She needs no help from you. There is nothing you can do for her."

No one could find anything to say to this. But Ailia had a sudden recollection of Ana's pale, tense face in the darkness of the storm-tossed ship, her odd withdrawn expression. She had thought the old woman was ill. And she recalled also how Ana had not let herself sleep on the journey, but remained awake all night to watch over the others. Perhaps because only *she* could deal with the dangers that threatened them? "Will . . . will Ana die?" she asked, frightened.

"No," said Mandrake with an odd vehemence. "Her powers are strong, and her body is too old and frail to withstand the stresses they place upon it. But she will not die." He straightened, towering in their midst. "Whatever possessed you to come up here in the first place? Why in Valdur's name can't you let well enough alone?"

"It won't be well enough if the Zimbourans get the Star Stone," countered Lorelyn. "Damion says there might be a war because of it."

"Far be it from me to argue with an authority like Damion." Mandrake cast a cold glance at the priest.

"We're going to go on and look for it," Damion said in a quiet voice. "And no one is going to stop us."

Mandrake's yellow, feline eyes narrowed to slits.

Damion had never had a close look at those eyes before, and he suddenly wondered if Mandrake was human, or related to the Anthropophagi. He did not really resemble the grotesque deformed creatures that had attacked them in the wood: but there were those unnatural eyes, those almost fanglike teeth. It was true that Ana said Mandrake had been born in Zimboura. But might not members of that strange inhuman race have fled to other lands in ages past? *No wonder Ana was so mysterious about Mandrake, back in Maurainia—I would never have believed her if she'd told me the truth. A descendant of a lost race—a bogeyman from a hearth-tale!*

A large sword with a dragon-patterned hilt hung sheathed at Mandrake's side, Damion noticed, but somehow he felt certain this man would be dangerous even without a weapon. He watched him with wary eyes, remembering that it was Mandrake who had abducted Lorelyn. *Why? Because the Tryna Lia's coming meant Trynisia would be rediscovered, taken back from Mandrake's people? The Zimbourans will destroy the Anthropophagi if they settle this island.* Now he understood. Mandrake must have heard of the Jana scroll and realized that its sea chart betrayed the location of his land and people. And so he had literally haunted the Academy, searching for the scroll; he had written the threatening letters that urged Damion to destroy it and break the vow that sheltered its keepers. And finally, in desperation, he had written to the Patriarch about the "heresy," and snatched Lorelyn away: all to put an end to Ana's Nemerei conspiracy, and the precious scroll that lay at its center.

Ailia took a hesitant step toward Mandrake. "Please—

couldn't you help us? I know you're not on the Zimbourans' side." She moved another step closer to him, her eyes pleading. "I believe Ana is important to you. She helped you, back when you were a child being mistreated by the Zimbourans. Don't you want to help her, and us? If the Zimbourans find the Stone, there will be a war—"

"Which is none of my concern."

Jomar glared at Ailia. "What are you doing? We don't need him. What about the old woman's Guardians?"

"Guardians?" Mandrake repeated.

"Ana spoke of an order of Elei," Damion told him, "sworn to stay in Trynisia until the Tryna Lia arrived to take the Stone."

"Here in Trynisia?" Mandrake raised his eyebrows. "There is nothing alive in this land except birds and beasts, and the hobs and Anthropophagi. The Elei are gone forever."

"They may be hiding in the mountains—" Lorelyn began.

"I have explored all this land, mountain and forest, hill and vale. No one lives here. I would have found them years ago."

The travelers all looked at one another in dismay. No Guardians! They had been so hopeful that they would have help once they arrived here. Now what were they to do? They could never get off the island on their own.

Unless Mandrake could be induced to help them, Ailia thought. She tried again. "You must have a ship of you own," she remarked. "You didn't come on the Zimbouran ships, did you?"

Mandrake's face was impassive. "No, I did not travel with them."

Damion stepped forward to stand at Ailia's side. "Listen to us, Mandrake. If you let us find the Stone and leave the island, I promise none of us will ever breathe a word about this place." Ailia winced, seeing her planned travel books evaporating before her eyes, but she remained silent as he continued. "We'll all swear to keep Trynisia a secret from the Commonwealth."

"And what of the Stone?"

"We won't take it back to Maurainia, I promise you that. We'll hide it—throw it in the sea—anything to keep it out of Zimbouran hands. Just help us to do that, and this island will be safe forever. King Khalazar will lose all his followers if he fails to find the Stone."

Mandrake arched an eyebrow at that, and seemed to consider as he looked from Ailia to Damion. "You argue like Ana already," he said at length. "Very well: I agree to your proposal. I don't usually take sides in these matters, but you have, between you, a sort of collective ineptitude that is somehow touching. I will accompany you, though, and keep an eye on you."

Jomar made an explosive noise of protest, but Damion turned to the Mohara man. "We don't want a fight, Jo. I suggest we let him help if he's willing."

Mandrake, watching Damion as though he followed the other man's thoughts, nodded in apparent satisfaction. "You may as well start out now," he said. With that, he made off at a brisk pace without glancing back to see if they were following him. After a moment they did. Jomar trailed along at the very end of the procession, wearing a baleful expression.

"I hope the dragon won't come back," Ailia said, her eyes searching the sky.

"The old woman said dragons were extinct," grumbled Jomar.

"She said there weren't any more *firedrakes,*" Ailia corrected. "Perhaps it was that other, older kind of dragon that she talked about. The ones the Elei worshipped—the Lords of Wind and Water."

"I thought those were just imaginary."

"She didn't say so—she talked about them as though they were real," said Ailia, remembering. "And didn't you notice that this one didn't breathe fire at us? I'm sure it would have if it could. It was one of the wind-and-water dragons, not a fire-dragon. The power it seemed to have over the weather—I feel certain it somehow *made* that rain cloud move toward us—"

"You're just imagining things," growled Jomar.

"No, she is right," Mandrake said, pausing and half turning toward them. "Dragons can gather clouds around them when they fly, concealing themselves. The ancients used to believe any oddly shaped cloud contained a dragon."

"But if they're all wrapped up in cloud, how can they see where they're going?" Lorelyn inquired.

"A dragon is not limited to the five feeble human senses," Mandrake told her in a lofty tone.

The group fell silent, concentrating on the slow ascent toward the summit. Damion kept casting sharp, wary glances up at the sky: it was now blue and clear for the most part, but there were one or two large sprawling cumuli in it that might easily hide a hundred dragons. And if they really were "wind-and-water dragons," might they not also be aquatic? Any of the deep sky-colored tarns they passed, cupped in the mountain's stony folds, might also be a lurking-place. Mandrake, however, did not appear in the least concerned. Damion glanced at the man's impassive profile. He flattered himself that he was a good reader of faces, but Mandrake's eluded him utterly. It might have been hewn from stone for all it revealed of its owner's emotions. Mandrake looked no more than thirty, and yet had the cynical, world-weary air of a much older man. Damion recalled reading that the Elei had enjoyed a longer lifespan than other human beings: was the same perhaps true of the Anthropophagi?

He glanced over at Jomar. That was another worry: his friendship with the Mohara man had begun to deteriorate. Jomar did not like Mandrake and made no secret of it. He plainly did not trust the man, and also seemed to feel that his self-appointed role as leader of the expedition had been usurped.

"Who is this Mandrake, anyway?" he demanded of Damion when their guide was a short distance away.

"I think he's an Anthropophagus," Damion began.

"Of *course* he's an Anthro-what-d'you-call-it—just look at those eyes of his! I meant who does he *think* he is—and what's his interest in this whole affair? I'd still like to know more about him."

"So would I," admitted Damion. "Ana didn't tell us much, did she? There's some mystery there. She didn't seem to want to talk about it."

"That old woman's always making a mystery of everything," Jomar grumbled. "If I were you, I wouldn't trust Mandrake any farther than I could throw this mountain. Remember what he did to Lorelyn."

"Perhaps he was only trying to protect her," replied Damion, trying to ease his own misgivings. "I think he was the one who told the Patriarch all about her and the Nemerei. Perhaps he felt obligated to keep her safe from the Zimbourans after that. Let's not antagonize him, Jo. We could be wrong about him."

Jomar's only response to this remark was a stony silence.

They were all very quiet as they approached the summit. There was something overwhelming about the mountain, now that field and forest had been left behind and its igneous bones were laid bare to their view. Sheer crags hung above, gray as louring clouds. Ailia felt increasingly timid under that granite scowl. She looked out on the ranges beyond, their slopes velveted with verdure, their peaks of layered rock etched with snow. Beyond these in turn were far-off summits completely mantled in glaciers.

Mandrake saw her looking at them. "The great ice fields," he said softly. "This land was once completely covered in ice, and nothing could grow here. The first inhabitants of Trynisia altered its climate long ago with the aid of sorcery. They placed crystals about the land that could warm the air around them for a considerable distance. The weatherstones are there still, but their power is weakening and will one day fail. And then Trynisia will end as it began: a frozen waste, its fields and forests buried in ice, its history forgotten."

Ailia shivered, thinking of the immense implacability of the slow-marching ice. The glaciers were merely biding their time until the day when they could devour Trynisia once more. She glanced at Mandrake's face and saw a peculiar expression on his features—"Sort of gloomy and gloating at the same time," was the nearest she could come to describing it later—and hurriedly looked away again.

The path wound on and up, steep as a stair. And at long last they saw above them a wall, built of the mountain's gray granite and blending with the crags so that it was nearly invisible. Atop the wall was a turret, its slit windows facing the road, and beneath the turret an archway opened, dark and deep. The path led through it; on the other side must be—

"Liamar!" Ailia breathed, breaking the silence.

CLOUD SWIRLED ABOUT the mountainside, bellowing with thunder; in its midst old Ana stood, leaning wearily upon a granite outcrop. Winged shadows swung through the grayness overhead, dived down, and then swerved away as she raised her free hand. But the dragons flew lower with every dive, as if an invisible ceiling positioned above Ana were subsiding along with her strength. Her eyes were closed, her head bowed.

He is with them now, the old woman thought. *He was right that I could not prevent it. Should I have warned them about Mandrake? But then they might have tried to fight him: Lorelyn is impetuous, and Jomar also.* There was a crack, and the world turned white, then dark; there was a smell of scorched air. They had cast a thunderbolt at her, trying to break through her shield. She straightened with a last effort as the dragons flew lower, so low that her hair and cloak stirred in the gusts from their wings. *No, they must not fight him. If the Tryna Lia draws on her untested powers, tries to use them against him, it will be her destruction. He would strike back at once with all the force he has. But for now, he does not fear her, nor she him. Let ignorance be her shield. She must not guess what he is, what threat he presents to her. Nor must she suspect who . . .*

Slowly Ana slid to the ground. Above her the dragons roared in triumph.

16

The Queen of Heaven

THEY STOOD TOGETHER INSIDE the ancient gateway, gazing out on a wilderness of tumbled and broken stone. Buildings stood cheek by jowl due to the scarcity of space, their walls weathered and crumbling, among narrow streets. Above the collapsed roofs the dome of the Temple of Heaven swelled like a rising moon. But its decorative gilding had long gone, and a great winding fissure ran up its southern face. They walked on into the desolate streets without speaking. They had expected ruin, but there was something in the atmosphere of the place that overwhelmed them. Due to its high elevation the city was nearly silent: only the wind made an eerie ululation, like a lament, through the gaping doors and windows of the empty buildings.

In the exact center of the city was a circular plaza

surrounded by shattered structures, a few foundations, and some broken-off columns like the stumps of dead trees, many blackened as if by a great fire. Here stood the Temple of Heaven, with the royal palace to one side. Ailia, looking at the latter, felt her initial euphoria fade. Tears pricked at her eyes. So this was all that was left of the palace of the Elei monarch, wonder of the world! Gone were the jeweled walls, the gold leaf, the mosaics: all the splendors of which Welessan the Wanderer had written with such enthusiasm. Only the stone skeleton was left, cracked and crumbling walls and a single lonely tower. It was all the more moving because some vestige of its old splendor remained, in the proud arches of doors and windows and the aspiring lines of the surviving tower.

"I wish I hadn't seen it!" Ailia burst out, breaking the silence at last. "If I hadn't, I could have gone on imagining it as beautiful and splendid, the way it was in the stories. Now I'll always think of it as a ruin." She looked around the lifeless city: it was like a cemetery, she thought, where all the hopes and dreams of a lost race lay buried.

"Well, let's get on with it," said Jomar. He spoke with an air of authority, determined to reestablish himself as the leader of the group.

"First we will find some shelter, a place where you can leave your gear," said Mandrake. He led the way to a ruined guesthouse. Jomar had no choice but to follow him with the others.

Mandrake led them along a maze of stone passages, their ceilings long since fallen, to a roofed room where they left their meager supplies and Greymalkin. At one end was a vast fireplace, large enough to stand up inside. "You will be able to sleep here in safety," he told them.

"What about dragons?" asked Ailia.

He seemed to find that amusing. "No dragon could fit in that narrow door. Now, let us go to the high temple and get this business over with. Bring a torch with you."

The columns, statues, and broken walls of the city cast long shadows toward the east, and the larger shadow of the western peak had plunged half of Liamar into premature darkness. They could see the six-pointed star formed by the outer fortifications, a turret at each point, and the radial pattern of the six main avenues centering on the temple plaza. Though it filled all of the plateau or broad hanging valley at Elendor's summit, Liamar was not very large: it could have fitted into Raimar many times over with ease. It had not perhaps been a city in the true sense of the word, for only the sibyls had lived here permanently, and the monarch in the royal palace—a palace much smaller than any royal residence of the modern world. The rest of the buildings, apart from the temple and the library, had been hostels and guesthouses for the pilgrims who journeyed here from all over the world.

They picked their way across the ruined plaza in the failing light, pausing occasionally at some intriguing sight. There was a long serpentine channel or conduit, for draining off rainwater perhaps: but it was dry as dust now. There were statues, a few still standing, though with lost limbs or heads. One was a magnificent equestrian figure, a king upon a mighty war horse. "Andarion," said Mandrake, barely glancing at the statue as they passed it. "It was raised after his victory in Zimboura, when he brought back the Stone." There was another statue farther on, this one of a woman on a tall plinth, crowned with stars and standing on an upturned crescent moon.

"Elarainia?" Ailia asked.

"No: that is her daughter, the Tryna Lia," Mandrake told her, pointing to the Elensi inscription on the side of the plinth.

Ailia stole a glance at Lorelyn, looking from girl to statue and back again, shaking her head. These two—the same person? Impossible! Lorelyn looked as grubby and unkempt as the rest of them: her long braids were unraveling, the freckled bridge of her nose was sunburned and starting to peel. There was certainly nothing particularly holy about her at the moment.

Lorelyn too looked pensive as she gazed up at the statue. "So these were my people," she said quietly. "I've always wondered where I came from, and who I was."

"I thought the Elei died out," said Damion.

"As a race, yes," confirmed Mandrake. "They are gone from the world. But their blood still runs in the veins of a few people living today."

Ailia looked at Damion. An incredible thought came to her, one she could scarcely suppress for excitement. His well-wrought features and those of the carved statues were so alike: could it be that he too was of Elei blood? Like Lorelyn, he had been left an orphan. If there were descendants of the Fairfolk still living in the world, why should Damion not have been born to one as well? She yearned to tell him of this idea, but on second thought she felt a little foolish and decided to say nothing.

Nearby three white pillars were joined at the top by a fragment of entablature, which Mandrake explained was all that was left of the Great Library that burned down in the Great Disaster, taking with it most of the ancient world's knowledge. They began to be glad of Mandrake's company, so fascinating were the pieces of information he shared with them, so vividly did he bring to life the history of the place.

Lorelyn pointed to the western peak. "I see two statues up there." Everyone looked, and saw that she was right: high up on the great horn of rock was a pair of figures about twenty paces apart, dragons attached to stone pillars.

"It's like those spirit-gates on the Kaanish islands," Damion commented, remembering the dragon pillars.

"That is the Moon Gate," said Mandrake. "The final stage of the climbing of Elendor. Most stopped with their viewing of the Stone, and went back down the mountain; but a few chose to go higher still in their quest for the Divine. They climbed to the very top of that highest peak, and then they walked through the gateway formed by those two pillars."

Jomar stared at the portal with an expression of mingled disbelief and disgust. "*Through* it—into what? The cliff's probably sheer as a wall on the far side. The drop must be seven thousand feet!"

"They went through the portal," Mandrake replied, "to be transported to what you would call Heaven—the realm of the stars."

"To Heaven!" exclaimed Damion, appalled. "You mean they died, don't you? They deliberately walked through that gate and fell to their deaths—a sort of ritual suicide—"

"No!" Ailia was aghast. "It can't be true! Welessan said nothing about that. How horrible!"

Mandrake wore a look of amused tolerance. "You misunderstand completely. If you walked through the Moon Gate *now* you would die. But in the days of the Elei that stone gateway opened onto a portal through the Ether."

"The what?" they all said.

"A plane that lies beyond the material world that you know. The Elei called it the Ethereal Plane. Through it one could pass from place to place without crossing physical distances. The ancient Elei sorcerers made large numbers of these portals, and taught the skill to Nemerei of other countries. The Kaans made portals of their own to link the many islands of their realm together, so that it would no longer be necessary to travel by ship. But in the end the gates became too dangerous to use, and all had to be closed. For just as mortals could enter the Ether, so . . . other things . . . from that dimension could cross over into ours. The Elendor portal was not closed, but its opening was moved: it no longer lies between the pillars, but high up in the sky above the mountaintop where only a skilled sorcerer can reach it. Real dragons guarded the portal once, to protect access to the higher plane. There was one special breed, the Imperial dragons, bred in ancient times as watchdogs. These were golden in color, with five toes on each foot instead of the usual three or four."

"Were they *tame?*" asked Lorelyn staring.

"They were biddable, yes: the Elei could even ride on their backs."

"*Ride*—on a dragon!" Ailia exclaimed. "How wonderful that must have been! To fly through the air—!"

"Yes," said Mandrake, and for the first time he smiled without mockery. "But the Elei used dragons for mounts only at need. They had other ways of traveling the skies, in greater ease and comfort."

"The flying ships," breathed Ailia. "The Ships that Sail Over Land and Sea—"

"Yes. They knew how to build ships with wings in place of masts, that could fly through the air like birds. Only a sorcerer could fly such a vessel, of course, but in those days sorcerers were common as salt."

Damion looked back over the desolation of the city and thought with sadness of the marvels it must once have boasted. "To think that the entire world was once united, under this city and its rulers . . . If the old Commonwealth had survived, I wonder where mankind would be now?"

"Probably right where it is at the moment," opined Mandrake. He had a cynical streak, in addition to the acerbic tongue that they were learning not to provoke. "The Elei were a clever race, but they were always intervening: they could never learn to leave well enough alone. They took too much on themselves, trying to impose their will on the world, to model it after their own ideals. And this is what came of all their efforts." His cold golden eyes swept over the ruined city: it might have been a trampled anthill for all the emotion he displayed.

Lorelyn spied a small wizened shrub growing up through a crack in the pavement, and paused to examine it. She saw that it bore both flower and fruit, like a tree of the tropics. The cream-colored blossoms had a delicate, spicy fragrance, and the plum-sized fruits smelled tantalizingly ripe. She was still famished after a soggy ship's-biscuit lunch. Surely it couldn't be poisonous, with such a wonderfully sweet smell?

"Look," she called to the others. "Is this edible, do you think?" She plucked off a fruit and held it up. It was semi-translucent, like a gem: the light flowed through its amber flesh, while the pit showed as a shadow deep within.

"I know what it is," said Ailia, quivering with excitement. "Food-of-the-gods—it must be the food-of-the-gods fruit. It grows on a tree called the tree-of-heaven that's found only in Eldimia, Welessan said. But the Elei brought a few seedlings with them when they settled in Trynisia. They grow small and sickly here—only the soil of Eldimia really suits them. But their fruit's still magical, or so he wrote. Anyone can eat the fruit, but if Nemerei eat it they will have visions."

"A drug," said Jomar, dismissive. "Like opium."

"I want to try it," said Lorelyn eagerly.

"Oh no you don't. Drugs of that kind are dangerous."

"But—"

"Jomar and Ailia are both right," Mandrake said. "The fruit is not safe."

"But I'm a Nemerei, and so is Damion. Ana said so. Maybe eating it will help us somehow."

"And maybe it won't. I would not try it if I were you. Let us go."

In silence they walked on to the Temple of Heaven. Spread-winged marble angels stood on the parapet of its tall portico, as though poised for flight. But they were not really angels, Ailia corrected herself: they were the El, the winged gods of the Elei—and their ancestors, it had once been believed. Some of the figures had broken wings and limbs, but their faces were in the main unmarred, bending on the city below the same serene and regal regard they had bestowed upon it in days of old, when it was filled with life and laughter and music. What scenes had those ancient stone faces gazed down upon?

"They were *not* gods," Mandrake said to her, seeing her staring at the statues. "The Old Ones were no more gods than you or I."

"Old Ones?"

"So the Elei once called the beings whom they worshipped as gods. The learned magisters of the Royal Academy would say that the Old Ones were only a myth, but the truth lies in between. I have found the evidence."

"What evidence? Tell us!" pleaded Ailia, her curiosity piqued.

"As if he needed encouragement!" muttered Jomar from his place at the rear.

Mandrake paid him no heed. "Long ago," he said, speaking softly, "before the human race arose, there lived in this land a great and sorcerous people. They were older than the Elei, older than any other living thing on earth: the beings you call gods and angels and faeries are myths that grew out of tales told about them. They learned to control all the elements and the forces of nature, bending them as they willed: that is how they created this warm verdant island in the far north. The so-called talismans—the famous swords and rings and so on that the Elei treasured—were actually artifacts created by these Old Ones. If you were to journey to the northern mountains you might still find some traces of their cities, buried beneath the glacial ice. And there would be treasures too, and other wonders you cannot imagine. In the ice caves of those mountains you can still find, perfectly preserved, the frozen corpses of creatures the world has never seen. Lion-eagles, winged serpents, beasts of strange hybrid anatomy: creations of the Old Ones, who long ago learned to manipulate the very stuff of life as they pleased. They fashioned the chimaera, a huge beast with a body like a dragon's and not one but *three* long necks, each ending in a different sort of head. One was shaped like a giant snake's, another resembled a lion's, while the third was like that of a goat."

"It *can't* have been real," stated Lorelyn, incredulous.

"No?" He raised an eyebrow. "I have seen its remains myself, preserved in an ice field in the mountains. Nature could never have produced such an oddity on its own. The Old Ones may even have learned to alter their own bodies with magic."

Ailia stared. "You mean . . . they might really have had wings?"

"Perhaps. We'll never know: the Old Ones lived many millennia ago. They were a long-lived race, I think, but they were still mortal. Some of them even stooped to taking mates from among the primitive peoples of the Continents, bringing their offspring back here to Trynisia with them. And so the Elei race came to be. The Fairfolk would later believe that their ancestors were gods. Not all of the Old Ones were benevolent, though. Their ruler Modrian, for instance, was as petty and tyrannical as any human despot."

"He was *real*—I mean, a real person?" exclaimed Ailia.

"I believe so. As was your archangel Athariel, and Elarainia the Morning Star Goddess, and all the divine beings in the ancient tales: they were probably all based on half-forgotten accounts of famous Old Ones. What the beings would have thought of their deification is anybody's guess."

"What became of them, then? Where did they all go?" Jomar demanded, a note of challenge in his voice.

Mandrake walked on toward the temple. "Legend had it that they were not of this world at all, but came from the stars and later returned there. But I think it is more likely they killed one another off in their wars. They never returned to reclaim their Star Stone, precious as it was to them. I believe they really did make it, rather than digging it out of the earth, for they could easily have learned to reshape nonliving as well as living matter. When they went to war, clashing with one another in the skies, the Stone fell from Modrian's coronet and landed on the mountaintop. The humans must have been too frightened to approach the gem at first. Later, they came and built this temple over it, and worshipped it."

They followed him toward the temple steps. "I don't believe it," Ailia whispered to Damion. "The angels flesh-and-blood beings, mortal like us—I *won't* believe it!"

"I wouldn't believe all he says," Damion whispered back. "He's very knowledgeable, Ailia, but he doesn't know everything."

Ailia gazed up at the temple's towers and façade. "The Last Level—oh, it doesn't seem right, somehow. We ought to have prepared for it, like the pilgrims."

"Nonsense," said Mandrake briskly, and strode on up the wide stone steps. They followed him to the pillared entrance. Two huge brazen beasts stood guard within the portico, fantastic creatures half lion and half eagle, with brazen bowls between their forepaws where sacred fires had once burned.

"Gryphons," said Ailia.

"Cherubim," Mandrake corrected her.

"But cherubim are angels," said Damion, puzzled. "The angelic order that guarded the gates of Heaven."

"So your priestly masters instructed you, but they were wrong. The cherubim were magical beasts, half lion and half eagle, created by the gods as guardians for their treasures. Dark Age writers like Bendulus who came across pictures of the creatures centuries later decided they must be monsters—hence your mythical gryphon. And artists who read the scriptures but had never seen live cherubim supposed them to be guardian angels, and portrayed them that way."

"Welessan the Wanderer said no one could see the Stone without first 'passing between the cherubim,' " observed Ailia, looking at the statues. "Was that what he meant?"

"No doubt." Mandrake turned toward the temple. "Shall we go in?" he suggested casually.

The others stepped forward, but Ailia hung back a little. "Welessan said that you had to be spiritually ready to go into the temple."

"More nonsense," replied Mandrake curtly. "Haven't you been listening to all I've been telling you? There are no gods or angels, Ailia: no holy places." The others trailed after him, Ailia still lagging a little. But even her apprehension could not have prepared her for what happened next.

As Mandrake passed between the brass figures, they came to life. Ailia distinctly saw one roll its brazen eye, glaring upon the party with the dark hole of its pupil. Too amazed even to scream or yell, she halted as, with a gritty grinding sound, the two giant beasts slowly raised themselves upon their haunches, spreading their metallic wings. Then they opened their eagle beaks and uttered a simultaneous rasping screech.

The travelers sprang back, clutching at one another. But the brazen beasts made no further move. Mandrake looked back over his shoulder at them. "Come along—it's perfectly safe."

"Is it magic?" Lorelyn asked, still staring at the statues.

"No, just a kind of elaborate clockwork. When you pass over the threshold your weight activates the mechanism. The Elei kings and queens had many such toys, in the old days. Queen Eliana had a tree of gold with mechanical birds in the branches that sang and flapped their wings when a lever was pressed."

"You might have warned us," Damion reproved, taking Ailia's arm comfortingly. She was trembling.

"I forgot," Mandrake replied smoothly, and vanished into the temple.

"Forgot, my eye!" growled Jomar. He too had been alarmed, and it made him angry. "He's just trying to unnerve us."

Then they entered the vast great central chamber of the temple, and what Ailia saw there drove all other thoughts from her mind.

All around that vast round space were giant arched niches, seven in all. In six of these were stone images, each many times the height of a living man. One was the statue of a youth in the act of leaping into the air, his hair flowing up like flames: he was carved all of red granite, and his flying hair plated with copper that must once have shone red too, though it was dulled now with verdigris. Next to him was a throned marble image of Elarainia, star-tipped scepter in hand. Her niche was painted blue and patterned with white stars and the figure of the Tryna Lia on her Moon Throne floating above. In the very center of the chamber stood a stone structure with a domed roof, like a small temple in its own right. The side facing the entrance was open, showing a dark space within. Atop the dome stood a female figure, more than life-size and covered in gold leaf: from her head radiated a halo of golden rays and stylized flames that flared into brilliance when the torchlight touched them.

"Elauria, the Sun Goddess," Mandrake said. "To the Elei the sun was female, not male. The circling sun shines in through the doorway in summer, lighting the Sun Goddess's statue." He waved his hand at the niches. "Those are the gods of the Elements, with their corresponding planets: the boy is Elarkurion, god of the closest planet to the fiery sun, sphere of the Salamanders; the one with the fish-tail is Eltalandria, who ruled the watery world of the Undines. Iantha was the air-planet, home of the Sylphs; Valdys the planet of the Earth Gnomes . . ."

The images were splendid beyond anything the travelers had ever seen. Eltalandria's upper body was of pinkish-white marble, veined like living flesh, and her piscine half was of dark green marble streaked with white. Her royal diadem was a frothing mass of pearls, some bubble-round and others formed like falling droplets; here and there upon her figure bright stones had been set, diamonds on her torso and emeralds among her scales and fins, to glisten in the light as though the dry stone bore a sea-wet sheen. In the next niche Elvaldys stood, his somber heavy figure hewn from a single block of gray-black granite, sparkling here and there with hoary flecks of mica. Eliantha, by contrast, was an airy form of alabaster and crystal, poised as if for flight with four diaphanous butterfly wings outspread. Around her shimmering tourmaline skirts smaller sylph-figures appeared to dance and dart like dragonflies. And in the largest niche of all stood the image of a woman of milk-white marble, so exquisitely carved that her white hair and robes seemed to stir in a gentle wind. Figures of animals—deer, lions, bears—fawned at her feet, and her arms overflowed with stone fruits and flowers. The travelers stood and stared up at the images in silence, and from their shadowed niches the cold stone eyes of the ancient gods peered back down at them.

Overhead the dome rose up in a swelling curve like a small and lesser sky, and they saw that it was in fact intended to be a model of the heavens, fretted and frescoed with stars and figures that represented the constellations. The great jagged fissure was visible from beneath, stabbing toward the apex like a black thunderbolt. Here and there, too, a gap showed in the ceiling where a stone block had fallen in and smashed on the floor beneath. At the zenith was a circular hole where the lantern would be in a temple dome, about ten paces in diameter, and unglazed; they assumed at first that the glass had been broken when the dome cracked. But Mandrake told them this round embrasure had always been open to the sky and the elements, and he pointed out to them the eaves in the roof of the central shrine, with carved lions' heads at the corners to spout rainwater and melted snow into shallow drainage channels in the floor beneath. Marveling at the building's design, Damion pivoted where he stood until the whole of the domed space seemed to revolve slowly about him, like the skies around the earth. Temples of the Faith had many round windows and ornaments to reflect the infinite Divine, but only the Elei had constructed a temple that was itself circular.

"I can see the polestar," he remarked, pointing up through the hole in the roof at the darkening sky. "Was that opening designed to frame it?"

Mandrake nodded. "Yes—but when this structure was first built there was a different star wheeling at the pole, and the constellations you know occupied other positions in the sky. It is that old."

Ailia walked back to the image of Elarainia. She felt drawn to the goddess somehow. She looked up at the serene marble face under its crown of stars—at the snow-cold features that were at once young and also conveyed untold antiquity. It was the face of a divine being—frozen in eternity yet still human-featured, unchanging yet also infinitely wise: old and young, virginal yet maternal. She thought how comforting it would be to pray to such a deity, to stand before it not as a supplicant, but as a child might seek solace at its mother's knee. Almost she yielded—almost she reached out her hand to touch the marble feet that protruded from beneath the stone robe. She noticed a difference between them: the right foot was carved with exquisite detail, even to the toenails and the straps of the sandal with which it was shod, but the left foot was worn quite smooth, as if by the touch of innumerable worshippers, and a longing filled her to lay her own hand there . . . Then a voice shrilled in her head:

blasphemy! The scowling bearded image of Aan, father-god of the Faith, interposed itself and she retreated in a confusion of guilt and dismay.

"Mandrake," Lorelyn said, "there's another place for a statue over there, but it's empty. Why is that?"

"The seventh niche is for Elazar—the deity of a planet your people haven't discovered yet. Long ago, Elei astrologers predicted that a strange star would one day enter the heavens, bringing with it a new planet. They created a niche for that planet, and placed an image there.

"But the new star, Azarah, and its attendant planet Azar passed through the great cloud of comets that lies far out in the heavens, and disturbed it: and for thousands of years comets could be seen streaking through the night skies. Azarah had disrupted the order of the heavens, which the Elei considered divine: and so it was declared to be an evil star, ruled by a corrupt spirit. Azar was also clearly a planet of malign influence, and they removed the image of its deity from the Temple of Heaven. Little did they know how catastrophic that disruption would yet prove to be. One fateful day several comets entered the atmosphere of Mera, and destroyed the lands they fell upon. The Great Disaster. Those who survived cursed the name of the Seventh Planet."

"*Seventh* planet?" repeated Ailia, looking about the temple. "But there are only five planets—apart from Azar, that is. Where is the other?"

"Right underneath your feet," Mandrake told her solemnly. "The world is a planet too, you know: the planet Mera, third from the sun. The Elei were well aware of that fact, though your enlightened astronomers have yet to stumble onto it. The woman of white marble in the big niche is Elmera, goddess of this planet and all that grows on it."

The world a *planet!* Ailia wondered what clever Janeth would have thought of that idea. It was too fantastic.

Jomar, who had paced in a restless manner while the rest of them admired the images, spoke up impatiently. "Where's this stone of yours?"

"It's underneath that shrine in the center," Ailia told him, pointing to the structure topped by the gold Sun Goddess. "That's the original shrine they built over the Stone; this bigger temple was raised around it, later."

Jomar peered inside the door of the shrine. "There's nothing in here."

"There's a stair. You go down it, and there's a sort of cryptlike space underneath, with the mountain's top for a floor. The Stone always lay right where it had fallen. Except for the Zimbourans stealing it, that one time, it was never moved."

Jomar raised his eyebrows skeptically. "You'd think any stone would shatter, falling from the sky onto a rocky mountain top."

"The Star Stone was supposed to be very hard—harder than diamond."

"Nothing's harder than diamond."

"Nothing on *earth* is," said Ailia softly.

"So where's the stair to get down?"

"I—I don't know," Ailia admitted. "There should be one. Welessan said there was."

"Are you sure it was inside the shrine?"

"No . . . Come to think of it, he didn't say exactly where it was. I just assumed it was in the shrine. He didn't go into great detail about it."

They all crowded inside the structure. It was like a smaller, cruder copy of the great temple, circular in shape, with stone carvings of the planetary gods all around its walls. But no stairway was anywhere to be seen; there was no room for one.

"Was it in the middle of the floor?" suggested Damion. "See that round patch, right in the center: the stone doesn't quite match there. It looks as though something was filled in, long ago."

"No, there was no stair. There *was* an opening there in the floor, a sort of round hole the pilgrims could look through to see the sanctum down below, where the Stone lay," said Mandrake. He stood in the doorway, watching them with the trace of a smile on his face. "The hole was filled in after the gem was recovered from the Zimbourans, to discourage any more attempts at theft. Later pilgrims had to enter the sanctum by its door if they wished to see the Star Stone."

"Well, where is the door?" demanded Jomar impatiently. But Mandrake merely shrugged his shoulders, then sauntered outside again to gaze at the statues in the main temple.

"Beast," Lorelyn muttered. "I'll bet he knows."

Damion sighed wearily. "Well, let's have a look around and see if we can find a way in."

They went back outside again and searched for nearly an hour, without success. There was no door to be seen in the shrine apart from the one they had entered, and no staircase anywhere in the temple, which also appeared to have only a single entrance. Discouraged, Ailia wandered back to the statue of Elarainia. "Please," she murmured, "please help us find it. We're running out of time. The

Zimbourans will be here soon." She knew she was praying to a pagan deity, but the situation was desperate, and Elarainia seemed the right one to appeal to. *After all, she's an angel in the scriptures,* the girl thought. And Welessan the Wanderer had said something about Elarainia being the way and the door for all who would see the Stone . . . She knelt at the statue's feet, gazing at the left one. On an impulse, she placed her own hand upon the cool stone. It was smooth as a sea-pebble caressed by countless waves.

Then she sprang back with a little startled cry. The foot had moved beneath her hand.

The cry, and the loud grinding noise that followed, brought her companions running. All stopped short, staring as the stone figure quivered, then began to move forward. Slowly, majestically, the carved throne advanced with a grating sound across the floor, bearing with it the Queen of Heaven still smiling her marble smile—a proud and gracious potentate commencing a regal processional. Then as abruptly as it had started, the stone chair ceased its motion, to stand several paces in front of the now-empty niche.

Lorleyn darted forward. "Look!" In the floor of the niche, exposed by the displacement of the stone image, was a square dark hole—with a flight of stone steps in it leading down.

"The door—the door!" Ailia cried, wild with excitement. "It leads to the Stone, I know it does! That's what Welessan wrote—Elarainia is the 'way and the door'! I *wondered* what he meant. Her foot is a sort of lever, see—you push down on it, and it opens the way to the staircase!"

"Good for you, Ailia!" said Damion. "Mandrake, hand me that torch, will you?"

One by one they proceeded through the archway and down the narrow spiral stair beyond, each of its steps worn to troughlike concavity by the treading feet of myriads of pilgrims. At the bottom was a passage, low-roofed and floored with the living rock of the mountain. They followed it to where it ended in a set of low, bronze doors.

"Look—do you see the difference in the stonework, there around the door frame?" said Ailia. She whispered, as though she were in a chapel. "That must be the foundation of the shrine—we're right underneath it!"

Damion passed the torch to Lorelyn, and he and Jomar tried without success to force the doors, first pushing at them, then trying to pry them open.

"I don't suppose you'd consider giving us a hand," snapped Jomar, glaring at Mandrake, who had followed them down and now stood watching them with a face as impassive as the stone gods'.

"It is your quest, not mine," he responded, indifferent.

"This is maddening!" Lorelyn exclaimed. "To have come so far, just to be stopped a few paces away from the Stone!"

"Wait a moment," said Damion. "I think I felt this door give a little."

Jomar joined him at the left-hand door and they both shoved. There was a gritty, groaning sound from the hinges, and then, so suddenly it startled them, the door gave way. It opened inward, onto a darkness that Lorelyn made haste to light with the torch.

Before them lay a scene of strange splendor. A blue-curtained canopy with stars wrought in silver arose before them in the gloom, and there were rich hangings of gold and red on the walls behind, and votive offerings of flower-wreaths and garlands were strewn upon the bare rock of the floor. For an instant the companions gazed at them in breathless silence. Then all at once there was a sighing sound and a rush of stale air. The flowers and hangings drifted into dust and the canopy sagged, disintegrating before their eyes. It was as if their intrusion had somehow profaned the sanctum, thought Ailia in dismay, as they backed away coughing at the roiling dust clouds. The torch fluttered fitfully.

"Be careful," Mandrake's voice came from behind them. "The air in there will be foul after all these years."

It was infuriating, but they had to retreat down the passage and wait some time for the atmosphere to clear. Then they ventured forward again, Jomar and Damion leading, and entered the ruined chamber. The Mohara man shoved the debris of the canopy aside: it crumbled to even smaller fragments at his touch. There was a pause. "Where's the Stone supposed to be?" he called out.

Ailia answered. "There's a pattern set into the floor, like a silver star, to mark the spot where the Star Stone landed. The Stone should be right at its center."

Jomar's voice sounded weary. "Well, it isn't here."

"The star?"

"No—the Stone. It's gone."

17

The Day of Disaster

THE TRAVELERS RETURNED to the guesthouse—without Mandrake, who continued to wander about the ruins on his own—feeling tired and depressed. *And I was just starting to feel useful,* Ailia mourned to herself. Night had fallen, and in the torchlight the ruins looked not so much forlorn as sinister. Between their worry over Ana, their disappointment at not finding the Stone, and their physical weariness, the spirits of the four were at a low ebb. Jomar and Lorelyn began sparring almost at once as to how to cook the thin, watery gruel that was all they had for the evening meal. The other two, tired of listening to them, retreated to the opposite end of the room and talked together.

"Are you *positive* that the Stone was in that particular chamber, Ailia?" asked Damion for the third time.

She nodded, too miserable to speak.

"There wasn't any other place where it was sometimes kept?"

"No—I'm certain Welessan said it was always in the one place."

That would make sense, if the Stone were the goal of so many pilgrims' quests, Damion reflected. They would have to know where to find it! "Could it have been stolen?" he asked aloud. "By Mandrake, perhaps?"

"Nonsense," declared a deep voice behind him. They all started and turned around. For such a large man, Mandrake could move very quietly: he seemed to have come right up out of the floor. Ailia half expected to see a trapdoor behind him like a pantomime demon's, belching infernal smoke. Greymalkin glared and rose, her fur bristling.

"If you'll think about that for a moment, you'll see how absurd it is," he told Damion matter-of-factly, neither anger nor indignation in his voice. "You saw for yourself how well-sealed the sanctum was. No one else could have entered it without disturbing the contents. Have you ever considered that the last of the Elei to leave Trynisia might have taken the Stone with them, against Bereborn's knowledge? It could be somewhere on the Continent then, or in the Archipelagoes."

"That's true enough," acknowledged Damion. Ailia's heart sank. She had so longed to see the gem.

"All this fuss over a piece of stone," Mandrake mused. "Lives lost, kingdoms overthrown, wars waged, and all for what? I don't know whether to call it comedy or tragedy. If it's any comfort to you, there's probably very little you could do anyway. It's been several centuries since the Zimbourans and the Commonwealth went to war. They are long overdue for another, Stone or no Stone."

"We should have a look for it all the same," Damion persisted. "It could be lying somewhere else in the city for all we know. I don't want to take any chances on the Zimbourans coming across it. We'll search all the ruins, just in case it's still here." Ailia's spirits lifted again.

A brief silence fell, and was broken by a fresh exchange between Jomar and Lorelyn. A strong smell of burning accompanied their repartee. "What happened to supper?" Damion asked.

"Her Highness the Princess of the Stars ruined it," Jomar replied.

"I did not," Lorelyn returned. "It was you said it ought to cook longer."

"It wouldn't have hurt to *stir* it. Don't you know anything?"

Seeing that they were about to recommence their argument, Damion intervened. "Well, it can't be helped now. Let's get out the other supplies. I think there's some dried fruit. Are you cold, Ailia?" he asked, seeing her shiver where she sat huddled in her cloak.

"No," she answered. "It's just that this place is so old and empty. It gives me an odd feeling."

He nodded, understanding. "Don't worry, Ailia. We won't be here long."

"Oh, I'm not frightened," she assured him. "It just makes me sad, that's all. I keep thinking of the people who used to come to this city. And now there won't be any more people here, ever again. No more pilgrims—no more queens or kings—"

"Except for Princess Lorelyn. And His Majesty here," sneered Jomar, jerking his thumb at Mandrake.

The tall man bowed, returning mockery for mockery. "I will take my leave of you now, since you seem determined to waste your time here," he announced, "but I will remain in the area should you require an escort back down the mountain."

Jomar bristled, but Damion made himself reply with courtesy. "Our thanks for your offer."

Mandrake cast a last glance over the small group. As he turned toward the fire its light kindled his catlike eyes. "You would be wise to accept it," he said.

Without another word he strode out of the chamber, his cloaked figure blending into the darkness beyond.

ALL THROUGH THE LONG ARCTIC day that followed they searched the ruins without success. It was a difficult, if not a hopeless quest, and they knew it: the Stone, if it were in Trynisia at all, could be buried anywhere under the heaps of rubble. But they knew that if the Zimbourans *did* succeed in unearthing it here—or even some other jewel that chanced to resemble it—a war might well be the result.

As the little group began rummaging in the rubble they kept a wary eye out for dragons, but saw none; the only other living things in sight were some small black birds—choughs, Ailia thought—which flew about the roofs of the ruins. At midday—or what would have been midday, had the sun stood at high noon instead of partway up the southern sky—they took time off for a meager meal, which they ate in gloomy silence, huddling together at the base of the statue of Andarion. Jomar in particular was frustrated and snappish—the idea of beating the Zimbourans to their precious prize had become something of an obsession for him. As soon as the meal was over they went back to searching, Damion and Lorelyn setting off to the remains of the palace, while Jomar combed through the rubble of another unidentified building across from the Temple of Heaven.

Ailia walked about the city on her own. Her back

ached from so much stooping and she stretched, lifting her face to the sky. High in that blue immensity she spotted a minute pinprick of pale light, shining faintly. Not the Great Comet: that celestial body had since passed out of the skies. It must be the Morning Star. Her father had once told her that it could sometimes be seen in daylight, when it was in opposition and brighter than usual. She felt a sudden, almost pagan impulse to revere that distant daystar. The words of a hymn to Elarainia that she had translated at the Academy now came unbidden into her head:

O how thou shinest in the height,
Thou beacon bright to saint and seer!
Thou art the very queen of Night
Enthroned within thy sovereign sphere.

While we who walked the starry strand
And meads of Heaven, flower-strewn,
Are banished to a lesser land
Forlorn beneath the barren moon.

As exiles from their native shore
Are parted by a pathless sea
So must we yearn forevermore
In halls divine to dwell with thee.

Night-blooming lily! Lady fair
Of lands unmarred by war or woe!
O Queen of Heaven, hear the prayer
Of thy lost children, here below!

It was called "The Lament of the Elei," and dated to a time just after the Great Disaster. Her own words, she thought with dissatisfaction, did not do justice to the original Elensi verses. She stood and watched the faint gleam of the planet until a scudding cloud blotted it from sight; then she gazed for a time at the sky itself, trying to determine what weather it foretold. Her father was able to read the sky, as sailors do: she wished she had learned the skill from him. She did know a few things. That high white streamer of cloud across the zenith, for instance, feathering at its edges, was the sign of a great wind in the upper air blowing cloud vapor before it as it swept down out of the north. But what coming change of weather it portended she could not tell. How beautiful, though, were those veil-fine wisps suspended in the blue! And how majestic the puffed and snow-white summits of the cumulus clouds, thousands of feet higher than the mightiest of the mountain peaks! That was another world up there, a land for gods to revel in: her eyes roved through it, among airy gulfs and pale knobbed cliffs where cloudy caverns gaped, gray-mouthed, revealing their dim inner chambers; through bays and inlets and wide lakes of blue sky hemmed in by misty shores. What wouldn't she give to have one of the Elei's marvelous flying ships! Or to be that bird up there, soaring with such ease through the heights where only her imagination could roam! It wasn't fair, she thought as she watched the winged shape plunge right into one of the gauzy cumuli and vanish from sight. As she gazed skyward in longing and delight she found herself trying to fit words to her feelings.

Look up, aloft! What wondrous weathers there,
What sky-scapes fleeting-fair delight the eye!

It had been a long time since she had attempted any poetry. Her lips moved, soundlessly shaping the words as they came to her.

What dove's-down drifts on avenues of air!
What cloudy castles lift their towers on high!

Was she mixing up too many metaphors? Ailia decided she didn't care if she was. Now for the next line—bear, glare, dare, fair (already used that), stare? Hair? Ah—

What silver swathes, like to an angel's hair
And wings, upon the firmament do fly!

Ailia sat down on a stone block, her disappointment in the unfulfilled quest for the moment dispelled, and tilted her head back so that the sky completely filled her field of vision. The far-off flying shape reemerged on the opposite side of the cloud, the sunlight flashing on the downstroke of its wings. What a very big bird it must be: an eagle perhaps? It must be large even for an eagle, though, to be visible from such a height . . .

Jomar's warning whistle pierced the calm of the mountaintop.

He had them all so well trained by now that they responded at once to the signal, scattering for cover like so many mice at the approach of a hawk. Ailia sprang to her feet, her heart lurching in her breast. The flying creature was descending with great speed, its shape now distinctly serpentine against the sky, undulating upon the air as its giant wings rose and fell. Realizing in panic that the roofless ruin offered her no shelter, she fled into the paved street. As she ran there came a noise from the sky like a succession of thunderclaps. She dared not look up, but she saw a darkness pass swiftly over the ground beneath her running feet, like the shadow of a cloud. Giant shadow-wings stretched from one side of the street to the other, and the dark outline of a long body—

"Ailia!" A hand seized her by the arm and yanked her inside a nearby building; she found herself staring up at Damion's blanched face. He did not look at her, but stared wide-eyed out the nearest window. She looked out the empty frame too, and saw the huge shadow sweep on down the street, together with a wind that set dust devils whirling up from the pavement. The thunderous wingclaps grew louder, then faded once more. She crept up to the casement and peered out.

And there was the dragon, winging away over the rooftops. The body of the beast was russet-colored above and golden beneath, the sunlight glancing off its scales as though off burnished metal. The four great limbs were drawn up against its underside with the claw-tips dangling, and she saw the horned head turning this way and that, as an eagle's does when it scans the ground for prey. Then the dragon dipped one wing and banked, and she saw the sharp dorsal scales, like a row of spearheads all along its spine; and the flat scales flanking them were not russet but red as blood, or roses, or rubies. She could see the webwork of veins in the giant crimson wings as the sun shone through them, standing out against the pellucid membranes like the veins of a leaf.

There were other dragons too, higher up—a dozen or so sinuous red-golden shapes had dropped out of the clouds above the mountains. For all their great bulk, they glided as effortlessly as swallows. The first dragon made one more pass over the city, and then rose to meet the others, his wings snapping like banners in a wind as they beat against the air. He was larger than the other dragons, and appeared to hold a dominant position among them, for as he climbed skyward they all turned and followed him. Ailia and Damion watched in breathless silence as the huge creatures swept low over the western peak in a tight arrow-formation, their great shadows flitting over the stark rock-faces. Then they flew on toward a neighboring mountain, plunging in and out of the trailing vapors that hung about its summit, stretching out their webbed wings to catch the updrafts rising before the sheer cliffs. How terrible, and yet how wonderful, to see these sky-gods at sport in their realm of air and stone!

"They're *beautiful!*" Ailia gasped.

Damion looked down at her in surprise. "I thought you were afraid of them," he said.

"Oh, I am!" she replied, in tones of ecstasy.

Damion leaned as far as he dared out the doorway. No wonder the Anthropophagi worshipped dragons. How terrible they were, beyond the terrors of all the rest of the animal kingdom, and yet—how magnificent, how graceful! The lead dragon in particular commanded his attention: he found himself thinking of a wolf leading a pack, a lion at the head of its pride. For sheer arrogant majesty they could not equal this creature, its air of owning the very sky through which it flew.

The Dragon King . . .

The dragons had ceased their play and were rising higher into the sky. In a few moments they passed above a shoal of thin fine cloud, becoming a phalanx of veiled shadows; then they disappeared altogether behind a dense mass of cumulus. Some time passed before they reemerged some distance away, now only a gleam of sun-reflecting scales in the blue.

Jomar gave the all-clear from his own hiding place and they ran out into the street, staring skyward and exclaiming.

"Did you see the big one? Did you see how close it came?" cried Lorelyn.

"Yes—what a monster!" Damion said, trying to sound cheerful. "I wonder if it's the same dragon that attacked us on the mountainside? It looked about the same size to me."

Ailia was silent, rubbing her hands together: the windowsill had left a deep imprint on each palm where she had clutched at it in her excitement. She could not find any words for the feeling that the dragons had given her: she was relieved that they were gone, and yet the memory of them held in it something close to elation.

"Perhaps Mandrake was right about leaving this place," said Damion, shaking his head. "It's much too dangerous."

"We can't give up now," protested Lorelyn. "We can't let the Zimbourans find the Stone."

"We won't." Jomar looked soberly at the rest of them. "But from now on we had better do our searching with one eye on the sky."

* * *

THE LONG DAY PASSED; the circling shadows followed the sun back toward its resting place. Presently Damion walked apart from the others, going over to the southern wall of the fortifications, where he stood at the arched entrance, looking out on the panoramic view of mountains and river valley and the ocean beyond, a few icebergs showing as minute white flecks against the blue expanse.

Mandrake was right: they were wasting their time here. It was mere foolishness to search for a gemstone that was probably long gone, or had possibly never even existed outside of legend. Their true priority was Lorelyn's safety. The Zimbourans persisted in believing that she was the Tryna Lia—or at least their mad king did: they would do all they could to recapture her. They dared not fail in this task, with their king right here in Trynisia with them. Some stone or other would be found by them—a white pebble, a shard of innocuous quartz—and presented to Khalazar as the fabled gem, along with the hapless girl. Then Lorelyn would die on the God-king's sword, before his watching and worshipping soldiers. And her death would only be the first in a tide of blood and savagery that would sweep the whole world.

He walked a little way down the hill and stood looking from one end of the island to the other. The hopelessness of the situation was inarguable. They could not escape, and they would run out of hiding places here eventually. Had he been alone, he thought, he would have given in long ago. But with the women here, and also Jomar, who still had not had his chance, despair was an indulgence Damion could not permit himself. Instead his mind ran over scheme after desperate scheme. Would it be possible to build a makeshift raft or boat? What of Eldimia—was it a real land? A place "beyond the world's end"—that was likely a poetic way of saying it was very far away from any other landmass. It was a depressing thought. Maurainia would be preferable, but how to get back there? Mandrake must have a vessel of his own hidden away somewhere, but while he claimed to be concerned about Lorelyn's welfare, could he really be trusted? Jomar had a low opinion of the man, and Damion too felt uneasy about relying on him.

He sat down on a flat-topped rock beside the path. A sweet scent came to him on the breeze, and he turned to see another little gnarled tree-of-heaven growing in a crack between stones. He reached out and touched one of its fruits. Was it true, what Ailia said—could the juice of these fruits really grant visions on demand? Had the sibyls used it for that purpose? What if he were to try one—would it grant him a glimpse of their future, give him some idea of what lay in store for them all? Jomar had dismissed the idea; Mandrake said it was too dangerous. But Mandrake's word could not be trusted on everything, and Damion was desperate enough now to try anything at all. In fact, the little golden fruit was in his hand already: it had dropped from its stem, ripe and heavy, at his touch, and lay now in his cupped palm, as though inviting him to give in to his desire—to taste it, to see for himself . . . He split the fruit's skin with his nails: it was succulent as a nectarine, bursting with a honey-colored juice that runneled down his fingers. He hesitated, then held them to his lips and licked away the moisture with the tip of his tongue. A sweet taste filled his mouth, piquant as a wild berry plucked in a sun-warmed meadow, and with it a sudden drowsiness came over him. He slumped down, propped against the side of the boulder.

WHEN HE CAME TO HIMSELF again it was to find that the sun had set.

The sky was darker than he had yet seen it here, blue-black and glittering with stars. The moon shone too: but it was no longer a waxing crescent. It shone now at the full. And it was not the moon he knew: the bright silver disc bore broad greenish patches, like tarnish, and was overlaid with many curious marblings and mottlings of white. And above it there were comets, dozens of them scoring the sky, trailing their blazing trains across its black vault. Some were huge as the Great Comet, some smaller, more distant perhaps. Never had he seen anything so beautiful, and so terrifying, as that sky.

He sprang to his feet. The mountainside below him was covered in a fresh fall of snow, yet he felt no breath of cold. As he gazed in bewilderment at the white slope he saw a man on horseback coming up it toward him. Already he was scarcely a bow's shot away. The rider was clad in jet-black armor and a helmet of strange design, the visor in the form of a man's face, with sculpted steel features and gaping holes for the eyes. The protective chamfron that masked his horse was shaped like a dragon's horned head. The knight spurred his steed straight at Damion, as if he intended to run him down. The priest leaped to one side and the horse galloped on past him, but its rider did not rein it in and turn again to the attack. He simply rode on, up the path toward the entrance of the city.

As Damion turned to watch, he saw that the cracked and crumbling turreted wall had somehow been miraculously restored. Faced now with fine marble, it gleamed before him in the strange moon's light. Staring, he too mounted the path to the gate. And walked through into the streets of Liamar.

The ruins had gone. All around him reared tall buildings of white marble. Beyond the snow-whitened rooftops swelled the great dome of the temple, undamaged now, showing gold between patches of snow. The pavements thronged with people, all clad in loose robelike garments and fur-trimmed cloaks, and the air was filled with a hive-thrum of activity. He was reminded of his last days on Jana. These people were fleeing the city—not in a panic, yet, but leaving as quickly as they could. There was a blast like a trumpet's behind him, loud and clear, making him start and whirl: he gaped at a huge lumbering shape approaching from the far end of the street. Its long serpentine trunk wove to and fro, giving off more trumpet-blasts, and the big rounded ears flapped like wings. The creature was covered in a thick pelt of brown fur. It was a woolly elephant, like those that roamed northern Shurkana. He had been told the creatures were untamable, yet this one had a mahout in fine livery straddling its neck, one hand resting on the shaggy domed head; and atop the sloping back was a crimson-curtained howdah of curious design. The giant beast strode past, the light of the strange stone lamps gleaming on its mighty tusks that did not jut downward like a common elephant's, but curved up in the shape of drawn bows. Damion craned his neck, peering up at the curtains of the howdah, but he could catch no glimpse of the interior and its occupants.

But he could see the people in the street, and at some of them he stared in wonder. For the first time, a man of his generation looked upon the Elei in all their glory. Damion's heart ached at the sight of them. It was not so much that they looked inhuman: rather, theirs seemed to him the true humanity, of which all others seemed but a poor and shabby imitation. They appeared to belong to no one race, their skin color ranging from porcelain-white to bronze, but they had, in addition to their unusual height, a perfection of proportion, a delicacy of feature seldom seen except in idealized statues. The stone images they had left behind had not flattered, but faithfully recorded, their appearance. Well might a primitive barbarian fall down before them, believing them to be divine! The pedestrians, for their part, neither looked at nor spoke to him. It was as though he were a ghost—and that least substantial of spirits, a ghost of the future. For these people, he did not exist, had never yet existed. If these fleeing pilgrims could see and speak with him, he could tell them of this city's fate, of the catastrophe that would befall Trynisia and the world beyond. *The Great Disaster.* He looked at marble walls and towers, seeing in his mind the desolate ruins they would become. He was a prophet of doom robbed of his voice. He walked on through the thronging streets, half expecting some shoulder to brush against his, some gaze to meet his own. Once, a lovely young girl with long golden hair, graceful in the flowing folds of a sky-blue gown, emerged onto the balcony of a guesthouse to look down into the street. She gazed in his direction; her anxious face glowed with relief and recognition, and he opened his mouth to speak—then he saw that her regard was not for him, but for a youth in a green cloak running up the street behind him.

This did not feel like the visions he had known before; all that he looked upon had the sharp, precise visual texture of everyday reality. The food-of-the-gods had given him his wish: he was an invisible observer in a bygone era, free to walk where he willed. He could go to the palace and see the Faerie Queen on her throne; he could go to the old library and glean the long-lost knowledge of the Elei. *And the Star Stone! I can go to the temple, and see the Star Stone! I'll know then what it looks like.*

He made off in haste through the streets, heading toward the great dome.

Entering the snow-whitened plaza, he saw to one side a huge pillared building that must be the sibyls' library. And at the other end rose a glory of marble-faced towers and flying flags: the palace in its heyday, seat of the ruler of the world, here in this city in whose tumbled ruins Damion and his friends would one day take shelter. He turned toward the Temple of Heaven's snow-pied dome. Atop its portico the stone angels stood with unbroken wings outspread. And there were the two gryphons—*cherubim,* he corrected himself—the brass of which they were made polished to a dazzling brightness, the bowls between their forepaws aglow with sacred fires. *The Guardians of the Light.*

Someone close at hand gave a cry and pointed at the sky. Heads turned upward, Damion's included.

A huge, blazing object plunged down through the sky, trailing a long plume of smoke and flame. And above it there was another, and yet another. They were shooting stars—but so huge! He stood transfixed as screams filled the air.

Even as he watched, the first burning sphere plunged toward the distant ice-strewn sea with a deafening roar and a tremendous billow of steam, silver-edged under the moon. But though its fire was quenched its mischief was not yet done. In a moment he observed, rather than felt, the tremor that ran through the mountain beneath him. People lost their footing in the snow and fell screaming. Cracks appeared in buildings, fires began to break out. He whirled, in time to see with a sense of doom the white-pillared library enveloped in a mass of smoke and licking flames, and the three pillars destined to stand alone forever afterwards become separated from the others by spreading fissures. The knowledge of the Elei died a fiery death within. To the south Damion saw columns of smoke and flame like gigantic bonfires rising from the doomed lowlands. But they would not burn for long. Even as he watched, horror-stricken, a moving mountain of water crested with raging foam descended on the coast.

Liamar meanwhile burned, its buildings turned to red-mouthed furnaces, its towers to spouting torches. Hot cinders spun across the night sky, carrying ruin to the few roofs that had yet escaped it. To watchers in the lands below, Mount Elendor must now resemble a volcano, belching forth fire and fumes into the night as the city on its summit burned to ashes. Melting snow poured in torrents along the gutters. People fled through the streets, screaming, heading for the gateway and the mountainside beyond. And there were other figures running through the firelit streets—men with malformed and brutish faces, inhuman and hideous, swords and clubs in their hands. They had taken advantage of the Disaster to wreak revenge on the Elei.

In the sky red flames leaped and glared: flames not born of the fires here below. A huge black shape flew down, tearing the smoke-pall to tatters. Its fiery exhalations mingled with the ruddy glow beneath, illuminating its vast ribbed wings and the scaly armor of its flanks. Low over the city it swooped, just as the crimson dragon had done in Damion's own time. But this dragon was very much larger, and black in color save for its belly, which was red as blood. Its head swiveled downward, and a gout of flame burst from its jagged jaws.

Firedrake. It was hard not to feel fear, even though he instinctively sensed that no harm could come to his incorporeal self. More of the creatures circled like gorecrows higher up, riding the hot updrafts from the burning. He wrenched his eyes from the appalling devastation before him, and broke into a run. He must get inside the temple.

On the top step he saw a tall slender woman gowned in white, with flowing silver-blonde hair beneath a golden fillet. The High Sibyl, perhaps, or a noblewoman: she wore no concealing veil. A company of the hideous beast-men rushed the marble steps and she drove them back, her hands outspread in calm denial, some strange power pouring from her invisible as wind. Her long pale hair blew back in the furnace-blasts from the burning city, yet even the flying embers could not touch her. Still her assailants did not flee in fear, but only drew back and waited. Did they sense that her strength could not last much longer?

Damion, however, could ascend the steps unchallenged. He raced up them. Within the great structure the forms of veiled and white-clad women milled in confusion. Many stood around the central shrine, which was surrounded by huge candles in golden holders, braziers and vases of flowers. As he watched, several sibyls ran toward the statue of Elarainia, and opened the door that led to the sanctum. He made haste to follow them. At the end of the corridor the bronze doors stood open. He saw the sanctum's interior, the garlands of fresh and living flowers, the blue starred canopy.

"The Stone!" a woman's voice cried. "The Stone!" And as he watched, fascinated, the sibyls parted the starry curtains and lifted out a small white casket of what looked like alabaster, carved with many-pointed stars. In there—the Star Stone was in there, in that little box! As they passed him he groped for it, futilely, with an insubstantial hand. The Stone was not in his time, but theirs. He could only watch in frustration as they bore it away.

Mandrake was right. The Stone *had* been taken from the sanctum. But *where* had the sibyls taken it?

He followed the Stone's bearers up into the main temple. A company of knights in silver-plated armor now stood there, their blue surcoats emblazoned with a white star. One of them received the casket, wrapping it in a fold of his cloak. The tall woman with the gold fillet was also there: she spoke to the knights, her voice high and clear but filled with urgency. "Go now," she urged, "and the protection of the gods go with you! I will remain behind, and let the enemy believe the Stone is still within the sanctum."

"Your Majesty." They bowed low before her, and

Damion gaped at her, realizing at last who this woman was: Eliana herself, ruler of the Elei and the old Commonwealth.

The cherubim screeched as the knights streamed out of the temple, swords drawn. The blades glittered in the light: they were not made of metal but crystal as clear as glass. He ran after them down the temple steps, out into the city. Staring down into the melee beneath him, he saw the mailed men hastening away across the plaza with their burden.

Follow them—follow! See where they take it!

Now that his head was level with the rest of the crowd he could no longer see the Paladins. He set off in the general direction they had taken, but it was some minutes before he spied them again, going down one of the narrow streets. He sped after them, glad that the crowd could not impede his progress, nor the Anthropophagi harm his immaterial body. The city smoked and spat embers like a forge, and in the sky shooting stars flared briefly as they fell. Wind-blown cinders rose and mingled with the stars.

Halfway across the plaza he saw the dark knight ride up, then rein in his mount: horse and man stood there for a moment motionless, like an equestrian statue of dull black metal placed there by some act of sorcery. Then a tremor shook the mountain, and the warhorse snorted and danced, its tossing head strangely reptilian in the metal mask. The man took off his helmet and sat for a moment looking toward the temple: the light of the conflagration shone directly on his features, and reflected from his eyes. Damion stopped short, staring. The long red-gold hair was swept back and tied with a thong, and the sharp, chiseled features showed clearly.

Mandrake!

Somehow, Mandrake was also here in the past, a part of this dream-vision. Had he too eaten of the ambrosia fruit? Damion called out to him.

"Mandrake—what's happened? How did we—"

Mandrake ignored him completely, continued to look across the plaza. He spurred his mount forward, and Damion stepped back as horse and rider moved past him at a slow walk, without so much as glancing at him.

"Mandrake!" he shouted, and ran after him. The man did not check his pace or turn around. Damion sprinted ahead, then swung around to bar his path, yelling and waving his arms. Mandrake continued to ride straight toward Damion. Again the priest jumped out of the way, but he reached out in an effort to seize the other man's steel-clad arm as he went by.

His hand passed right through the arm, as it had passed through the casket that held the Star Stone.

Damion stared as the other man rode on across the plaza; coming upon a group of armed Anthropophagi, he stopped, barked something at them in an unknown tongue. The hideous warriors listened, then bowed their heads. He put on the helmet and rode away.

Damion gasped. Mandrake was no ghostly visitor here, like himself. The other Anthropophagi had reacted to him, and Damion was not able to touch him. Somehow, by some unimaginable feat of sorcery, the Nemerei had *entered* the past—become incorporated into it. Damion made as if to follow him again, but then the thought of the Stone-bearing knights made him reconsider. He turned, to see the Paladins running around a corner and disappearing from sight. Cursing softly, he set aside the mystery of Mandrake and ran after the Stone.

He raced around the corner, just in time to see the Paladins waylaid by a great force of Anthropophagi.

He stood watching helplessly, unable to intervene. Before his horrified eyes sword-blades swung to and fro, reddened by more than the firelight. The crystal blades of the Paladins' swords were hard as any diamond: they bit deep into the bodies of the attackers, sheared away limbs, snapped the blades of the steel swords wielded against them. To Damion's eyes they seemed to flash with blue fire as they were raised and swung. But as soon as an Anthropophagus was killed he was replaced by a dozen more. One by one the knights fell, overwhelmed, and the fires reflected in the red, spreading pools that stained the snow beneath them. All but one: the knight in the cloak, the bearer of the Stone, fought still like a man possessed. He cut his way free of the hordes, and as Damion watched he ran for the western peak of the summit. Why there? Then Damion saw that there was a cave mouth high in the rock-face, and the lone Paladin was heading toward it. A few Anthropophagi saw him break away and pursued him. The rest, however, were intent on the spoils of their battle, and howled with glee over the slain Paladins, tearing off their silver armor, taking up their weapons, searching their still-warm bodies.

Up by the mountain peak the handful of Anthropophagi who had chased the surviving knight fought for their lives, unnoticed by their fellows. There were too few of them to face this man. The crystal sword flashed like blue lightning, cleaving their weapons asunder, and two of them already lay dead at his feet. The others retreated, reconsidered, fled back to their comrades. Their cries of alarm at last caught the other Anthropophagi's attention, and as one they turned to see the knight running for the cave.

"The Stone—the Stone!"

Did that cry come from his own throat, or another's? He was never afterwards certain. In the next instant the vision was mercifully gone . . .

. . . AND HE OPENED HIS EYES, stirred, realized that he was once more sitting by the stone on the mountainside. The shadows had not moved, the sun still blazed down upon him. No time at all had elapsed during his visit to the age of the Elei. And the horror that lingered in his mind vanished, swept away by a wave of wonder and triumph.

His wish had been granted. He knew where the Stone was.

18

The Dragon King

"YOU EXPECT ME TO believe that?" exclaimed Jomar, incredulous.

The Mohara man was tired and growing cross; he had

worked even harder than any of the others, so determined was he not to give the Zimbourans any chance of victory. Now here came Damion, wandering into the ruins like some moonstruck witch doctor, claiming to have seen the location of the Star Stone in a miraculous vision.

"Mountain air can make people see things," Jomar told him. "Things that aren't there. Lots of the soldiers saw illusions when we crossed the Kanja Range, back in the Winter Campaign in Shurkana. High elevations have thinner air: it does strange things to people's brains."

"It wasn't mountain air," said Damion, and told him about the fruit. "Lorelyn was right all along. The tree was the answer."

"Answer? You drugged yourself," said Jomar in disgust.

"It wasn't a drug, it was magic," Ailia corrected.

"There's no such thing as magic!" Jomar shouted.

"Jo," Damion said, "I don't expect you to understand it. I don't understand it myself. But drug or not, I'm convinced the Stone is inside the mountain peak. I've climbed up there, and there *is* a cave mouth, with a sort of tunnel at the back of it."

"You must have seen it before."

"I swear to you I didn't."

Damion looked back at the ruined city. It was bare as bone, picked clean by the passing ages of any trace of life. No hint remained here of the horrors past—the horrors he had beheld—nor any hint of the beauty that had been. But he had *seen* those people, seen them live and die before his eyes: he almost felt that he knew them. What had become of the sibyls—of the girl in the sky-blue gown and her lover? If they had all perished, it should not have been in vain. "We've searched the city: it's not here. We'll need torches—"

"We?"

"Come, Jo—at least give it a try! Then if I'm right we'll have it, and if I'm wrong you can gloat. Or have you got a better idea?"

Jomar hadn't. Unable to come up with any major flaw in Damion's, he began to niggle at details. "Well, how can you be sure it wasn't taken from the cave later on?"

"The only way to find out is by looking." He avoided mentioning the sight of Mandrake in the past. Jomar's credulity had been stretched far enough for one day, and he himself was no longer certain that the man he had seen was Mandrake. After all, it was said that everyone had a double somewhere; it could even have been one of Mandrake's own distant ancestors he had glimpsed. "I'd prefer not to go alone, though," he continued, "in case there's a cave-in, or pits in the floor, or something."

"I'll go with you," said Lorelyn.

"No, it might be dangerous. Let Jomar and me check it first."

"All right," Jomar said in resignation. "It can't be much worse than digging around in a lot of rubble. I still think you're crazy, but I can't think of anything else to do. Let's go."

Ailia bit her lip. "What if the Zimbourans come, or—"

"We won't be that long," replied Damion. "Cheer up! Stay here, and keep an eye out for Ana. She may yet find her way up here, and we might have the Stone when she arrives."

* * *

ON VENTURING INTO THE TUNNEL at the back of the cave, the men discovered that it divided in two. One passage was carved with steps: it rose in a steep spiral, and the two men guessed that it led to the "Moon Gate" high atop the peak. The other had a rough floor, and led downward. Jomar and Damion chose this one. Clutching the torches they had taken from the Zimbourans' packs, they carefully began the descent. The ceiling was low, and they were obliged to stoop for much of the way.

The passage seemed to plunge straight down through the bowels of the mountain, its frequent tight turns making the men feel slightly dizzy as they followed it. After what seemed an age they came to the end of it, finding themselves in a large cave. Above them was a ceiling of rugged rock; to the right, another tunnel leading into blackness.

"Not another passage!" Jomar complained. "It just goes on forever. Maybe we should stop here."

"We've *got* to go on, Jo. You wouldn't want the Zimbourans to find the Stone, would you?" Damion was close to wheedling now in his desperation. Jomar was ominously silent for a moment, staring into the dark mouth of the tunnel.

"I'm beginning to feel as if I don't care anymore," he grumbled. "That it's really all for nothing. Khalazar is probably going to declare a war no matter what happens: I doubt anything we can do will make any difference."

"That's what Mandrake said," Damion told him, pouncing. "You don't agree with *him,* do you?"

Jomar's jaw tightened. He would do almost anything rather than agree with Mandrake.

"Khalazar can declare all the wars he likes," Damion

went on, "but that doesn't mean the soldiers will obey him. You've been in that army, Jo. Do you think those men would go to war if they weren't afraid of their leader? Imagine Khalazar coming back from this little trip empty-handed, after all his boasts. It would be the end of him."

Jomar said nothing. Then, still without speaking, he walked on, leading the way through the second tunnel. It was as the Mohara man said: there seemed to be no end to the passages. Damion was reminded of the catacombs and could feel that same panicky sensation beginning to stir again, the longing for a sight of sky and trees. He fought to keep this feeling under control, but it was an effort. It was close to overwhelming him when the tunnel terminated in a cave, larger than the first. He and Jo stood still for a long moment, peering into its depths. They were rendered speechless by the sight that lay before them.

Treasure beyond imagining filled this cave from end to end, lying in loose piles upon the floor: ancient wealth of the Elei. There were coins, arm-rings, chalices, and crowns: gold gleamed seductively in the torchlight, jewels flashed like frost. There were huge cloudy crystal globes, urns brimming with pearls, necklaces like cobwebs dewed with diamonds, carved rubies red as fire and uncut ones like clots of blood. There were the huge curving tusks of woolly elephants, the ivory intricately carved; and great tears of honey-colored amber; and enormous geodes split open like pomegranates to show the crystals clustering beneath their stone rinds. There were knights of marble or obsidian standing erect beside their stone steeds, every detail of men and beasts carved to give the exact semblance of life, save that the former lacked arms—for these were mere mannequins, designed to support treasures greater still: tall crested helmets and coats of silver or golden mail or plate armor, surcoats and caparisons of woven gold and scabbards from which the jeweled hilts of swords protruded. Ceremonial armor, it must be: such beauty was never meant for fields of battle.

The huge chamber was utterly silent, save for a faint soughing sound that might be the wind playing in some hidden crevice high above. For a long moment they stood motionless; then as one they rushed forward.

"The royal treasury—of course!" Damion exclaimed. "That's why my knight came down here! Where better to hide a gem than in a roomful of gems? It could take years to search through all this—and you might never know if you'd got the right stone!" *And how are* we *going to find it*? he wondered. *If it's even still here?*

His companion was not in the least interested in the fabled gem, now that many more surrounded him. His dark eyes gleaming, he rummaged through the glittering piles, stuffing his pockets with gems, brooches, rose-pink pearls the size of grapes. "I don't believe it! I could have bought my freedom with even *one* of these!" Jomar crowed, taking up a gold ingot from a pile and hefting it in one hand. "And look at this—and *this!*" He caught up a ruby-studded dagger and pored over it by the torchlight. Sullen red lights in the gem's depths, awakened by the flames, seemed to glower back at him. Then he dropped the dagger to seize hold of a marble knight's jeweled sword-belt. Setting his torch down, he grasped the scabbard with one hand and pulled on the exposed golden hilt with the other, drawing out the sword. The blade glimmered strangely in the torchlight, and he saw that it was made not of steel but of clear crystal or glass.

Jomar blinked. "Now what in the—?"

Damion stared at the weapon. The golden hilt was decorated with the sinuous forms of dragons, coiling around the handgrip. It hardly seemed right to call this thing a weapon: it was more like an exquisite work of art.

Jomar shrugged. "Glass blade. Some kind of ceremonial sword, obviously. Pretty, but useless."

"No, Jo—that's a Paladin's sword."

"You can have it if you like. *I'd* rather have a sword that really cuts."

Damion set his torch down on the floor and took up the sword. It was much lighter than the Zimbouran weapon: he needed only one hand to heft it. "It cuts, Jo. The Paladins all carried swords like this, and they did use them in war. The blade isn't glass, it's adamant: a kind of gem, like diamond, that can cut through anything." He touched the glittering edge lightly with his finger, drawing a drop of blood despite his care. "It could even be King Andarion's own weapon. His had a gold hilt with dragons, like this—or so the stories say. Here, take your sword and hold it out toward me."

"What are you babbling about?" grumbled Jomar, but he unsheathed his Zimbouran weapon and held it out. Damion raised the crystal sword above his head and swung it down. There was a clang and a spurt of blue sparks—and Jomar leaped back with an oath. The Zimbouran blade was broken neatly off at the hilt, sliced through as though it were a stick of soft wood.

"There, you see?" Damion removed his own Zimbouran weapon from its scabbard and tossed it to Jomar. "Adamant. The blades were supposed to run with flames when they were wielded by a Paladin."

"Valdur's *teeth!* I don't believe it," Jomar rasped, still gaping down at the shattered steel. Damion took up his torch in his left hand and walked on through the cave. His eye had been caught by something else—something small and pale that glimmered in the dim light. His eyes widened. "Jo!" he gasped, dropping the crystal-bladed sword on the rock floor. "That's it!"

"What's it?"

"The Stone," Damion replied, beginning to walk toward the object. "That's the casket, the little box that it was in. The one I saw in my vision—"

"What? *Where?*"

Damion did not reply: in his eagerness he had already begun to walk toward the main mass of treasure. As he drew near, the light of his torch gleamed upon a vast heap of red gold, shining in the torch-glow: at its far end lay what looked like a fist-sized opal, the torch's light rousing its veiled fires. Next to this the tips of two great elephant tusks—or perhaps they were rhinoceros horns—jutted upward from the pile. But Damion's mind did not dwell for an instant on these things. It was the little casket on the floor that drew his eyes.

It was the same one, he had no doubt. The Anthropophagi must have missed it in their search of the treasury. The little alabaster ark that contained the Stone—still here, after all this time.

So great was his excitement that he did not at first notice that the booming, gusting sound seemed louder at this end of the cave, nor that there was a strange smell, sweet and pungent as incense, hanging in the air about him. He took another step—and then stopped dead.

The heap of red gold had moved.

It was not a trick of the flickering torchlight. As he stared, another slow, shuddering motion ran along the vast refulgent mound, and there was a clink of displaced coins and gems. The portion on which the opalescent gem and the two ivory horns lay began to stir. It rose slightly, then subsided again with a sigh and a low rumbling noise.

He was staring at the horned head and sprawled body of a dragon, asleep there upon the treasure mound.

Damion stood transfixed. He could see an eye now, covered by a thin ruby-red lid; and a scaly red-golden flank that rose and fell rhythmically. The windy soughing sound was the monster's breath. He looked back at Jomar: the Mohara man too stood staring at the beast, now that Damion's torch revealed it for what it was. Jomar gestured frantically and mouthed the word *Run!*

Damion hesitated. Jomar was right, he must flee before the creature woke. But what of the Stone?

The alabaster casket lay only a few paces away, encircled by the dragon's body. The Stone of the Stars: he had risked death, even killed for it. How could he walk away and leave it now?

Damion took an unsteady step forward, then stopped. The casket was very close to the dragon, rather nearer the head than the tail; in fact, it lay not an arm's length from the very jaws of the beast, and about the same distance from the nearest of the forelegs. But the dragon was asleep. It might just be possible to steal up quietly, snatch the casket, and whisk it away without waking the monster. If it *did* wake . . . but he must not think of that. The thing must be done, and done now. Slowly, he advanced. His heart, he noticed vaguely, seemed to be beating in his throat, of all places.

Behind him Jomar stood motionless, staring in disbelief as Damion drew closer to the dragon. The Mohara opened his mouth and then shut it again, knowing that if he called out the beast might wake. Laying his hand on the hilt of the Zimbouran sword, he eased it slowly from its scabbard so as not to make any sound, and moved closer to the dragon.

Damion was only dimly aware of Jomar's presence behind him. The dragon's tail, thick as the trunk of a small tree, lay in front of him: he stepped over it, into that dread circle, then stood still. *What if it smells us?* he wondered, sweating at the mere thought. He doubted Jomar could kill the dragon: its scaly plates looked as hard as any armor, and if he were to strike at it he would likely only wake it and seal his fate and Damion's. The young priest hesitated a moment, then advanced again. Six paces away, a scythe-shaped talon flexed, scraping the cave floor with a sound like steel on stone. He shut out the dragon from his thoughts and vision, concentrating solely on the white box, measuring the distance he still had to go. *You could hop, skip, and jump that in two seconds flat!* he told himself. *Come on—come on. You can do it!*

There was no sound from Jomar behind him. Had the Mohara man given up and retreated? He hoped so—for the sake of the women, one of them must survive. He didn't dare turn around to look, but continued to walk forward. Two paces more, and the Stone would be in his hand. He would thrust it into the travel-pouch hanging at his side, and run and run and run . . .

The dragon's coiled body lay all around him, and he could not help but look at it now. It was perhaps the size of an elephant, but leaner, and very much longer. The huge head with its long jaws and scaled skin was reptilian, but there were the great yellow oxlike horns, and a pair of pointed external ears. Behind the head was a neck-frill, then a ruff of what looked like rufous fur: there was also tuft of red hair upon the chin, like a goat's beard. The wings resembled a bat's, but for their color and their size: great sails of semi-translucent crimson membrane, stretched over attenuated skeletal claws. They were half-furled now, lying in heavy leathery folds upon the beast's back. A thick mail of lapping scales covered the dragon's body, reddish-gold along the flanks and deep carnelian-red upon the back, with broad ventral plates beneath like armor of beaten gold. The row of knife-shaped dorsal scales ran along its spine from the base of the neck to the end of the tail, which spread in a multifoliate fan like the tail of a heraldic fish.

Reptile, mammal, bird, fish: it was like a peculiar mixture of all of these, and yet it reminded Damion more than anything of a gigantic insect. The giant red wings held a metallic iridescence like a butterfly's, or like the wing cases of a beetle; a pair of long whip-shaped barbels projecting from the nostrils waved from side to side with a slow somnolent motion like antennae. The round, opalescent scale on the forehead that he had taken for a gem seemed to stare at him, like a third eye. Huge, strange, utterly alien, the dragon loomed before him, perilous even in sleep. He stared at it, fear and wonder blended in equal parts within his mind.

The casket! It was right there at his feet. Scarcely daring to breathe, he stooped and picked it up, feeling the warm blasts of the dragon's breath upon his face. He longed to open it and look on the Stone, but it was imperative to get clear of the dragon first. He began the long backward retreat, still not taking his eyes off it, feeling his way across the floor.

The dragon's eye opened.

Damion froze.

For what seemed an eternity he looked into the great, unlidded orb. Its pupil was black as obsidian, black as the darkness of the mountain's heart, surrounded by a thin ring of gold: it gaped before him like a hole opening onto unfathomable deeps. His head began to swim strangely: his feet were rooted to the floor.

"Damion!" The cry came from somewhere behind him; it was Jomar's voice. He shook himself free from the spell and stumbled back, as if from the edge of a precipice. Shoving the casket into his travel-pouch, he turned to flee. Jomar was at his side now, sword raised against the menace before them.

With a slow, almost leisurely motion, the dragon raised its head, and opened its wings with a leathery rustle. The tremendous span of them seemed to fill the cavern, an overarching roof of shimmering scarlet silk. Then it folded them again and began to crawl forward, its huge bulk gleaming dull red in the torchlight, mimicked by its tremendous shadow upon the far wall.

Jomar gave a yell, but the monster ignored him, its attention all upon Damion and the casket. Slowly, slowly it moved forward, with the slinking deliberate motion of a cat intent upon its prey. The long stalking was somehow worse than any sudden charge, though at any moment Damion knew it could become one, an onslaught of violence swift and terrible as a thunderbolt. He retreated, it advanced, all in a horrible near-silence broken only by the monster's rumbling breaths.

Damion dropped his torch and ran for the adamantine sword. He flung himself toward it, falling and rolling, his hands closing on the hilt and lifting it even as the dragon lunged at him. Its jaws sprang open. Warm breath blew into Damion's face, carrying not the rotting-meat stench of a carnivore's mouth, but a sickly-sweet, cloying aroma that made his head swim and his vision blur. As he stumbled before it the monster lashed out with a foreclaw: it did not strike him, but the sword was knocked from his hand and went clattering along the ground. He staggered back, staring wildly about him.

"Run!" Jomar shouted, rushing forward with his own sword held out.

The dragon halted, crouching. As he stared up at it, the creature laid its ears back and slitted its eyes, looking for an instant more feline than reptilian. The mane of fox-colored fur seemed to bristle. From its jaws issued a series of hissing snarls that sounded eerily like speech, a mad incantation in some arcane tongue. The great eyes flashed, all darkness and fire, as though they were themselves vast, malevolent gems unearthed from the mountain's depths. It glared—not at him, but at the crystal sword. The blade was glowing, not with any reflected light, but with a pale blue-white radiance of its own. The adamant burned, as if with an inner flame.

Damion, overcoming his own amazement, lunged for the weapon again and made a thrust with the blazing sword-blade. The volume of the dragon's hissing increased, and it drew back. Then with a shout Jomar seized him by his other arm, dragging him back.

"Follow me!" he yelled, gesturing to the far wall of the cave. There was an opening there, an entrance to yet another cave or tunnel, just visible in the torch-glow. An entrance too narrow for the dragon's giant body . . .

They ran for it together, sprinted down the passage beyond as the dragon bellowed after them, the cavern resounding with its rage like the crash of surf in a sea-cave. They fled down the passage, leaving the horrific sounds far behind.

WHEN THEY WERE TOO EXHAUSTED to run any farther they collapsed panting against the side of the tunnel.

Damion," said Jomar as soon as he could speak, "I take back everything I ever said about you. No, shut up—I'm trying to apologize. I was wrong about you, priest. That was the craziest, stupidest, *bravest* thing I've ever seen."

Damion was warmed by these words, but honesty compelled him to say, "It wasn't really I who saved us, you know. It was the sword itself that did that. There's a kind of . . . power in it." He looked at the weapon in wonder. The strange blue fire had died out of the blade, leaving it once more clear as glass.

"I know, I saw it. Now where's that box?" asked Jomar. "Let's have a look at this Stone we've risked both our lives for."

Damion took the alabaster casket from his pouch.

Though it was small, it was quite heavy. He hesitated, almost reluctant to open the lid. When he did so, he would look on what no man now alive had ever seen. Would it be a wonder, like the adamantine sword—or a mere gemstone like any other?

"Come on, open it," urged Jomar impatiently.

Damion lifted the lid, holding his breath as he did so. There was a silence as the two men looked into the casket's interior.

"Empty!" said Damion in despair.

19

The Moon Gate

LORELYN . . . LORELYN. ARE YOU THERE?

Lorelyn raised her head at the summons. The voice spoke to her as it had done before, in the castle cellars: not verbally, but communicating directly to her mind. "Mandrake?" she replied, speaking aloud. "Where are you?"

Very near. In a moment you will see me.

Lorelyn sat bolt upright, listening. There was no sound in the main room of the ruined guesthouse or outside it, save for the soft slow breathing of Ailia, who had lain down for a rest on a blanket and had fallen into a doze. Greymalkin had gone—out hunting, probably. Lorelyn felt very alone.

Presently she heard a soft footfall in the stone corridor outside. She sat up, peering through the half-light at the dark figure that approached and paused in the doorway. She could not see his face in the shadows. His silent summons brushed at her mind, a mental caress, conveying urgency and concern for her. *Lorelyn, you must come with me.*

"Why are you using the mind-talk when you're right here in the room with me?" she asked, suspicion stirring.

He spoke aloud, but softly. "Hush—don't wake Ailia. I must talk with you, Lorelyn. Will you come outside with me for a while?"

She hesitated, glancing at Ailia's pale, exhausted face. It *would* be a shame to wake her. "All right—just for a moment," she said, reaching for her travel-cloak.

They walked out into the street. The sky was heavy with clouds, and a few flakes of snow fell around them and settled on their heads and their cloaked shoulders. "Lorelyn, the Zimbourans are not far off," said Mandrake. "I have seen a large force of them approaching the mountain. We must leave this place."

"The Zimbourans!" she exclaimed. "But we can't leave yet—the Stone, we still haven't found the Stone. What if the God-king—"

"The Stone is gone, Lorelyn. It was taken from Trynisia centuries ago. You will never find it; but neither will your enemies. You have no reason to linger here."

"Where can we go, though? We're not really safe anywhere on this island. Unless you can take us all back home . . ."

He turned to face her, laid his hands on her shoulders. "I can take you to the island of Eldimia, Lorelyn—the land where you were born. Where descendants of the Elei—your people—still live."

"Eldimia! You really can take us there?" Lorelyn asked. He nodded. She searched his face with her eyes. "Mandrake, tell me—do *you* believe I am the Tryna Lia, too?"

He sighed heavily. "Yes, I do. I have known it for some time, in fact, and I hoped to free you from your fate by taking you somewhere safe and hiding you. I see now it was no use. I have been trying, like a fool, to fight against destiny. I will fight it no longer."

"So you'll take us away on your sailing ship? I must go fetch Jomar and Damion—they're exploring a cave in the mountainside. And Ana still hasn't turned up—"

"I will not take Ana to Eldimia—nor any of the others."

"What!" She stepped back, shaking off his hands.

"Lorelyn, try to understand. Ana must go back to her own people, to the Nemerei. They need her. And Damion and Ailia have friends and family in other lands. Jomar can go with them. He will have to make a life for himself, now that he is a free man, and he wouldn't care for Eldimia."

She backed away, looking at him warily. "That's nonsense. How can the others get back to their homes without a ship? We can't just *leave* them here!"

He glanced away from her. "I am not alone in this land. I have allies and servants here. They will convey your companions back to the Continent, at my bidding." Mandrake moved a step closer. "Will you trust me? Your enemies are drawing nearer as I speak. Ana cannot help you now. Believe me—I don't want you to die."

His tone was gentle and persuasive. Yet still Lorelyn retreated. "Who *are* these servants of yours? Are they here?"

He raised his right arm, pointing skyward. "One is coming now. Look!"

Lorelyn looked up, and gave a cry of alarm. A dragon spiraled down out of the clouds, a swooping shadow, huge wings spread in a motionless glide.

"Do not be afraid," soothed Mandrake, taking her hand. She tried to pull away, but he gripped her fingers tightly. "He won't harm you."

"*He*—?"

"Trust me."

She could not free her hand. She watched wild-eyed as the dragon planed down and alighted in the plaza. The chill blast of wind from its wings lifted Mandrake's long hair and made his cloak billow up as though he too were winged. Releasing her hand, he walked toward the huge, copper-colored creature without fear. Its black mane and beard flowed in the wind as it turned its great head to look at him. She saw the cold glitter of its eye. Lorelyn cried out again, this time in utter amazement. The monster stood before Mandrake tame as a horse, softly blowing through its nostrils. He stood, wreathed in its steaming breath, and laid his hand upon the scaly neck.

"It's not possible," she breathed.

"And why not? Did Ana not tell you I was a sorcerer? You have always been eager for adventure. Would you not like to ride a flying dragon, and be taken to the fabled land of Eldimia?" He advanced toward her again, holding out his hand.

"No!" she cried. "I won't go and leave my friends behind, in danger!"

She turned and began to run. But he was swifter: he came up behind her and caught her by one arm, then seized the other hand as she spun around and tried to hit him. The gentleness was gone from his voice and hands. "I am sorry. But you really haven't any choice," he said.

AILIA WOKE WITH A START from a shadowy dream. She sat up for a moment blinking, wondering where on earth she was, then groped for a candle and tinderbox. The trembling light brought little comfort. She found their current quarters disturbing, shivered to think of all those empty chambers in the guesthouse—those cold, silent, history-haunted spaces. Even in her sleep she was uneasily aware of them. She held the candle up. Then she saw that Lorelyn was not in the room, and had not set out any bedding for herself.

Perhaps she just wasn't sleepy, and has gone out for a breath of fresh air instead, Ailia thought. But worry stirred deep inside her. Looking around, she saw no sign of Lorelyn's travel-cloak.

The fire that the men had set in the huge fireplace had died down to a few sullen embers. On the mantel a carved monster's head, like a heraldic lion with curling ram's horns, seemed to watch her with a sardonic expression as she paced and fretted. "Oh, Ana, why don't you come back?" she moaned. "I'm no good at all at this sort of thing. Ought I to go and look for Lori? Whatever shall I do if . . . if the men don't come back?" How long had she been asleep? Had Damion and Jomar been gone a long time—*too* long, perhaps? There were times when a vivid imagination could be a curse, she reflected, as appalling visions of disaster filled her mind. Ailia knew she was getting, in her mother's phrase, "all of a swither." There was no point in assuming the worst. It was likely Lorelyn had just grown tired of trying to sleep. But she would go and look for the girl anyway, just to set her mind at rest.

Ailia walked down the outer passage, the flame of her small candle making the darkness behind and before her seem all the darker. However, when she went outside she found that she no longer needed it. A light snow had fallen, but the night sky was cloudless now and many stars were out. She set the candle down on a stone block and stood looking about her. The mountain's two peaks were hooded with white, and their deep seams and shelving strata supported long thin drifts like lines of pale script. The snow-clad city looked as though it had regained its marble pavements, and its worn masonry glittered with jewels of frost; in the clear cold air the Mountains of the Moon beyond showed every detail, every fold and crevice and shadow of their forest-mantled slopes and their jutting icy crowns. A half-moon hung low over the northern battlements, looking so large and so near that it was easy to fancy she really stood at the threshold of Heaven itself, within reach of the First Sphere. High above was the constellation of the Lantern Bearer, with the polestar in his hand. As she gazed, there came a red glow from behind the mountains like a great fire, and then up rose an ice-green shaft that shimmered, elongated, turned into a wide wheeling shape that spun across the zenith: the aurora borealis, brighter and more vivid than she had ever seen it, despite the pallor of the sky. It must be directly overhead.

It was all so beautiful that her fears left her. She watched the auroras until their elfin glow faded, leaving the sky to the stars and the falling halved moon. No wonder the Elei had believed themselves divine, living so close to the sky! Here, on a mountain's summit, one was as high as a human could go: only a winged thing, a bird or dragon, could go any higher than this. And then she remembered the tales of the Elei's winged ships, and what Mandrake had said about them riding on the backs of tame dragons. Oh, for a flying ship or a friendly dragon now, to take her up, up into that shining sky!

Looking down at the snow, she saw that she had not one shadow but two: a faint moon-shadow, and another fainter still. Of course, the second shadow was cast by the Morning Star. Arainia's blue-white brilliance tonight rivaled that of the half moon. Ailia looked, fascinated, from her faint star-shadow up to the planet.

But the sight of it set her to thinking of Lorelyn again. She glanced around her. The snow was undisturbed by any tracks, so the girl must have left before it fell. The roofless ruins were utterly still. Ailia walked the snow's white carpet through still-stately halls and chambers, alone under the high silence of the sky.

"Lorelyn, Lorelyn!" she called softly, uncertainly. There was no answer. Could the girl have gone up to the cave, following the men? It was just the sort of mad, unpredictable thing she would do. Ailia retraced her steps, looking up at the dark hole into which she had seen the men disappear earlier. She did not like the look of it at all. *I can't go in there!* she thought, appalled. *I can't!*

She stood for a moment, trembling and irresolute. She longed so to hear the men's voices again, feel their comforting, capable presence. They would know what to do about Lorelyn's disappearance, they would come back and take charge and everything would be all right again. She wouldn't be alone anymore . . .

She went back for her candle and scrambled up to the cave mouth, peering in. There was the tunnel: she ventured in, shielding her candle-flame, and followed it until it divided.

The stone stair could only go up to the Moon Gate. They would not have gone there. After some hesitation, she took the passage that sloped downward.

She could never afterwards say how long it was that she journeyed downward. Once she called out, urgently: "Damion, Damion!" But the shout echoed from the rock walls around her and died in the darkness. She had always been a bit afraid of the dark, ever since she was a child. Now as she journeyed down into the mountain's depths, the hand with which she held her candle shook, throwing wild shadows on the walls . . . *Steady, now,* she told herself, biting her lip. *There's nothing to be afraid of!*

At last when she was certain she must be at the mountain's very roots the steps came to an end and she found herself in a larger space. She noticed worriedly that her candle-flame burned very low. Why on earth hadn't she thought of bringing a spare? If she didn't find the men soon, it would go out and she would be surrounded by darkness . . .

To and fro she went, in and out of the seemingly endless passageways, calling her companions' names. At length she came upon the passage that terminated in a wide cave mouth, and she peered inside, then leaped back, nearly dropping her candle.

She had read about treasure troves, but for once reality exceeded her imaginings. The small timid glow of her candle glanced upon gold and silver and flamed in the hearts of cut gems. She ventured into the great room, going from pile to pile, running coins and jewels through her hand, though she did not pocket any. It was not the treasure's value that moved her, but the presence of such rare and beautiful things in such staggering abundance. *Did the men come here too, before me? Did they see all this?*

"Damion! Jomar!" she called. There was no reply: the chamber was deathly silent. She started forward, her candle held out . . . and tripped on a burned-out torch that lay in the shadows.

Her candleholder went flying, striking the stone floor with a tinny, desolate sound. The little flame flickered fitfully, guttered, and went out.

Darkness rushed in upon her like a flood, and with it a terror unlike anything she had ever before experienced. One of the earliest fears of her childhood had come true: she was lost, lost and alone and in the dark . . . In the terrible moments that followed she called, desperately, for Jomar and for Damion—only to stop, frightened at the echoes her voice awoke. How was she ever going to get through those passages and back up that stone stair in the pitch darkness? "Damion—Damion, please hear me!" she called. She expected no answer now, and none came.

Then as her eyes adjusted, she realized that the chamber was not, after all, completely dark. A faint, pale light shone through the gloom. It looked to her rather like starlight—filtered, perhaps, down to these depths by some crevice high above. Then it occurred to her that the light did not seep down from above; the rays appeared, rather, to come from behind one of the piles of treasure.

Ailia stumbled toward the treasure heap, instinctively seeking the source of the light. And when she found it at last, lying between the mounded mass and the wall, she forgot everything else.

It was as though a hole smaller than the palm of her hand had been gouged into the rocky floor—into the very fabric of the world itself. Through this tiny aperture floods of light poured in white, whelming torrents, from some realm of pure radiance outside the world of matter, a universe of light. Ailia gasped and dropped back, blinking. For a moment she could see nothing but the imprint of that radiance on her retinas, a small violet spot such as one sees after looking inadvertently at the sun.

A small round spot . . . A circle, a round object—could it be . . .

"The Stone," Ailia breathed. She dared to look again, and as she did so the light changed, seeming not so much to grow dimmer as to soften, and she could gaze now, without being dazzled, at the small round object at its heart.

It was a jewel, a little globe carved with many facets, of crystal clear as water. At its center was a core of white light, like a star within its shining halo; from this the tide of radiance poured. Like the Tryna Lia herself, it was a thing of Earth and Heaven: stone and starlight. Its radiance was reflected by other gems in the hoard all around, repeated within their own gleaming centers, until it seemed as though she sat surrounded by stars of a hundred hues. Ailia put out her hand toward the crystal, then snatched it back.

"No," she whispered. "Oh, no, I can't. *I couldn't.*" She trembled. She was not afraid that the Star Stone would harm her. Rather, she feared what she might do to it, with her profane and unhallowed touch. She recalled the precious relics in the temple sanctum, sagging into dust and ruin at the travelers' intrusion. Surely her hand would sully and besmirch this shining thing.

She folded her hand in a corner of her cloak, making an improvised glove. Then, timorously, she reached for the radiant gem.

THE STONE ITSELF LIT HER way back, through the long tunnels and up the passageway, casting its unearthly radiance about her. It would tolerate no darkness, but sent its searching beams into every dark corner and crevice she passed, driving out the shadows and Ailia's fears along with them. It was as though she were not alone after all, but accompanied by a powerful, living presence. Her heart sang as she ran out of the cave into the ruins. "I've found it, I've found the Star Stone," she whispered. "And it's real, it's everything I dreamed it would be . . . everything and more."

Its light filled the guest chamber, so that the walls themselves seemed to glow. But the men were not there. Disappointed, Ailia stood and wondered what on earth to do next. Lorelyn still had not returned either. There was nothing for it but to sit here and wait. "Guardians of the Stone—where were you? Why weren't you here?" she whispered. "We needed help so badly."

Did she imagine it, or was there a sudden brightening of the Stone's soft radiance? She remembered the legends of the Paladins' pilgrimages, of the heavenly apparitions that had hovered about the holy gem. "Please—help us!" she begged. "If there are any protectors of the Stone, if you really *do* exist, then come to our aid—now! Don't let the Zimbourans win . . ."

And then she heard it: the sound of many booted feet approaching. Her heart leaped. For an instant she half imagined that her invocation had summoned the guardian-knights out of the dead city. She thrust the Stone into a travel-bag, then sprang up and hurried down the passage to peer out the main entrance. Yes, there were torches in the ruins! She stole cautiously toward them, keeping to the shadows, peering from behind broken walls. Were these friends—or foes?

A strange voice barked something, in a language that was neither Elensi nor Maurish. Ailia halted in her tracks, now staring in horror at the group of men standing in the snow—men who could only be Zimbourans. As she stood there, several more appeared—an entire company of soldiers.

She whirled, fleeing back the way she had come—and ran straight into another armed troop.

FOR AN INSTANT they were as motionless and startled as she. Then their leader strode forward. It was Zefron Shezzek. "You!" he said in thick-accented Maurish. "No, do not dare to run, little one, unless you want a spear in your back! Tell me where the others are, and we may spare your life."

Ailia gave a gasp of pure fright and stumbled backwards. Disregarding his words, she turned and fled.

No spear or arrow flew after her; she heard only shouts

and then the pounding of booted feet. They meant to take her alive. *Of course, to make me talk . . .* She tore along a passage with many doors opening out of it at either side. But her speed was her undoing: her toe caught on a broken stone concealed under the snow and she staggered with a cry of pain, then fell to her knees. At once she was up again; the shouts and heavy footsteps of the Zimbourans were right behind her. Had they heard her cry? She ducked into one of the doorways, but it led only to a small chamber. She backed into a shadowed corner and huddled there. It was no use: they would find her cringing here, and drag her out. She could already feel their rough strong hands upon her . . .

Something brushed against her leg, and had she had the breath she would have shrieked: instead she recoiled. In the next instant she saw that it was only Ana's cat. Greymalkin purred and rubbed her furry sides against the girl's ankle again, as if offering comfort. Ailia shrank into her dark corner as a man's harsh voice shouted in the passage, just outside.

The gray cat suddenly darted through the doorway and into the passage, yowling at the top of her lungs. There was another shout, followed by a spate of angry words from more than one voice, farther down the corridor. And then, incredibly, the booted feet moved away again.

Ailia sat in a daze, hardly able to believe it. Saved—by a cat! Seeing Greymalkin run from the room and hearing her caterwaul, her pursuers must have assumed that it was the cat that cried out. They were not going to search this room after all. Ailia had a chance now to escape, to flee the ruin, to make her way back down the mountainside in the concealing darkness.

But what of the Stone? It was in the travel-bag in the fireplace room, in plain sight.

In slow-dawning horror Ailia now realized what it was that she must do. Greymalkin had shown her, quite unwittingly, how the gem might yet be saved. All it would take was a distraction: as the cat had led the enemy away from Ailia, so she too must lead them out of the ruin, away from the roofed sleeping-chamber where the Stone lay. She was too cold, too tired, to evade the soldiers for long. But the Zimbourans must not find the Stone. There was still time: if she ran now they would follow, not linger here in the ruins.

She drew a deep breath, feeling the chill air fill her aching lungs. Then she burst from her hiding place.

At the sound of her fleeing footsteps shouts arose: they were not far away, and she knew that the Zimbourans would soon be close behind her again. She sprinted out of the building's doorless entrance and across the street. Her chest still felt raw and the muscles in her right side seemed to be pulling apart. But she forced herself on, and on. For the men had seen her now.

A visceral, animal panic seized hold of her, lending her a swiftness she had never known she could achieve. But she could not sustain it. Within moments the brief spurt of speed was over, and she was near the end of her endurance: her lungs burned with every gasping breath, a painful stitch spread along her side.

There—the cave mouth in the peak yawned darkly ahead of her. She could hide in there, somewhere: the men would come upon the treasure hoard, and perhaps they would even forget all about her in their greed and excitement at its untold riches. She drew a breath that seared her throat, and scrambled up to the tunnel entrance, feeling her way through its dark maw. Here were the stone steps that led upward. She hesitated. Perhaps she should go up, not down? If she took the lower passage she might be trapped in the cellarlike spaces below: treasure or not, eventually she would be caught and cornered. But there might yet be an escape route at the top of the peak—some little trail or sloping rock-face she could climb down. She half crawled up the stone steps in her weariness, groping for them with her cold-numbed hands. Soon there was a faint light spilling down the stair. It grew steadily stronger as she ascended.

She emerged from a square hole at the top, into a flat space in front of the portal, or rather what remained of it. The rock floor was covered in shallow drifts of snow, and on a low platform at the far end were the two damaged pillars with dragons wound around them, framing empty air. To one side, near the threshold of the portal, was another dragon, this one of brass or possibly gold. It was curled up in its own coils like a serpent, with its head resting on its tail: and it was huge, larger than the stone dragons, larger even than the living dragons that she had seen fly over the city.

Ailia threw a desperate glance around the mountaintop. She knew at once she had done the wrong thing in coming here. There was no place to hide, and the light of moon and stars glancing off the snowdrifts lit the whole place. She might conceal herself behind the big dragon statue or one of the stone pillars, but these were such obvious hiding places: it would take the men no time at all to find her.

Shouts came from below: the soldiers had divided up,

and by the sound of it several of them were running up the stairs. She whirled, staring about her. There stood the Moon Gate—but she was not yet desperate enough for the hopeless escape it offered. She heard the heavy boots at the entrance to the stair, and then they charged up through it, yelling in their harsh native tongue as they caught sight of her. She crumpled to her knees in the snow, watching helplessly as they ran toward her, their weapons at the ready.

Then one man yelled in fear and pointed with his sword toward the platform.

The biggest dragon statue, the gold-plated one, was moving. There was a rattling of metal on stone as its great coils stirred, its head came up, its folded wings unfurled. Its eyelids opened to reveal cold shining eyes of emerald, their depths luminous in the torchlight. Ailia gaped. Of course: it was a mechanical statue, like the gryphons at the temple door. As the Zimbourans recoiled, howling in terror, the golden dragon gave a grinding roar, its teeth flashing in the starlight like the heads of spears. The men turned tail and fled for the stair. Ailia laughed weakly. She was saved again, this time by a statue. She began to struggle to her feet.

And then she saw the glistening cave of the monster's mouth: the long lashing tongue, the breath that mounted up in a steaming cloud. Slowly it uncoiled itself and stretched out its golden length upon the rock.

Alive—it was *alive.* Not a statue after all. This was a real dragon, roused from its slumber here on the mountaintop. Ailia staggered back a few steps, and dropped to her knees again.

20

The God-King

"I CAN'T BELIEVE WE RISKED our necks for nothing," Jomar grumbled.

They had paused for a moment after wandering for what felt like hours through the twists and turns of the tunnel. Having left their torches behind in the hoard-chamber of the Dragon King, they had only one small candle from Jomar's pouch to light their way, and they made slow progress. Their fears that the tunnel would come to a dead end had not come to pass, but its rough rocky floor began to show an unpromising downward slant.

"It never occurred to you to look *inside* the box first?" Jomar complained as they sat with their backs to the tunnel wall, taking a rest.

Damion bit his lip. Being trained as a priest of the Faith left one with a small store of available expletives, none of them satisfying. "Well, if that doesn't take the biscuit!" he burst out at last. "I was somewhat preoccupied with a large, dangerous animal at the time—or didn't you notice?"

"Well, it doesn't really matter, anyway. *I* never cared a straw for that stupid stone. We didn't find it, but neither did the Zims."

"But they still might! If the container was there, the Stone must be too. It's in that hoard, somewhere—"

"Well, I'm not going back there! Not with that monster waiting for us! Let the Zims tussle with him if they want to."

Damion said nothing for a moment. He did not want to face the dragon again either. He stared into the darkness of the tunnel beyond the candle-glow: it reminded him suddenly of the dragon's huge dark eye, and in his mind he confronted it again. It was that eye, even more than the creature's jaws and talons, that filled him with fear: that bottomless pupil, with its glint of malevolent intelligence. For the merest of instants he had seemed to sense behind it a vast inhuman mind, a labyrinth of shadowy caverns and tunnels of thought. He could not rid himself of the feeling that the dragon in its turn had known his mind, perceived his intent, and reacted, not as a dumb brute instinctively defending its territory, but in anger at his attempt to take the Star Stone. *Was* the Stone there, somewhere in the treasure chamber—and if so, was the Dragon King's possession of it merely an animal's mindless fascination with some glittering bauble? Or was it something more?

"Jo," he said in a low voice, "you may think this sounds foolish, but—I think the dragon understood why we were there in the cave. Somehow, it *knew.*"

Jomar groaned. "Not those faerie tales again! They're only animals, Damion!"

"Are they?" Damion countered. "How can you be sure? We know nothing at all about the creatures—they aren't like anything else on this earth. Who's to say that they might not be intelligent—almost as intelligent as a man?" He thought of the dolphin that had swum alongside the ship, looking up at him with its large, wise eye. "The Dragon King might even be attracted to the Star Stone—"

"Dragon King?"

"That's what Ana called him. The Trynoloänan."

"You're as bad as Ailia, believing all that rubbish. They're just *animals,* Damion. How could they have a king?"

"Bees have queens, haven't they? It's just an expression. And that one did seem to be dominating the other dragons—"

"As for all that about the dragon *wanting* to keep the Stone," Jomar went on, ignoring him, "it's just ridiculous."

"Is it, though? Lots of animals collect bright, shiny objects. Magpies, for instance. And a dragon must be far more intelligent than a magpie."

"Don't be stupid. He's—*it's* just an animal and nothing more, I tell you!" snapped Jomar. He added morosely, "We'd better get out of here before we *both* start to go insane. I say we keep on going."

"Jo, we could wander through this mountain's innards forever. You said so yourself. We don't even know if there *is* another way out."

"There's still a chance if we take this way. Back there, with the dragon, there's no chance at all."

Damion sighed and said no more, but leaned back against the rock wall and closed his eyes. There must be a way out: of that he suddenly felt certain. They had come so far, overcome so many obstacles, that like Ana he had begun to see something else at work behind their own efforts: not fate, nothing so remote and indifferent, but a benign and guiding influence of some kind—the hand, perhaps, of the God he had so nearly abandoned. He reached out with his mind, hoping for another vision or some minor miracle, trying to make contact once more with that mysterious providence he had felt or imagined.

"You can at least show some interest," snapped Jomar.

"Shut up, I'm praying," replied Damion without opening his eyes.

"A lot of good that'll do!"

"Well, what good will you do sitting there pickling your wits?" retorted Damion, opening his eyes again to look accusingly at Jomar.

The Mohara man shoved his liquor-flask back into his pouch. "All right! I don't know what to do either. But I don't see any point in going back the way we came, past a large and angry dragon."

Damion sighed and rose. "Very well, we'll keep going."

They rose and walked on, and presently the tunnel began to level out again, widening until it resembled a gigantic rabbit-run. Soon it terminated in a gaping hole, lit by a strange deep blue glow—

"The sky!" cried Damion. He ran eagerly forward, Jomar following, and the men found themselves emerging from a wide cave mouth onto the northern face of the mountain. It was very steep here, an almost vertical slope of scree: but the two peaks and the north wall of Liamar lay only a short distance above them.

"There now!" Jomar crowed. "What did I tell you?"

Damion couldn't smile. They had not brought back the

Stone, and this second disappointment was almost more than he could bear.

"LORELYN? AILIA?"

No one answered their calls. The sleeping-chamber was empty: both girls had disappeared. "What in the—? Where are they?" exploded Jomar, staring around the room. "They were told to stay here! Don't tell me they've gone off exploring by themselves!"

"Lorelyn!" Damion called, running through the passage. "Ailia, where are you?" The dark, frigid rooms echoed his voice, but there was no other sound in response.

"Why would they leave the ruin? Did they go looking for us?" He went cold at the thought, remembering the dragon in its lair.

"Maybe something frightened them, and they had to get away fast," Jomar suggested.

"We'd better go look for them," said Damion wearily.

They went back outside. The snow outside the ruin was well trodden, with more than one set of tracks. "One person, though," Jomar said, studying them intently. "Going and coming, and—yes, going again. The tracks don't look big enough to be Lorelyn's, so it was Ailia. But then where is Lorelyn? I don't understand this at all."

The two men followed the tracks. One set led toward the peak, another into the plaza. Jomar decided this latter set was fresher. He and Damion followed it until they came to a place where the snow had been trampled by many feet. Booted feet. They looked at one another.

"Anthropophagi?" asked Damion.

"No," replied Jomar, examining the tracks. He

straightened, looking grim. "These are Zimbouran bootprints."

"The Zimbourans!" Damion exclaimed. "They've caught up with us and captured the girls! We should never have left them on their own!"

"Calm down," Jomar replied, though he too looked miserable. "Ailia ran right into them," he added

Damion's heart gave a sickening lurch as he looked at the small footprints vanishing among the larger ones.

"If Mandrake had anything to do with this," Jomar vowed, "I'll have his head . . . Unless they got him, too," he said, looking slightly cheered at the idea. He walked on, staring at the ground, then gave a shout. "Wait, Damion—look over here! They *didn't* get her. She ran away!"

As he moved to inspect the trail Damion heard a curious whistling sound, followed by a faint metallic clink. He stared at the base of a broken pillar. An arrow lay before it in the snow.

"Hold!" shouted a voice.

Figures came swarming out of the ruins: Zimbouran soldiers in their black leather garb. Damion and Jomar drew their swords, but a quick glance told them it was no use. They were hopelessly outnumbered, and swords were no use against bowmen.

"Well met!" growled a voice at the rear of the group. Damion and Jomar both went rigid at the sight of the thickset figure to whom it belonged. "Now then!" said Shezzek, stepping forward. "Let's have no nonsense, and you'll not get hurt. For the moment, anyway."

The weapons were struck from their hands; then Jomar and Damion felt their arms seized and pinioned behind them. There was a sound of hooves muffled in snow: another group of soldiers appeared out of the ruins, leading horses by their reins. One of them was Artagon.

"Traitor," Shezzek hissed at Jomar. "Where is the gem?"

"You're wasting your time," the Mohara man responded in a bored tone. "We don't know where it is, any more than you do."

Shezzek struck him across the face. Damion winced, but Jomar was evidently accustomed to this kind of abuse: he did not even groan, but stood silent and mutinous, glaring at his former captain.

Shezzek directed his next question at Damion. "Where are the others?"

Damion's failing spirits leaped at those words. *The others! Then they didn't catch the women after all!*

"Answer me!" Shezzek shouted. "The Princess and the old witch, where are they?"

"It's no good asking us," Damion answered, surprised at his own temerity. "The truth is, all the women went off without us."

"That's your story, eh? Well, we'll see what the other girl says," the half-breed said, leering.

The other girl. Damion felt a stab of anxiety. "What have you done to Ailia?" he shouted, caught between fury and fear.

"Nothing yet; the young fool ran away, but my men are hunting her in the ruins. When we catch her—"

"Let her alone!" interrupted Damion. "She's not a part of this. She only fell in with us by accident. She's no use to you at all."

"You think not?" Shezzek studied Damion's face.

"You seem very concerned about the girl. She is important to you, perhaps? That is useful. Perhaps when we put her to torment in front of your eyes you will remember where the Tryna Lia girl is—and where we can find the Stone."

Suddenly, and with all his might, Jomar brought his right foot down on his captor's, twisting free as the man howled with pain, and snatching his sword up from the snow. Almost in the same movement he swung around, slashing at the Zimbouran who held Damion. The man leaped back, forced to release his captive in order to grope for his own weapon. Jomar lunged, laying open the man's sword arm from wrist to elbow as Damion dived for the adamantine sword. The wounded man screamed and dropped to the snow, nursing his arm, but the other soldiers closed in, making a bristling wall of blades. Damion and Jomar stood back to back, panting, trying to face all their foes at once.

"Sorry about that," Jomar muttered to Damion, "but I prefer to die fighting. It's a Mohara tradition."

"You fool," rumbled Shezzek, and gestured to his men.

One of the soldiers attacked Jomar, bringing his blade down upon the Mohara man's. Jomar parried the blow and responded with a vicious thrust of his own. Now two men rolled in agony at his feet. Damion waved his own sword about wildly, hoping that he looked formidable. The Zimbourans jeered and closed in, then howled in shock and dismay as the crystal blade sheared through their steel. But more men moved to flank him, forcing him to swing the sword from side to side in an effort to fend them all off. It was hopeless: even with the Paladin weapon he could not fight more than one man at a time. And the archers were raising their bows.

A wavering, inhuman cry rose from the temple behind them.

They all whirled, attacked and attackers alike, to face the dark doorway. A slight figure stood there, long silvery hair flowing about it. The woman's right arm was upraised in a warding gesture, and at her feet stood a gray cat with eyes that burned red in the torchlight.

"Children of Valdur!" cried the apparition in Elensi, to the accompaniment of another yowl from the cat. "Begone from this holy place, or know the anger of the Elei gods!"

"It's Ana!" whispered Damion in disbelief.

The soldiers backed away, but Shezzek recovered himself, barking something in Zimbouran at the men. They advanced with reluctance. The woman lifted both arms toward the sky, and called out again. "Beware! You may not enter the temple of the Elei. The gods will strike you dead where you stand." Greymalkin yowled again, a high, bloodcurdling sound.

Two soldiers raced up the steps toward the old woman, swords in their hands. But as they passed the threshold the two gryphon statues rose onto their haunches, spread their brassy pinions, and uttered deafening screeches.

Howling with terror, the men retreated, one of them stumbling and falling backwards down the steps. The men surrounding Damion and Jomar scattered. Shezzek held his ground uncertainly for a moment, but without the protection of his men his courage failed him, and he too turned and fled the scene.

"Damion! Jomar! Come with me quickly!" Ana cried.

They bounded up the steps, ignoring the screaming cherubim. Ana stooped to pick up her cane from the stone floor, her long white hair brushing the pavement. Her left hand held something that glittered like a piece of ice.

"How did you get here?" exclaimed the Mohara.

"We mustn't stand here talking, Jomar. Zimbourans are very superstitious, thank goodness, but King Khalazar is on his way."

Damion could not move, however. He stood staring at the object in her hand, unable to take his eyes from it. Now that he was closer he could see that it was a great crystal, clear as a diamond and carved with a myriad of facets. "Is that *it?*" he asked. "How in the Seven Heavens did you find it?"

"It is the Star Stone, yes." She thrust the gem inside a pocket of her gown, then bent down again to pick up the growling Greymalkin. "And I just found it a few minutes ago, when I was looking for you. I followed your tracks here, and saw that you were having some trouble. Now, quickly! We must find a place that is safe and secure, while we wait."

"Wait for what?" demanded Jomar. But she merely said, "Hurry, hurry."

They fled into the portico. Jomar gestured to one side. "In there—the tower that's still intact."

They hastened up the spiral staircase. Halfway up, a doorless archway opened from the tower onto the roof of the portico. Upon the parapet the stone angels stood with their winged backs to the travelers. Behind them swelled the mighty dome, a rounded mountain of marble.

There was no entrance other than the tower staircase: on one side was a steep drop to the pavements below. The roof was just wide enough for two people to walk abreast. Once it had joined both the front towers, but a portion of it had fallen in, and now this segment on which they stood was isolated. It would be easy to defend, Jomar declared. The Zimbourans couldn't reach them from the other tower. They would have to mount the staircase in single file, so the defender at the door never need fight more than one man at a time. Jomar and Damion could take turns, each spelling the other. But even as he said this they all knew it was no use. The Zimbourans could simply wait for them to grow too tired and famished to defend themselves.

"What about Ailia?" Damion asked, worried. "They must have caught her by now."

Jomar frowned at that. "They can use her as a hostage, to make us surrender."

"They haven't got her," Ana replied, that strange far-seeing look coming into her misty eyes. She set her cat down and reached into her pocket again.

"They said the soldiers—"

"They have not captured her—nor will they."

Damion knew better than to argue. His gaze went to the glowing jewel she cradled in her hand. "Where did you find the Stone, Ana?" he asked.

"It was lying in a bag, in the chamber where all your gear was."

"In the chamber?" Damion stared at her. "But who . . . how . . . ?"

Jomar looked over the battlements, then turned to the others, his face grim. "I can see them coming back. They won't take long to find us."

They watched as armed figures began to pour across

the snow-covered plaza, their boots churning its whiteness to a gray slush. At their rear rode a man on a large black horse.

Damion saw Jomar's face go hard at the sight. "Khalazar," he muttered.

"Rescue is on the way," said Ana.

"If you mean the Guardians, there aren't any," Jomar snapped, turning on her. "According to Mandrake they're long gone. *He's* in Trynisia too, by the way."

No surprise showed on Ana's face. "He was," she answered. "In fact, he was the power, the danger I told you of before. I tried to draw his attention away from you, but in vain. He attacked me again and nearly destroyed me, sending his dragons upon me and leaving me so weakened that I could scarcely move. I could not warn you about Mandrake when we parted. If I had, you might have tried to fight him and aroused his anger. It was better that you not defy him: he was less likely to harm you if you seemed harmless. Nor could I tell you where the Stone lay, for he would surely have attacked you had you tried to take it. But I see that one of you succeeded in finding it all the same. As I said before, it was meant to be."

"He almost had us convinced that it wasn't here at all. So where is Mandrake now?"

"I'm afraid he's gone again. That is why I am free to rejoin you: his power no longer threatens us. But he has taken Lorelyn with him."

Damion reeled where he stood. "He's abducted her *again?* Where has he taken her this time?"

"To the land of Eldimia."

"Eldimia? Why would *he* take her there?" asked Damion, puzzled.

"I know Mandrake well. He always has several plans laid, in case one of them fails. His scheme to hide Lorelyn away was thwarted back in Maurainia. Now he is trying another plan. He will place her on the throne of Eldimia, but remain by her side, forcing her to do his will. In the end it will be Mandrake who rules Eldimia, and not the Tryna Lia." She looked away over the dead city, spoke as if to herself. "Ah, how clear it all is now! Why did I not see before? He means to make use of her, for his own ends!"

"So *he* wouldn't be interested in helping us," said Jomar. "Or is it Ailia who's going to come bounding to our rescue?"

"No, not Ailia," Ana replied. "The Stone has its own Guardians, pledged to protect it in the hour of need."

Jomar stationed himself by the doorway, his drawn sword in his hand. "Guardians be blasted! I told you, old woman, there *aren't any Guardians!* We're going to have to fight for ourselves. Not that there's much point to it now. We won't be able to hold the Zims off forever." His black eyes blazed. "But they won't kill me until I've taken a few of them first."

"Hold them off for as long as you can then," said Ana. She turned her face toward the mountains as if in prayer. "I will await the Guardians." She closed her eyes once more, and cradled the gem at her breast.

"Then you'll wait a long time. They died off, centuries ago."

Ana's eyes did not open. "No, the Guardians of the Stone never died. They live still."

"What do you mean? It's been five hundred years! No one could live that long—"

"The Guardians could. They are not human," she interrupted.

"Not human?" echoed Damion. A hideous doubt assailed him as he stared at the aged woman, her long hair blowing in wild strands around her face. "You said . . . I thought you said they were men. Human beings, who could help us . . ."

Ana opened her eyes and looked at him. "I did not say so; but I'm afraid I let you interpret it that way. You would never have believed the truth: that the Guardians are not of this world at all." Her clouded eyes seemed to gaze at the marble angels poised upon their pedestals.

Damion's knees sagged: it was all he could do to remain standing. So this was how it would end. They were all going to die here on the battlements, just as Jomar had said.

AILIA RAISED HER HEAD SLOWLY. The dragon was still there, huge and silver-gold in the light of stars and moon: it had coiled its long snaky body upon the dais again, and its head was turned toward her. Now that its wings were furled and no longer filled the air with thunder, it seemed smaller than before, though it was still the largest living thing she had ever seen. It lay panting gently, its breath rising in white clouds of steam; occasionally it would raise a clawed foreleg to scratch the side of its neck. Seeing her move, it uncurled its great long body and rose to all fours once more. Ailia froze. She could never outrun the creature, even had she the strength to make the attempt. Lying very still, she watched as it approached on its great clawed feet. She noticed, in a detached kind of way, that its toes were shaped like an eagle's: cruel, curved talons.

Ailia had by now reached that state in which a victim abandons fear together with hope. To her dazed mind the number of talons on the dragon's feet seemed to have some immense significance: she counted them in her head as the beast approached her. Five talons to each foot; it was important somehow that there be five. She stared at them stupidly. Then her eyes strayed to the pillars where the carved dragons coiled and snarled. Imperial dragons: what had Mandrake said about them, about their claws? That they alone bore five talons on each foot . . .

Tame dragons.

Ailia lifted her gaze to the meet the dragon's. It halted a few paces away, watching her. She dared to stir, to rise slowly to her feet, without taking her eyes from the dragon. It did not move; its green gaze was fixed upon her, but without the hostility it had shown the soldiers. The steaming breaths gusting from between its mighty tusks warmed her shivering body: they had a strange sweet smell, like incense-smoke. It had a ruff of thick fur about its neck, she saw now, rather like a lion's mane, and a bearded chin.

The beast raised one mighty foreclaw, and she cringed: but instead of attacking her it scratched the side of its neck again. And then she saw that the dragon was chained to the right pillar. There was a loop of heavy black iron behind its head, like a tight-fitting collar. It was this chain, she realized, that had produced the metallic rattle she had heard when the dragon first moved. But who could have done this to such a powerful creature?

She stepped forward. The dragon watched her approach, still with no sign of anger.

"You *are* tame," she breathed. "He tamed you, didn't he? You're Mandrake's dragon."

The great beast clawed at the iron chain, grunting as though it were in pain. The leathery wings upon its back stirred and rustled, then abruptly they burst open. A great double canopy of translucent gold, ribbed with bone, rose in two arches high above Ailia's head. She gasped. The wings spanned the width of the mountain peak, sixty paces from end to end. For a moment they hung there, quivering, blotting out the sky; then they sagged, collapsed, and furled onto his flanks again. This dragon was earthbound and helpless as any hobbled beast of burden. Mandrake had made him a prisoner. The poor creature. He belonged to the air, to the sky, and only the chain kept him here: he could not break its iron links with his talons or fangs.

But she could undo it for him. There was no escape for her, not now: but the dragon at least could go free. He had saved her from the Zimbourans, she owed him that much.

Another remembered voice spoke in her mind: it was Ana's this time, and she spoke of dragons and earth-magic. *"Lying for days upon a hoard of gold and silver augmented a dragon's powers, giving it the ability to fly and to use sorcery. Dragons did not care for iron, however. Iron is too potent a star-metal: the magic in it is so concentrated that it overwhelms and negates any other sorcery."* So it was no use loosing the chain where it was fastened to the base of the pillar. That would still leave him bound at the neck. Pure, "cold" iron negated sorcery—and dragons flew by sorcery, so Ana had said. If he was to be freed, she must unfasten the collar. There was a clasp on it, she saw, like the one on a necklace, too small for his mighty claws to manipulate. She could undo it. But that would mean going right up close to his gigantic head.

She approached him, timidly but with resolve, and he seemed to guess her intent: he stood still, lowering his head so that the chain's clasp was on a level with her shoulders. Reaching out, she caught hold of the chain. She felt his neck beneath her fingertips, and to her surprise his scales were warm and dry: she had thought they would be cold and slimy like a fish's. She seized the little metal lever that released the clasp, drawing it back. With a clang the iron chain slithered to the stone floor and lay there like a long black snake.

Shouts arose behind her from the entrance to the stair: the Zimbourans were returning, in greater numbers by the sound of it. "Fly," she whispered to the dragon. "You can fly away now. Go on!"

But he did not open his wings again. Instead he stood looking at her; then he folded his forelegs under him, and sank down until his head and neck lay flat upon the rock. For an instant she fancied that he was actually thanking her: it looked very like a bow. But after a moment he rose again, took a couple of steps closer to her, and repeated the gesture, this time with his head lying next to her feet.

She had a sudden memory of an oddly similar picture: a lady in a graceful gown, with a palfrey kneeling before her. Some horses were trained to go down on their knees so a rider could mount: did tame dragons do the same thing?

Angry yells filled the air: she saw a whole troop of soldiers running toward them. She leaped for the proffered neck, gripping handfuls of the tumbled mass of the mane. The dragon walked slowly and carefully across the rocky floor, bearing her along on its neck like a Zimbouran elephant carrying its mahout. Ahead of her were the curving horns, behind her the long scaly back and folded wings. She looked down, and saw the creature's giant shadow striding along beside them on the snow. Behind, the men were standing in a line, arrows taking flight from their bows. The dragon roared as several shafts struck him: she saw the steam of his roar rise up, felt the throbbing in the massive column of his neck. But she was strangely lightheaded and not afraid at all. *Go on!* she urged her strange steed. *Fight them, beat them!*

But the dragon strode on toward the portal. And now Ailia saw the cliff beyond, the moonlit ground terminating before a terrible gulf, its depths lost in darkness. The dragon passed between the pillars, up to the very edge, and she gripped handfuls of his mane as the long neck thrust out over the abyss and she found herself looking down on blue deeps of air—down to where the jagged rocks lay, and the forest grew like moss upon the mountainside. Fear came to her again, but still with that odd undercurrent of exhilaration. An arrow flew over her head, and she heard the wind whistle in its feathers, saw it fall into the gulf, down and down.

There was a creaking and rustling behind her, as of canvas sails mounting a mast. It was the dragon's wings unfolding again. She felt the huge animal crouch and gather himself. And then the ground was no longer there. The snow-covered rock fell away: there was only the dark rushing up at them, the shriek of the wind in her ears, a blast of cold, a horrid plunge into nothingness that turned her stomach to a bottomless pit. For a dreadful instant they plummeted into the depths.

There was another sound, a great booming noise like the wind in a ship's sails: the dragon's wings were beating. Still, for a moment the iron of the discarded chain on the mountain top worked its malign influence, and they continued to fall. The icy air roared about them. Then the wings beat again, harder this time, with more strength and confidence. They were out of the iron's range, free to fly with the aid of sorcery. The dragon rose, soaring up to meet the stars, while behind him the crag dwindled away, the figures of the Zimbourans like black ants clustered at its edge between the two tiny pillars.

Ailia shrieked, not altogether from fear.

She was flying. *Flying!*

The huge wings beat in strong steady rhythm, bearing them both up until the mountain itself diminished, merely one of many that jutted from the earth's surface. Range upon range appeared, rising one behind the other like waves in the sea, and then there was the real sea in the distance, and the white waste of the ice, and far down below there was the river, running like a thread of silver through the dark tapestry of the forest.

And still the dragon sought the sky, until the land tilted below them and began to fall away as the mountain had done. From this godlike point of vantage the mountain ranges now appeared as little more than an upheaval of the island's surface, like the broken earth behind a plow. In a few moments they had passed down the whole length of the river valley—the journey that on land had taken days—and were out over the sea. Ailia looked down and caught her breath at the sight of the rim of white waves, nibbling the shore . . . Something gray poured past like smoke, hiding the view, and then they flew into a cold mist in which Ailia could see nothing but the vast vanes of the wings, moving up and down. She remembered the cloud that had engulfed the mountaintop. *Clouds! I'm in a cloud—*

They burst out into clear air again, above a second sea—a sea made up of white misty shapes, reefs and anvils and mushrooms and mesas poised upon the air. Between these vast masses were strung finer filaments: wispy faerie bridges that spanned great gulfs with dark depths as of water, save that at the very bottom of them she glimpsed the real sea, all diamonded with light, and here and there a glitter of floating ice. She raised her head higher, bracing herself on a horn to look about her, and then she gasped. She could not breathe: her lungs labored and her throat strained. Cold speared her body, cleaving her to the bone, and the cloudscape before her dimmed into a sparked and seething darkness. She sagged back down into the dancing strands of mane—and found her head was clear again. There was air around the dragon, and warmth as well. They wrapped him in an invisible cocoon, an atmosphere that he bore with him as he flew, but its outer limit was only a couple of feet away from his body.

Feeling dizzy, Ailia shut her eyes. When she dared to look down again it was to find the clouds diminished in their turn, as the mountains had been: they looked to her like clouds reflected in a pool, or like a snowy, furrowed field seen from the top of a high hill. Awe again gave way to terror. She clutched tufts of shaggy mane, wondering how one commanded a mount like this. Were words enough, or did one need magic to guide a tame dragon? How could she get him to fly back down to earth again? As she pondered this there came a blush of fiery color beyond the eastern end of the world—which to Ailia's eyes now had a perceptible curve—and with the swiftness of a thunderbolt the sun sprang into the sky.

Ailia and her dragon mount were so high that they had surprised the dawn that lay in wait behind the horizon, and they soared now through a morning not yet come to the lands below. Yet in the sky above her she could still see the stars. As the things of the earth became smaller, so the things of the sky seemed to grow: these stars were not wavering points of light but discs that shone steadily, and the moon low on the rounded horizon was a shining semicircle no longer but a globe half steeped in shadow, while on its sunlit face all its pits and vales and dark mottlings were plainly visible. Almost one might reach out and touch it . . .

If we fly any higher, thought Ailia, *we will be in Heaven itself—*

And then the air opened up in front of them in a blazing tunnel of light.

21
The Palace

DAMION PEERED OUT from behind a stone angel at the enemy below. Ana waited motionless nearby, though her head was bowed now. Greymalkin perched on the parapet gazing down at the Zimbourans, her tail twitching. At the tower door Jomar suddenly went rigid.

"I hear them. They're coming up the staircase!"

The two men began to prepare themselves for combat—not, Damion thought in dismay, that they had much of a chance, with the odds so heavily against them. The Stone, in their possession for so brief a time, was now as good as lost.

He glanced down over the edge of the parapet. A dragon had flown over minutes ago, surging into view over the western peak: a huge beast, bigger than any he had yet seen, with scales that glittered silver-gold in the starlight. He had hoped that the sight of it would frighten off the Zimbourans, but in vain. It merely soared away into the sky and vanished. The soldiers looked frightened, but none of them fled. King Khalazar waited below, mounted on his horse: a large heavyset man clad in rich robes of scarlet and gold beneath a black fur cloak. His fleshy face sported a full black beard arranged in tight curls. On his head was a tall scarlet headdress, in his hands a naked sword with a long curved blade.

For Lorelyn, Damion thought. Thank God she wasn't here: he could almost feel grateful to Mandrake, now, for spiriting her away.

A red glow touched the undersides of the clouds. What a bitter irony that the end should come for them now, just as day broke—a day whose ending none of them would live to see. Ana lifted her head once more and stared skyward with her veiled eyes, her lips moving as if in prayer. She held the great crystal up before her face, and the blood-colored light filled its heart.

There was a sound of booted feet advancing up the tower stairs, and Jomar looked down it, raising his sword. "One more step and you'll be a foot shorter," he threatened. The boots only ascended faster: Jomar lunged at the doorway, stabbing with his sword, and there was a howl of pain and fury followed by a loud commotion of voices. Jomar laughed wildly.

"Ha! Come and get it, you Zimbouran dogs!" he roared.

"Jomar!" came a voice from the stairwell. "You're already a traitor. Don't be a fool as well!"

"Oh, you're there, are you, Shezzek?" returned Jomar. "Safe at the back as usual! Why don't you come on up and face me yourself—sir?"

Shezzek's voice answered. "Mohara, there is still time. There is no hope for your companions, but if you throw down your sword and come quietly—"

"All will be forgiven," Jomar sneered, and made another thrust with his sword. A second yell rang out.

"Take him, you cowards!" shouted Shezzek, adding a torrent of Zimbouran words.

And then Jomar leaped back with a terrible cry. To his

horror Damion saw the shaft of an arrow protruding from Jomar's upper back, just under the right shoulder.

"No!" Damion cried.

A triumphant shout made him whirl about distractedly; he saw several bowmen ranged in a row atop the broken stump of the western tower.

"Archers! Ana, get down!" he yelled, then ran to Jomar's aid. The Mohara man staggered backwards, clutching the arrow's tip with his free hand: it protruded from his chest. For a fraction of a second his eyes looked into Damion's, wide and filled with pain. Then his legs gave way beneath him, and he fell.

"Jo." Biting back his anguish, the young priest ran to take Jomar's place at the tower door. But it was too late: a soldier had already leaped through onto the roof, followed by another. Throwing himself in front of his fallen companion, Damion brought his blade down on the first soldier's with all the fury of desperation. The steel gave way before the gleaming adamant, and the man recoiled in fear. But out of the corner of his eye Damion saw the second man slip past and head for Ana, who still stood facing the sky as though oblivious to the struggle taking place behind her. And now all those behind swarmed out onto the roof. As he faced one attacker another lunged in with lightning speed: white-hot pain shot up Damion's sword arm, and his weapon dropped from his hand. He ducked under the second, sweeping blow designed to hack off his head, dodged to one side, and succeeded in scooping up Jomar's fallen sword. Holding it out in both hands, he managed somehow to block the next follow-up thrust, but the sheer force of it propelled him backwards. The parapet was close behind him now, it would only take another heavy blow to send him tumbling over it. Damion's knees bent under him, and his eyes swam. As he raised his arms again, he saw that his right sleeve was slashed and dyed a bright, shocking scarlet with his own blood.

The Zimbouran struck at his sword-blade again. He had not the strength, with one wounded arm, to withstand the clash of steel on steel. The sword dropped from his hands. As he collapsed back against the parapet Damion saw Shezzek step out of the doorway. Behind him came a large robed figure: King Khalazar. The latter's small black eyes went to Ana, still standing motionless with the Stone in her hand. The gem blazed like flame as the rising sun reflected from its facets. Khalazar's face grew ugly with triumph, the fleshy mouth widening into a wolf's grin. On the battlement the gray cat shrilled in impotent fury as Shezzek, at an impatient gesture from his king, drew his sword and strode toward the old woman.

The sun stood above the snowy peaks, and between its light and his tears Damion's eyes swam in a wavering haze; but he could make out several gleaming shapes hurtling through the air above the Mountains of the Moon. He blinked: for a moment he lost them in the brilliance. They seemed to be flying out of the sun itself. Huge, winged things, approaching with the speed of thunderbolts. Shrieks of fury echoed from crag to crag as they converged on the summit of Elendor.

Dragons. Shezzek and Khalazar and the other men looked skyward in fear, arrested in their tracks.

Damion closed his eyes, dragged a deep breath down into the bottom of his lungs. Then he surged to his feet, ran at the Stone, and snatched it from Ana's hand. She called out to him, but he ignored her. Stuffing the crystal in his pocket, he swung away from the parapet with its towering angels and ran in the opposite direction: toward the great curving swell of the temple dome.

The Zimbourans started in surprise, belatedly taking their attention from the flying monsters to the priest. Ignoring the old woman, they turned to pursue Damion—as he had intended. He climbed the curve of the dome on hands and knees, crawling up it like an insect: it was not a proud perfect hemisphere like that of the High Temple in Maurainia, but was more flattened in shape, and the cracked and weathered surface offered him many hand- and footholds. But its upper portion was slippery with snow. Fortunately the archers were focusing all their efforts on the approaching dragons: as he scrambled and slithered up the stone slope he was aware of the huge shapes swooping down out of the sky.

Cries arose from the enemy. He dared risk one rapid glance backwards, and saw that only two men were after him: Shezzek and one of his soldiers.

There was no time to see more. He could only hope Ana was safe from them for the moment, now that she no longer had the Stone. Damion struggled on up the side of the dome. He clambered past one of the square gaping holes where a stone block had fallen in, and glimpsed the dim interior far below. If another block should give while he crept over it—but he would not think of that, nor of the men now closing the distance behind him. He could hear their hoarse strident breaths, like the panting of hounds in the chase. He was wounded, and they were not: it made all the difference.

He had now reached the point where the dome's upward swell began to level slightly, like the bottom of an inverted bowl. Not far ahead of him was the great round hole, ten paces across, that gave light to the sanctuary beneath. He got to his feet and began to run, his arms outspread for balance. In a few moments his pursuers would be running too, and they would have him. And the Stone.

"Stop!" Shezzek roared after him. "You fool! What do you hope to gain—"

Damion ran on. The hole was there in front of him, looking far larger than it had from beneath. He made for its stone rim, placing its rounded width between him and Shezzek. Far below he could see the domed shrine with the gold Sun Goddess on its roof, gleaming in the faint light.

"Give me the Stone," ordered Shezzek. He started to move around the hole, and Damion at once ran the other way. Back and forth they went, alternately changing direction—Damion had a blurred boyhood recollection of playing tag around a table. The stalemate could not last, though. The other Zimbouran was just a few paces away, and a second foe would quickly end the game. Damion broke and tried to run, but only succeeded in staggering a few steps: he was light-headed from loss of blood. He would never get down the other side of the dome: his last burst of energy was spent.

"It is over." Shezzek began to walk around the hole. "You only delay the inevitable."

Damion drew the Stone out of his pocket. Khalazar had seen it in Ana's hand—that was good: the God-king would not now believe that any other gem was the one he sought. Damion darted back to the roof-hole. They would not be able to stop him in time—

"What are you doing? You think to bargain with us?" hissed Shezzek. He stood still, on the other side of the gaping hole, and waved to the approaching soldier to stop his advance on Damion. "No! Do not throw the Stone down there. I will spare your life, and the old woman's too, if you give it to me now."

Damion looked back at him. "No bargains," he said. "I wouldn't bargain with you even if I trusted you to keep your word. There's no hope for my friends or me now and I know it. But I also know that my friends would all agree to die before they would let you have this." He held the crystal out over the hole. Surely it would not survive the plunge to the marble floor forty paces below. His hand trembled; he hesitated. If it was *not* destroyed, and the enemy went into the temple and seized it . . . then all this had been for nothing.

At least Lorelyn escaped, he thought. It was one small crumb of comfort at the end.

The soldiers climbing the slope of the dome shouted; over their voices rose a piercing high-pitched screech. The sound grew louder, nearer: something whirred over the top of the dome, the cold wind of its passage nearly blowing the men off balance. Damion's head jerked up. The creature that glided down to land ten paces away was not a dragon. It was the right size, but its shape was all wrong: the great outstretched wings were not leathery, but plumed like a bird's, the primary feathers standing sharp as swords against the sky, the sunlight fanning through them in long rays. Yet the creature's body was not plumed but furred, the four massive legs ending in broad lion-like pads. He saw the head turn sideways, showing a silhouetted profile of hooked beak and feathery crest and sharp pointed ears.

Shezzek and the soldier behind him screamed and leaped back. The other man lost his footing and went rolling back down the slope of the dome, wailing as he went. Shezzek turned to flee, only to see more of the winged beasts that Damion had taken for dragons flying straight toward him. He leaped backwards, then before Damion could shout a warning he teetered on the rim of the gaping hole, flung up his arms, and fell in. His terrified wail echoed through the vast space below and then ended in a sickening thud as he struck the stone floor. The remaining Zimbourans gained the top of the dome, their swords flashing in the sun as they drew them; but the other flying beasts swooped down upon them, and with wings, tails, and talons sent them fleeing or tumbling away. One beast alighted on the tower where the archers stood: they panicked and tried to flee, colliding with one another, and then plummeted howling to the ground. The winged creatures exchanged high, wild, wordless cries as they swooped and soared like avenging angels about the temple's dome and spires.

Damion became aware of something shining brightly, down by his feet: an object bright as fire. The Stone! He had dropped it when he retreated from the first beast, and it had fallen not into the hole but onto the stone surface of the dome. As he stared at it dazedly, it seemed to him that the gem was not merely reflecting the light of the sun now, but glowing with its own internal radiance.

A flying monster landed on the dome not five paces away, furling its giant wings. It turned its head sideways and the great iris of its eye, golden and spoked like a prayer-mandala, gazed full at Damion.

The priest, his mind clouded with pain and loss of

blood, was still trying to think where he had seen something like it before when the whole world faded from his sight, and he felt himself slip away into darkness.

WHEN AILIA CAME BACK to herself again she realized that she lay on something soft and warm. A soothing heave-and-sigh like the breathing of the sea was in her ears, and the warm surface rose and fell with it.

Blinking, she sat up. She and the dragon were in a cave: she was sprawled against the side of the dragon's neck, the soft fur of the mane beneath her, the great body curved around her in a circle. The enormous animal, she saw now, was fast asleep, its sides gently heaving. Steam rose from its nostrils: the air around them was cold and thin, like mountain air.

Ailia turned her attention from the dragon to the cave mouth close at hand and the view beyond. They were high on the side of a hill or mountain: far below lay a vast plain, gray and very flat. Hill and plain were barren and utterly devoid of life, animal or vegetable: there was not so much as a lizard or a lichen in all that austere landscape. It was very still too: no insect hum, no murmur of a stream invaded the silence. There was something else about the scene that struck her as peculiar, though her still-dazed brain was slow to grasp it. It was night, the sky was dark—quite the darkest sky that she had ever seen, almost black—and the stars were all out, shining as she had never seen them shine before. The Morning Star showed as a distinct disc, its pale bluish-white light deepened to the hue of sapphire. The hills and the plain beneath were bathed in a harsh, white light, stronger than moonlight, and the shadow of every rock and stone stained the gray-white ground black as ink. She went to the cave mouth, looked out, and was almost blinded by the blazing sphere of the sun.

The sun—in a night sky? Sun and stars shining together? Ailia could make nothing of it. She felt curiously light-headed—no, more than that; her whole *body* felt light, as though it weighed half as much as usual. When she tried to walk she found herself skipping, her body lifting into the air with each step, though it took no effort at all.

Wherever am I?

An anxious perusal of the landscape revealed nothing, only presented more mysteries. The hills were arranged in a long, curving arc. A few paces away a small crater with a raised rim steamed like a cauldron on a fire.

A soft sound from behind made her turn around, to see the dragon now awake and gazing at her. She felt no fear of it, only a sense of wonder at being so close to so large a living creature. The wings were neatly folded, furled back to the bone like sails upon the yards of a ship. In the sun's light the dragon's scales gleamed like gold coins, while the pale ventral plates below showed the soft iridescence of nacre. The dragon's head glittered as it moved, like some huge golden ornament studded with jewels: jewels that were its eyes, and the white opalescent lump above and between them that shimmered with half-hidden fires. The face was long and wise, and whiskered like a carp's. The mane that framed it was all bronze and tawny-gold and auburn, chrysanthemum-colored; but the tuft of beard on the chin was pure white.

The dragon turned its emerald eyes toward the steaming

crater, then back toward her. It seemed to be urging her to do something.

She walked, or skipped, out of the cave, and then stopped short, arrested by yet another wonder. In the sky above her hung a colossal, impossible moon, more than twice as large as normal and far brighter. It was half-lit, and its illuminated hemisphere was not whitish-gray but a beautiful sea-blue in color, with streaks and whorls of dazzling white.

She went to the edge of the round, steaming pit, and found it was full of water. Hesitantly, she dipped her finger in: it was not hot, but pleasantly warm. Rolling up her sleeves, she sank her arms in to the elbows, splashed some of the water on her face. At once a tingling sensation spread through her whole body. It was not like the Pool of Purification, that brought peace and tranquillity: this hot spring awakened in her a sudden vigor and renewal of energy, a healing of the body rather than the mind. The aching tiredness left her muscles, the assorted scrapes and bruises she had suffered during the course of her travels ceased to hurt. She felt rejuvenated, full of strength and life. *I'm not dead, then—I certainly don't feel like a spirit! But where am I? What is this place?*

She looked up at the huge blue hemisphere again, noticed for the first time that there were large jagged patches of color on it, beneath the white markings: patches of green and brown and rust-red. They seemed somehow familiar . . .

Ailia caught her breath.

For a long time she stared at those sprawling shapes, unable to believe her eyes. For she knew them, had studied them years ago on her father's old maps and navigational charts. The borders were not there, nor the pastel colors that identified them, but these jagged outlines were as familiar to her as the features of her own face. There, unmistakably, was the coastline of Maurainia, the long green strip of the East Coast . . . There was Great Island, half obscured by a swirl of cloud, and parts of the Northern and Southern Archipelagoes lying scattered across the blue of the ocean . . . The Antipodes were hidden from her view on the far side of the globe, lost in the vast shadow that was night. Her eyes moved to the north pole, traversing in the merest fraction of a second the thousands of leagues that the galleons had taken weeks to cross: and there was Trynisia, a lone green land surrounded by white ice . . .

The world. She was looking on the world itself, from some unimaginable height.

Then I really am in Heaven. It wasn't at all the way she imagined the Afterlife—this dreary, empty wasteland. Where were all the other spirits of the departed—the angels—the Celestial City?

The dragon emerged from the cave and stood gazing at her. There was a jewel-glint of benevolent intelligence in the green depths of his eyes. "Oh please—am I dead, then? Can't I go back home?" she entreated, moving toward him.

His pointed ears pricked forward, like those of a dog or horse when it is given a command. Then the dragon stretched out his long neck upon the ground, inviting her to mount again. She did so, clutching at the chrysanthemum mane as the dragon rose and walked carefully to the edge of the hilltop. She felt again the tensing of his enormous muscles; then the great forward spring as the wings lifted behind her.

And they were airborne again, soaring over the dreary desert. She could see the dragon's wide-winged shadow gliding along the gray plain beneath them. Nothing else moved, not even a wind stirred to blow the dry dust.

And yet there had once been life in this desolate place. As they flew over the gray wastes she saw, far away beyond the high hills, shallow depressions and meandering gullies that must have been the beds of lakes and rivers. The plain or basin below was completely surrounded by the hills—in fact, the chain was almost perfectly circular, she saw with surprise as they gained altitude. In the center a hill of gray rock rose abruptly from the flatness of the plain. Tall, steepling shapes surmounted it, at which Ailia stared in puzzlement: they were not like any natural formation.

Then as they passed over the hill she caught her breath. Those pinnacles of rocks were not natural at all: they were the towers of a palace such as she had never seen before in her life. It was not like a Maurish or Elei structure; it seemed a palace built for gods or giants rather than mere men. Very tall and narrow in shape, with high steep walls, its towers were slender as spears, thin and attenuated: their long stark shadows lay broken upon the rugged rock beneath, where a causeway led to the distant hills. And on one hillside she thought she glimpsed a gateway very like the one on Elendor: two tall white pillars rising from the ground.

The bowl-shaped plain had been a lake once, the central hill an island. Her gaze swept back in wonder to the palace: the whole structure looked strangely top-heavy to her. Shouldn't those impossible, needling towers have fallen long ago, dragged down by their own weight? The walls beneath, she saw, were breached in places, as though by some invading force; and beyond these jagged wounds, and through the peaked windows and the high gaping gates, lay a darkness dismal and profound. A sense of ancient disaster, of some incomprehensible catastrophe, haunted her as she and her strange steed flew over the courtyard that was half plunged in the shadow of the high walls.

Perhaps it was only a trick of the eye, or a wraith of dust raised by a random eddy of air; but for an instant Ailia thought she saw a figure go striding across the court beneath—a figure far too tall to be human, all swathed about in gray-white robes that trailed behind it like cerements. She blinked—there was nothing there but the bare pavement of the courtyard. And then the strange palace with all its grandeur and mystery dropped behind, and faded into the desolation of the landscape.

The deserts now lay spread beneath her, and she could see the odd circular basin in its ring of hills, and hundreds of other ring-shaped ranges like it, some gigantic and others quite small, some overlapping at the edges like rain-rings in the surface of a pool. They reminded her of the craters she had seen in Trynisia, gouged into the ground by the fallen stars. But there were many more of them, and they were much larger. The whole of the gray waste was pocked and pitted with them as far as the eye could see.

But only when the horizon bowed into a curve, and the pale shining place beneath her took on the form of a vast half-sphere, did she realize where she had been. And the knowledge made her grow faint even as the air opened up before them again in a chasm of light.

SOMETIME LATER SHE AWOKE again to find herself lying on soft cushions. Sunlight beat upon her face; the air was warm, and smelled of flowers. Somewhere birds sang.

Ailia opened her eyes and sat up. She lay on a cushioned divan, in a little gazebo or summerhouse built of what looked like marble. Where was she? Had she fallen asleep? She sat very still for a moment, trying to sort out her memories and make sense of them. She recalled the dragon, and—with a slight shiver—the dreamlike strangeness of the lunar landscape. The scene she now looked on was as far removed from it as possible.

Where the moon-country had been bleak and barren, this land was lush and verdant, full of life. All about her were tall, graceful trees, heavy with blossom: the scents blowing from these were sweet, penetrating, seductive in their intensity. The grass underneath them was clipped short, like a lawn of green velvet. The sun was close to setting, in a flood of soft, apricot-colored light behind a distant range of mountains. It looked enormous, perhaps because it was so low in the sky. The vault above was a mass of clouds, dyed pinkish-gold on their undersides by the sunset, and above them she glimpsed a pale band, like a cloud only more solid-looking, and more remote than the loftiest cirrus-strands: it was arch-shaped, following the curve of the sky's dome. She puzzled over this for a few moments before turning her attention back to the mountains. They were tall, towering shapes with sharp-pointed summits, higher even than the Numiendori.

She was no longer on the moon, at least, but neither

was she back in Trynisia. *I'm in a sort of park,* she thought at length. The grounds were well kept, the trees and shrubs had a healthy and well-groomed appearance. Could this really be Heaven at last? Had she traveled bodily to those celestial realms that Welessan was able to visit only in visions? *The moon—the moon was the First Heaven. The one above it was the sphere of Arainia, the one with a paradise in it. Is that where I am—in the Second Heaven?*

There was no sign of the dragon anywhere: she was completely alone. She rose and began to walk through the neat, ordered groves, looking about her in wonderment. It was difficult to feel alarmed in a place so beautiful, so manifestly made for pleasure. She kept stopping to smell the flowers, to caress their moist petals and hold them to her face. One leafy hedge was covered in white rose-shaped blooms with a citrus smell so sharply sweet that it made her mouth water. A more delicate aroma came from a grove of trees beyond it, laden with oranges and pale blossom. It might be spring in the northern lands of her world, but here in this unknown realm summer was in full flower.

The flight of a bright-breasted bird overhead caught her eye. Glancing up, she saw through a gap in the foliage above a smooth-sided hill, and standing atop that hill a palace: no sad and empty ruin this time. Its white walls and towers were whole and undamaged, softly radiant in the sunset. They were to the eye what a trumpet fanfare is to the ear: they took her breath away. Here was a palace out of the faerie tales, out of her daydreams, and she knew in the instant she saw it that she must go there: somehow she felt certain that the answers to all her questions lay within its walls. She need not reason it out; already, before the thought completed itself, her feet were pointed in that direction, drawn irresistibly toward the palace of her dreams.

The gardens seemed to become even more luxurious as she walked: there were bowers, shady benches, the occasional small pavilion or round pillared temple. There were boxwood hedges, and topiary clipped in fabulous shapes: globes, pyramids, birds, beasts. There were rose arbors, and huge stone urns. There were avenues of stately cypress, and one lane of very tall and slender trees with bark like the husks of pineapples and high crowns of plumose leaves. Wasn't there a name for these trees like enormous feather dusters standing on end? *Palm trees,* that was it. She had seen pictures of them in travel books, but never laid eyes on a real one, nor imagined that she ever would: they added to the unreality of it all.

There was not a human being in sight. Once she was startled to see a female figure standing in the bushes only a few paces away, staring out at her, but in the next moment she saw that it was only a marble statue—a graceful young girl in a loose-flowing gown with a pitcher in the crook of one arm. Other statues too, were dispersed about the grounds: men and maidens, gods and goddesses, lions, hounds, deer, stallions—a veritable menagerie of marble and verdigrised bronze. Groups of statuary stood in pools, which must be fountains: chariots drawn by swans or prancing horses, groups of cavorting nymphs. But the fountains were still, the water beneath them mirror-smooth. They must be a splendid sight, she thought wistfully, when the water ran through them.

Presently she came upon a path that wound in careless meanders through the gardens until it led her to a lake—a small artificial lake, completely covered in the pads and blooms of water lilies, white and gold and wine-colored. Beneath them, through green gaps of water, swam golden carp with wise whiskered faces. A slow-moving stream fed the lake. Beyond lay another lake, larger and without any lilies: here swans idled regally with arched necks, seeming to admire their own elegant white reflections. Peacocks strutted on the lawns, blue-breasted ones with green tails and white ones with tails like lace fans.

And then she became aware of a distant sound—a low, constant, rushing roar, as of cataracts pouring over rocks—and turning toward it she glimpsed a dance of whitewater through the trees. She ran forward eagerly.

Here, at last, was a functioning fountain: a huge and splendid one, all mermaids and dolphins and hippocampi, with plashing plumes of water playing around them. The flying spray dewed her cheeks as she walked forward, while the roar of the water, now that she was close to it, at once overwhelmed and exhilarated her. It was, above all, a comforting sign of habitation. *Someone* had set this fountain in motion; the place could not, after all, be altogether deserted.

Ahead of her and slightly to the left rose the green hill, a narrow road winding up its side. Above it the palace's towers seemed to float in the waning afterglow, weightless as the clouds above them: brightly-colored banners flew from them like flames. She forced down a sudden feeling of unease as she set her foot upon the road and began her ascent.

22

East of the Sun, West of the Moon

WHAT AN AMAZING DREAM THAT WAS, Damion thought.

He stretched, yawning. "Jo?" he said, without opening his eyes. "Jo, wake up, you're snoring again . . . Do you know, I had the strangest dream last night—just like one of those stories Ailia tells . . ."

His voice trailed away as his eyes opened. For a minute or so he lay quite still, staring at the ceiling above him. It was white, with decorative moldings of leaves and flowers. He and Jomar lay in neat white beds, in a spacious room with large-paned windows through which the golden light of late evening flowed. Sitting up, he saw that he was clad in a loose white robe, and there was a faint, pale scar on his right arm.

And then he noticed the range of mountains outside the windows.

Where and when had he seen mountains like these before? Taller than they were wide, their pointed summits free of ice and snow, they prodded his memory like goads. He leaped out of bed and ran over to the windows. They were open, a balmy breeze blowing through them. This was not—could not be—Trynisia. He looked out on smooth-mown lawns, shady trees, flowerbeds, and a few benches. The vegetation was all of the lush, feathery variety he had seen in the tropics. Beyond a white-painted wall rose the tops of more trees and the roofs of other buildings.

As he leaned out of the window, he caught sight of another enigma. Low in the reddening sky, shining through a gap in the sunset clouds, was an atmospheric effect of some kind. It was like a rainbow, a vast arc that curved up from the horizon to vanish in the masses of rose-gold cumuli above. But it could not be a rainbow, for it had no color: it was a pale silver-white, with little glints here and there as though it were dusted with diamonds. Nonplussed, he turned his attention back to that evocative range of mountains, the one feature in all this strangeness that seemed familiar. Bracing himself on the window ledge, he leaned farther out.

And then he saw the palace.

It was off to his left, beyond the roofs and trees, perching on its steep-sided hill. There could be no mistaking it: it was the many-towered white palace from his vision.

"Where in blazes are we?" He turned to see Jomar sitting up in bed, tousle-headed and frowning. He wore a robe like Damion's, and a white cloth bandage stretched across his chest. "Where are we?" Jomar repeated.

Damion hesitated. "I think," he said, "we must be in Eldimia."

"What—*how?*" Jomar frowned. "What happened? The last thing I remember was fighting the Zims up on the roof. How did we get here?"

Damion decided not to tell him about the winged creatures. He still wasn't sure himself whether they had truly existed, or merely been a figment of his pain-clouded mind. He hedged, "I'm not certain—I think I lost consciousness shortly after you did."

At that moment the door opened, and a slight, white-clad figure entered and stood smiling at them. It was Ana: but she seemed changed. She was no longer bent with age and weariness, but walked nearly upright, and she no longer used a cane. Her gown was of some soft, fine fabric, and her hair was once more neatly rolled into a bun atop her head.

"Ah! I thought I heard voices!" she said. There was a loud meow and Greymalkin darted through the door. The cat sprang up onto Jomar's bed, purring.

"Where in the Pit are we?" demanded Jomar.

"In a hostel," Ana replied. "You were brought here to be healed."

"I meant what *country* are we in? Is this that other country of yours—Eldimia?"

"It is indeed. We are safe now, Jomar. There is no pain or discomfort now where you were wounded?"

Jomar's hand went to his chest and the cloth bandage there. "Wounded . . . I remember. An arrow hit me . . . But how did we get to Eldimia? And where in the world is it?"

"Eldimia," said Ana slowly, "is not *in* the world at all."

They stared at her, speechless, and she sat down on the edge of Jomar's bed, petting her cat. "Oh dear, it's so hard to explain . . . You see, we have moved beyond the world that you know, and passed into another."

"You mean—we're in Heaven?" asked Damion, almost whispering.

A smile touched Ana's lips. "In a manner of speaking—yes."

"Heaven!" Jomar scowled at her. "What are you saying, that we're all dead? We died back there, in the ruins—that arrow killed me?"

Ana laughed. "Dead? My dear Jomar, how could that be?" She laid her hand on his arm. "You're too solid for a spirit—and entirely too talkative for a corpse. No, Jomar, we did not die. You were gravely wounded and we were all in peril of our lives, but the Guardians of the Stone saved us. They were convinced at last that we were the Tryna Lia's companions, and had a right to the Star Stone. At my asking they conveyed us safely to Eldimia, along with the gem."

The two men stared at her as she went over to the nearest window and stood looking out of it. "This may be difficult for you to understand, but I will try my best to explain. Eldimia lies in the Otherworld: the realm beyond the world's end, between the sun and the moon. The world, as you know, is round, and so you might say it has no edge or end: but it has, for all that. The world's end, its outer boundary and the limit of its influence, lies at the orbit of the moon. In the airless void beyond are the planets: the so-called higher spheres that the Elei journeyed to long ago with the aid of their magic. The planets are not part of some spirit-realm, you see. They belong to our own material universe, and so a mortal may travel to them without suffering death.

"Welessan the Wanderer spoke of these things. Much of his account was wrong, but through no fault of his own. His mind was influenced by the cosmology of his day—the seven heavens and the five elements and so on. He thought the strange lands he glimpsed in his vision must lie within the fabulous crystal spheres he had been taught about as a boy: heavenly realms, the abodes of immortal spirits. But they actually lay within the planets themselves. In the Second Sphere, as he called it, he saw not an immortal paradise but a real land in a real world."

She gestured to the garden, to the roofs and trees lit by the crimson afterglow. "Here dwell the Elei who fled your world in ages past, along with people of many other races. Here in this city of Mirimar, on the island-continent of Eldimia, in the planet of Arainia that you call the Morning Star."

THERE WAS A LONG SILENCE. At last Damion asked in a low voice, "How did we come here?"

"As I told you, the cherubim who are the Stone's appointed Guardians brought us here," Ana said. "They accepted that the Tryna Lia had come at last, and so they were free to surrender the Stone into her keeping. But she was carried off to Eldimia, so in order for her to claim the gem they had to transport it here. Like dragons, they have the power to move between planets by entering the Ethereal Plane. When they saw our plight they would not leave us behind, but bore us with them through the Ether. Since we are the true Tryna Lia's companions, they were allowed to intervene."

The cherubim, Damion thought. *Eagle-winged and lion-bodied: the servants of the Old Ones, the Guardians of the Light.* "I saw them, on the temple roof," he murmured. "I thought it was all a dream . . . But what of the others? *Is* Lorelyn here? And whatever became of Ailia?"

"They are both here in Eldimia. But they are not yet safe," said Ana, suddenly becoming brisk. She left the window and came to stand before them. "The real fight still lies before us. We have the Stone; but Lorelyn is in Mandrake's power. He is holding her in the palace of Halmirion."

"Mandrake!" Jomar's face turned fierce. "I'd forgotten about him. Wait till I get my hands on him—!"

"You cannot fight Mandrake," said Ana with unwonted sharpness. "He is more dangerous then you can possibly realize. King Khalazar and his men are nothing next to him. He might have pretended to be your ally on Elendor, but he is the true enemy, the great prince we are destined to fight." Sadness passed across her face, like the shadow of a cloud, and was gone again. "I must go now. King Tiron—the father of the Tryna Lia—and those Nemerei of this world who are loyal to him intend to challenge Mandrake, and I must be with them. But it will take all the strength we can marshal to defeat him."

"Wait a moment! I want to go too!" protested Jomar.

"So do I," Damion added. "We've recovered from our injuries."

"No, this battle is not for you, my friends," Ana replied. "It cannot be fought with any weapons you possess. I am sorry, but I must ask you to remain here."

With that, she turned and walked out of the room, leaving them to stare after her.

THE PALACE WAS EVEN more imposing when Ailia finally stood in front of it in the gathering twilight.

Had its tremendous gates not been flung wide in open invitation, she would never have dared to enter. She crossed the forecourt, noting the stables that stood to one side. Many splendid carriages were housed there: warm lamplight glanced along gilt and glass and fine wooden trim; from the stalls came the snorting and stamping of horses. But there was still not a human soul to be seen. Before her broad marble steps led to a grand entrance, the doors open wide as the gates had been.

It's just like walking into one of my own stories, Ailia marveled as she went in.

The entrance hall was of white marble, and the ceiling was molded and gilded in circular patterns of floral designs and the shapes of beasts and birds. There was no one in sight, not a single guard or servant. She stood for a moment, deliberating. Two corridors led to the right and left, while straight ahead of her a magnificent staircase, lit by marble figures holding aloft giant candelabra, led up to a landing, then divided in two and rose to a second story. In the wall of the landing a huge window framed a view of towers and trees: a courtyard must lie beyond.

"Hello? Is anyone there?" she called out nervously. Her voice echoed from the walls and faded. *Where could everyone be? I can't believe everyone in such a grand palace would be away. Shouldn't there at least be a maid or two about?* Ailia, as unnerved by her prolonged solitude as by the grandeur of her surroundings, began to hunger for the sight of a human face.

She was not at all loath to go farther into the palace, however. She chose, at random, the left-hand corridor and hurried down it. Her footsteps sounded very loud in the silence, but still no one came to challenge her. Marble figures stared at her out of tall niches with white, vacant eyes. She thought she heard a distant music of stringed instruments, so faint and far off that she half wondered if she imagined it. The corridor led to a set of two gilded doors before turning to the right, and looking down its length she saw a series of steps leading up to another pair of doors. She decided to try the first set. Pushing one door open, she slipped inside and looked about her.

She was in a chapel, but a chapel many times larger than the Royal Academy's. Its walls were white marble warmed by the light of many lamps, the ceiling was painted with clouds in a blue sky, and in the sanctuary there stood, not a portal with carved battlements or an image of the robed and bearded God Aan, but the statue of a blue-gowned woman on a rounded plinth. Her face was serene, its white stone features eternally young and untroubled, her gilded hair rippling to her feet. In her marble arms were garlands of real flowers; at the skirts of her gown images of children and fawning beasts; on her head gleamed a crown of stars. Elarainia, the Morning Star Goddess.

Where was this place? Could she be having a vision of the distant past, like Damion's? But he had said he could not touch anything in his dream, while everything here felt real. She reached out, laid a hand on the nearest pew: its wood was hard and solid beneath her palm.

The chapel too was empty, neither priests nor worshippers to be seen. It contained only the hallowed hush found in sacred places, that seems to deepen when the occupant is alone. But the flowers in the statue's arms were fresh, the lamps lit against the coming of night. Someone had been here, and recently.

She decided to go on up the hall and try the second set of doors. These too were open. A huge banquet hall stretched before her, with long rows of dark wooden tables and a dais at the far end. On it stood a high table with several chairs, including one tall majestic one that had the air of a throne. The hall was hung with banners and tapestries, its high windows were of tinted glass, and at this end was a minstrel's gallery. On the tables were more cut flowers in vases, as well as bowls of every kind of fresh fruit, pineapples and pomegranates and jade-green grapes, and others that she did not recognize. There were spun-sugar follies shaped like castles and swans and sailing ships; and trays of rainbow-hued sweetmeats; and tall pitchers of jewel-colored cordials. As she gazed at them Ailia's stomach cramped with hunger. It seemed a very long time since her last meal of soggy ship's biscuit, but she dared not steal from any of the dishes. *It's exactly like a faerie tale. If I touch the food those great doors will be flung open behind me, and an ogre will come in—or a loathly Beast, or a Black Knight . . .* She glanced back at the doors, half expecting to see some such faerie visitant appear even without provocation. But there was no one there.

And then the music started again.

It was louder this time, and nearer. In the wall behind the dais, she noticed, was a half-open door, and through this the music drifted. Ailia advanced slowly toward the dais. This was one of those grand places that even when empty have a presence about them, so that one feels one must show respect. She hesitated before mounting the steps of the dais. But the music drew her on, with its yearning beauty and its promise of human company. If indeed those musicians were human. Peering around the door, she saw a stone staircase spiraling up. The music cascaded down it like a waterfall.

There must be another large room above this one,

where some kind of revel was taking place. She hurried up the stairs. And oh, there were human voices now, she could hear them: the distant murmur of conversation! Ailia suppressed a near-hysterical cry of relief and longing as she raced up the stone flights. To see people again, any people—! The spiral stair was enclosed within a column of carved stone; at the landing a door opened out of the column, and small glass panels were set in it like windows. She stepped out of the doorway and found herself in a hall. At this end it vanished around a corner, while at the other it ended in a wall with a window. But halfway down another doorway opened on a large hall or chamber: and it was filled with people.

Ailia was suddenly smitten with shyness. It was such a very grand place, at least as large as the banquet hall below. She peered around the doorframe. The hall was opulent beyond belief, white with ornamentations of gold leaf. But just as impressive were the people currently occupying the chamber, standing about in whispering groups. They were arrayed in the finest fabrics: silk and brocade glistened wherever she looked. Arms and necks were adorned with precious gems, each glinting with its core of captive fire, so that all the hall seemed to dance and flicker with faerie lights of every imaginable hue. Yet the people themselves were the most magnificent of all: their features reminded her of the Elei statues in Liamar. *Elei!* she thought. *They must be! There really are Elei left in the world . . .*

There were other, more ordinary-looking people there too, clad in simpler clothing and standing near the back of the hall. *So that's where all the servants are—they've come to see whatever is happening here! It must be terribly important.* Much as Ailia longed for company, she did not dare burst in on this grand gathering. These people, resplendent in their refinery, must be nobles and dignitaries, assembled for some momentous occasion. She noticed that they often glanced toward the doorway, evidently waiting for someone to pass through. She shuddered to think of the sensation she would create should she appear there, an uncouth intruder in her torn and travel-stained attire. She shrank back, very glad that they apparently had not seen her gawking around the doorframe.

And now a cry rang out from the end of the corridor: "She comes, the Lady of light comes! The daughter of Heaven, the Tryna Lia!"

The Tryna Lia?

Ailia bolted back into the stairwell, looking out through the little window-slits as the curious procession appeared around the corner. First came a group of women, robed in white with veils before their faces, carrying silver candelabra. Surely these were sibyls, like the ones of elder days. That ancient order, too, still existed in this place.

Four of them held aloft a blue starred canopy. A figure walked beneath it, surrounded by a floor-length veil so that at first only a dim outline could be seen, obscured as if by a pillar of misty light: a feminine form, tall and slender, clad in flowing white. On her brow a diadem flashed and gleamed, while about her a mantle of gold hung—no, that was the woman's hair, long blonde hair hanging to her knees. Then as the veiled figure drew near Ailia was able to see her face. She gasped, and sprang out into the hallway.

"Lorelyn? Lorelyn!"

"Ailia!" The veil was flung back and Lorelyn stood there, gowned in pearl-white, her unbraided hair falling free. She was so magnificent that for a moment Ailia could only gape at her, open-mouthed. The procession halted in confusion. The retainers, a group of grand-looking men and fine ladies, exchanged puzzled glances and murmured to one another.

"Lorelyn—is it really you?" Ailia cried. "Are you the Princess?"

"So they tell me," the other girl replied, waving her hand at the group of retainers. "It looks as though Ana was right."

"Then—this is *your* palace! But where are we, Lorelyn? What is this place?"

"We're in the land of Eldimia. Ana was right about that too."

Eldimia! So it was a real place, after all—as real as Trynisia. How much time had elapsed between her flight from Mount Elendor and her arrival here? Ailia felt dizzy with wonderment.

"But however did you get here?" Lorelyn burst out, seizing Ailia's hands. "Mandrake brought me here on a flying dragon—it came at his command, and let us ride on its back! We flew here through something called the Ethereal Plane—a strange sort of place, all filled with light. Mandrake explained it, but I couldn't quite understand it. You'll have to ask him. He is a great sorcerer, Ailia—and he's on our side after all. I'm sorry I was so suspicious of him. He's going to help me here, help me learn to rule."

"I was brought here by one of his dragons too," Ailia

told her. "I suppose he must have trained it to fly here. I can't recall much of the journey, though." She did not mention the dreamlike sojourn on the moon: she was no longer certain that it had really happened.

"We're in another world now, an altogether different one," Lorelyn told her. "I couldn't understand that part, either! But here we are, and here we must stay, I suppose: unless you can get Mandrake to send you back home."

"Another world—?" Ailia echoed. She saw now that Mandrake was in the group of retainers, clad in a dark blue doublet and hose and a flowing black mantle lined with red silk. The warlock and the Island girl stared at each other: for the very first time, Mandrake looked taken completely back.

"What is this?" he demanded, turning to one of the men beside him. "I gave strict orders that no one be admitted through the main gates aside from the chosen emissaries."

"No one of this description came in by the outer gates, my lord," the man answered. "I cannot say how she came to be here, unless she was already in the grounds before they were sealed."

"But you're all alone!" Lorelyn said to Ailia, ignoring Mandrake. "What became of Damion and Jomar, and old Ana? And the cat?"

Mandrake strode forward and, pulling the veil back down over the face of the protesting Princess, pushed her back under the regal canopy. "Carry on," he directed her retinue curtly. "The people are waiting." And they obeyed him, as if in a daze: the unseemly interruption of their solemn procession had disconcerted them. Mandrake remained behind, facing Ailia.

One look at his narrowed eyes was enough. Ailia's protests died in her throat and she whirled, fleeing back down the staircase.

DAMION AND JOMAR WALKED in silence along the streets of the city. They were clad now in fresh new clothes, tunics and trousers of soft fabrics provided by their hostess, the owner of the hostel. She and her assistants spoke few words to their guests, but looked at them with open curiosity and something like awe. Damion had been hard put not to stare back. For the woman was an Elei: very tall, fine-featured, with luxuriant russet hair that hung loose down her back. She was a healer by trade, it seemed, and she had left the house with Ana and several other people, most of them Elei, though one of the company was a diminutive Kaanish man with a long white beard and another was a tall, dark-haired man whom Damion recognized from his vision of the palace and the infant Princess. King Tiron, Ana called him.

"He is not like your hereditary kings," she told them. "He was crowned as the consort of the Tryna Lia's mother, Queen Elarainia, and his title is honorary as was hers. He holds no real power. But he is much loved by the people here." The man had not changed a great deal from the time of Damion's vision, save for some silver hairs at his temples that might well have been put there by sorrow and stress rather than age.

Damion and Jomar had waited until Ana and her companions left, then they too departed the hostel. There was no need for either of them to speak: each read his own thought in the other's eyes. They were going to go to the palace despite Ana's warning, to offer what help they could. Each of them put on his sword-belt, and these drew many a curious glance from pedestrians they passed in the streets. They themselves stared in wonder at the scenes surrounding them. Mirimar appeared to be at least twice the size of Raimar in Maurainia, but it was more orderly and serene. There were no beggars, no refuse in the gutters, no dank dark alleys anywhere to be seen. There were fountains, verdant parks, tree-lined avenues, elegant houses and mansions. There was a predominance of marble, most of it white. Pillared courts gave onto gardens, which breathed forth a paradise scent of blossoming trees and flowers. A giant, white-domed structure larger than Raimar's High Temple dominated the city. Damion looked up at towers that exulted skyward, in seeming defiance of the binding earth. No mortal hand could have raised this city up: surely it must have grown as a forest grows, in groves of living stone and glass and crystal that burst of themselves into a bloom of steeples, cupolas, minarets. He and Jomar passed under a tall triumphal arch covered in alabaster, inlaid with patterns formed by many-colored gems. Sapphire, emerald, lapis lazuli, jacinth, chalcedony: Damion heard the words echo through his head. These were the stones that adorned the Heavenly City in scripture. Had those descriptions been based on this place?

Looking at the faces in the crowds, Damion was struck anew by the beauty of the Elei, who appeared to make up about half of the citizenry here. All of the people were clad in the clothing of a bygone age: the men arrayed in doublets and hose, the women in long flowing cottes. It was as though he had reentered his vision of Trynisia's past; but now the Elei could see him, he could meet their eyes and exchange pleasantries as they walked past. Intriguing scenes surrounded him on all sides. In one park people gathered to listen to a bearded old man—a poet, a prophet, a philosopher?—holding forth in Elensi. In another a group of children played with a strange shaggy beast, like a cross between a dog and an ape, while others danced to the music of a strolling minstrel. The general atmosphere was that of a festival: bright banners and buntings were strung over the streets, and the air rang with voices and laughter.

"Why do you look so solemn?" asked a woman in the crowd, dancing up to them with her arms full of flower-garlands. "Have you not heard? The Tryna Lia has returned to us from the heavens, to dwell at Halmirion again!"

"Can we get in to see Lor—the Tryna Lia, I mean?" asked Damion.

The woman shook her head. "Only emissaries and those of high office may enter—and King Tiron, of course. I hear that he passed through the streets just recently, on his way to Halmirion. The Princess, they say, has many evil enemies who would do her harm if they were allowed near her, and so her guardians must be careful. But have no fear: she is in safe hands. For she has with her a sorcerer, so it is said, a master of the Ether: the magic he wields is beyond compare, and he can travel wherever he wishes, even to realms outside the world. He brought her here, from her exile in the Blue Star." She placed a garland around his neck and passed on.

The Blue Star . . . Damion looked up into the night. A point of sea-blue light hung in an opening between the silver-limned clouds, bigger and brighter than any other star: the Evening Star, he would have called it back home in Maurainia. But that star was not the planet Arainia: Arainia was all about him, it was the city and the mountains and the ground on which he walked. Which meant that the Blue Star . . .

Damion stared up at the great blue light shining above the streets and shivered. He had managed to make himself believe what Ana told them—that this city and the countryside in which they now walked belonged to another world, that a mortal man might pass beyond the bounds of his native earth and set foot on another planetary sphere. That the people who walked and talked and held their revels all around him were the descendants of those who, by arts unknown, had traversed the void between the worlds to settle in Arainia. This much he could grasp, but the other . . . To believe that blue star was his world—that Trynisia and Maurainia and Zimboura, all their cities and forests and deserts and plains, the oceans and the Archipelagoes, the monastery where he was raised—that all he had once called "the world" was somehow compacted within that minute and distant point of light—

"You're not listening to me," Jomar accused.

Damion gave him a blank look. "What?"

"What's the matter with you?" snapped Jomar. "You're behaving like someone with a bad case of sunstroke. You don't actually believe all that rubbish about planetary spheres, do you? This may be a different country, but we're still in our own world."

Damion said nothing. This was not, could not be their own world. For one thing, there was that curious light feeling he had, as though he weighed a little less than before, and which made everything from walking to climbing a set of steps far less difficult than usual. There was the fine rare air—like mountain air, except that they were at sea level. There was the sky: when they had arrived at Mount Elendor the moon was in its first quarter, but this one was round and full, and a curious color—a shade of pale blue. And the stars—never before had he seen them shine so brightly, nor with such clear and vivid hues. Anatarva glowed a warm yellow, the stars in the Unicorn were white and blue, the red star Utara in Modrian-Valdur burned like a brand. And these were the constellations of late summer, not of spring. There were many other stars, faint and small among the larger lights, stars that he had never seen before. The strange white sky-bow was still there as well: with the clouds beginning to pull apart he could now see that it made a perfect arch across the sky from the eastern to the western horizon. Its glittering span appeared solid, with distinct hard edges that did not waver or fade.

And there were the Elei themselves, long vanished from the world he knew . . . But there was no time to argue the point with Jomar. The man was more tense and irritable than ever before: perhaps the thought of being in an alien world frightened him, and he denied it so that he could focus on the conflict awaiting them. Fighting was something that he understood, indeed it was what he knew best.

The two men could see now that the hill on which the palace stood lay just outside the city limits, in a large wooded enclosure like a private park surrounded by a white wall. At its golden gates stood men in blue-and-silver livery.

"We'll never get in there," Damion said, stopping short at the sight.

Jomar's teeth flashed in his old snarling grin. "You think not? That wall isn't very high, and there are no spikes or anything at the top! No sentries anywhere except at the gate, either. These people know nothing about securing grounds. Come on, let's see how it looks on the far side. We could climb up and over easily enough: if we can get a barrel or something to stand on, and I get on your shoulders, I can pull you up after me."

"What might be inside, though?" Damion asked. "Patrolling guards? Dogs?" *Dragons? Three-headed monsters?* he added in his thoughts. Who could say what lurked beyond that harmless-looking white wall? Perhaps it had no iron spikes or sentries because they were not needed . . .

Jomar shrugged, his eyes still fiercely bright. Now that he had a plan of action, nothing was going to dissuade him. "We have our swords."

He strode forward, and Damion followed him. Together they walked on toward the walled enclosure, and whatever awaited them within.

23

Darkness and Light

AILIA AWAKENED TO A PAINFUL throbbing in her left temple. There was a lingering unpleasantness at the back of her mind, too—like that left by an uneasy dream.

And then she remembered.

Mandrake!

She shivered to recall the look on his face when he had come toward her down the corridor—that look of surprise and fury in his catlike eyes. She had stumbled as she fled him, falling down the staircase and striking her head on a step: she remembered nothing after that. He must have carried her away while she was unconscious. Opening her eyes, she looked fearfully around her, blinking as her surroundings became clear.

But she recognized this room . . . This red-curtained bed on which she lay, the stone walls, the tapestries. *It's that strange room in the castle cellars,* she realized. *The dungeon room, where Mandrake kept Lorelyn and me. However can I have got back here?*

She sat up, massaging her aching temple, and saw that she wore a nightgown of some rough gray material. As she sat there fingering its unfamiliar fabric the door opened, and Damion came in. He was clad in ragged clothing and his face was unshaven and weary. There was something strange about him, something odd about the way his blue eyes met hers.

She jumped up, then staggered as pain wracked her head again. "Damion! How did we get here—to Maurainia? Did that dragon bring me here? How did you—"

Damion stood with his arms folded across his chest, staring at her with those cool, distant eyes. "So you've come back to us," he said briskly. "We didn't know what to do with you."

"*Do* with me? I don't understand." Why was he looking at her like that, as though he barely knew her? She felt confused and disoriented. "Damion? Please, tell me what's happened. How did we come here?"

He sat down in a tapestried chair. "Ailia—what is the last thing that you remember?"

"Remember?" She cast her thoughts back. "The palace—I was in a beautiful palace, in a strange country. Eldimia. And Lorelyn was there too. She is the Tryna Lia, Damion—she really is!" She paused and frowned. "And Mandrake was there."

"Anything else?" The blue eyes bored into her.

"A . . . a dragon. That's how I got there. It saved me. We flew up into the sky, up to the moon—" She broke off as his eyebrows lifted. "Damion, it's *true.* After you and Jomar went into the cave—"

"I and *Jomar?*" He repeated her words with a look of puzzlement. "What cave? Ailia, you don't know what has happened, do you?"

"Happened?"

He rose and paced to and fro. "You and Lorelyn were held here some weeks ago, by a man called Mandrake—"

"Yes—the sorcerer."

Damion shook his head impatiently. "Not a sorcerer—just an ordinary man. He was trying to keep Lorelyn away from us—"

"Us?"

"Us witches." He stopped and looked at her directly. "All right, I'll begin from the beginning. There's a coven of us who meet down in the catacombs. Ana is our leader, and Lorelyn is the one we've chosen to be the next leader of the coven—our high priestess, if you will. That's why I brought her out of the Archipelagoes in the first place. The silly girl keeps resisting the idea, but we'll have our way with her yet."

Ailia stared at him. "This isn't true," she said in a low voice. "It didn't happen this way."

"Mandrake found out about us, and betrayed us to the Patriarch, who turned up with a rabble from the villages to drive us out. Some of our members have been getting a little careless—burning barns and so forth. They found me and Ana in the ruins, and you and Lorelyn as well. And that turncoat Jomar—he ran back to the Zimbourans, of course, as soon as he saw which way the wind was blowing. But we got away from the guards, and we've been in hiding down here ever since. As soon as everything calms down, we'll take Lorelyn and go into the mountains. With any luck we'll get safely to Marakor."

Ailia leaped up. "No! I don't believe you! This is all wrong!" Panic filled her. "We *didn't* get away from the guards—they took us on board their ship, took us north to Trynisia. It was *then* that we got away from them—and Jomar joined us, and helped us—and we searched for the Star Stone . . ." Her voice trailed away as he continued to stare at her.

"Yes, you've been raving about that for some time. It's that herbal potion we gave you."

Potion? She sank back onto the bed, feeling shaky. There was a pounding sensation in her head.

"We've had to hold you down here for the last three weeks—and a very noisy and uncooperative prisoner you were too. We gave you the potion to try and pacify you, but it only made you delirious. We can't let you go yet. We must get Lorelyn out of the country first. I will go tell Ana you're awake at last." He turned as if to leave.

"Delirious. Then . . . none of it was real." The ocean voyage—the quest for the Stone—her flight on the dragon's back—the beautiful Elei palace. And Damion's friendship. This cold, brusque young man was not the Damion she had known. But that Damion, it seemed, was nothing but a dream.

"No," she moaned. "Oh, no." She looked up at him desperately. "It can't all have been fever dreams! It can't have been—" She broke off, put her hands to her face. Of course it had all been a delusion. Hadn't she suspected it all along? Lorelyn—old Ana—Damion—the Stone, the faerie island. Oh, it was easy to see how her febrile brain had put the whole thing together, weaving together strands from her own experience and the old stories she loved! "But it felt . . . so real," she said in a halting voice. "The voyage, and the journey to the mountain—and then finding the Star Stone! It was just the way I'd always imagined it . . ."

"Exactly. You *did* imagine it. You haven't been anywhere, Ailia Shipwright. You've been down here all this time. The potion has taken away some of your memories and replaced them with delusions. Ana said that might happen. Does your head hurt?" Wordlessly she nodded. "She said there might be a headache, afterwards. It's the herbs, Ailia." He leaned forward. "Can't you recall your real life? Tell me, where are you from?"

The words fell from her lips like lead. "Great Island."

"So you haven't lost that memory. Good. Now where were you born? Who were your parents?"

"Bayport village—on the south coast. My father is Dannor Shipwright, and my mother's name is Nella."

The flame-blue eyes burned through her. "Go on—back to the beginning. What is the first thing you remember?"

"I . . . don't know." The blood drummed in her temples. She could not think.

"Come, everyone has a first memory. Find it, Ailia. Remember who you are."

Her head was swimming, drooping. She cradled it in her hands. "Leave me alone. Why are you asking me this? Leave me alone!"

"I'm trying to help you. You'll just have to trust me—"

"Trust you!" she exclaimed, overcome with pain and bitterness. Was this the real Damion Athariel, then—this cold young man, this liar? If so, it would have been better to stay delirious. "And you call yourself a priest!" she burst out, in anger and despair.

"Not anymore I don't. I became disenchanted with the priesthood. I made no secret of it: everyone knew. And I was only ordained a year ago, after all."

"*Two* years," she flashed back, then stopped.

The room had gone very still all of a sudden. The walls quivered before her eyes, as if from a haze of heat. She began to rise from the bed, still staring at the man who stood before her.

"Your memory's playing tricks again," he said. "Do you think I wouldn't know my own ordination day?"

But she had seen it—the moment's hesitation before his reply. "What was the name of the boy who was your best friend at the orphanage?" she asked.

He said nothing, glaring at her. "What of it?" he snapped at last. His eyes turned to ice.

Now she was certain. "You don't know!" Ailia set her feet on the floor. "Well, I do. Lorelyn told me. His name is Kaithan." She stood, confronting him. "You're not Damion."

"Ailia, don't you think you—"

"*You're not Damion!*" she screamed. This man looked like him, and yet not: that was not Damion's soul that looked out at her from the cold blue eyes.

Then he threw off the disguise, like a man shrugging a cloak from his shoulders: Damion's likeness fell away from him, and it was Mandrake who stood there before her.

"You little fool," he hissed. "You won't let me make this easy for you, will you?"

The walls quivered like curtains in a wind, swaying and melting into air. And then they were gone, and she was in a different room: a lavishly appointed chamber with a high molded ceiling. Outside its tall windows she could see turrets against a dark sky. *I'm in the palace still!* She looked at the man who stood in front of the door—it was an elegant door now, tall and gold-trimmed with decorative carving at the lintel. "Illusion—that was all an illusion of some kind, wasn't it?"

He nodded. "I was trying to help you. I meant to return you to Maurainia, to the ruin at the Academy. You would have awakened there, and fled back outside, and for the rest of your life you'd have believed your journey to be just a hallucination—"

"And you'd have let me believe all those horrible lies about Damion and Ana!"

She backed away from him as he advanced upon her. She saw that she was clad not in the gray nightgown, but in her travel-stained postulant's dress. Hysterical laughter effervesced in her throat. It was real, it had all been real, the adventure of the Stone *had* happened!

"Ailia, listen to me," said Mandrake. The anger was gone from his voice; it was soothing now, and gentle. "I meant you no harm. The illusion was only intended to make your return to Maurainia easier. I am trying to help you, to set you back on the right path—"

"Why are you here, with Lorelyn?" she countered. "Where are the others? Did you do something to them too?"

"It is time for you to go home, Ailia. You don't belong here."

She must not listen. His voice was low, hypnotic, and with every sentence he took another step toward her. He was only two paces away. She must do something—but what? Desperately she thought of the old stories, of the heroes and heroines whose pluck and resourcefulness she had so admired.

She turned away from him and darted over to the nearest window, which overlooked the forecourt. "The dragon!" she cried. "The tame dragon that brought me here—it's flying this way!"

"Do you think I would fall for a trick like that?" he said, his tone contemptuous.

"But he's really there!" She struggled with the window-latch, making the tall pane swing outward. "Here—I'm here!" she screamed into the night. Out of the corner of her eye, she saw Mandrake stride toward one of the other windows facing the court.

At once she bolted for the door.

It was not locked; she had it open in less than a second and raced away down the hall. She heard him calling after her and frantically increased her speed. The hall dead-ended behind her and turned a corner up ahead, but halfway along its length it became an open gallery with railings, and a double stair of marble steps led down under a carved ceiling. Of course—that grand front staircase. Holding up her ragged skirts, she tore down it, certain that Mandrake was behind her, though she dared not even a quick look over her shoulder as she ran. She flew out the entrance and into the paved forecourt.

It was still empty of all but horses and carriages: there would be no help here. But no hindrance either. She ran on, ignoring the muscle-stitch that was spreading again through her side, through the great gates and toward the winding road as if all the demons of the Pit were after her.

Above her the sky was very dark, with clouds scudding over it to hide the stars. A storm was on its way: she heard thunder boom overhead as she ran. She did not know where she was going and in her extremity she did not care. Her one thought was to escape from the sorcerer. Could she hide from him, somewhere in the grounds? There were all those pavilions and gazebos and things . . . She did not see the man beside her until he caught her arm in a grip that was strong enough to stop her, though not to hurt her.

She screamed, struggling with all her might, but could not break his hold.

"It's Ailia all right!" exclaimed a voice in her ear.

She knew that voice—it was Jomar's! The Mohara man was right there beside her. But was he real, or only another illusion?

"Ailia!" exclaimed a second voice, and Damion appeared out of the dark. He came up to her and put his hands on her shoulders. "We heard you shouting. What have they been doing to you in there?" he demanded.

Ailia relaxed. It was no illusion this time, she was sure. This really was the Damion she knew and trusted and loved. How he had come to be here, she neither knew nor cared: it was he. She leaned into his arms and closed her eyes.

"It would appear," said a voice from behind them, "that I have visitors."

They all turned with one movement, to see Mandrake standing in the gateway to the forecourt.

"Not unexpected visitors, at any rate," he continued, walking toward them. "I knew you would come, once Ana revived. I spared your lives and hers in Trynisia, in payment for an old debt. But there is nothing to hold me back this time."

Jomar stepped forward and drew his sword. "If you want a fight, I'll be happy to oblige."

"Don't be foolish," returned Mandrake, his tone icy.

There was a scraping sound as Damion drew his own

sword, a weapon that Ailia had not seen before, with a blade that shone like diamond. He moved to stand at Jomar's side. The sorcerer stood his ground as the two men advanced upon him, regarding them with undisguised disdain.

Ailia called out, "No! Damion—Jomar—stop! He's right, you can't fight him!"

Damion was within two paces of Mandrake when he heard her warning cry. But his eyes were riveted on his enemy's face. In the dim light Mandrake's eyes were a strange sight, the slit pupils enormously dilated so that they all but eclipsed the irises. When had he seen eyes like that before, deep night-black eyes surrounded by thin bands of gold . . . ?

Mandrake reared up to his full height, his arms outstretched, and the long cloak with its lining of blood-red silk lifted on the rising wind like wings. From out of nowhere a mist formed, seething up out of the grass, an unnatural mist that did not bend before the wind but boiled up into a dense white column. Within it the dark towering form of the sorcerer seemed to grow larger before their eyes. And those *were* wings that spread behind him, wings red and shimmering and bony as a bat's . . . And his face had changed: the dark dilated eyes were huge now, horns thrust out from the tossing mane of hair. The hands were tipped with talons, reaching out to seize them.

As if in a nightmare, they saw forming before them in the mist a vast shape—fire-colored, scale-armored, with wings that blotted out the sky, and a horn-crowned head whose eyes blazed down upon them. It was no *glaumerie* cast to confuse them: the creature was there, it was real.

The earth trembled beneath it as it moved. Damion stared at the monster, stunned. It seemed even larger than when he had last encountered it in the mountain cave. Its baleful black-and-gold eyes flared into lambent discs. *Mandrake's eyes.* But there was no time to ponder the terrifying transformation; already the Dragon King was upon them.

Behind him Ailia cried out, and the sound galvanized Damion into action. He held up his sword, remembering the creature's seeming fear of it in the caves. The Dragon King halted in mid-charge. His burning eyes narrowed, focusing upon the sword with malevolent intensity.

Then he reared up, roaring in rage, as Jomar, recovering from his own staggerment at the sorcerer's transformation, attacked from the side. Turning on his assailant, the dragon lashed out with a claw and sent the Mohara man flying.

Damion rushed in as the dragon turned, following Jomar's lead, and got in a blow at the left flank.

But the Dragon King was no mere beast, to be thus outwitted by his foes. Roaring in rage, he leaped into the air, striking from above with teeth and tail and talons. His fury filled the night with noise, and still he barred the way to Halmirion.

There were people streaming down the front steps of the palace and across the forecourt, alerted no doubt by the noise outside. They stopped short when they saw the dragon. Lorelyn was in their midst, and with a cry she elbowed her way through the crowd, gripping her long white skirts in her left hand. In her right she held something that shone in the lamplight with a glassy glitter.

Ailia stood rooted where she was, in terror. She saw

Jomar lying on the ground, and Damion waving his sword wildly at the jaws that snapped at him from above. She forced herself to look at the giant flapping shape above: it was the dragon, but it was Mandrake also. The two were one and always had been. Ana's voice spoke in her memory: *"The celestial dragons could change their shapes at will, becoming anything they wished—bird, beast, or human being."* As she watched in an agony of fear, Damion aimed a slash at a claw that reached down for him. He did not see the tail scything forward at the same time.

"Damion, look out!" Ailia screamed.

The middle part of the tail, thick as her waist, struck Damion in the back and knocked him off his feet. The adamantine sword flew from his grip.

"*No!*" Lorelyn raced over the grass, the Star Stone in hand.

The dragon dropped back to earth and faced her. The atmosphere, already charged with the stress of the storm, became electric as the two confronted each other. Tension coursed between them like lightning.

Lorelyn was very pale, but she placed herself between the monster and the two prone men, still clutching the Stone in her hand. She held it out in a warding gesture, but its crystalline depths did not kindle as before with the starlike radiance. It was only a clear gem, cold and lifeless in her hand. The dragon took a step toward her, its scaly neck thrust out, undaunted.

With a shout Lorelyn flung down the Stone, then, darting to one side, she pounced at Damion's sword of adamant where it lay gleaming on the grass. Seizing the jeweled hilt in both hands, she raised the blade to meet the dragon's charge. It blazed with blue fire, and he roared and spread his wings.

No, Ailia thought. This was wrong: the Tryna Lia was supposed to face the dragon with the Star Stone. She could not win otherwise . . . Lorelyn took a spirited swing at the monster's outstretched muzzle. But he pulled his head back and leaped up into the air again. Her golden hair streamed back in the wind of his wings as he hovered over her.

"Lori, no! The Stone—use the Stone!" Ailia looked wildly about her. The crowds on the steps were still huddled in fear. On the ground Damion stirred, looking dazed, and tried to rise. Jomar too was struggling to regain his feet, shaking his head groggily and looking about him for his sword.

The Star Stone—it was the weapon Lorelyn needed, that she was born to wield. Summoning all her courage Ailia ran toward the discarded jewel. It was beginning to glow again, with a pale light like the moon half veiled behind a cloud. Ailia dropped to her knees and closed her hand around the cool hard crystal. At once the light grew stronger, brighter—blinding. She averted her eyes.

The Dragon King plunged earthwards again, and his great head lashed out quick as a striking snake's. Still Lorelyn stood firm, sword outheld—but his attack was a feint; as she thrust the blazing blade at him he swerved sideways. In her long gown she could not keep her balance: she stumbled as she whirled to face him. Before Ailia could cry, his left foreclaw had struck the girl. The sword dropped to the grass as she fell and rolled over once, twice, then lay still.

"Lori, the Stone!" Ailia shrieked. "Take it, take it!"

But the other girl lay motionless. Ailia began to run toward her, waving the incandescent gem.

"Ailia, no!" yelled Damion in horror as the dragon turned to face her.

Lorelyn still lay unmoving—was she unconscious, dead? Ailia shook her shoulder, then turned to the horror of horns and scales and talons not five paces away. The gem in her hand burned white, banishing the night from around her: the radiance beat through her blood-red fingers and spilled between them in long rays. The radiance blazed into the dragon's eyes, making the great black pupils contract into slits, deep crevices through which malevolence glared out at her. But he was afraid: she could see it. Afraid—not of the Stone, but of the light within it.

With all her might, with all the strength of her desperate fear, she ran at him and thrust the jewel at his scaly face.

The monster roared and recoiled. She advanced a step, her hand held palm outward, letting the Stone-light blast forth, holding it at as a shield between the dragon and Lorelyn. Again he retreated. Damion and Jomar took advantage of his momentary distraction to seize their swords and leap to their feet again, attacking from right and left. Damion's blade found a chink between two of the ventral plates under the flank and bit deep, while Jomar's blade tore at a flailing wing. Blood flowed, darker red against scarlet scales: the dragon bellowed and pulled away, yanking Damion's weapon from his grasp.

With the sword still embedded in his side, the huge creature sprang into the air. But he was unable to fly: his slashed wing crumpled like a storm-rent sail, and he was forced to plane downward, vanishing into the thick vegetation that clothed the hillside. A crashing commotion marked his descent.

"After him!" called out Jomar hoarsely. He plunged down the slope, his sword outheld. Damion hesitated, then followed him. The light of the Stone did not reach this far, and the hillside was a tangle of shadow. They plunged through shrubs and thorny rosebushes, brushing the clinging branches aside as they followed the broad swathe of crushed greenery.

Halfway down the hillside the trail of blood and destruction abruptly ended: here they found Damion's sword, lying with gored blade upon the grass. About the weapon a white mist seethed like smoke, wisping away and dissipating even as they rushed through its pale tendrils. Damion bent to pick up his bloody sword, then stared at Jomar, who gazed mutely back. Beyond this point there were no more gashes from the giant claws, no trace whatsoever remaining of the dragon. He had vanished utterly.

Overhead the storm clouds parted and dwindled, and the stars came out again.

Slowly, wearily, they climbed back up the hill to the palace.

Lorelyn was groaning and sitting up, her hand to her head. Ailia still stood like a statue, motionless and pale, the Star Stone glowing in her hand. A crowd had gathered around her. Ana and King Tiron were there, but they made no move toward her. Damion went to the girl, touched her shoulder: she started, looking up at him.

"Ailia," he said softly, wonderingly. "Ailia, you're one of them—you're a Nemerei."

Ana came forward now with the king. The dark-haired man trembled. "It is she, it is she!"

"Gently, Majesty!" Ana admonished. "Do not frighten her. Ladies and lords," she said, turning to face the silent crowd upon the pavement, "I have the honor of presenting to you Elmiria—daughter of Queen Elarainia."

They were all looking at *her,* Ailia realized, not Lorelyn. "What do you mean?" she asked in sudden panic. The Stone fell from her hand into the grass as she slowly backed away. "I don't know what you mean."

Ana looked solemn. "*You* are the Tryna Lia, Ailia. We have been seeking you for years, ever since your mother fled with you. You have come home at last."

"Come *home?*" Ailia whispered. She looked up at the pointed towers of the palace, lit like lanterns against the evening sky; at the familiar stars blazing down at her, and the sapphire moon winning free of the swathing clouds.

"Home," she murmured again, in wonderment.

24

The Princess of the Stars

"YOU SEE," SAID ANA, "it was of vital importance that the Tryna Lia should not know her own identity. As long as she was kept in ignorance, she was safe from all her foes . . ."

The companions walked together through the palace grounds. In the sky above the strange moon shed its azure glow, while another paler radiance came from the silvery sky-bow. The Elei called this the Arch of Heaven, Ana told them, but it was really a system of rings that encircled the planet. Beneath that luminescent sky all the land was awash in blue and silver. It seemed to the travelers as though they had, indeed, come to the end of their lives and arrived in Heaven, the world of all their fears and sufferings left far behind. Ana walked at the head of the little group, Damion and Lorelyn not far behind. Before them Greymalkin leaped and pranced like a kitten. King Tiron walked at Ailia's side, his arm about her shoulders, as if fearful that she might somehow be spirited away and be lost to him again. Ailia glanced from time to time at the strong bearded face in a dazed way, and thought, *He is my father?* He was very handsome, she thought, dignified in a quiet way, with his dark hair and the deep gray-purple eyes that were so like her own. He did not look quite old enough to be the father of a grown woman. For

Ailia was, it seemed, older than she had thought: this was part of the deception that had been woven about her from her earliest years, the deception that had saved her life. She had always looked young for her age, and she knew now that what was said of the Elei was true: that they lived beyond the normal span of years allotted to the human race, and aged at a slower pace.

And what of that other family, still in the troubled world of Mera, whose encircling love had fostered and protected her? Nella and Dannor, and Jaimon and the others, who even now must be wondering what had become of their daughter, niece, cousin—their Ailia? *Am I even Ailia anymore?*

Her thoughts were interrupted by Jomar. Uncharacteristically quiet and subdued all this time, he suddenly demanded of Ana, "Why didn't you tell us all this before? About Arainia, and the other worlds?"

"Because you would not have believed me. So long has it been since anyone traveled between the worlds that such travels have become the matter of myth. You would have thought me completely mad, and refused to trust in me. Even now I don't think you quite believe that you are really here." She smiled.

A brief silence followed, during which they were aware of the curious hush of expectancy that lay over the land—an expectancy that had in it something more than the mere approach of dawn. Out in the city beyond, and in the palace from which they had just come, thousands awaited their first sight of the Tryna Lia since her infancy. This brief, moonlit idyll was the last moment of tranquillity Ailia and her friends would know for some time.

"This is a great day for the people of Arainia," Tiron—*her father*—said in his deep soft voice. "For two decades they have waited to see the Moon Throne filled. When you were born here at Halmirion, Ailia, people rejoiced that they should have lived to see that day. You are no mere ruler: there have been no true kings or queens in this world for many an age, and its people are governed by a council. Your role is a spiritual one, as was your mother's. The people believe you are sent to save them from a coming danger. And not this world alone, but also the world of Mera from which you and your companions have come, will rejoice when you take your throne. Your role, Ailia, is to free both these worlds from the followers of Valdur: to fight those who would take Arainia, and save Mera from the forces that enslave it."

"You mean the Zimbourans? But I can't do that on my own," Ailia said.

"No: but here in Arainia you can assemble an army for that purpose, and send it across the void to free Mera. These people will flock to your call, for you are the leader they have long awaited. They yearn to be reunited with their sister world of Mera. The champion of the light has come, the enemy of all those who serve the Dark One."

Ailia looked down at the ground. "I still can't understand it," she whispered. "Why *me?*"

Ana smiled at that. "Ailia my dear, people have been asking that question since ever the worlds began. Andarion asked it in his time, and so have all who have ever been called to a life of great deeds and service. I cannot speak for the power that guides the cosmos on its course, but I can pose you another question: why should it *not* be you?"

"When did you first know that I was—*who* I was?" Ailia asked.

"I first had an odd feeling about you when you came to me at the Spring Fair. I was screening the general populace for potential Nemerei, under the guise of a little harmless fortune-telling. When you entered my tent I sensed in you a power at rest, waiting to be wakened—like the spring itself sleeping in the earth. It was not until you ended up in Trynisia that I truly began to suspect who you were, though as yet I had no proof. When a celestial dragon personally conveyed you through the Ether to Arainia, that was another sign. It wanted only the last test—the test of the Star Stone—to prove it beyond doubt. The Stone shone only for you."

"But how did it all happen? If I was born in this world, how ever did I come to live on Great Island?"

"The truth of that tale," Ana replied, "is known only to a retired sailor by the name of Dannor Shipwright and his wife. I think, however, that I know enough now to put the pieces together.

"Eighteen years ago, the Queen Elarainia took her little daughter from Halmirion and fled her world by magic, taking refuge in the neighboring world of Mera. Her father remained behind in Arainia, to watch over the safety of the people there, and to prepare for his daughter's return. Both knew that the servants of Valdur, and Mandrake too, had an interest in capturing their child. They knew she had to be hidden away until she grew old enough to develop her full powers, and protect herself from harm. But no place on her home world was safe. In any case, the Star Stone was in the world of Mera: her weapon, and the one thing that could protect her.

Therefore, Elarainia chose to do what no one in her world had done for centuries: journey to another world by flying ship, sailing her winged vessel through the Plane of the Ether and into the skies of Mera.

"But the ship was caught in a great tempest that raged through sky and sea: perhaps a natural storm, and perhaps not. For all Elarainia's skill, her vessel could not stay aloft, but fell into the sea off the coast of Great Island."

"The shipwreck on the south coast!" Ailia exclaimed.

Ana nodded. "Only fragments of the ship were found, no doubt: not enough to tell the islanders that this was no common sea-vessel but a craft made to sail the sky. And there was but one survivor—an infant, washed ashore perhaps on a piece of wreckage, or rescued from the waves by an Islander. Dannor Shipwright took her in. His wife, it seems, was barren and overjoyed to have a child, and they reasoned that as the child's family must all have perished in the wreck—since no one ever inquired after the little girl—they had a right to keep her." Ana turned to King Tiron. "I am sorry if this pains you," she said gently.

"I have known for some time that my Elarainia would never return to me," King Tiron answered slowly. "Indeed, I believe she foresaw something of the sort when she departed Halmirion. She was in such a strange and sorrowful mood when she bade me farewell . . . And now she lies beneath an alien sea."

"Perhaps not," said Ana looking thoughtful. "She may well have gone into hiding somewhere, having placed her child in safe hands. We can still hope, Tiron."

"I remember her," said Ailia softly. "At the convent I had a dream of a beautiful woman, a queen, with golden hair falling to her feet. But I never thought of it being the same dream as Lorelyn had."

"Many of us Nemerei had that dream, or vision," Ana told her, "but in your case it was born out of a memory, long suppressed."

"She *was* very beautiful," said Tiron, "and a great sibyl and sorceress. I had never seen such beauty, nor such power, in any human being. Well might the people here have taken her for the Goddess incarnate! And there is something of her in you, daughter." He looked down at Ailia. "Though you are not like her in coloring or in height, yet there is a hint of a resemblance in your face. And I heard you speak with her voice—her very voice."

"That explains one thing that's been puzzling me," Damion commented. "You always looked familiar to me, Ailia—I'd assumed I must have noticed you at the Academy and remembered you, but now I know the real reason. You reminded me somehow of the woman in my visions."

Ana gave him a thoughtful look. "There may be more to it than that, young Damion. It may well be that you and Ailia were intended to meet—that your soul knew her on sight. You and Lorelyn have played significant roles in her life so far: I cannot believe that is an accident."

"Perhaps—nothing would surprise me now! But there's still one thing I *don't* understand," he continued. "I saw the infant Princess very clearly in my second vision, and I'm certain that she had blue eyes like her mother's—not purplish-gray ones like Ailia's."

Ana smiled. "I had forgotten what sheltered lives you priests lead! My dear Damion, *all* babies have blue eyes at first!" Her face and voice grew solemn once more.

"Neither Mandrake nor my Nemerei knew anything of what had happened. But we all heard, many years later, of a young girl brought from the Archipelagoes of Kaan, who had been left at a monastery as a child—seemingly abandoned by her parents—and was gifted with mind-speech. The Nemerei felt that this girl might well be the one whom they sought. Mandrake believed this also, and decided to steal her away before the Nemerei could get her to Trynisia and give her the Stone.

"Mandrake, you see, grew away from the rest of the Nemerei long ago, questioning their beliefs, and their strict laws governing the use of sorcery. So it was that he came to see the Tryna Lia as an enemy, a being who would come to dominate the worlds and persecute rogue Nemerei like himself who would not abide by the laws. The Star Stone was to him an extension of her power, a tool of the Old Ones that she would one day use to augment her own sorcery and conquer any rival. He knew where that Stone lay, for he had been to the forgotten isle of Trynisia and learned all its secrets. But he could not destroy the gem. It would have taken the greatest of sorceries to do that, a power to unbind matter itself. Such an act of sorcery also destroys the one who performs it. And in any case the Stone had its Guardians. The cherubim will not interfere with ordinary mortals, but they have leave to defend their treasure from any dark sorcery, and they would have done so without hesitation. Rather than battle them for it—a battle he could never have won, so much greater is their power than his—Mandrake had to content himself with posting dragons to guard the cavern where the Stone lay. The cherubim watched the watchers, but made no move against them. And he himself stood guard in the cavern when we approached the mountain, meaning to drive us away—and the Zimbourans too, if they came too close. He did not intend that the Star Stone should ever leave the mountain."

She turned to Lorelyn. "My poor child!" she said. "When I think of all the dangers to which you have been exposed! And yet you have paid the Tryna Lia the greatest service of all: by keeping her ignorant of her own identity, you have helped to save her life. That is why I asked if you were certain you could risk your own life for another's. You see, Mandrake eventually came to suspect that you were not the one he had sought, but through your innocent belief in yourself he thought to make use of you. Any Nemerei here in Arainia would have seen that belief was true and unfeigned: you would have passed all their tests, and been accepted by the people as their savior, and you in turn would have been ruled by Mandrake. When the real Tryna Lia came here with the Star Stone, she would have found her throne already filled, and many loyal subjects ready to fight to keep you upon it against the supposed 'usurper.' Oh, it was well planned indeed! Yet it worked against him in the end. Your belief and that of the others—Ailia included—ensured that the real Tryna Lia would be safe. Innocence was her shield, and it withstood the keenest probing. Mandrake himself, for all his skills at illusion and deceit, found only the memories of a simple Island girl when he questioned her here."

Ailia shuddered, remembering the interrogator with Damion's voice and face. "So that was why he wanted to know what my first memory was."

"You are right," Ana nodded. "It was a near escape. Who can say what early recollections he might have dredged up from your mind? But fortunately you resisted him." She turned to Lorelyn. "I must now ask your pardon, dear, for allowing you to go on believing you were the Princess. But had you ceased to believe it, Mandrake would have detected the change in your mind, and from that change begun to draw conclusions of his own. He might then have suspected much sooner who the real Tryna Lia was."

"I don't care," replied Lorelyn indifferently. "I never wanted to be the Tryna Lia anyway."

"Oh, Lorelyn—" Ailia turned to her. "You really don't mind?"

"Mind? Why should I mind?" Lorelyn retorted. "I think it would have been an absolute bore! I'd have been locked away in that palace—trapped within walls *again!* Now I can do as I please, for once, and be whatever I want to be. I'm going to be a knight."

Jomar snorted at that. "You can't be a knight. You're a girl!"

"I'll be anything I want to be, Master Jomar," retorted Lorelyn.

The others moved ahead, leaving the quarrel behind. "If those two don't stop bickering," observed Damion mildly, "they'll be married before a year is out."

They walked on in silence for a while. A warm subtropical breeze wafted past bearing with it opulent scents of jasmine and gardenia—and other, alien fragrances. The blue moon Miria was near setting now; the Arch of Heaven, partially obscured by the planet's shadow, shone still, but its pale radiance too was growing dim. Ailia, looking up, was glad that she could still see the stars above, so safe and familiar. The Evenstar was Mera now and the polestar was not the same, while the constellations moved not westward but toward the east—but they were still the old beloved constellations she had known from childhood.

"The Celestial Empire," she breathed. "I used to look up at it when I was on the Island, long ago. But it never looked so bright and beautiful there. Oh, Ana—*did* the Elei journey to the outer stars, as it says in the faerie stories? All the other lovely things are true—surely that one must be as well!"

"Yes, it is true," Ana confirmed. "With the aid of the magic they inherited from the Old Ones, the Elei were able to pass through the Plane of the Ether and reach the stars. That is not so strange a thing as you might think: for the stars themselves are suns like our own sun, and many have worlds about them like Arainia and Mera. The Arainians were starfarers long ago: your ancestors walked once beneath the moon-trees of Miria, and visited their kindred in Mera and the other planets, and traveled to worlds of far-distant stars. Arainia was then part of a great stellar Empire, ruled by a Celestial Emperor in a far-off world. But on Mera the Great Disaster and the Dark Age obscured its memory and turned it into a myth. That Empire still exists however, and the Emperor still rules on his Dragon Throne. I believe, Ailia, that one of your tasks will be to reestablish not only the ancient commerce that once existed between Mera and Arainia, but the ties of both with the star-realm beyond. Remember, it was said in the prophecy that the Tryna Lia would 'reconcile Earth and Heaven and make them one.' "

"I'll do whatever I must. There are all those poor people back in Mera, slaves like Jo, and Lorelyn's monks on Jana. And I so want to see Jaim again, and my parents—my foster parents, I mean—to tell them I'm all right, and to thank them. I miss them terribly, and they must be so anxious."

"Of course: they were your family for most of your life, and Mera was your home—your true home, in every sense of the word. But this is the world of your birth, and the seat of your strength. That is why the Dragon King could not prevail against you, for all his superior powers."

Ailia shivered slightly. "The Dragon King . . . Was Mandrake really a dragon after all, then—never a man?"

Ana took a little while to answer. "No," she said at length. "He was man and dragon both. You were all quite wrong in thinking he was an Anthropophagus—where you got that idea, by the way, I simply can't imagine . . ."

"My fault, I'm afraid," said Damion guiltily. "It seemed a reasonable explanation at the time."

"It was true what I told you earlier: I found him as a young child in the land of Zimboura. Mandrake's mother was a Loänei, a Wer-worm as they used to be called: a magician who could take the shape of a dragon at will. She was a daughter of the old imperial house of the Antipodes, who claimed transformed Loänan among their ancestors." Her eyes grew distant, far-seeing. "So there was always a dragonish side to Mandrake's nature: he inherited a dragon's eyes, and its powers, and its longevity. A Loänan can live a thousand years and more."

"I saw him," said Damion, "in Liamar, in the days of the Great Disaster. I thought he'd somehow managed to get into the past."

"When in actual fact he was there, five centuries ago. He went often to Trynisia," Ana said, "in olden times, when he was known as Morlyn."

"Prince Morlyn!" Ailia gasped. "Andarion's son!"

Ana nodded.

"Then—he *wasn't* killed in the battle with Sir Ingard," she said.

"And he wasn't destroyed here in the gardens either, was he?" said Damion. "He got away from us, in the end."

"I'm afraid so. I think we have not seen the last of the Prince," Ana answered. "And we will have to do something about him later. Until now he has kept to himself, and has not posed a threat. But your coming, Ailia, is a sign that he is changing his ways, and means to become what the prophecy foretold: a powerful mage and warlord, the servant of our enemy. You will be the protector of Mera and Arainia, challenging his plans to dominate them. He has failed to keep you from your throne, and he will be more ruthless in future. But he will not dare to attack you again in your own realm, Ailia. Now, shall we return to the palace?"

"Just a moment, Ana," said Damion "There's something I don't understand. You say that you knew Mandrake—or Morlyn—when he was still a child."

Ailia looked at her wide-eyed. "But . . . but then you must be hundreds of years old too! You must be—"

"Eliana." Tiron spoke the name softly, behind them.

Ailia and Damion stared at old Ana standing before them, the light of the pale blue moon shining on her white hair. She smiled at them.

"An old name," she said. "And one I have not used for

quite some time. You might as well go on calling me Ana."

AILIA WAITED IN THE CORRIDOR outside the high doors of the great hall. She was clad in the formal attire that had been brought to her by the sibyls, and over which a small army of seamstresses had labored during three long Arainian days: a gown like those worn in days of old by Elei ladies in Mera, with long pointed sleeves that trailed to the floor. It was of white samite, sown with patterns of pearls and diamonds that danced with light whenever she moved, and its train swept out behind her like a comet's tail. Her hair, neatly combed, hung loose down her back, and over it the women had draped a sibyl's veil, floor-length and fine as a mist. A chaplet of lilies held it in place. It would be removed later, when the circlet of royal argent was placed on her head.

With the veil before her face she felt somewhat removed from her surroundings; and she still felt slightly dazed. Most of the previous three days had been taken up with visits by her father's family, anxious to view their lost relative: voices and faces and names that crowded upon her dazzled senses, and blurred one into another. Only a few hours were left for her to rehearse this ceremony, with a cloth from a banquet table pinned to her dress to give her the feel of the royal mantle's length and weight. She had felt very nervous about the whole business, constantly repeating to herself the detailed instructions the palace officials gave her. But now none of the pomp and ceremony seemed to have anything to do with her; it was larger than she, and she merely moved through it, as though she walked in her sleep.

There came a ringing fanfare of trumpets from within, that made her start slightly. And now the doors opened, the procession started forward. A regal canopy of blue cloth woven with stars was brought by four ladies-in-waiting—themselves great noblewomen of this world—and held on its poles high above her head. Veiled vestals with ceremonial candelabra in their hands passed through the doors chanting; her canopy-bearers moved to follow, and she had to move with them, into the Thronehall of Halmirion.

The hall was huge, as large as the great chapel. Its walls were of white marble, its windows tall panels of crystal, while the ceiling, like that of the chapel, was frescoed with clouds so superbly painted that one half-thought to see them move: at first glance, it seemed as though the hall were open to the sky. Angels sported amid those clouds, and cherubim and dragons, and gods in airy chariots. At night, she was told, the fresco was lost in shadow and there shone down instead a thousand stars: for the ceiling was studded with constellations of *venudor* crystals that gave forth a radiance of their own. At the end of the hall was a dais, and on the dais was a throne. On the wall behind were more luminous crystals carved like five-pointed stars, while an enormous upturned crescent moon raised its gleaming horns behind the throne, so that the occupant would seem to be seated in the midst of the starry heavens. The throne itself was all carved of semi-pellucid white quartz. No one else had ever sat upon it, she realized in awe, not even her mother: this was the Meldramiria, the Moon Throne, made for Ailia alone. All through the ages it had waited: before the Elei fled Mera, and all through the Dark Age and the Age of Enlightenment; it had waited for her when she was a child on the Island, and when she had lived at the Academy, and when she journeyed through Trynisia with her companions. In the wall to her left Ailia glimpsed the outline of the door that led to the palace's private apartments: into it she and her friends and attendants would go once the ceremony was concluded, and there would be feasting and entertainments and laughter. How she hungered now for that safe haven—to be away from all these watching eyes!

The walk up the aisle, past the assembled people, seemed to take forever. All those eyes upon her, and not theirs alone; many of those present were Nemerei, passing on all they saw in the form of waking visions to other Nemerei all over this world. There were many people gathered on the dais as well: priests and priestesses of a dozen different orders, of whom, as chief priestess of the sovereign deity of Arainia, she would be the titular head, symbolically uniting in her own person all the different sects and temples of this world. This was difficult to imagine now, as she found all these robed majestic figures thoroughly intimidating. There were also many secular officials, governors and administrators of territories, and the chancellor of the world council with his jeweled golden chain. Her father was there too, and she was glad to see her friends standing with him: Ana wearing a plain white robe, with her cat, resplendent and smug in a diamond-studded collar, nestled in her arms; Jomar, looking ill at ease in his fine clothes and trying hard to hide it; Lorelyn tall and graceful in a golden gown, her face aglow with excitement. And there was Damion, in elegant attire like the others, also wearing a cheerful expression that somehow put all the pomp into perspective. Seeing her look at him, he grinned encouragingly. She flashed a smile back at him.

The High Sibyl said something. Then the sibyls and other clerics approached the starry canopy and lifted the veil from her head. She heard the great sea-sound the crowd behind her uttered as their Princess was at long last revealed to them, and felt horribly exposed, and not a little glad that her face was turned away from them. She knelt, very still and quiet, as they laid the royal mantle on her—a great sweep of midnight-blue material, over twelve paces in length, embroidered with silver stars. The weight of it nearly bowed her shoulders.

Several robed clerics then brought to her a great oaken chest, and, setting it down before her, they opened it and took out a silver scepter tipped with a six-pointed star in whose center shone a diamond big as a hen's egg. Receiving it in her right hand as she had been instructed, she was surprised and relieved to find it not nearly so heavy as it looked. And then they brought out the royal Diadem, a circlet of wrought silver: her mother had worn it before her, and as it was placed upon her head she found that it fit her perfectly. It was all encrusted with diamonds and pearls and star sapphires, and at the front the Star Stone was set, with its dew-dazzle of flashing facets. She trembled at the thought of him on whose brow that gem had first been bound.

But then the High Sibyl motioned for to her to rise and go to the Moon Throne. All alone she went forward now with the mantle rivering behind, and took her seat upon the throne. She faced the crowd now. Gazing out at that living sea, she tried to isolate faces in its immensity. Here stood a little child—there a tall, weathered man—there a graceful Elei lady . . . At last she understood. She had only to be there for them, the tangible embodiment of their longings, a symbol of all they most valued. Theirs was the real power: they were the light, and she but the lens through which it shone, the mirror that returned their own brightness to them. In that instant there burst forth from the Star Stone a pure white radiance, and some there thought that they saw in the midst of it—brighter even than the surrounding incandescence—the shape of a bird of fire.

The Tryna Lia had come at last to the throne destined to be hers; and there was rejoicing in Eldimia and beyond.

Here ends The Stone of the Stars, *Book One of* The Dragon Throne.
The second volume, The Empire of the Stars, *will continue the story of Ailia's reign, and the battle to free the world of Mera.*

APPENDIX

Pronunciation of Elensi Words

I have rendered as English the various languages of the peoples of the world of Mera, with the exception of the ancient "dead" language of Elensi. In Ailia's time this language was no longer spoken except by the priests of the western Faith in their temple rituals, though scholars were obliged to learn it in order to study ancient texts, and traces of it were still to be found in many place names and in people's proper names passed on by tradition. These names and a few other terms I have simply rendered phonetically, rather than translating their literal meanings. I have done the same for proper and place names in other tongues, such as Zimbouran and Kaanish.

Elensi words are pronounced as follows:

Vowels

A—always has the short sound, as in *flat*

AA—has a long, drawn-out "ah" sound; before R, pronounced as in *car.* (In some instances I have rendered it as A for easier reading, as in *Aana–Ana, Loänaan–Loänan.*)

AI—as in *rain*

AU—another "ah" sound; before R, pronounced as in *oar*

E—always has the short sound, as in *bed*

EI—like the German *ei*, an "eye" sound

I—like the French I, an "ee" sound

O—always has the long sound, as in *bow,* except when it is the penultimate letter in a word (i.e. *Damion, Halmirion*), in which case it has the short sound as in *iron, lion*

OA—not a diphthong as in *road* but two distinct sounds, as in *coagulate*

U—always the long sound, as in *tune*

Y—always a vowel, never a consonant: has the short I sound as in *win,* except before E, when it takes the long sound, as in *wine*

Consonants

G—always pronounced like the G in *goose,* never as in *gin*

S—pronounced as in *so,* not the Z sound as in *phase*

TH—always pronounced as in *thin,* never as in *then*

Note: these rules do not necessarily apply to words in languages other than Elensi, i.e. Zimbouran, in which the letter Y *is* a consonant.

Glossary of Extra-Terrestrial Words

Aan: (AHN) Elensi. Literally "Lord." In western theology, the Supreme Being, creator of Heaven and Earth.

Ailia: (AY-lee-a) Elensi *ai* + *lia,* "lode star." A young girl of Great Island who joins the quest to find the Star Stone.

Almailia: (al-MAY-lee-a) Elensi *Alm'ailia,* from *alma* + *ailia,* "sea lodestar." Here translated "Star of the Sea." One of the Goddess Elarainia's titles.

Ana: (AH-na) Elensi. Wise woman and guide to the Tryna Lia.

Andarion: (an-DAR-ee-on) Elensi *aan* + *darion,* "Lord Knight." Title given to King Brannar of Maurainia in the Golden Age.

Arainia: (a-RAY-nee-a) Elensi *ar* + *ain-ia*, "bright homeland/sphere." Second planet in the Auria system.

Arkurion: (ar-KYOOR-ee-on) Elensi *ar-kuri + on,* "bright torch bearer." First planet in the Auria system.

Auria: (OR-ee-a) Elensi *aur + ia,* "place/sphere (of) life." Elei name for the sun.

Azar: (AZ-ar) Elensi *àzar,* "calamity." Name for the planet of the dwarf star Azarah. See below.

Azarah: (AZ-a-ra) Elensi *Azar'ah,* from *azar + rah,* "bringer of calamity." Name of a small dim star that became trapped in the Auria system's gravitational field. See Glossary of Terrestrial Terms: *Disaster, the.*

Damion: (DAY-mee-on) Elensi *dai + mion,* "welcome messenger." (I have simplified the spelling of this name from the phonetic *Daimion,* as there is an English name, Damien, pronounced similarly.) Priest of the Faith and companion of the Tryna Lia.

Elaia: (el-LAY-a) Elensi *El'aia,* from *el + laia,* "lower gods."

Elarainia: (el-a-RAY-nee-a) Elensi *el + Arainia.* Name of the goddess of the planet Arainia; also, the mother of the Tryna Lia.

Eldimia: (el-DEEM-ee-a) Elensi *Eldim'ia,* from *el + dimi + ia,* "(the) gods' beauteous country." Land in the Otherworld to which the Elei fled after the Great Disaster.

Elei: (EL-eye) Elensi *el* + *ei,* "children of the gods." Ancient race now vanished from Mera. They had special powers of the mind, believed by them to be the result of a divine ancestry.

Elendor: (el-EN-dor) Elensi *el* + *endor,* "holy mountain." Sacred mountain in Trynisia, on whose summit the holy city of Liamar was built.

Elensi: (el-EN-see) The language of the Elei. From Elensi *el* + *ensi,* "holy tongue," or "gods' tongue."

Eliana: (el-ee-AH-na) Elensi *el-i* + *aana,* "lady (of the) spirit host," or "queen of the faeries." Queen of Trynisia during the Golden Age.

Elmir: (EL-meer) Elensi *el* + *mir,* "spirit power." The concept of Spirit, represented in Elei art as a bird. See *Elvoron.*

Elvoron: (EL-vor-on) Elensi *el* + *vor* + *on,* "containing spirit and matter." Elei concept similar to yin and yang, and ascribed, as with all their knowledge, to the teachings of the gods. The Elvoron is traditionally represented as the Elmir bird (spirit, heaven, sacred time, order) and the Vormir dragon or serpent (matter, earth, profane time, chaos), often with the former at the top and the latter at the bottom of the Tree of Life. In Elei philosophy the opposition of Matter and Spirit is nullified by the power of Mind, which bridges or "reconciles" them.

Elyra: (el-LIE-ra) Elensi *El'yra,* from *el* + *lyra,* "higher gods."

Haldarion: (hal-DA-ree-on) Elensi *hal* + *darion,* literally "Castle Knight." The old fortress of the Paladins in Maurainia, later the site of the Royal Academy.

Halmirion: (hal-MEER-ee-on) Elensi *Halmiri'on,* from *hal* + *Miria* + *on,* "Castle Moonbearer." The palace of the Tryna Lia in Eldimia.

Iantha: (ee-AN-tha) Elensi *i-antha* + *a,* "of many clouds." The sixth planet of the Auria system, a gas giant.

Ingard: (EENG-gard) Elensi. Famed knight and friend of King Andarion.

Jomar: (JOE-mar) Moharan. One of the Tryna Lia's companions, a warrior of mixed Moharan and Zimbouran heritage.

Kaan, Archipelagoes of: (KAHN) Kaanish. Kingdom between the western and eastern continents of Mera, composed of many chains of islands.

Kaans: (KAHNS) Kaanish. The inhabitants of the Archipelagoes.

Kantikant: (KANT-ee-kant) Elensi *kanti* + *kant,* literally "many-books book" or "book (of) many books." There are seven sections, or "books," in the Kantikant or Holy Book of the western Faith. The three oldest writings are of Elei origin: the Book of Beginnings, which recounts the story of creation and the fall of the rebel gods (this word was later altered to "angels"); the Book of Chronicles, an account of Elei history later dismissed as mythology by Maurish scholars; and the oracular Book of Doom, believed to be of Sibylline origin. The other books are later Maurish writings: the Book of Songs, an ancient hymnal; the Book of Wisdom, a collection of proverbs; the Second Book of Chronicles, an account of Maurish history; and the Book of Being, a vision of Earth, Heaven, and perdition by the prophet Orendyl. Owing to its eschatological theme the Elei Book of Doom was placed at the end of the canon. See Glossary of Terrestrial Terms: *Scriptures.*

Khalazar: (KHAL-a-zar) Zimbouran *khal* + Elensi *Azar,* "born under Azar." Name of the king of Zimboura in Ailia's day. The "kh" sound is pronounced like the "ch" in the Scottish *loch.* (The western peoples, who had no such sound in their language, pronounced the name "Kalazar.")

Liamar: (LEE-a-mar) Elensi *lia* + *mar,* "star city." Holy city atop Mount Elendor in Trynisia.

Loänan: (LOW-a-nahn) Elensi *Loänaan,* from *lo* + *an* + *aan,* "lord (of) wind (and) water." See Glossary of Terrestrial Terms: *Dragon.*

Lorelyn: (LORE-el-in) Elensi *Lor'el'yn,* from *lora* + *el-lyn,* "daughter of sacred sky (heaven)." Name of the young woman believed by many to be the Tryna Lia.

Marakor: (MA-ra-kor) Marakite. Country to the south of Maurainia.

Maurainia: (mor-AIN-ee-a) Elensi *Maur* + *ain* + *ia,* "homeland (of the) Maur (tribe)." Principal kingdom of the western continent.

Meldramiria: (mel-druh-MEER-ee-a) Elensi *meldra* + *Miria,* "throne (of the) moon." The Tryna Lia's throne in Eldimia.

Mera: (MARE-a) Elensi word for "earth" or "soil," also used by the inhabitants of the third planet of the Auria system as the name for their world.

Meraalia: (mare-AWL-ee-a) Elensi *Meraal'ia,* from *mera-al* + *lia,* "star stone."

Merendalia: (mare-en-DAL-ee-a) Elensi *Merendal'i'a,* from *meren-dal* + *lia* + *a,* "highway of the stars." The Milky Way as seen in the night sky, believed by the Elei to be the abode of the highest gods.

Miria: (MEER-ee-a) Elensi *miri* + *a,* literally "of radiance." Elei name for Arainia's moon.

Mirimar: (MEER-eem-ar) Elensi *miri* + *mar,* "radiant city." Capital city of Eldimia.

Modrian: (MO-dree-un) Elensi name for a deity, chief of the sky gods (but subordinate to the supreme deity of High Heaven). Said to have rebelled and been defeated by the other gods of earth and sky, who confined him in the Pit of Perdition. See *Valdur.*

Mohar: (MO-har) Moharan. Country south of Zimboura, now an occupied territory.

Mohara: (mo-HA-ra) Moharan. A people of the southern Antipodes.

Moriana: (mo-ree-AN-a) Elensi *mori* + *aana,* "lady/mistress of the nights." A title given to Mera's moon deity; also the name of Brannar Andarion's queen.

Morlyn: (MORE-lin) Elensi *mor* + *lyn,* "night sky." Son of King Brannar Andarion and Queen Moriana.

Morugei: (MOR-oo-guy) Elensi *Morug'ei,* from *moruga* + *ei,* "children (of) the night-haunts." Also Demonspawn. The mutant humanoid races that worship Valdur. These creatures are reputed to be the misshapen offspring of true humans and evil incubi. They include numerous races, whom I call here Anthropophagi, Trolls, Ogres, and Goblins. The first three subspecies breed "true," passing on their characteristics to subsequent generations, but among Goblins no two individuals are alike, and even their offspring do not resemble their parents. However, the Goblins have a higher intelligence than the other races, and are more skilled in the arts of sorcery.

Nemerei: (NEM-er-eye) Elensi *ne-Mera* + *ei,* "child/children (of the) not-world." ("*Ne-Mera,*" "Not-world," is a literal translation of the immaterial dimension here called the Ether.) Beings able to communicate with their minds alone, in addition to other psychic powers.

Numia: (NYOO-mee-a) Elensi. Elei name for Mera's moon.

Numiendori: (NYOO-mee-en-DOR-ee) Elensi *Numi'endori,* from *Numia* + *endori,* "mountains (of the) moon." Mountain range in Trynisia to which Mount Elendor belongs.

Raimar: (RAY-mar) Elensi *rai* + *mar,* "city (of the) flame." The capital city of Maurainia; site of High Temple of the One Faith and the Sacred Flame of Orendyl.

Rialain: (REE-a-lain) Elensi *Riala* + *ain,* "home (of the) Riala (tribe)." Country north of Maurainia.

Selenna: (sell-LEN-a) Elensi *sel* + *enna,* "mist mantle." Highest mountain of the Mari Endori range in Maurainia, once sacred to the Elei.

Shurkana: (shur-KAN-a) Shurkanese. Country to the north of Zimboura in the Antipodes.

Talandria: (tal-AN-dree-a) Elensi *Talandri'a,* from *tal* + *an-dri* + *ia,* literally "all salt water place/sphere." The fourth planet of the Auria system.

Tanaura: (tan-OR-a) Elensi *Tan'aura,* from *tana* + *aura,* "tree of life." See *Elvoron.*

Tiron: (TEER-on) Elensi *tir + on,* "blessing-bearer" or "blessed one." Name of the father of the Tryna Lia.

Tryna Lia: (TRY-na LEE-a) Elensi *Tryna Li'a,* from *tryna + lia-a,* "princess of the stars." Prophesied ruler awaited by the Elei, said to be the daughter of the planetary deity Elarainia.

Trynisia: (try-NEE-see-a; try-NEEZH-ee-a) Elensi *Tryn'isia,* from *tryne + is + ia,* "royal beloved country." Land of the Elei in Mera, abandoned after the Great Disaster.

Trynoloänan: (try-no-LOW-a-nahn) Elensi *tryno + loänaan,* "dragon prince/ruler." A male leader of the Loänan.

Valdur: (VAL-dur) Elensi *val + dur,* "dark one." Name given to the god Modrian after his fall from grace. Later appropriated by Zimbouran clergy as the name for their chief deity.

Valdys: (VAL-diss) Elensi *val + dys,* "dark dwelling." The fifth planet of Auria's system.

Vormir: (VOR-meer) Elensi *vor + mir,* "matter power." The material universe symbolized as a dragon or serpent. See *Elvoron.*

Zimboura: (zim-BOOR-a) Zimbouran. A country in Mera's Antipodes.

Glossary of Terrestrial Terms

The words below are taken from our own terrestrial myths, languages, and cultures. I have utilized them for parallel concepts found in the worlds and cultures described in this book.

alicorn: the horn of a unicorn. It was said to have a precious gem at its base, and to possess miraculous curative powers.

Anthropophagi: deformed humans, one of the races of the Morugei. This name (meaning literally "eaters of men") belonged to a similar race featured in medieval European mythology.

Apocrypha: a term used for numerous old Elei writings that for various reasons were not accepted into the canon of the western Faith's holy book.

Archons: a term used for an ancient race of beings that once dominated the galaxy and were worshipped as gods.

Believed by some to be the origin of the Elaia, "lower gods," in Elei mythology.

avatar: a term taken from Hindu tradition, here meaning either the physical manifestation of a god or else its representation by a mortal being in such a way that the divine being can be said to be literally present.

Celestial Empire: the realm of the stars and planets; the galaxy.

cherubim: gryphons; winged creatures who serve the heavenly powers as steeds and guardians. The word "cherub" comes from ancient Hebrew mythology, and was used for a divine gryphon-like creature (not to be confused with the Renaissance version, a Cupid-like winged figure).

Commonwealth: a term here used for two different unions of friendly nations. Meran history is divided into two eras, the Old and the New. The Old is that period predating the founding of the old Commonwealth, comprised of the Seven Kingdoms (Trynisia, Rialain, Maurainia, Marakor, Kaan, Shurkana, Mohar). The New Era begins with this union, and continues through its dissolution after the Dark Age in the Third Millennium N.E. to its partial reinstatement as the Western Commonwealth (Rialain, Maurainia, Marakor). The events related in this book take place during the early years of the Fourth Millennium N.E.

demon: an Elaia: spirit closely linked to the plane of matter. The word is here used at times in its classical sense, the "daimon" of Greek myth being a supernatural, but not necessarily malevolent, being; very different from our modern understanding of demons.

Disaster, the: I have translated the great cataclysm of 2497 N.E. as the "Disaster," since it literally involved an "evil star." Approximately ten millennia ago, a small "rogue star," Azarah, probably a brown dwarf, entered Mera's solar system and became caught in the sun's gravitational field. In passing through the cometary cloud, it sent dozens of comets plunging toward the inner planets. This bombardment continued sporadically over thousands of years. From descriptions of the Disaster in Mera—"stars falling from the sky," earthquakes, volcanic eruptions, dust clouds obscuring the sun (hence the appellation "Dark Age")—it would appear that one or more fragmented cometary nucleii impacted with the planet. The damage to the moon and other planets is also consistent with a cometary bombardment.

This accords well with the mythical account, in which the god Modrian-Valdur sent his lieutenant Azarah to destroy the world; all such higher spirits being associated with stars. Azarah also brought with it a single planet, the ill-omened Azar of Elei lore.

dracontias: according to folklore, a "magic stone" or jewel that lies inside the head of a dragon. There is in fact a crystalline substance located in, and extruding from, the Loänan braincase, which is said to amplify the creature's extrasensory powers.

dragon: the oldest intelligent race in the known universe, the dragons, or Loänan, are giant saurians that do not in the least resemble the monsters of Western myth but are closer to the *lung* dragons of China: supremely wise, almost godlike beings, benevolent in nature (with a few exceptions). They are able to shape-shift, can exercise power over the elements, and may live for a thousand years or more. They come from the area of the galaxy known to Merans as the constellation of the Dragon, and travel between the stars by entering a hyperspatial dimension known as the Ethereal Plane.

Ether: a dimension of pure energy beyond or "above" the material plane.

faeries: the Elaia; sometimes used of their mortal offspring, the Elei.

Fairfolk: a term sometimes used for the faeries in Celtic traditions, here applied to the Elei race.

glaumerie: an illusion cast by faerie beings on mortals. Some human sorcerers are also able to create illusions.

gods: see *Powers.*

heavens, the: a term applied by the Elei to the three planes of existence: material, ethereal, and spiritual. The first, "Lesser Heaven," incorporates all physical phenomena, the stars and planets, and the vacuum that surrounds them. The second, "Mid Heaven," is a dimension inhabited by "ethereal" beings such as the Elyra and Elaia.

Such beings can move in and out of Mid Heaven at will, seeming to appear and disappear mysteriously in our material plane. The third, "High Heaven," is home to the most exalted spirits. Elei art portrays the three heavens in the form of three concentric circles, with High Heaven forming the outer sphere, like the Primum Mobile of medieval European cosmology. (Perdition, the domain of Modrian-Valdur, does not appear in the Elei model because it is considered a realm of Non-being.) As in our medieval models, the universe is considered to be a closed, self-contained system. But unlike them, the Elei design is not intended as a literal depiction of reality; Elei cosmology teaches that the three planes are not separate, but fluidly coexistent, an arrangement impossible to portray in visual art.

Early Maurish astronomers adopted the term "Heavens" to describe their system of concentric "planetary spheres," which was very similar to medieval understandings of our own solar system. See *spheres, the.*

Hobgoblins, Hobs: small hominids related to human beings, inclined to mischief but not actually evil, and not to be confused with the more dangerous Goblins. Many possess sorcerous powers.

Holyday: a day of rest, similar to Sunday or Sabbath, observed by Meran peoples who followed the old Elei calendar. The Meran year is thirteen days longer than ours, and the Elei divided it into fourteen months of twenty-seven days. Each month was divided into three weeks containing nine days. Finally, the weeks were themselves partitioned into triads, two "low days" for regular work, followed by a "high day" on which laborers could take either the morning or afternoon off. On the third high day of the week, "Holyday," no work at all was done and the people attended services in the temples.

Mandrake: (*man* + *drake*) English equivalent for the Maurish name Jargath, "dragon-man."

Otherworld: a term used for the world of Arainia to which most of the Elei fled after the Great Disaster in Mera.

Powers, the: the Elyra and Elaia, entities worshipped as gods by the Elei, later reinterpreted as angels by followers of the western Faith. It was believed that the Elyra inhabited the stars, while the Elaia dwelt in the earth and moved among mortals, taking human or animal shapes. They even interbred with humans, it was said, and so created the race of demigods known as the Elei. The Elaia were also believed to linger in certain places as invisible spirits ("genius locii") and to be attracted to material objects of a "harmonious" nature, such as the crystal lattices of gemstones.

quintessence: the "fifth element" in old Meran cosmology, a substance superior to the four material elements of earth, fire, water, and air. Celestial objects and divine beings were believed to be composed of quintessence. It most likely derives from the old Elei concept of *elothan,* what we might call "pure energy."

scriptures, the: This term refers to the holy book of the western Faith. See *Kantikant.*

sibyls: prophetesses; holy women of the old Elei faith who communed with the gods and received from them visions of the future. They dwelt in Liamar, the holy city of the Elei.

spheres, the: Like our own ancestors, Maurish astronomers once believed, erroneously, in a system of concentric celestial spheres in order to account for the orbits of the planets. In their case the spheres were seven in number. Each sphere was believed to be formed of pure crystal (to account for its invisibility) and constituted a separate Heaven, as well as containing one of the five known planets, the moon, or the sun; the world of Mera lay at the center. This mistaken belief gave rise to such tropes as "planetary spheres" and "the seven heavens." (In his own account of his journey through the seven spheres, Welessan Dauryn added the three heavens of Elei cosmology, for a total of ten heavens.)

Tree of Life: the food-of-the-gods-tree; also, the symbolic representation of the universe as a tree. See *Elvoron, Tanaura.*

About the Author

Alison Baird is the author of *The Hidden World, The Wolves of Woden, The Dragon's Egg,* and *White as the Waves.* She was honored by the Canadian Children's Book Centre, is a Silver Birch Award regional winner, and she was a finalist for the IODE Violet Downey Book Award. She lives in Ontario. Her Web site is: *www.alisonbaird.net.*

More
Alison Baird!

Please turn the page
for a preview of

The Empire of the Stars

available in trade paperback

and

The Archons of the Stars

available in trade paperback.

1

The Empire of the Stars

THE FIRE-RED DRAGON BURST OUT of the Ether high in the upper air, his entrance into the skies of this world a bright flash hardly to be seen amid a shimmer of many-hued auroras. All the lands below him were shrouded and still, bound in the ice and silence of Winter-dark. Nothing moved here save for him, and a few furtive creatures in the snow-clad forests, and the remote flickerings of the Northern Lights. Impervious to the bone-bitter chill, he flew on toward his goal: a mountain that stood apart from the rest of its range, as though singled out by fate for the role it had played in history. Its double spire of granite did not reach as high as most of the cloud-piercing peaks beyond it, yet it was by far the most famous. In days of old it had been called Elendor, the Holymount.

To the Elei people who had once dwelt in the valley beneath, its two peaks had loomed like living sentinels: a pair of great beasts or vigilant giants, keeping watch over the city that lay between them on the mountaintop. But Liamar had long since been reduced to ruin, mere fragments of walls and buildings interlaced with shadow. The stone sentinels guarded nothing now, and the people were long gone from the island. All the Elei's fabled treasure lay piled within an immense cavern deep inside the mountain: they had placed it there for safekeeping, ages ago, but now that their ancient race was gone the dragon had claimed their gold and jewels for his own. He dived down to settle on the lower of the two peaks, mantling his wings about him, and staring at the ruins.

There were cries in the sky above him, high and wild: other Loänan, celestial dragons, greeting him as they flew past and acknowledged his authority. He was their Trynoloänan, their master and ruler. They thought him one of their own. None guessed at his kinship with those who had dwelt in the city below, none knew that even in this shape he had the soul of a man. His dual nature was a secret he guarded as jealously as any jewel-hoard. But while he wore this form it wracked him with a torment very near to pain, as though mind and body were being wrenched asunder. Once he had dwelt as a man among men, heir to a distant kingdom: Prince Morlyn of Maurainia. In that far-distant land his name was still known, his tale told as legend.

He recalled a time when the city below him bustled with life—for he was old, at least as humans count time: five centuries had passed since his birth, although in draconic reckoning he was not yet in his prime and even in his human shape preserved the vigor of youth. Here in Liamar the Elei had kept the Star Stone, which they cherished above all their other treasures: the enchanted stone of the gods, cast out of Heaven in their last great battle. Indeed, the whole city had grown around it, shrine and fane and lodgings and fortifications spreading outward in concentric rings from the place where it fell. But Liamar was empty now, a setting without its jewel. He had been here in the land of Trynisia when comets rained down on this world, and he had seen, without regret, the old Elei realm fall in ruin. The Stone had then been taken from its sanctum, and hidden in the secret cave. There he had guarded it after the people fled, and set dragons to watch the hoard when he was not present. And there it had lain for centuries . . . until all his plans went awry.

He recalled other scenes more recent in time, shared with him by the witnesses through the joining of their thoughts. He beheld soldiers of a foreign land pursuing two men and one aged woman, the latter bearing the Star Stone in her hand. Winged beasts—not dragons, but strange creatures half lion and half eagle—stooped down upon the armed invaders as they followed the fugitives up to the roof of the central temple. Driving the men back, the creatures took up the Stone's bearer and her companions and flew them away to safety. Lastly he saw a young girl run out onto the top of the taller peak opposite his stony perch, with more soldiers in pursuit. And he watched as she too fled the mountain on the back of a golden dragon, outflying the arrows of her foes.

The images faded away from his inner sight, ghosts returning to the past.

The Tryna Lia. Five hundred years ago she had been only a faceless figure within his mind: his prophesied antagonist, according to the Zimbouran priests who had raised him. Over the ensuing centuries he had been able to forget her, but now the shadowy threat had at last become a reality. And yet superimposed on these fearful thoughts was his memory of this girl, whom he had first encountered in the country of Maurainia, then again here on the Isle of Trynisia: a seemingly ordinary young girl, guileless, naive, utterly innocent of her own destiny. But in the hands of old Ana and her sorcerous conspirators, young Ailia was even now being corrupted, carefully shaped into the living weapon that would one day threaten the realm of the god Valdur's servants—and, if prophecy was to be believed, his own life as well. Nor had she any choice in the matter. In the eyes of the Nemerei she was bound to her fate as surely as he, and there was no escape for either one of them but the death of the other. He must find a way to draw her out of her own world, into another where her powers were not so strong. And prophecy said that she would come to Mera with an army, to deliver it from Valdur's servants. If he could but force her hand, make her attempt to fulfill that prophecy before her powers were developed enough, he might perhaps defeat her.

He sprang off the peak and soared skyward on his flame-colored wings, as though seeking to leave his thoughts behind. For if he continued to muse along these lines he might begin to pity Ailia, and in the conflict to come pity was an indulgence that he could ill afford. He wasted valuable time in brooding here. As the other dragons turned in their flight and tried to follow him, he warned them off with a roar and they retreated reluctantly. He had a journey to make, and allies to seek far beyond the frozen sea. Swifter than any wind of that world he flew southward, until the sun returned to the sky, and still he flew on, barely pausing to rest. He left behind the spinning stars of the pole, passing on through the tropics while the moon tilted above him, until at last it stood inverted amid the bright-burning constellations of the Antipodes.

IN THE LAND OF ZIMBOURA, high in the topmost tower of his old stone keep, the God-king Khalazar was at work upon a spell.

It was night and the chamber was swathed in shadow, its one narrow window showing only a few stars, its only other source of illumination a few guttering candles. Their fitful light played upon a profusion of curious objects on the shelves along the walls: black-bound volumes of gramarye, bunches of dried herbs, wooden wands, astrolabes and orreries, crystal globes of many sizes. There were bones of birds and animals, and several human skulls staring dully from dark corners. On one large oaken table were ranged all the tools of the alchemist's trade: beakers, retorts, crucibles; but all of these were now filmed with dust and strung with cobwebs. The potentate of Zimboura sat cross-legged in the center of the floor. His flowing black hair and beard were touched with gray, and deep lines of discontent were engraved on the face grown fleshy with middle age. His hand, as he traced in blood the outline of a magic circle on the floor, was far from steady. The spell was new, and much hung on its success:

"Akhatal, azgharal, Gurushakan rhamak ta'vir . . ." It was a spell to summon the ghost of Gurusha, ancient demon-king of Zimboura: for the task at hand no lesser spirit would suffice. If he could not succeed in this, he would know that he was not in truth the Avatar his people sought.

All was not well with his young empire. The northern

plains and forests of what had once been the neighboring country of Shurkana were his, along with their vast yield of wheat and wood. But Shurkanese bandits based in the mountains continued to bedevil his troops. The Archipelagoes of Kaan were his, but to the west lay an unconquered continent, whose people had defeated his own in battle centuries before, and could well do so again. The northern island of Trynisia was his, but the oceans that divided it from Zimboura were impassable in winter, and it was populated only by hideous and hostile savages. The fledgling Zimbouran empire was stretched to its limit, thin and vulnerable, its few troops unable to control the restless and resentful populations of its conquered countries.

And now, even here in the capital city of Felizia, bread riots and other minor insurrections were breaking out like wildfires among his own subjects. He badly needed allies, but in all the world there was not one to be had. So he had turned in desperation to the only other world that he knew of, the world of the spirits: day and night he had performed incantations designed to summon supernatural aid. Yet no spirit would answer his call, not the most minor imp or incubus.

It had been Khalazar's belief for many decades that he was no mere mortal, but the earthly incarnation of a god—and no minor deity, either, but that highest of all deities, his people's primary god: Valdur the Great. For years he had felt the utmost certainty concerning his godhood. As a boy he had smiled to himself whenever he heard the priests of Valdur speak of the god's coming incarnation—knowing that *he* was the one, that he was already come. He had despised his predecessor, King

Zedekara, even while he served him, for that monarch had merely feigned divinity in order to impress the mobs. When Khalazar and his followers rebelled against Zedekara's rule, he took his victory for granted and was unsurprised when it came. And when news was brought to him that the location of the Star Stone—the enchanted gem preordained to be wielded by the avatar of Valdur—had at last been discovered, he took this as yet another sign that his destiny was at hand.

But then he had lost the Stone. An old woman had seized it, a witch with the power to summon terrifying winged genii out of the heavens; and one of her companions was a young girl claiming to be the Tryna Lia herself, daughter of the Queen of Night incarnate in human form. After they escaped him Khalazar had retreated to his homeland and fallen into despair, until it occurred to him at length that this too was in the prophecies—the other gods of the pantheon would do all they could to thwart Valdur's rise to power, and the Tryna Lia was their chosen champion. The avatar of Valdur must expect to confront her—so was her appearance not in fact an *affirmation* of his identity?

But if he were the Avatar, a tormenting voice now whispered in the king's mind, why could *he* not summon genii at command? Should not the incarnate Valdur also exercise authority over the spirit-world? Was he *not* Valdur, after all? The thought tortured him throughout every waking hour. He had turned to necromancy, seeking counsel from the spirits of the dead, who as all men knew were party to secrets unknown to the living. For many months he had practiced incantations on a collection of corpses (easily obtained in this violent land), but none could be induced to speak. Now in growing desperation he had turned to this alternative necromantic practice, the summoning of ghosts from beyond the grave. And as he recited the incantation, he thought that he did, in fact, hear a faint rustling sound within the chamber, though he dared not pause in midspell. Only when the incantation was properly concluded did Khalazar lower his hands and open his eyes. The chamber was empty and still as before. With an oath he sprang up, and was about to quit the magic circle when a slight movement in a far corner made him start and whirl.

A figure stood there at the dark end of the room: a tall man, or the shade of a man, clad in a hooded robe the same hue as the shadows in which he stood. The door was still barred from within; the intruder could not have entered that way. The window was open, but it was fourteen stories above the ground and the tower's smooth walls offered no purchase to a climber. As Khalazar stood gaping the figure came soundlessly forward. The beardless face within the cowl was white as death, and the eyes of the apparition burned like yellow flames. Beneath their unnatural glare the king shivered from head to toe. A spirit beyond a doubt, but this was not, could not be Gurusha: that was not a Zimbouran face within the hood.

"Avaunt!" Khalazar screamed, cowering within the circle. "Avaunt—I did not summon you!"

The specter put back its hood, letting long lion-colored hair tumble about its pale face. "Come, Khalazar," it said in a deep reverberant voice, "you are in no position to reject any help. Be sensible."

"Who are you?" rasped the king, unable to retreat any farther without leaving the protection of the circle.

"My name is Morlyn," the specter replied. "I was a prince of great renown in days of old. Surely even you in Zimboura have heard of me?"

Morlyn: the dark sorcerer-prince of Maurainia, dead now for five hundred years. Even as he sweated and trembled before the strange figure, Khalazar felt a minute flare of elation deep within his mind. He had summoned a spirit! Not the one he had sought, but a real spirit nonetheless—and a great one, the ghost of a warrior and archmage! A thin cackle of triumph escaped his shaking lips.

"Well?" the apparition said, folding his cloaked arms. "Have you nothing to say, King, now that I am here? What would you have me do?"

"Destroy—destroy my enemies," Khalazar croaked.

"A large task, that. You appear to have quite an abundance of them." The one who called himself Morlyn walked slowly around the perimeter of the magic circle, his fiery eyes fixed mockingly on Khalazar's. "Shall I start with the Shurkanese? The Western Commonwealth? Not to mention all those here in Zimboura who have designs on your throne? And then there is that little matter of the Tryna Lia."

Khalazar pivoted fearfully, trying to keep his face always toward Morlyn. The spellbook had said that spirits were always obedient to their summoners, yet this one showed little respect or subservience. "How can you help me?" he demanded, trying to give his voice an edge of authority.

"We can help one another, Khalazar. Unite against our common foe. I bear no love for the Tryna Lia, and would gladly see her and her followers destroyed. Will you accept my offer?"

Khalazar stared at him in perplexity. With a sigh of impatience the dark figure stepped forward, and very deliberately placed his booted foot within the ring of blood. The king recoiled with a cry, but a long-fingered hand closed like a claw upon his forearm, preventing his escape. He writhed, torn between terror and outrage. This was not possible! No spirit could enter an enchanted circle—and that hand on his arm was surely flesh and blood! Peering up into the dead-white face, Khalazar saw that the "flaming" eyes were in fact reflecting the candlelight, like a cat's: they were golden in color, with slit pupils, the eyes neither of a genie nor a man, but of a beast.

"What *are* you?" he gasped.

"An ally, Khalazar of Zimboura."

For an instant Khalazar thought he must be swooning: the walls seem to reel around him. Then he blinked, dazed and disbelieving. The chamber had vanished, and with it had gone his castle and, it seemed, all of Zimboura. He and his inhuman companion drifted through an unfathomable darkness, pierced only by the silver points of stars. Stars above—and stars *beneath*!

"Where are we?" he shouted wildly.

"Have no fear, Khalazar—you are in your chamber still; at least your body is. We journey now in spirit, through the great void that lies outside the world. Look."

A long arm stretched out, and following where it pointed Khalazar saw a great blue globe suspended in the dark, half in shadow.

"That, King, is the world you know—the world you would have for your own. And now look around you! Here in the great Night, the stars lie thick as dust. They are suns, many of them greater and brighter than the sun you know, and many circled by worlds like your own. How little your ambition is, that you should be content to rule *one* world only!" The arm pointed again. "Far away, so far you cannot see it, is another, smaller sun that orbits this sun of yours, and circling that sun in turn is a world—Azar, the planet for which you were named. You have wasted your time in seeking to summon little genii of earth and air, when the great spirits, the sovereign lords of the spheres, await your bidding! Elazar, and Elombar ruler of the planet that circles the red star Utara—all the celestial thralls of Valdur dwell here in the heights. But you have foes here too."

Again a sweeping gesture of the cloaked arm. "Do you see that planet there, near the sun—the blue-white one that shines so brightly?"

"I see it, spirit."

"That is Arainia, which you of this world call the Morning Star. But it too is a world, and in it your greatest foe dwells."

Once again Khalazar felt a sense of vertigo; once again he blinked and stared about him. The stars were gone. He stood in broad daylight in a park, lush with verdure, feathery fronds waving against the sky, trees in light green leaf and slow-unfolding flower all around him. Beyond reared the towers of a city—a city such as Khalazar had never dreamed of: vast and sprawling, yet orderly, encircled by no protecting wall, filled with stately mansions and pleasure-gardens. In the sun fountains leaped, glittering.

Morlyn led him along a path to the gate of the park, and out into the city. Khalazar followed like a man in a trance; though he seemed to be walking, he felt nothing under his feet, and neither he nor the tall figure before him cast any shadow in the sun. The streets into which they entered thronged with people clad in garments of brilliant hues, tall, graceful men and women, unlike any he had ever seen.

"What city is this?" he cried as the strange people walked past him unheeding. "I have never seen the like—"

Morlyn led him to the gateway of a mansion. "Look," he said softly. "These gates are gold, Khalazar—*gold,* of which the people in this world have such an abundance that they use it even in their children's toys. And on the gateposts, embedded in the marble—do you see the many-colored patterns, the intricate floral designs? Look more closely, and you will find that each leaf and petal is in fact a gemstone: emerald, ruby, lapis lazuli. These gates alone are worth a whole Zimbouran city . . . and this is but the house of a modest merchant." The Zimbouran king tried in vain to prize a gleaming emerald leaf from its setting, swearing with frustration as his insubstantial fingers passed through it.

"Look!" Morlyn waved a white long-fingered hand toward the rooftops, and Khalazar lifted his eyes and saw a great palace with towers reaching to the sun, all alabaster and gold. It perched upon the summit of a green hill, like a sailing ship mounting the crest of a wave. "That, O King, is Halmirion, palace of the greatest sorceress in this world: the Tryna Lia. She is not that rather simple young woman whom you encountered in Trynisia: that was, I fear, a case of mistaken identity. The true Princess dwells here: Ailia Elmiria, daughter of Elarainia the Queen of Night."

Khalazar fell silent, seized with sudden dread as he gazed up at those towers, so bright and confident beneath the sun. How many times had he reassured himself that his foe was but a woman, weaker in body and mind than he. Should they ever meet face to face in mortal combat, the advantage would surely lie with him. But now his heart sank. Who could defeat a monarch of such power, such inexhaustible wealth? She need never face him at all: she could surely raise a hundred armies to his one, and defeat him utterly upon the field of battle. And she had other allies, like the fearsome genii he had beheld in Trynisia . . .

"Help me," he grated, wrenching his gaze from the hateful sight. "If you have the power, then help me defeat this evil sorceress!"

"You shall have my help," Morlyn answered. "And that of the Valei, the servants of Valdur in other spheres, who hate this world of Arainia and its people more than you can ever know. But you have power too, Khalazar: in your armies, in the devotion you can inspire in them. Once your armies are joined with those of the Valei we will have a force that Heaven itself may fear, O Avatar of Valdur! This world is as rich and fair as Zimboura is dry and desolate. Only do as I advise, and its gold and jewels, its forests and game, its people—and its Princess—shall all be yours."

"Agreed!" the king cried.

And then the echo of that cry was ringing from the stone walls of his chamber; he had been returned to his palace, to his own corporeal form. He spun around. No dark-cloaked figure was anywhere to be seen in the room, so that he might almost have been tempted to think the visitation a delusion or a dream. But from outside the open window there came again that soft rustling sound, like a bird's wings beating in the night.

1

The Archons of the Stars

"SHE STILL HASN'T AWAKENED?" Jemma asked, coming into the sickroom where her aunt sat next to the bed. Nella shook her head, not taking her eyes off Ailia. The girl's eyes were shut fast and shadowed beneath, and her skin waxen pale. From time to time she moved restlessly, her hands twitching on the coverlet, but she did not wake.

Jemma took the seat next to Nella. Ailia's fever had broken at last, and it seemed she was on the mend. But how had she come to be lying in the hostel, and where had she been in all this time? And all that strange, delirious raving . . .

"She has changed," said Jemma presently. "Her hair is more golden than it used to be. It was more, well, mousy before. And I swear she's grown taller. If she were standing up she'd be taller than I am, and we used to be the same height."

Nella still said nothing, and after a moment her niece got up again. "I must go feed the hens," she said. "And see if they've laid any eggs."

"I'll come with you," said a voice from the door. Her brother Jaimon stood there, looking in at them.

They went out the back door together, into a little yard where a few scrawny chickens peeked about in a desultory way. Jemma sighed as she opened the grain bin. "We're lucky to have these. Poultry are priceless nowadays. But I don't know how much longer we will be able to feed them, Jaim."

He nodded. "I know it's a great temptation to kill and eat them, but as Uncle Dannor says, better an egg a day than one meal of meat." He stooped to pick up two eggs. "Though if they don't lay more we'll surely have to kill them."

All the city of Raimar seemed hushed and subdued this evening. New rumors had come to Maurainia of war in the east. First there had been insurrection in the streets of Zimboura, then the fall of King Khalazar. No one in the western lands was sorry to hear of that, but now it was said that two rival powers were fighting for supremacy in Zimboura: yet another man who claimed to be the God-king, and his rival, a sort of desert prophet called the *Zayim* who worshiped a goddess, of all things. Whichever one triumphed, the Continent would surely be attacked. Here in the capital, people were desperately afraid. The ones who had not fled into the countryside beyond the mountain barrier had bought and hoarded foodstuffs.

Presently Jemma spoke again. "I am so glad Ailia is back safe with us again, and feeling better. And yet—everything still seems wrong, somehow! I'm afraid, Jaim. It's not just the wars and the talk of invasion—there have always been wars—but now there's *that,* as well." She raised a hand, pointing. They both looked up at the night sky above them, wondrous and terrible with its shower of many long-tailed comets. "Some people say this means the world is ending."

"I don't believe in portents and prophecies," said Jaimon, as they returned indoors and placed the eggs on the kitchen counter. "I don't think the comets mean anything at all. They're just a phenomenon of the skies," he declared, following his sister into the sickroom.

"What's that?" said Nella, looking up as they entered.

"We're talking about the comets," said Jemma. "But, Jaim, what if one of them falls to earth? It would be like the Great Disaster again." She shuddered. "Whole lands burning up. Comets are made out of fire, after all—"

"Ice," Ailia murmured, moving her head from side to side on the pillow.

"What did she say?" Jaimon asked.

Nella hastened to the girl's side. "Something about ice—perhaps she's turned feverish again?" She felt Ailia's brow. "No, she's just a little warm, but will you get her a wet cloth for her forehead, Jemma?"

Ailia stirred and spoke again. "Ice . . . Comets are made out of ice, not fire."

"She's raving again," said Jemma anxiously.

Seeing the tears gathering in her niece's eyes, Nella turned brisk. "Just get me the washcloth, please."

"I'm sorry, auntie—it's the worry getting to me. Poor Ailia being so ill, and folk going on about the end of the world—"

At that moment Ailia's eyes opened, and they all fell silent as she lay gazing upward. Her gaze shifted from the ceiling to their faces, and recognition dawned on her face.

"Mama? Jaim, Jemma—is it really you? Or am I dreaming still?"

Nella took her hand and held it close. "We're really here, love—you're back with us again. Oh, we have been so worried, Ailia!"

"But where am I, and how did I come to be here?" Slowly, assisted by Nella, she sat up.

"We found you in the hostel. You were suffering from fever, and you have been asleep or delirious for nearly two days now. How are you feeling, love?" she asked, placing a woolen shawl around Ailia's shoulders.

Ailia looked up at her foster mother and smiled. She was still pale from her illness, but her eyes were brighter. "I feel a bit weak—but quite wide awake. I think I shall be all right. I am used to warmer climates now, so I expect I catch chills and fevers more easily." She coughed and pulled the shawl closer.

"But wherever have you been all this time?" Jemma burst out.

Ailia avoided her eye. "In a—another land. Far away."

"We never gave up hoping you would come back to us," said Jemma. "I used to dream about it. I cried a lot at first. Some folks said you were dead, lost forever. But deep down, I just knew you were all right. Ailia, *why* won't you say just where you've been? Can't you remember?"

Ailia closed her eyes against the visions that arose before them. Remember? If she could only forget!

Nella watched her with concern. "You raved something awful when you were feverish—all about people and places we've never heard of."

"Fever dreams," said Jaimon.

Ailia said nothing. She could not bear to look back at those bleak, black days in Zimboura, the grief of Damion's loss still fresh and searing in her mind, the turmoil of hate and fury and desire for revenge that had filled her nights and days with misery. And all the time people speaking of her as a goddess! Had they only known what a goddess she might have become! She shuddered now to recall the things she had been capable of in that dark period, but not—thank Heaven!—actually done. She could never have lived with the guilt. Mandrake had called her a monster. How right he had been! With the powers now at her disposal, she could have wreaked such havoc on the rebels of northern Zimboura that future generations would look back on that time and tremble. She could have used her weather-powers—withholding rain and then sending down lightning bolts to consume the parched land with fire. Or she could have sent rain—weeks of it, drowning homesteads, swelling rivers from their beds. Or created cyclones that would strike at her command, tearing towns to matchwood. She'd have taken draconic form, striking with claws and jaws. Had that in fact been Valdur's intent? To take Damion from her in order to drive her to such savage acts of vengeance?

No—she would not think of these things. She was with her old familiar Meran family again. She was safe . . .

Jaimon approached her bedside and stood gazing down at her. "Those people who came to us wouldn't say where you were, either—they went all evasive when we asked."

"People?"

"They were an odd lot—beggars and villagers mostly—but they all claimed to know what had been done with you. They said you had been carried off by Zimbourans."

The Nemerei! "Yes—I and several other people. We were charged with witchcraft, but it was all nonsense. We—we were able to make our escape, but not until we'd been taken by our captors to a foreign country and we couldn't return home. Months passed, and then years—but I never stopped thinking of you all." How could she ever make them understand the whole truth? They would think she was merely raving again.

"But how did you manage to return?" Jaimon pressed.

Nella interrupted him. "Don't pepper her with questions, Jaim. Let her get her strength back first."

"Tell me," Ailia said, "what has been happening here? Have you stayed in Maurainia all this time? I was dreadfully worried about you, too."

"Dannor and your uncle Nedman came over to join us, when things got rough," Nella explained. "And Jemma's husband came later. The men are all working down at the wharves, except Jaimon. He's signed on to sail with the Royal Navy, and is leaving in a few days." Her voice trembled a little.

"There, aunt, it's all right," Jaimon comforted. "I will be careful."

"But what use is the Navy now?" asked Nella tearfully. "And the seawalls? Now that our enemies can attack from the air."

"The air?" repeated Ailia. "You mean—flying ships? Here?"

He nodded. "We see those things flying overhead all the time now. People scream and run at the sight of them. No one knows how the Zimbourans made ships with wings. Some old-timers out in the countryside say it must be done with black magic. But most say they've simply learned the trick of flight from watching birds. Magisters at the Royal Academy have been trying to do that for years."

In fact, it is both—magic and machinery, Ailia thought. Aloud she said, "Do you remember the old tales of the Elei and their flying ships? Zimbourans may be flying in them, but others devised those ships, a very long time ago."

"Anyway, the air-ships began to appear not long ago—the first were sighted on the eve of Trynalia."

Trynalia, the winter solstice. Her enemies must have chosen that date on purpose, as a provocation. Trynalia, the festival of the prophesied Princess. When dark curtains hung at every window until midnight, and then the door of each house was flung wide open to welcome the Tryna Lia in . . . The old rituals reminded her once more of what she was, while she shrank from the knowledge, the faces before her filled her with pity and tenderness. She said, "Don't be afraid. We have friends and allies who are fighting for our cause, even now."

"Who? The western countries stand alone now. We've no allies left in the world. Unless you mean divine intervention?" said Jaimon, raising an eyebrow. "Cherubim and seraphim?"

"Cherubim, anyway," said Ailia, and the merest trace of a smile flitted across her lips. Then she turned serious again. "The comets aren't omens. They were disturbed from their normal orbits long ago, by Azar and Azarah, and are just reaching us now—"

"Azar and what?" Nella asked, bewildered.

"Oh, I forgot—the Maurainian astronomers haven't discovered them yet."

There was another puzzled silence, which was broken by the sound of the front door and two voices, a woman's and a child's. "Ah—there's Betta back from the wharves." Nella stood. "She will be glad to hear you are recovered, Ailia dear."

The voices came closer, and Ailia's aunt entered the room, along with a small blond boy who began to jump about in excitement and shout. "She woke up! Look, look, she woke up again!"

"Lem?" said Ailia, smiling and putting her feet on the floor.

"No, that's Dani," Jemma told her, stooping and putting her arms around the child.

Ailia blinked. "Baby Dani—but of course, it's been so long, I had forgotten Lem would be much bigger now."

"Lem is with his papa, down on the docks," Betta said. "He wanted to stay and watch them work."

"I should get our luncheon," Nella said, rising. "What is left of it."

"The men were paid today," Betta told her. "Ned gave me his wages. We can go to the market later."

Dani ran to Ailia and looked up at her with bright brown eyes. "You talked when you were sleeping. We listened to you talk."

"What did I talk about?" she asked.

"Funny things. You had a dragon who was your friend, and you lived in a castle. And the castle was in a star. You told stories when you were sleeping. Will you tell some more now you're awake? Will you tell me all about Arainia?"

Jaimon frowned. "Don't pester her, Dan! Run along now."

"Oh, let him be!" Jemma intervened. "Goodness knows we could all use a little fancy these days. Here Ailia, I'll brush some of those snarls out of your hair. It's gotten dreadfully matted."

Ailia leaned back and tried to think of Arainia, as she had before on this Island, but now those memories seemed faint and unreal next to the harshness of winter and poverty here. She could half wonder if she had imagined them all. But as Jemma combed out her tangled hair with firm capable hands, Ailia was soothed. She began to talk slowly and softly, not caring if she were believed or not; merely to speak of Arainia eased the ache within her. Jemma listened quietly along with her eager son, never interrupting, nor did her hands cease their soothing motions.

"It's very beautiful there. It's always warm, because it is so near the sun. And the mountains there are taller than the ones here. And there are wonderful creatures—like the giant birds called rocs, that could carry off an oxcart if they chose. But all the beasts are tame. And there is a great city, and a palace with glorious gardens." Her voice grew soft and dreamy. "And the sun rises in the west and sets in the east. And the moon is blue."

Jaimon shook his head and went out to the kitchen to join the two older women.

"You must tell her, Nell," he heard Betta say.

"Tell her what? That I and Dannor have lied to her all these years?"

Jaimon stepped forward. "Aunt, if you know something about all this, you must tell us all. Not just Ailia, but Jemma and I. What do you mean you 'lied to her all these years'? Has it anything to do with Ailia being taken away? Tell me now!"

Nella stood for a moment with downcast eyes. Then she said, "Come outside, so she won't overhear."

They followed her into the hens' yard and stood looking at her. Nella twisted her work-coarsened hands together, then spoke again. "There was a shipwreck, many years ago. On the south shore."

"Yes, I've heard of it," Jaimon replied. "The older folk are rather close-mouthed about it."

"I'm not surprised, for the wreck, you see, was all covered in gold plate. The pieces are probably still lying in cellars and smugglers' caves all over Great Island. Oh, yes; we never told you young ones the truth of it. Terrible strange it was—a wreck like any other, we thought at first. But the pieces of the ship that washed ashore were all golden. They must have been wondrous rich folk that went down with that ship and yet no one came looking for them. And old Jeb that lived down on the shore, he alone saw the ship before she sank. He swore up and down that he saw that ship sailing through the *sky,* like a ghost ship out of the old tales, before it fell into the sea. He wouldn't have nothing to do with the wreckage, gold or not. Said it was unlucky. Many came to be believe him, and they hid or buried what they'd salvaged, and never spoke of it again."

"Jeb! Wasn't he the town drunkard?" said Jaimon.

"He wasn't drunk that night. No doubt that ship *was* sailing the sky—for it must have been the same as these flying vessels we've seen since. Though I still don't know why no one ever came to claim its wreckage—or the babe."

"The babe!" said Jaimon.

"We found her on the shore, too. Just a tiny child she was, barely old enough to talk and toddle. But her little dress was all embroidered with thread of gold. We kept that dress for years, in case her kin ever came to claim her, and then finally we threw it away. You see, we'd begun to think of her as ours, and we didn't want Ailia herself to think otherwise. I couldn't have babes of my own, so for me she was like an answer to a prayer. If she'd found that dress, she might have started asking questions we didn't want to answer."

"But if Ailia came off a flying ship she could be anybody! I've said it before, Nell—if her clothes were worked with gold she must be a lady. Maybe even a princess!" said Betta.

"A princess!" Jaimon snorted. "Of what country? If anyone was missing a *princess* we'd surely have heard of it!"

"Still, she must be told the truth at once," Betta's voice was firm.

"Yes, that I agree with." The two of them turned to Nella, who made no answer. She was gazing at the cold winter sky, and suddenly she stiffened. A fiery red glow flared briefly behind a cloud—and then another appeared, away to the east. Jaimon, following her glance, started and seized each of them by an arm. "Is it more flying ships? Into the house! Quickly!"

They ran back in, to find Ailia and Jemma standing in the kitchen doorway staring at them. "We heard you shout," said Ailia, leaning on the doorjamb for support. "What is it?"

"Ships, I think," Jaimon answered. "We saw fire in the sky—"

Ailia reeled against Jemma. "Yes—the real enemy is here, at last. It has begun. There's snow on the roofs still," she added. "That may give some protection to us all. But it won't be enough—" She moved forward, swaying slightly, then stood very still in the center of the room, her fists clenched and eyes shut, as if she were praying. Then they heard the rushing sound overhead, the flapping as of tremendous wings. Red light flared out through the windows, and shadows leaped along on the walls. Jaimon ran to the windows. "There's a fire up the street—I can see the smoke and the flames—" He headed for the door.

"Don't!" cried Jemma. "Don't go out there, Jaimon!"

"They will need help putting the fire out—"

A great clamor erupted from the streets outside as they followed him to the door—all but Ailia, who remained where she was. Over the snowy rooftops the shape of the domed high temple appeared black against a red glow.

"Fires! There are fires everywhere!" shouted Jaimon.

Looking up, they saw something moving rapidly through the ascending smoke—a black, flapping shape. Then Jemma screamed, "All the ships in the harbor are on fire! I must go there. Lem is down on the wharves, and Arran—"

Jaimon pulled her back inside. "No—it's too dangerous! It's an attack of some sort. But how are the Zimbourans doing it? Is it burning pitch?"

Ailia stood alone in the main room and felt the energy draining out of her. Nell ran to her while Jaimon kept watch at the door. Suddenly he gave an exclamation.

"What is it now?" cried Nella, cradling Ailia who had collapsed.

"Rain! An absolute tempest, out of nowhere—it's sending up clouds of smoke and steam. I can't see a thing—"

"It will put the fires out," Ailia stated, and with that she slid into a deep sleep.